# *The* FOUR STREETS

NADINE DORRIES grew up in a
working-class family in Liverpool.
She trained as a nurse, then
followed with a successful career in
which she established and sold her
own business. She has been the MP
for Mid-Bedfordshire since 2005
and has three daughters.

# *The* FOUR STREETS

## NADINE DORRIES

HEAD
*of* ZEUS

First published in the UK in 2014 by Head of Zeus Ltd.
This paperback edition first published in the UK in 2014 by
Head of Zeus Ltd.

9 7 5 3 1 2 4 6 8

A CIP catalogue record for this book is available from
the British Library.

ISBN (PB) 9781781857595
ISBN (E) 9781781857571

Typeset by Ed Pickford

Printed in the UK by Clays Ltd, St Ives Plc

Head of Zeus Ltd
Clerkenwell House
45-47 Clerkenwell Green
London EC1R 0HT

WWW.HEADOFZEUS.COM

For my beloved and much-missed brother, John

1960–1986

*Chapter One*

L ET ME TAKE you by the hand and lead you up from the Mersey River – to the four streets, and the houses stained black from soot and a pea-soup smog, which, when winter beckons, rubs itself up against the doors and windows, slips in through the cracks and into the lungs of gurgling babies and toothless grannies.

In May 1941, Hitler bombed Liverpool for seven consecutive nights.

All four streets survived, which was nothing short of a miracle.

Home to an Irish-Catholic immigrant community, they lay in close proximity to where the homes of families far less fortunate had once stood. Life on the streets around the docks was about hard work and survival.

Children ran free, unchecked from dawn until dusk, whilst mothers, wearing long, wraparound aprons and hair curlers, nattered on front steps and cast a distracted eye on little ones charging up and around, swallowing down the Mersey mist.

They galloped with wooden floor mops between legs, transformed into imaginary warhorses. Dustbin lids became shields and metal colanders, helmets, as they clattered and charged along back alleyways in full knowledge that, at the end of the day, they would be beaten with the smelly mop end.

The women gossiped over backyard walls, especially on wash day, whilst they fed wet clothes through a mangle and then hung them on the line to dry.

In winter, the clothes would be brought in, frozen and as stiff as boards, to defrost and dry overnight on a wooden clothes maiden placed in front of the dying embers of the fire.

Such was the order of life on the four streets. All day long housewives complained about their lot but they got on with it. Through a depression, war, illness and poverty they had never missed a beat. No one ever thought it would alter. Their way of life was constant and familiar, as it had been as long as anyone could remember. When little boys grew up, they replaced their warhorses for cranes and, just like their da, became dockers. Little girls grew up and married them, replacing toy dolls with real babies. Neighbours in Liverpool had taken the place of family in Ireland and the community was emotionally self-supporting.

But this was the fifties. The country had picked itself up from the ravages of war and had completed the process of dusting itself down. Every single day something new and never before seen arrived in the shops, from Mars bars to Hoovers. No one knew what exciting product would appear next. Liverpool was steaming towards the sixties and the

Mersey beat. Times were about to change and the future hung heavy in the air.

It smelt of concrete new towns and Giro cheques.

The economic ebb and flow of daily life on the streets was dominated by the sound of cargo ships blowing their horns as they came into the docks angrily demanding to be unloaded. A call for the tugs meant money in the bread bin, which was where every family kept their money. An empty bread bin meant a hungry home.

The main source of income for each household came from the labour of the men who lived on the four streets. Liverpool stevedores were hard men, but the bosses who ran the Mersey Dock Company were harder. Wages were suppressed at a level that kept families hungry and men keen for work. It was a tough life for all. Childhood was short as everyone pulled their weight to live hand to mouth, day to day.

Each house in the four streets was identical to the next: two up, two down, with an outhouse toilet in the small square backyard. Upstairs at the top of the landing, a new enamel bath, courtesy of the Liverpool Corporation, stood exposed under the eaves. The water to the bath was supplied via rudimentary plumbing in the form of two pipes that passed through the landing roof into the loft and attached straight to the water tanks.

Although some homes had discarded kitchen ranges for electric cookers, and back boilers for the new immersion heaters, those on the four streets enjoyed no such new-fangled innovations. The open range remained, doubling as a back boiler and a cooker.

Running past the back gate to each house was a cobbled alleyway known as 'the entry', which was odd as it was in fact 'the exit'. People only very occasionally entered by the front door, and they always left by the back, although nobody remembered how the habit had begun. No one ever locked their doors; they didn't need to.

The entry was a playground to the street children as well as the large brown river rats that grew fat on the spewing contents of the metal bins overturned by hungry dogs and cats.

At the top of the four streets lay a grassed-over square of common land known as the green, which in school holidays hosted the longest ever football matches, sometimes lasting for days on end. Rival teams were formed from each of the four streets and were in perpetual competition. Matches would begin with a nominated goal counter, who at the end of each day would collapse in his bed, exhausted and mucky, with the score scrawled on a precious scrap of paper tucked under his pillow, ready to resume playing the following day.

St Mary's church, which stood at the end of Nelson Street, was visited at least once a day by every woman on the four streets. No one missed mass. The priests were hugely influential amongst the community and combined the role of law keepers, teachers and saviours of souls.

No two front doors in close proximity were painted the same colour. Black followed blue, followed brown followed green. On almost every window in every house hung a set of net curtains, each with a lace pattern different from any other window in the street. Even in homes that could boast nothing in terms of material wealth, individuality fought to be expressed and admired.

Aside from the practical function of the nets, their existence played a significant role within the community. The degree of their whiteness and cleanliness invited verbal judgment to be passed upon the woman responsible. They had to. Women needed a yardstick by which to measure one another's competence as wives and mothers. Men didn't wash nets. That was women's work. Men were judged only on the number of sons they spawned. For women, it was the nets. A barometer and a source of gossip, which was essential. Gossip was the light relief between household chores. Football for men. Gossip for women. Religion for all.

Maura and Tommy Doherty lived in Nelson Street. Although they had a brood of children, they continued to breed, and were passionate, loving and caring neighbours to everyone in the streets. Tommy was short and muscular. If he hadn't been a docker, putting in ten hours a day of hard manual labour, he would have been short and fat. He was bald on top and sported a Friar Tuck band of hair around the back and over his ears. As a result, he was very attached to his cap, which he wore indoors and out, rain or shine. Not one of his children had ever seen him without it, except when he slept. If Maura hadn't insisted he remove his cap before he got into bed, often flicking it off herself, he would have worn it there too. Tommy had vivid, twinkling blue eyes, the kind that can only come from Irish roots, and his eyes reflected his personality, mischievous and kind. He was a proud and devoted husband and father, and was possibly one of the few da's on the streets never to lay a finger on any of his children, a fact that bore testament to his temperament. All he desired in life was peace and quiet.

Tommy had grown up in Cork and had travelled to England to work on the roads. On his first night in Liverpool, he was waylaid by a prostitute at the Pier Head. On his second, he met Maura. Penniless by the third, he got taken on at the docks and, to his great sadness, had never been home since.

Maura was thin, taller than Tommy by a good two inches and, as Tommy often joked, her almost-black hair and eyes were proof that her granny had lain with a tinker: a joke that often resulted in Tommy being chased around the kitchen with a wet dishcloth.

Maura liked to travel, sometimes managing the whole mile and a half into Liverpool city centre, known to everyone as 'town'. She had been born and raised in Killhooney Bay on the west coast of Ireland and, until the day she left home to work as a housemaid in Liverpool, had never ventured any further than Bellingar, on the back of a mule and cart.

'Sure, why would ye need to go into town?' Tommy could often be heard exclaiming in surprise when Maura told him she would be spending extra on shopping that week and would be taking the tram. 'Everything a man could want can be got on his feet around here.'

Without fail, an almighty row would ensue and Tommy could often be spotted running out of the backyard gate as though the devil himself were after him, when it was in fact

Maura, brandishing a rolled-up copy of the *Liverpool Echo* to beat him around the head with, the children scattering before them like cockroaches in daylight, in case they got in the way and copped it instead. He regularly sought refuge in the outhouse, one of the few places where no one troubled him, and took his newspaper for company. Tommy may have craved peace but, with seven kids and a wife as opinionated and as popular as Maura, it was just a dream.

He didn't much care for the news, although he read what he could understand. His relief from hard labour was to check out the horses running at Aintree and to study their form. Tommy had spent his entire childhood helping his father, a groom for a breeding stud. He knew something about horses, did Tommy. Or so he thought. It was his link with home, his specialist subject, which made him feel valued when others sought him out for his opinion or a tip. He was right more often than he was wrong. In his heart, he knew it was the luck of the Irish, combined with Maura's devotion to regular prayer to the Holy Father, far more than his dubious unique knowledge, which sustained his reputation. He still lost as much money at the bookies as every other man on the streets.

If there was anyone in the backyard as Tommy left the outhouse, whether anyone looked at his *Liverpool Echo* or not, or was even paying him a second's attention, as he walked to the back kitchen door he would nod to the newspaper in his hand and loudly pronounce, 'Shite in, shite out.' Social skills were strangers.

Life was lived close to the cobbles.

Maura was, without doubt, the holiest mother in the street. She attended mass twice a day when everything was going well, and more often when the ships were slow to come in and work was scarce.

She was the person everyone went to for help and advice, and her home was where the women often gathered to discuss the latest gossip. On the day one of the O'Prey boys from number twenty-four was sent to prison, the mothers ran to gather around Maura's door, each carrying a cup of tea and a chair out onto the street to sit and gossip, watching the children play.

'I'm not surprised he's gone down,' Maura pronounced to the women sitting around, whilst standing on her doorstep, arms folded across her chest, supporting an ample bosom. Hair curlers bobbed with indignation inside a pink hairnet whilst, in order to dramatize her point, two straight and rigid fingers waved a Woodbine cigarette in the general direction of the O'Prey house. 'Look at her nets, they're filthy, so they are.' In Maura's eyes, there was a direct connection between the whiteness of the net curtains and the moral values within. No one ever challenged her assertion.

The women turned their heads and looked at the windows as though they had never noticed them before.

'Aye, they are that too,' came a murmur of acknowledgment, led by Peggy, Maura's next-door neighbour. They all nodded as they flicked their cigarette ash onto the pavement and took another long self-righteous puff.

The mother of the son who had provided a poor household with stolen food was damned by dust. But Maura's condemnation wouldn't stop her sending over a warm batch of floury potato bread, known as Boxty, as an act of commiseration when she made her own the following morning, using flour that was itself stolen from a bag that had fallen off the back of a ship in the dock. Maura was as kind and good as she was opinionated and hypocritical.

# Chapter Two

J ERRY AND BERNADETTE DEANE lived across the road from
Maura and Tommy in number forty-two. Like many of
the men on the four streets, Jerry had arrived in Liverpool
from Mayo, hungry for prosperity and advancement that
weren't to be found in rural Ireland, where levels of relative
poverty remained almost unchanged since the sixteen hun-
dreds, and where, right into the winters of the nineteen-sixties,
children still walked to school barefoot through icy fields. It
was as though the land of his birth were caught in a time
warp. The outside privies on the four streets were a luxury
compared to the low stone-and-sod houses of Mayo, where
an indoor toilet of any description was mostly unheard of in
many of the villages.

Jerry and Bernadette had met on the ferry across from
Dublin to Liverpool on a gloriously sunny but cold and very
windy day. Jerry spotted Bernadette almost as soon as he
boarded the ferry, her long, untameable red hair catching
his attention. Jerry was mesmerized as, from a slight distance, he watched Bernadette do battle with her hair, which
the wind had mischievously taken hold of and, lock by lock,

teased out from under her black knitted beret. She struggled hard to force it back under the hat.

Jerry had been on his way to the ship's bar when he caught sight of her, her beauty stopping him in his tracks.

'Jaysus,' he would often say to anyone who was listening, 'she took the eyes right out of me head, so she did.'

Instead of moving into the bar for a pint of Guinness to settle his stomach, he sat down on a painted wooden bench, bolted to the wooden deck, to watch the young woman standing at the ship's rail and wondered to himself why she didn't step indoors and into the warm. Surely, it would be much easier than taking on the sea wind and trying to tame a wild mane of hair outdoors?

Her already pale complexion turned a ghostly ashen as she gave up on her hair, staggered forward a few steps and grabbed the rail with both hands, looking more than a little queasy.

Aha, Jerry thought, seeing an opportunity in the girl's problem, thank ye Lord, a hundred thousand times, for here's me chance. He embodied everything everyone knows to be true of an Irishman. He was as bold as brass, full of the blarney and didn't know the meaning of the word shy. That was until he met Bernadette.

Taking the initiative, Jerry nipped into the café, bought an earthenware mug of steaming-hot sweet tea and took it over to the strange but beautiful girl. In his grinning, cheeky Irish way, he tried to introduce himself, but he was so struck by the size and the blueness of her eyes that, for the first time in his life, he could say nothing.

Bernadette didn't notice Jerry as he approached her, so focused was she on holding onto the rail of the ship and on keeping in her stomach the fried eggs and bacon she had enjoyed that morning. She was sure she might faint, and was wondering how she would cope all alone if she did, when she saw Jerry's tall, broad form standing next to her. It was hard to look up as it meant breaking her concentration, but she managed for a few seconds even though she felt like throwing herself overboard. A slow watery death was surely more pleasurable than feeling as she did right now.

She was distracted by his large black eyes that made her forget her sickness for all of thirty seconds. 'I felt as though they were burning into me very soul,' was how Bernadette described her first meeting with Jerry, wistfully and often, her eyes welling up at the mere memory of the day.

It was obvious to everyone who knew their story that Jerry and Bernadette had benefited from that all too rare but wonderful thing, love at first sight.

He realized as he walked over to her that there was no reason on God's earth why he, a complete and total stranger, should be taking a mug of sweet tea to a woman he had never met in his life before and might never meet again. Jerry introduced himself, as best he could, but it came out as a prolonged and indistinguishable jabbering.

Holy Mary, he thought to himself, where the feck has me sensibility gone and why is me hand shaking like a virgin on her wedding night, spillin' the bleedin' tea everywhere?

Although Jerry was talking gibberish, Bernadette could tell he was offering her the tea. So desperate was she to feel better that she accepted it, assuming that he could see how ill she felt.

'Thank ye,' she whispered, as she took the mug out of his hand, managing a very thin and feeble smile that she didn't for one second feel herself. 'I'm so glad there is someone who knows the cure for how bad I feel.' She tried to improve the smile and look grateful, whilst her stomach did an Irish jig in her belly.

Jerry's stomach also began a jig, but it had nothing to do with feeling seasick. He smiled to himself at how it seemed to have gone into free fall, something he had never experienced before.

Bernadette was doubly grateful for the tea as she had only half a crown in her purse and hadn't wanted to waste a penny. She wasn't sure if drinking tea with milk was the right thing to do in the circumstances, but she trusted him. He looked trustworthy – and gorgeous; even through her sickness she could see that. And why shouldn't she drink the tea in any case? In Ireland, strong, sweet tea was the cure for everything from scurvy to colic.

As she drank slowly and tentatively, Jerry studied every detail of her profile, her neck and her hair, which kept blowing across her face, covering it like a lace veil. Finding his sea legs at the same time as his courage, Jerry played the fool with his best show-off jokes and Bernadette tried her best to laugh at his audacity. After all, he was outrageously flirting with a sick woman. Suddenly, without warning, they both saw the tea again, all over the deck and Jerry's shoes.

Jerry sprang into action. The wind had met its match.

He gathered Bernadette's flyaway hair together and spun it into a knot, before tucking it back under her cap as tightly as he could, for fear she would vomit straight onto it. Bernadette was beyond caring that a stranger was stroking the back of her neck and whispering soothing, comforting noises into her ear. Her eyes had filled with tears of shame and she looked as though her knees were about to buckle at any moment.

Jerry kept hold of Bernadette, and her hat, keeping her hair away from her face for almost the entire crossing. The seasickness claimed her as she vomited over the rail all the way to Liverpool during the notoriously choppy journey across the Irish Sea.

As deathly as the seasickness made her feel, Bernadette had noticed Jerry's black wavy hair and, for an Irishman, his unusually broad shoulders. He wore a typically oversized cap, which, although pulled down low over his forehead against the wind, blew off to the other side of the deck so that Jerry, thrown from side to side by the rocking of the boat, had to run like a madman to rescue it. Despite how ill she felt, she laughed. It was impossible not to laugh at this cheeky Irishman.

They didn't leave each other's side for the entire crossing. If they had, Bernadette might have fallen over. By the time they docked at Liverpool, she felt she had known him all her life. To be fair, she had: not necessarily Jerry, but many young men from home just like him. However, it was the fact that there was something very chippy and confident about Jerry that made him different and extremely attractive, despite her self-imposed intention to meet a rich American traveller who would sweep her off her feet and carry her off, away across the Atlantic, to the country where so many of her Irish ancestors had emigrated to live.

'Never worry, Mammy,' she had said to her mother, who was upset at the thought that soon all her children would have left her to work abroad. 'I'll send ye me pay and when I'm in America, oh sure, won't ye be the grandest woman in all of Killhooney Bay, I'll be able to send ye so much.'

Bernadette was confident that she would be massively successful in the land of milk and honey, and her generosity was such that she was determined everyone she knew would benefit too.

She already had a job waiting for her as a chambermaid in Liverpool's Grand hotel, with staff accommodation provided in the maids' dorm under the roof, boiling in summer and freezing in winter. Bernadette did not care. This lowly position did not deter her from her grand ambitions. She would have work. That was something many in rural Ireland did not. It hadn't stopped raining in Mayo for weeks before she left, and although she loved her home, she was looking for adventure and a way to earn a living, not to grow a set of gills.

But she hadn't reckoned on meeting Jerry and she also hadn't expected to fall in love within minutes of her feet leaving the Irish shore. It wasn't the most romantic or conventional beginning to what became the deepest and truest love affair, but it forged an immediate deep bond.

Jerry told Bernadette he was off to stay with a widowed aunt who lived on the four streets. Although he didn't have a job already lined up, he knew there was plenty of work in

Liverpool for strong Irish navvies. Work on the docks, the roads or building the new houses was not too difficult to come by and a slice of a pay packet earned in England could transform the life of a family back home.

As soon as they docked and Bernadette set foot on dry land, she started to feel better. On board the ship, she had felt as close to death as it was possible to be, having vomited what felt like the entire lining of her stomach. Never had she experienced anything as unbearable. She knew if it hadn't been for Jerry's company and the fact that he had looked after her, it would have been a million times worse.

Jerry turned to look at her and laughed. In the five minutes since they had docked, the colour had risen in her cheeks. Her eyes had begun to take on a sparkle and her smile was less forced. Jerry didn't want to part from her. He needed to know the Bernadette who wasn't distracted whilst vomiting over the deck.

'Let's go in here,' said Jerry, pointing to a rough-and-ready portside café. 'Ye need to get a lining on your stomach before ye set off to your hotel, and I sure need to eat before I set off to look for work. Let's grab a bite together, eh? It'll set us both up for what lies ahead for the rest of the day.'

Bernadette willingly agreed. She had no idea when she would get the chance to eat again, and she also wanted to spend some time with this handsome young man when she wasn't embarrassing herself and could act in a more dignified and ladylike manner.

The café smelt of damp wool, stale bodies, fried steam and blue cigarette smoke. They walked across its floorboards to a newly vacated table with a red gingham tablecloth, next to the open fire. The waitress came and removed the overflowing ashtray, replacing it with a clean one as she took their order. Jerry offered Bernadette a cigarette, a Capstan Full Strength, which made her choke, and both of them laughed a great deal as they began to talk.

Very shortly a large brown earthenware pot of tea was placed on the table with a plate of thickly sliced white bread and butter, followed by two plates piled up with chips and two fried eggs on top. Bernadette hadn't realized how hungry she was until they both devoured the food.

Finally, Jerry plucked up the courage and, cheekily, reached out and took one of Bernadette's hands in his own. She didn't pull away.

'Does ye not know any modesty at all?' she chided playfully, hitting the top of his hand with her free one as though to knock it away, something she had no intention of doing.

Bernadette might have been play-objecting to Jerry's romantic advances but really she was giggly and delighted. They talked about their homes and family, the places they both knew and the people they had in common.

'Do ye know the O'Shaughnessys from Mayo?' asked Jerry.

'Ah, sure I do, from Bellingar, I know the mammy and daddy and their daughter Theresa,' replied Bernadette. This was Ireland. In the rest of the world they say you are only ever six people away from someone you know, but in Ireland it has to be two.

Jerry was nervous, turning his teaspoon over and over

between his fingers, making a constant tinkling sound as it tapped the cup. On a normal day, he found it hard to remain serious for more than a few minutes and here he was, for the last hour, pouring out his life plan to a woman who had thrown up over his feet. He had never before had a conversation in which he talked out loud about the things that made him hungry for the future. Jerry was stupidly happy. They both were. Emotions were gripping them both so fast they had no idea what was happening but neither resisted.

By the time Jerry delivered Bernadette to the tram stop for the hotel, he had decided she was very definitely the woman he was going to marry. There was no doubt. She was the one. It was just a matter of time until she realized it too.

As they said their goodbyes, neither could believe what had happened. A few hours ago they had boarded a boat to take them to Liverpool and a new life, and here they were, both without a shred of doubt that, just those few hours later, they were in love; their new life had arrived. It had jumped up and whacked them both in the face with no notice whatsoever. Things were about to change, forever.

Jerry promised to call at the staff entrance of the hotel and find her at the weekend. They walked away from each other, waved, then both looked back and laughed. Jerry ran back.

'This is ridiculous,' laughed Bernadette. 'I don't even know ye.'

Parting was physically painful. Both were secretly worried they might never see the other again, that the magic bubble might burst. As Bernadette turned to walk away for the second time, Jerry reached out and grabbed her by the wrist, and that was when Jerry, in broad daylight, with people walking past and with the Mersey River watching and a thousand seagulls soaring, kissed his Bernadette for the first time.

It was a kiss that was so daring, Bernadette often recounted it to her friends.

'Sure, he was so bold I had no idea what was coming and when he kissed me, I lost me breath and almost fainted, so I did.'

It was very different from what Jerry told his friends. 'She was so keen, she couldn't keep her hands off me and begged me for another, in front of everyone and in broad daylight too. I thought we was going to be arrested right there.'

If Bernadette heard him, it would be followed by squeals and play fighting. No one ever knew which version was true and no one cared. Their storytelling infused everyone with warmth and laughter.

When they finally parted, Jerry went straight to his aunt's house, deposited his bag and, after a quick greeting, took himself straight down the steps at the end of the street to the docks. Dock work was casual. He would walk the entire length of the waterfront and visit every dock if he needed to in order to be taken on. He now had a new imperative, a spring in his step. A reason to find work and good, well-paid work.

As he ran down the steps whistling, he couldn't get Bernadette out of his mind. For what felt like every moment until the weekend, he relived each second of their conversation. In bed, in the minutes before sleep, he relived their kiss as his stomach churned at the excitement and expectation of another. Might there be more? Could this be possible? Could life really be that good? Could Jerry, a farmer's son from Mayo, really be this lucky?

He was. They met almost every night until the day they married, even if it meant Jerry had to walk to the hotel when Bernadette had only her break time free. He would stand at the staff entrance until she could slip out, just for a snatched kiss, to reassure himself she was happy. On her day off she would run down to the docks and spend it at his auntie's house on the street, enjoying the comfort of having a place where she could spend her time and wait for Jerry to finish work. On Sundays they would attend mass at St Mary's church together and walk along the shore as far as Waterloo.

They were blissfully in love and, after nearly a year of steady work, Jerry asked Bernadette to marry him. He popped the question in the café at the Pier Head where they had their first proper date. Bernadette could not have been happier. He even got down on one knee as the customers and staff cheered and clapped. They both cried a little as an elderly man from Eire came up to them on his way out of the café and pressed a brown ten-shilling note into Jerry's palm as he left.

'For the babby when it comes,' he said, and winked as he left.

They both thought they would burst with joy. But this did not distract them from the plans they had. Jerry and Bernadette spent a great deal of time mapping out their future. When Jerry's aunt suddenly died, it was a shock to everyone, but luckily, shortly after Jerry had moved in with his aunt, she had put his name on the rent book, which meant that he could remain in the house without question. The houses on the streets had transferred from one generation to the next in this manner ever since the first wave of immigrants had flooded through the gates of Clarence dock during the potato famine.

However, the pressure was too great for Jerry and Bernadette to put off the wedding until after the full twelve-month mourning period. Bernadette was helping Jerry to cook and clean and look after the house, and not being able to run up the stairs was driving them both mad with desire. But Bernadette was a good Catholic girl and she was taking no chances with sex before marriage. No shotgun wedding for her. Suddenly, being alone in each other's company in the close proximity of a bedroom was becoming an almost unbearable temptation. Bernadette would never stay overnight and the pressure built to an almost unbearable pitch.

'Just stay tonight,' Jerry begged, one Sunday night as Bernadette was leaving. 'Please,' he murmured into her ear in the midst of a very passionate kiss. 'I promise I will be good and ye will still be a virgin in the morning.'

'Not at all!' replied Bernadette forcefully. 'Are ye crazy? Can ye imagine what they will be saying here in the streets tomorrow when they see me leaving in the morning?'

Her resolve did indeed drive Jerry crazy. He wanted to put his fist through the wall, but he also knew she was right. They were married within three months.

During those three months Bernadette got to know everyone on the four streets as well as she did her neighbours back home. Bernadette and Maura came from the same village, Killhooney, and had known each other since Bernadette was a baby. You didn't need to travel far in Liverpool before you met someone from back home. The two women became special friends, which extended to Tommy and Maura's children, especially their eldest daughter, Kitty, who spent as much time with Jerry and Bernadette as she did in her own house.

Although Maura was older, she and Bernadette had attended the same school, knew the same families and had a shared history. Their deep yearning for home had drawn them together from the first day Bernadette had arrived in the street. Maura was daily homesick. Both their families came from the sod houses, close to the coast. Every day they talked about how there was no better view of the Atlantic than that from the cliffs overlooking Blacksod Bay. No better dancing at a ceilidh than that to be had at the inn. No better fish to be tasted than salmon poached from the Morhaun River or fish from the Carrowbay Loch. They had so much to talk about and their conversations about home acted as a salve to Maura's always aching heart.

Neither mentioned the poverty, the lack of shoes, the rain, the hunger or the wet ceilings. The sun always shone on Mayo when it came to the reminiscing.

Bernadette spent hours talking about her work to Maura, who loved to hear the chambermaids' tales about the guests staying in the hotel. Stuck in a life that would never alter, Maura found every detail fascinating, from what the ladies wore to the staff-room gossip, especially about the head housekeeper, Alice Tanner, who had worked at the hotel since she was fifteen and who was legendary for never having taken a day off or having had a visitor since Bernadette arrived.

'Sure, that Alice is a mean one altogether!' Bernadette would exclaim, at least once a week, as she flounced into Maura's kitchen. 'I cannot wait until Jerry and I are married and I can give in me notice. She would drive a saint to drink. I have never given out like some of the others, Maura, but God help me, I will one day soon.'

Maura was all ears.

'She knew Jerry was coming to the staff entrance for me last night and she deliberately sent me off on a wild-goose chase across the hotel to make me late for him. Out of my half-hour break I got ten minutes with him. Jeez, that Alice Tanner is a spiteful bitch. She never sets foot outside of the hotel, and no one ever comes to see her. She's just wicked jealous, so she is, and here's me, always protecting her from the others. So help me God, I cannot any more, the witch.'

Maura loved these days. She would make Bernadette a cup of tea, sit at the kitchen table and listen to her talk for hours on end. The most interesting conversation Maura ever had with the other women on the four streets was how to keep your milk from drying up when you had half a dozen kids to run after, with not enough food to go round for everyone, and how many black eyes there were in English potatoes. Bernadette's chatter was a ray of sunshine.

Just talking to Maura would calm Bernadette down and they would move onto the more interesting gossip, such as the wedding that took place at the hotel on the Saturday. Maura could not believe the things they did with a salmon at the Grand and who knew people ate lobsters?

Everyone on the four streets looked forward to Jerry and Bernadette's wedding with huge excitement. There was something special about them both. They were always laughing and making everyone else laugh either with them or at them.

There was no salmon or lobster to be had at the Irish centre, but the Guinness flowed as fast as the laughter was loud.

The wedding reception had been in full swing for just a few hours when Jerry dragged Bernadette away to carry her over the threshold. The gentle ribbing from their family and friends carried them down the street as they ran giggling to number forty-two.

'What in God's name will they all think?' protested Bernadette, tripping on her new heels. 'Running away to me marriage bed and not staying until the end.'

Jerry's response was to scoop her up and sprint with her across his arms the rest of the way. A Lord Lochinvar stealing away his princess.

The river was black and still. Watching and listening. Holding onto what it knew ... and their shrieks and squeals of laughter echoed out across the water and were surely absorbed into eternity. They were, after all, the happiest couple to have ever run along the river's bank.

The wedding reception carried on way into the early hours, long after their marriage had been consummated a number of times.

In the early hours of the morning, spent and exhausted, Jerry and Bernadette made plans for the future yet again. They knew they were special. They knew they were different. They knew that the brightest future awaited them.

They also knew they were lucky to have a house of their own, even one owned by the Liverpool Corporation. It was the norm for young couples to begin their married life by moving in with their parents. Bernadette and Jerry were a novelty. Jerry's aunt had been barren, and had lavished her attention on her immaculate home, on the rugs she had been able to buy at the docks and the nice chest of drawers from Blackler's department store. Although slightly fancy and dated for Bernadette, with far too many fringes around cushions, lampshades and curtains, it was still the best-furnished and decorated house on the street.

Bernadette strove to be different. From the day they married, she learnt how to sew and cook, acquiring any little skill she could master to keep them one step ahead. Life had yet to wear Bernadette down, to disillusion her, to possess her womb. She embodied the arrogance of youth, combined with a hungry, impatient aspiration for a better life away from the four streets, although she and Jerry were yet to work out how it would be achieved. Even when there were only two of them, a docker's wage merely covered the bills and provided food, with just a little left over. Most couples in the streets had at least six children, which made life much harder than it should have been.

The neighbours nicknamed her 'Silver Heels', so grand were her dreams. Bernadette was aware that she had almost set herself apart from the community by talking about the future she wanted. If she hadn't been so popular, she might easily have succeeded in this. But how could anyone dislike Bernadette and Jerry? They were so in love, so idealistic, so happy.

A natural good neighbour, she always helped her friends. Whether it was to take a crying baby into her house to give a mother in the street some time off, or buying a few sweets for the children on the green. She attended mass every day and never gossiped – her heart was pure.

'Bernadette, ye are too good for this world, so ye is, sure ye must be an angel come to spy on us,' said Maura, who said she sinned so often she needed to go to mass twice a day. 'Feck knows, if ye are, I'll never get through them pearly gates now, no matter how many times I go to confession. I don't confess everything, ye know!' Maura would exclaim in mock indignation every time Bernadette refused to join in the gossip or say anything unkind about another woman in the streets.

Bernadette was godmother to the Doherty twins, which made her broody for her own, but with an iron will she maintained her plan to have everything in her house perfect and some money saved before a baby arrived. And besides, she and Jerry loved their Saturday nights out, and their short trips back to Ireland to visit their families and to take home presents. The young married couple with no babies and a bit of money were accorded a similar status as the film stars of the day. They knew that once babies arrived, all that would stop.

Jerry was so content that he could find nothing to complain about, no matter how hard he tried. Whereas many men feared going home on a Friday night after they had drunk half of their pay packet, Jerry ran home to his wife. He took a great deal of ribbing from the other dockers, but they all wanted to be him. Why wouldn't they? He never stopped grinning. He and Bernadette were the only couple on the streets never to be heard having a row.

The fact that they didn't have a baby straight away was the subject of daily gossip amongst the women.

'He must be jumping off at Edge Hill,' was a theory thrown over garden walls by women with a dozen children each.

Edge Hill was a train station just a few minutes outside Lime Street station in Liverpool city centre, and 'jumping off at Edge Hill' was the colloquialism used for the withdrawal method of contraception favoured by the Pope. Not that the Pope ever had to use it, despite being such an expert. It was highly unreliable; even more so when practised by dockers who selfishly, after a few rum toddies, forgot to jump off and went all the way to Lime Street.

Jerry never forgot. Life to him and Bernadette was about careful planning and being responsible. They were going to get on in life and nothing, but nothing, was going to be left to chance.

When Bernadette finally became pregnant, there was no one on the four streets who was not caught up in the joy of the news. Babies were not an uncommon occurrence on the streets, but the arrival of Bernadette and Jerry's first baby had everyone excited.

'That child will be surely blessed when it comes,' said Maura. 'Was there ever a child more wanted or which could bring more joy?' No one could answer that question. It was as though Bernadette was the only woman ever to have been pregnant.

Bernadette had broken the news to Jerry whilst they were in Ireland visiting her family. They were standing on the cliff at Killhooney, overlooking the inky depths of Blacksod Bay. Jerry had almost fainted and had to sit down.

'Oh my God, Bernadette, are we to be a mammy and a daddy?' He took off his cap and rubbed his hair before putting it back on. Bernadette tucked her calf-length skirt in behind her knees as she sank to the ground to sit next to him.

'We are that,' she replied, looking shocked, and then they both began to laugh and cry at the same time. They kissed and hugged each other as the sea roared with laughter all around them. That night, the villagers attended the ceilidh in the pub arranged with an hour's notice and, pregnant or not, Bernadette danced into the small hours.

When the time came for the baby to be born, news had spread fast that Bernadette was in labour and that she and Jerry were at the hospital. Already the women were falling over themselves to help. They let themselves into the house by the back door, cleaned it from top to bottom despite the fact that it was unnecessary, stocked up the fire ready for a match to be thrown on and left a stew on the side of the range. Bernadette was one of their own, a young woman from the bogs in search of a better life. Disappointment would certainly be just round the corner but, until it came, she had friends and the four streets to count on. Whilst the women were being good neighbours and dusting down her new cot, Nellie Deane made her entrance into the world.

Jerry had been absolutely convinced that Bernadette had been carrying a boy, and the fact that it turned out to be a girl threw him, but only for the few seconds it took him to fall madly in love with his new baby daughter.

For hours, he had nervously paced up and down, waiting. There were no mobile phones then and although there was a public payphone in the hospital entrance, no one they knew could afford a telephone. All communication was by word of mouth or letter. Everyone knew it would be over a week before their relatives in Ireland received the news announcing that Nellie had arrived.

Jerry was beside himself with excitement. Their new baby's birth was the manifestation of his and Bernadette's life plan. He had the perfect wife in Bernadette, and at last he would have the perfect baby. For months he had told everyone he was going to have a boy. That was all forgotten now.

'Jeez, I knew from the day she told me she was pregnant it would be a baby girl,' said Jerry in a very matter-of-fact way to the midwife. 'I have always wanted a beautiful daughter.'

'Oh my,' laughed Bernadette, 'have ye indeed, is that why ye have been saying for seven months ye can't wait to get him to the football, was that our little girl ye was talking about then?'

Moments after she had given birth, they were both laughing together. He and his Bernadette, with her long red hair and bright blue Irish eyes, had spoken in detail about this day ever since they had first known she was pregnant. Not a drink had passed Jerry's lips from that time, as they had saved every penny to buy a cot and turn the second bedroom into a nursery fit for their child. They had managed to completely refurnish and decorate their home. Each time a room was finished, almost forty couples traipsed through the rooms to ooh and aah. Bernadette was meticulous. She fought the dock dust and smog hand to hand; the windows shone, the nets gleamed and pride reflected from her white windowsills.

Once Bernadette had been cleaned up, Jerry was allowed into the labour ward. He had paced the corridors the entire length of the hospital during the birth, desperate for it to be over so that he could be allowed back at Bernadette's side. No father was allowed in a delivery room in the nineteen-fifties. The baby business was women's work. He held his precious bundle in his huge muscular arms, more used to lifting cargo than babies, and could barely see her little face through his tears. Being careful to protect their tiny, fragile scrap, he turned towards his wife and their eyes met.

'She looks like ye,' whispered Jerry. His voice was thick with emotion as the tears trickled down his cheeks. 'She is the most beautiful baby in the whole world.'

Before Bernadette could protest, she gave in and didn't argue. Was there ever a man who could love his new daughter more? Let him think what he wants, she thought.

'Ye will have your lad next,' she said with a smile and such confidence, he believed her without question.

She smiled up at him tenderly, her love for this man who was different from all others pouring out despite her exhaustion. He leant over and kissed her dry lips, thinking that he had never seen his wife as lovely as she looked right now, after twenty-four hours of hard labour and no sleep. His tears wet her face and as she laid a hand on the side of his cheek, she kissed them away and tasted the salt on her lips. Between kisses, they were quietly sobbing and laughing at the same time, flooded with the love their new baby had brought to them as her gift. Jerry hitched the newborn up so that she was wedged between them both and they each gave a nervous laugh as they leant down and kissed her too. The three of them, wrapped in one warm embrace, filled with the smell of the newborn. They were both high on the miracle of life.

'I feel so scared,' confided Bernadette to Jerry, looking up at him. 'We have this little life to look after, she needs us for everything, Jer, we can't fail her.' Bernadette spoke with a degree of urgency, referring to the conversation they had had many times into the small hours of the night.

'Shh, I know, my love, and we won't,' said Jerry. 'She will be a princess, she will have everything she needs. I will never be out of work or let her down.'

Bernadette smiled up at him again. She felt safe and secure. She had no idea how happy one could possibly be, but she couldn't help worrying about money.

Worry was in her Irish DNA. Famines had left an invisible footprint. Jerry and Bernadette had plans for their baby daughter. For months they had talked and plotted about how their children would be schooled. Regardless of what the priest said, they would have just the two, so they weren't reduced to total poverty. They wanted their children to live a better life than their own had been and that of others on the streets. Bernadette was surely right: a son would be next. Jerry did not want his son to have aching bones every day from a lifetime of hard toil, or to be injured in one of the accidents that happened all too often on the docks, or to develop premature arthritis due to the excessive wear and tear on his joints from manual labour. He wanted his daughter to be more than a shop assistant or a cleaner. He wanted her to be a lady, a beautiful, kind lady who possessed all her mother's gentleness, but who could grasp life's opportunities and make something of herself.

Leaving them to have a few private minutes alone, the midwife went to fetch them both a cup of tea and some hot buttered toast. This baby had been a tricksy delivery and at one point she thought she was going to have to call for the doctor to assist. But just at the last minute, with the help of a pair of forceps, the baby shifted position and made its entrance into the world. The midwife had been touched by the obvious love and affection Nellie's parents had for each other; knowing that the special first hour with a first-born came only once in a lifetime, she made herself scarce as quickly as she could.

Even though he had been up all night, Jerry would save the bus fare and walk back home. He could not remember ever having been as hungry as he was right now. After he had eaten breakfast he would change into his work clothes and be in time to clock on at the docks for the first shift. This was no time to miss a day's pay.

Exhausted from her long ordeal, Bernadette lay back on the hospital pillows, feeling drowsy. She turned her head to one side and smiled at her husband, the man she loved more than life itself. Jerry had moved and was sitting on a chair next to the hospital bed, cuddling their baby, still unable to stop looking at her tiny face. Bernadette's eyes were still full of tears as she gazed upon the manifestation of all their hopes and aspirations for the future, the baby, who was falling asleep on his chest, flooding his thoughts, absorbing every ounce of his new love and devotion. Watching them together increased her happiness, if that was at all possible.

As sleep fought to claim her, she tried to say his name and to reach out and gently stroke his hand. She looked down at her arm in confusion. Her hand was like a lead weight and, no matter how hard she tried, it wouldn't respond. Unnoticed by Jerry, who at that very moment had eyes only for his new baby, panic slipped past him into the room and settled itself down upon Bernadette.

She tried to open her mouth, but it wouldn't work, and despite her best efforts, her arm would not move.

Jerry's name urgently beat against the sides of her brain but could get no further, as she managed to part her lips and move her tongue, which felt twice its normal size. But no sound escaped. A black haze had begun to blur the edges of her vision. She struggled to maintain her focus on the adoring father and their baby lying in the cradle of his arms, trapped in their bubble of wonderment. She lay, silently imploring, desperately willing Jerry to move his gaze away from their baby girl and to turn round. Her mind screamed: Look. Look. Look. At. Me. He didn't hear it as he kissed the downy hair on his baby's crown.

Bernadette's head became lighter and the sounds around her more acute. She could hear people outside in the corridor, giggling and talking as though they were standing right next to her bed, laughing at her.

And then, suddenly, she sank. The screaming in her head ceased. She felt as though life itself were draining out of her very soul as a chill sped upwards from her toes and fanned across her body like an icy glaze. She could no longer move her tongue and her eyelids felt leaden; there was no energy left to fight, no will to prise them open as she wearily succumbed to the dark cloak that enveloped her which was so heavy, so oppressive, that, try as she might, she just couldn't lift it off.

'She hasn't even murmured a sound yet, she just has these great big eyes lookin' at me now, just like her mammy,' said Jerry, as he turned himself and the baby towards Bernadette.

The last thing Bernadette saw, as her eyes slowly closed, was the smile evaporate from Jerry's face and transform into a look of horror as he suddenly looked down at the floor and saw a steady stream of blood, dripping from the corner of the bed sheet onto the floor, as though it were running from an open tap on a slow flow, creating a puddle of blood that had reached his own boots.

*Chapter Three*

IT WAS BITTERLY cold in the early morning half-light as heavy rain washed over the streets on the crest of gales swept up from the Mersey River. A fresh squall every minute relentlessly pounded any unfortunate soul who had reason to be outdoors.

'It's as though an angel is chucking a bucket of water down the street, so strong it is,' said Peggy to her husband Paddy, as in her half-sleep she opened the bedroom curtains.

Peggy was a plain woman, with a face that had never experienced even a touch of the cold cream currently flying off the shelves in Woolworths in town. Peggy had no beauty routine. Peggy had no beauty. What she lacked in looks she complemented with a mental denseness that made much of what she said hard to comprehend and frequently funny. Peggy was also a stranger to housework and, unlike the other women on the streets, made no effort to dispel the English urban myth: that the Irish were a dirty breed.

Peggy hurriedly drew the curtains again when she remembered that they had been closed all week as a mark of respect and needed to remain that way for another day. She peeped through the side of the curtain and stared at the fast-flowing rivulets of water gushing down the gutters on either side of the entry.

Paddy turned over. He wasn't going into work this morning. He and Peggy were a good match. Paddy wasn't a pretty sight at any time of the day. With red hair and cheeks to match, from his high blood pressure brought on by over-eating, over-drinking and over-smoking, he had aimed high with Peggy and got lucky.

'The ships will wait,' he had announced as he turned out the light the night before, which of course they wouldn't, because their time in dock was dependent on the tide, not Paddy. This morning the men and boys who normally struggled to be taken on by the gaffer would fill the places of those from the four streets.

Peggy lifted the net and raised her hand in a half-hearted greeting as she saw Maura run down the entry and in through her own back gate from early-morning mass. Maura's head was bent against the wind and rain and she was holding onto her hat, but as she put her hand on the gate latch, she looked up towards Peggy, as though she knew she were watching.

If Peggy pressed her face full against the net and onto the glass she could just see halfway up Maura's backyard to the outhouse. An acute nosiness, born from an idle existence, forced her to strain to see if that was where Maura went next. Peggy knew Maura was returning from six o'clock mass and felt guilt stir itself somewhere in the depth of her belly. Maybe she should have made the effort for first mass today. Sure, didn't she have enough to feel bad about, without having seen Maura playing the Mary goodwife? She made a mental note to attend mass in the evening, after the funeral. A note she would have lost by the end of the day.

For every other street in Liverpool, it was a day of heavy rain. But those who lived by the river had to contend with the squalls that battered the docks on a regular basis. The four streets took the brunt of every storm that had gathered pace and momentum across the Irish Sea, only to be broken up and dispersed when buffered by the houses. They stood out against the tempest like a policeman's upturned outstretched hand, yelling 'stop' to the wind and rain as they whipped round the houses and then subsided into a flimsy breeze, on their way across the city.

Peggy and Paddy were right to be surprised by the weather. It was one of the worst days anyone on the four streets had seen for many a long year. But the residents weren't fazed. Those from the west coast of Ireland had seen as bad, if not worse.

Just as Peggy was putting the kettle on and beginning to make the watery porridge that passed as breakfast in her house, Maura was on her knees in front of her kitchen range, sobbing again, struggling to light the fire, which had gone out overnight.

Her children were yet to leave their dreams behind and the baby, just into its third month, slept in a small cardboard box, wrapped up in a multicoloured, hand-crocheted blanket, made from scraps left over from knitted baby cardigans and school jumpers, with odd ends of yarn salvaged from the wool stall in the market. The box was pushed securely to the back of the armchair, one of only two comfy chairs in the house. It was upholstered in a bottle-green knobbly wool, flecked with the occasional splash of dark orange. The legs were chipped, the wooden armrests worn and two of the springs, covered in brown rubber, which ran underneath the cushion, had snapped. This meant that anyone who sat on the chair sank down into the middle and, having been grabbed on all sides by the cushion and springs, found it difficult to get up again. The baby was just a scrap and the weight of the box was evenly spread across the chair, so the infant was safe enough.

Maura had only a cardboard box in which to put her baby girl, her seventh child, Niamh. For the first, Kitty, there had been a Moses basket, which had fallen apart after both sets of twins and had never been replaced. Maura had thought the twins were to be her last. She had assumed that every baby after the twins was to be her last and then came Angela. However, her Tommy's virility showed no sign of waning and they had coped up to now. Maura's baby might have been in a box, but she was warm, clean, dry and well fed.

Even indoors Maura was still battling the elements, as the wind blew the thick white smoke back down the chimney, refusing to allow the fire to draw and forcing the smoke to billow back into the living room, making Maura cough and splutter. She was shivering, cold and drenched to the skin, having just run the hundred yards or so from the church to the house, far enough for the rain to have found its way through her coat. She thought about the expression she had just glimpsed on Peggy's face at the window. She had raised her hand in greeting. But for both women there had not been a hint of a smile.

A less devout person than Maura would have skipped mass in this foul weather and, indeed, there were only half the usual numbers for the early-morning mass. Shame on them, Maura thought, as she took communion. Today was not a day to skip mass. By the time it was over, Maura would have entered and left the church four times, regardless of the weather.

'There's already more water running down these gutters than they can cope with, without you adding any more,' said Tommy, as he passed behind her on his way to the outhouse, carrying the *Daily Post*.

Maura sat back on her heels and covered her face with her hands. 'I just can't stop meself,' she whispered back to him through the gaps in her fingers, catching a sob at the end of her breath.

Tommy knew that if he put his arms round her, she would disintegrate. Better to keep her mind busy on the important daily routine. The things that mattered.

'Two rashers, two eggs and fried bread in ten, thanks, Queen, once you get that fire going, mind,' he threw over his shoulder as he bustled past her to the back door.

Tommy was the only person in the house to eat meat and eggs for breakfast. For the rest of the family it was bread in watered-down warm milk. Tommy had to unload a cargo ship each day. Without decent food of some kind he would slack and be laid off. As he was about to make his way into the yard, he was hit by a wall of water as though it had been waiting for him to open the door at just that second. Maybe Maura's trip to mass hadn't been in vain after all. Retribution.

'Fecking holy fecking Mother of God!' she heard in decreasing decibels as his blaspheming words were snatched away from him by the wind and rain and flung into the air. The back door slammed shut with such force that the sleeping baby startled and jumped in her box. Her eyes opened wide and her little arms were rigid as they shot upwards with tiny fists clenched. Her lips puckered up and for a second Maura thought she was about to wake and cry.

'Please, God, no,' she whispered, 'not today, I need another hour to get everything done.'

She stroked the back of the baby's hand, making gentle shush, shush sounds to try to prevent her from waking fully. It worked; as she leant across and looked into the box, the baby's eyes slowly closed, her arms softened and dropped gently back down to her side, her face relaxing into a dreamy smile as sleep and innocence won the battle with the slamming door.

Today, as Tommy used the outhouse for his morning ablutions, he was more preoccupied with the state of Maura's mind than on the running order of the horses.

His reverie was suddenly broken by an urgent call from his oldest child.

'Da, will yer hurry now, I'm desperate!' shouted Kitty, her voice cutting through the wind and rain from the back door. On a finer day, she would have been knocking on the outhouse door itself, giving him no peace.

Kitty was his eldest; she was five going on fifteen and, now that she was in the infant school, had refused to use the pot that was kept under the children's bed. Kitty might have been only five but, as the eldest of seven, she could change a nappy and soothe a crying baby as well as her mammy. With her auburn hair and her mother's eyes, she was one of the prettiest and sweetest little girls on the four streets and definitely took after her father in temperament.

The sleeping arrangements were cramped, with the girls in one bed and two sets of twin boys sleeping behind a curtain in another. The new baby would join the girls' bed soon enough and be trusted into Kitty's care.

'I'll be out in a minute, Queen,' shouted Tommy loudly.

He would do anything for their Kitty, his first-born and the apple of his eye. He would even abandon his normal morning routine of studying the horses' form whilst sat in the outhouse with a pencil behind his ear, ready to mark out a promising filly. As he prepared to vacate his throne for Kitty, Tommy wondered, yet again, what they were going to do to prevent Maura getting pregnant again. It wouldn't be long before all the children were refusing to use the pot and demanding the outhouse, his morning sanctuary. Seven little ones in their two up, two down, was as much as the place could take.

Tommy had a great deal to concern him today. He was also worried about the tears that had poured continuously down Maura's face during the six days since Bernadette had died. It was too much. She had cried for too long. One of the neighbours had told him that she felt Maura was making herself sick. What could he do to stop her?

Last night, when they were in bed, Tommy had clutched at straws. He was lying on his back and Maura on her side, her arm propped up with her hand behind her head.

'If ye keep on crying like this, the upset will get through to the babby and make her ill,' he told her.

He was no master of the art of child rearing, despite the fact that they had so many of their own, but he had heard enough women in the four streets say exactly the same thing to Maura over the last few days to know it was a comment that carried some collective weight. And anyway, imparting such wisdom made him feel authoritative and useful, rather than just criticizing Maura for crying all the time, and, other than Tommy, God alone knew how much she had cried.

His stress management technique was rewarded as Maura responded, 'I know. I feel so sick and I can't eat for crying. I know ye are right.'

Her breast had fallen free from her nightdress, which was still open from the baby's last feed, and lay bare against Tommy's chest. That was enough. His hand moved from stroking her arm to stroking her breast for just a minute, which was all it took.

As she quietly sobbed into his chest he pulled his arm from underneath and rolled her over onto her back. He kissed her lips gently as he lifted up her nightdress and parted her legs with his knee.

Somewhere in his Guinness-addled brain, Tommy

thought sex would help Maura. It was life affirming, it was comforting, it was a relief in the midst of despair. For Tommy, that was. For Maura, it just made her feel more isolated and bereft.

As soon as he had finished and heaved his last sigh, Maura left the bed for the bathroom. As she stood to go, with her back to him, Tommy slapped her backside playfully.

'That's a good girl, now isn't that more like it, eh? Bet you fecking loved that. Now if you're still feeling bad tomorrow I'll give you another.'

She heard him chuckling to himself in the thirty seconds he took to fall asleep. She looked back over her shoulder. He had no idea. She watched him beginning to snore as he fell into the first folds of sleep, pleased with himself, a self-satisfied grin on his face.

She would always be with Tommy, she knew that. She loved him. He wasn't perfect, but he wasn't bad either. He was a man with simple needs, who had no idea how to emotionally support his wife, but tried his best, even though sometimes he got it horribly wrong. She knew she would never have emotional support, unless she asked for it to be expressed physically. Tommy thought that making love to Maura was the best and only way to show his love and, in doing so, in the years they had been married had knocked her up five times and impregnated her with two sets of twin boys. A double feather in his manly cap.

Before she went to the bathroom, she wondered how he would react if she were to die tomorrow. Would he be a shadow of himself in the way Jerry was?

When Maura returned to the bed she moved against Tommy to be wrapped in his arms, the only place she felt any comfort or relief. The only place where her tears stopped flowing, even if only for a few minutes. He would hold her tight across her back and she would inhale the smell of him deeply as each breath brought with it a wave of calm and sweet relief to her anguished heart. Maura knew she wouldn't sleep tonight. How is anyone going to sleep, she wondered, as she thought of Jerry and his mammy and daddy in the house with baby Nellie. She felt their heartache as raw as her own and began to cry again.

Tommy knew Maura had hardly slept at all since they heard that Bernadette was dead. Later that same night, somewhere between sex and dawn, he had been woken by her sobbing as he had been every night since Bernadette's death.

Tommy was confused. At a loss to know how to comfort her, he had tried everything he knew. He had felt irritated and impatient with her one minute and overwhelmed by love and compassion the next. He desperately wanted normality to return as soon as possible. Life was hard enough, working on the docks every hour God sent, without the unexpected calamities that were thrown in their path every now and then. Sure, Tommy was upset too. Who wouldn't have been? Kitty and the other kids were also distraught. There wasn't anyone on the four streets that hadn't cried and wailed upon hearing the news. Bernadette was a legend.

The women all liked her, the children loved her and the men lusted after her. There wasn't a man who hadn't envied

Jerry, the man who had it all. No kids until he wanted them, a bit of money in his pocket for the extras, a trip home to Ireland every now and then, and as much Guinness as he could drink. Aye, Jerry had had everything, the lucky bastard, until now.

'Come here, Queen,' he had whispered to Maura in the dark of the night as she woke him with her muffled sobs.

There was the slightest hint of exasperation in his voice. He knew she was trying to do everything she could not to wake him and yet he wasn't sleeping as well himself. She shuffled over from her side of the bed to his and laid her head on his chest as he put his arm under her back and round her shoulders. With his free hand he stroked the cold out of her other arm, which lay on top of the blankets. And there he had lain, holding onto his Maura until the sobbing had passed and she had fallen into a fitful sleep, until the baby, who was in her box on the floor down at the side of the bed, had woken them both for her feed at five.

\*

As he did every morning, Tommy lay on his side watching Maura feed the baby. Maura lay on hers. They were facing each other with the baby resting on the mattress between them. The room smelt of warm milk, wet nappies and lanoline. Tommy stroked the baby's head but she didn't break her stride to look at him as she sucked furiously at Maura's breast. Even at three months, she knew the rough scaly hand stroking her downy dark hair was only that of her da; it was

45

something he often did when she was lying in her box. Maura and Tommy smiled at each other and that was the last Tommy knew until Maura woke him again just before six.

'The baby is in her box, she's all fed and changed and will sleep now. Look after her, I'm off to mass.'

It wasn't yet six o'clock. Tommy smiled. If anyone got to heaven it would be Maura. There was no better Catholic than his wife. She set the standards in the street for the other women to follow and she was definitely Father James's favourite.

When Maura returned from mass, she quietly checked on the other children, who were all sleeping soundly. It was still early and what she couldn't get done in the hour after mass and before they woke wasn't worth doing. Whilst Tommy was in the outhouse and she waited for the fire to catch, she leant over to check on the baby in the box. The child was full and sleeping, but that didn't stop Maura from picking her up and holding her against her whilst she rocked. Although the baby needed no comfort – not a sound did she make – Maura did and the only solace she could take right now was to hold her sleeping baby close.

The fire suddenly caught as flames raced up the chimney. The bricks on the inside heated quickly, chasing the smoke back up the stack and out of the top to mingle grey smoke with grey mist. Maura was now shivering violently. Putting the baby back, she jumped up quickly and pulled off her coat, which smelt of wet wool and stale chip-pan fat.

Both she and the other women had agreed the previous day to send the children off to school early and to keep the little ones indoors. Today was no day for footie games or laughter on the green, regardless of the weather.

She looked up at the clock on the mantelpiece above the fire, next to a pair of Staffordshire pot dogs. They were the only things of value in the house, although they spent more time in the pawnbroker's than on the mantelpiece.

The morning routine of feeding and dressing seven children began in a hurry. Kitty took Angela, and Maura the twins. Tommy helped today as he was at home, and took over from Maura as baby Niamh had her next feed. Kitty took the twins to school and then returned to help look after the little ones until Mrs Keating, a neighbour, came in. The teachers wouldn't bat an eyelid. They were all from back home and knew of the terrible tragedy that had struck the four streets.

Tommy had brought chocolate back from the newsagent's, something they had only ever had at Christmas before.

'Don't let them have any until ye see us turn the corner at the end of the street, now, Kitty, do ye hear me?' Maura said as soon as Kitty came back in through the door. 'What did Miss Devlin say to ye? Was she all right now about ye coming back home?'

'Aye,' said Kitty, 'she was grand, Mammy, and she asked me to tell ye she would be putting in a prayer card in St Mary's for Bernadette.'

Kitty was smart and older than her years. Her childhood was doomed to be short as she shouldered the responsibilities of an elder sister. She didn't need to be asked or told anything twice.

The church bell began to ring out the death knell. A Liverpool funeral wasn't worth having without the solemn, dramatic accompaniment of the slow, steady call to a requiem mass. They told everyone on the four streets it was time to leave. Put on your coat. Check your lipstick. Put on your hat. Leave the house.

Maura looked out of the window to see if anyone else had begun to drag their hard-backed kitchen chairs outside into the street. The rain had petered out into a drizzle. How did anyone cope in this life without prayers to be answered, she thought. She put on her funeral black coat and mantilla, shouting to Tommy to come and help her put their own chairs out onto the pavement.

As she stepped outside she looked towards the top of the street and noticed that the dogs had ceased to bark, the tugs had stopped blowing and every curtain in the street was drawn in respect. Most houses had been in darkness with their curtains drawn for the last six days and no curtains would be opened until after the interment.

The cranes, visible on even the murkiest day, stood motionless like dormant lighthouses in relief against the flat landscape of the harbour. Even the dockers who didn't live on the four streets, and who hadn't known Bernadette, knew Jerry. They wanted to pay their respects and show solidarity in his worst hour. The Mersey Dock Company, the stevedore bosses and even the gaffers knew this wasn't a time to pull rank or to lay down the law. The faces of the men were too grim, too set to challenge. The docks were as silent as the four streets.

A hush had fallen over the cobbles and the only noise was that of wooden chair legs being scraped across the pavement as they were dragged outside to be lined up in a row along the pavement edge. Along with softly falling tears and the occasional sob, this was the only sound to be heard. No one spoke, but everyone crossed themselves each time they looked towards Jerry's house.

There were no words to be said. The feeling of loss was so acute, the shock so profound, that normal chatter had ceased.

People were used to grief. Everyone knew at least one person who had suffered as a result of the war even if they hadn't lost someone of their own. Infant mortality rates were high and maternal death from childbirth the biggest single killer of young women, particularly those from impoverished backgrounds like their own. Death was no stranger to the families on the four streets but, still, they hadn't expected it to snuff out the very brightest light that burnt in their midst. They were grappling in the dark. She was too vibrant, too noisy, too vital to be lost.

It was nine-thirty as everyone took their seat and lined the pavement in a guard of honour. At just that moment, the clouds parted and a ray of sunshine broke though. The older neighbours, who weren't going to the church or the grave-yard, came out, the women with their headscarves fastened over hair curlers and heavy dark woollen coats flapping open on top of faded nightdresses or, for the men, stained pyjamas. They wore outdoor shoes with bare legs and no stockings, or work boots unlaced with no socks. The laces flapped around bare ankles and soaked up the rain from the pavement. No one batted an eyelid at the coats worn over nightwear. Every-one had wanted to say a last goodbye to the young, exuberant girl with the flaming red hair and the infectious laugh.

The women took their places on the chairs lined up in the street as their men stood behind, holding onto the backs. Some were shaking, some were tearful, and all were in shock. Today was a day they all wanted to be over as soon as possible. Even Maura. Despite her inner torment, her unstoppable tears and the acute pain in her diaphragm, the survivor in her knew that once a line could be drawn under today, she could take a fairy footstep towards normality. Life had to move on. She had her own children and family to hold on to, and if there was one thing she had learnt from death, it was to love and appreciate those around you because you never knew what tomorrow would bring.

None of the women were strangers to death from child-birth; Bernadette wasn't the first woman on the four streets to meet her maker that way. But Bernadette had done something different: she had chosen the hospital over a home delivery.

'I'm taking no chances,' she had told her neighbours. 'It's all the rage with the fancy women,' she had declared, laugh-ing her decision off when the others asked why a home birth wasn't good enough.

'Ooh, get you, Silver Heels,' they had all teased her.

But Bernadette hadn't cared; she thought no ill of anyone for laughing at her. She had just wanted the best for her baby. None of the other women had a clue what plans they had in store for their child's future, and for Bernadette a hospital birth would lay down the first marker of change.

It would be the first of many steps she wanted to put in place to break with the past. Their child would not be living its life on the four streets, but she couldn't share that desire with anyone. Never mind the fact that she knew, Bernadette just knew, that life for her baby would be very different from that of any of her neighbours' children.

They heard the horses' hooves before the gleaming black and glass hearse reached the top of the road. The first thing they saw were the white bouncing feather plumes attached to the horses' brow bands as they came into sight and turned the corner. Bernadette was coming home, back to the door of her proud, pristine house for one last time. She was coming to say one last goodbye to them all.

The men removed their caps and, casting their eyes downwards, clutched them to their chests. The women held each other's hands along the row, like children in a playground, and sobbed. Squeezing each other's hands tightly, they were holding one another up. The sudden emotion that had flooded the silence of the street as Bernadette had turned the corner was in danger of knocking them over, of taking one of them down. The shock of knowing that she was only feet away from them, that they could reach out and touch her coffin if they so tried, had brought up sharp the reality of her loss. There but for the grace of God could go any one of them. Most of them had at least half a dozen children each. At the rate they turned out babies, on any week Bernadette's fate could be theirs.

At the top of the dock steps, they heard the slow, steady ascent of footsteps as, one after another, dockers appeared and removed their cloth caps as they gathered along the top, stood in silence and watched.

As the carriage horses slowed to a standstill, everyone's eyes were on the house as Jerry's front door opened. For a few moments there was nothing. Not a sound. It looked as though the door was going to close again without Jerry coming out; then suddenly he stepped out with his baby cradled in his arms. For a second, he held onto the door frame, then looked down as his foot came off the front step and he stood in the street.

Hardly anyone other than Maura and Tommy had seen Jerry since Bernadette's death. The neighbours had been in and out of the house but it was Jerry's parents, who had got straight onto the ferry as soon as they heard the news, who had sat and talked with neighbours for hours, entertaining in true Irish tradition. No one had paid their last respects at the house and left without a glass of Irish whiskey and a sandwich in their insides.

Jerry had lost a great deal of weight and seemed ten years older than his age. His face looked grey and lined, and his red eyes were sunken and surrounded by dark circles from lack of sleep and continuous crying.

'Have ye ever seen a man so heartbroken?' Peggy could be heard to whisper.

She said that at every funeral of every widow, and it could have been the case; however, on this day, it was a fact. The truth. A statement exaggerated in a way only the passionate Irish could manage. Truly, had anyone ever seen a man more bereft or heartbroken?

Jerry's mother and father stood one each side of him and, without touching, were providing the invisible support to keep him upright. They were coping and giving no sign of being under stress themselves. Jerry's mother, Kathleen, the true matriarch of the family, was doing what all mothers do, being strong for her boy. No one could have mistaken Kathleen for anything other than an Irish mother. Fair, fat and looking like fifty. Her once light strawberry-blonde hair was partly grey and fresh out of rollers. Her eyes were also heavy but shone with a determination to get her son through this awful day in one piece.

Behind them came Bernadette's brothers. As soon as they had heard the news, they had packed up and made their way straight to Liverpool, just as they knew their mammy and daddy, who had both passed away, would have wanted them to do. The landlord at the Anchor pub on the Dock Road had rung the owner of the pub in Bangornevin, who had sent out a cellar boy on a donkey to the pub in Killhooney Bay, where there was no phone, who had sent out Celia, their cleaner, who was related to Bernadette's brother's wife, to break the news. The Irish mule telegraph. Both families had all arrived by coincidence in Liverpool on the same boat three days later.

In the meantime, whilst Jerry had waited for family help to arrive, Maura had kept him fed, watered and sane, but only just.

Each morning when he woke he felt a huge shock as the realization washed over him that Bernadette was dead. In the first few seconds as sleep half left him, he would reach out to scoop her into his arms; sometimes he would smile to himself, believing her still to be there. Every day since their wedding, he had woken as the happiest of men. But now, leaden dismay slowly descended upon him as it filtered through the haziness of sleep until suddenly, as though he had been slapped on the face, his eyes opened and the adrenaline kicked in, ready to help his body handle the shock, as fresh every day as it had been on the first.

It began with a hint. A small clue. A question. An odd pain between his ribs. A feeling that all might not be quite right and then, with a rush, the thought, *she's gone,* would flood in so quickly that even the adrenaline had no ability to protect him from the sudden pain and outpouring of tears.

If it weren't for Maura and Tommy, he would never have got out of bed in the morning. One or the other was always there, shouting up the stairs, telling him the kettle was on and the fire was lit or there was a stew or a pie on the table. How did they manage to smile and laugh as they did, as though nothing had happened? Had they cared nothing for Bernadette? Did they not understand his agony?

The hospital had insisted on Nellie remaining there until Kathleen arrived. 'Ye cannot be dealing with managing a first newborn now, in the midst of all ye grief,' the Irish ward sister had told him kindly. 'I do know what I'm talking about. Now, get yer mammy and daddy over and come back to the hospital, and by then baby Nellie will be settled on a bottle and ye can take her home.'

Jerry felt as though the hospital were kidnapping his baby. No. No. No. The words screamed in his mind. This is not what Bernadette wanted. This is not what she had planned.

'Now come along,' the sister said kindly but firmly. 'If Bernadette were here, both of them would have been with us for a week. Nothing is different for the baby.'

And so he had returned home alone. He had walked the full length of the city back to the four streets, unaware of where he was going. Unable to see through his tears. Unable to comprehend what was happening. She had been dead for only an hour and here he was, out on the street alone.

When he had spotted the blood pouring onto the floor, he had slowly stood up and, disbelieving, taken the three steps from the chair to his wife.

'Bernadette,' he whispered. 'Bernadette, what's wrong with ye?'

Only minutes before they had been kissing, crying and laughing, and now she lay deathly silent with a complexion of sallow wax beaded with clammy cold perspiration. He reached down and took her hand to shake her awake but dropped it just as quickly as the wet, unnatural iciness seeped from her fingers into his.

He ran into the corridor screaming for the midwife. In what seemed like seconds, it was as though all of hell had broken free. They no longer cared whether or not he could hold a baby's head properly as they had done only minutes earlier, as he was yelled at to take Nellie and to get out of the labour room.

Doctors in white coats stampeded down the corridor, with nurses running after them, pushing metal trolleys, their shoes on the floor sounding like waves of angry thunder coming towards him. He saw his beautiful wife thrust out of the room on a gurney and he wanted to shout at the doctors to be careful as it smashed against the side of the narrow corridor, leaving black rubber skid marks on the pastel wall as hospital staff became clumsy in their haste. Bernadette was as white as the sheet upon which she lay, with her long red hair splayed over the pillow, as the nurses, with panic running alongside, yelled at people to get out of the way.

It was too late. Within six minutes, she had haemorrhaged to death.

And at that very moment, as the last breath left her body, Bernadette heard their baby cry for the very first time ... as though Nellie knew and were calling her back.

As Jerry left the hospital, the only lucid thought he had was to get to Maura's house. When he got to the back gate, he staggered and almost fell through into the safety net of their yard. Maura ran out of the back door, wiping her hands on her apron, imploring him to tell her what was wrong as, not knowing why, she began to cry herself, fearing the very worst, which transpired to be worse than even she, in those few seconds, had imagined.

On the second day, Maura and Tommy left yet another meal on Jerry's kitchen table. He didn't want to go back to their house. He couldn't face leaving his own or having to speak to anyone – he felt an inner resentment at their ability to carry on as though the most tragic, world-stopping event had not occurred. He wanted to scream and shout at them: 'Don't you both know she is dead? How can you both be so heartless? How can you just carry on with your lives as if nothing has happened?'

But he couldn't shout that, because they were there, at the beginning and the end of every day, acting normally, giving him quiet and unobtrusive support as though nothing had really altered, as though life must go on just as it had before. Except he knew that could never be the case.

*

He fell into step behind the funeral cortège, with Nellie in his arms. 'Here's yer mammy,' he whispered into the side of her face as he lifted her up onto his shoulder. With one hand on the back of her head and the other across her back, he cradled her to him. He was the only person who felt Nellie should be at the funeral. Every other woman on the four streets thought it was wrong and that a funeral was no place for a week-old baby. She shouldn't even breathe fresh air until she was a fortnight old, or so the mantra went.

He wouldn't give in. Nellie was Bernadette's daughter. She had been the most important person in their lives whilst she had been growing in Bernadette's womb. To Jerry, for Nellie not to be there was as odd as it was to the other women that she was. Nellie was going, in his arms, and that was all there was to it.

Bernadette was now only two feet away from them both. He wanted to rip open the wicker casket in which she lay and touch her. He wanted to stroke her hair, to look at her. He wanted to join her, to lie down next to her. He wanted to die and to be with her. He knew that in less than an hour she would be underground. Somewhere he and Nellie could never reach her, buried beneath the dirt, in the eternal darkness.

Tommy was at his side, and behind him four other men from the street who were acting as pall-bearers. He was about to carry his wife for the last time. The moment was coming when she wouldn't be there any longer, when his mind would have to let go and accept there was nothing else he could do for her. He had chosen flowers for her grave, picked a dress from her wardrobe for her to be buried in, combed her hair when she lay in her casket.

Every little thing he had done since the moment she had died was for her. He had given their baby her bottle, for her. He had cleaned the house, for her. 'She would want me to keep the place clean, Jaysus, she would go mad if I didn't,' he said to Kathleen who was making a good job of cleaning up whilst he insisted on feeding the baby.

He was about to take Bernadette in his arms for one last time and then she would be gone and there would be nothing left for him to do for her. He wouldn't be carrying her as his bride, shrieking and laughing down the street. Not as the girl he sometimes playfully carried upstairs and threw on the bed with her squealing, 'Put me down, put me down, you animal,' as she pounded on his back, unable to squeal for long, laughing so hard she had no breath left for words. None of that would ever happen again. It was gone forever.

He also knew, without any doubt whatsoever, that distraught with grief and desperation as he was, Bernadette would never forgive him if he didn't look after their precious daughter with every bone in his body. Bernadette would never rest if Nellie wasn't well loved and cared for by him and him alone. His life was to be a living nightmare as there was no escape for him. He could not die. He couldn't follow Bernadette. He could not stay with her. He had no option. Here, looking after their child, was where he had to be. There would never be a way out.

He knew this because he had dreamt it, as though Bernadette had lain next to him and whispered it with imperative urgency into his ear when he slept last night. The dream was so real, it had given him some comfort. It hadn't taken away the pain, but he felt as though she were, somehow, somewhere near. When he woke, he thought he could smell her. The room felt as though she had just walked out and was standing at the top of the stairs. He was sure that if he shouted her name, she would shout back, 'Yes, I'm here, Jer,' with her tinkling laugh.

Only in the dream, she hadn't been laughing. She had been urgent, imploring, instructing him to take care of Nellie. He had felt her fingers intertwining with the hair on his chest. He had felt her leg cross over his as she kissed his ear and her free hand stroked his hair, just as she always had. She was loving him in his sleep and giving him a list of instructions. These instructions were about Nellie and, when he woke, he could remember every single one.

The dream had given him purpose. He had been starving with grief and, in his sleep, Bernadette had fed him. That was his job now, to look after Nellie in the way Bernadette would have wanted. She was their legacy. This was his purpose. When he felt sorry for himself and trapped in a living nightmare, he would remember that dream.

Nellie began to whimper against his chest.

'It's yer beautiful mammy, don't cry,' he croaked. His throat had closed; it was on fire, thick with distress. He could say no more. His legs felt like jelly and his arms began to shake. 'Oh God, make me strong, let me cope,' he quietly prayed. He looked up and could just make out all the familiar faces around him, down the street, at the top of the steps and on the green. Neighbours who had spent hours talking to Bernadette. She had been in every house and had dispensed her own kind words to almost everyone in front of him.

For every woman who had cried tears of exhaustion, Bernadette had lent a hand.

She had hugged away the fears of some of the wives and laughed with the men as easily as he did.

His own eyes swam with tears to see so many people lining the street to say goodbye. As he looked towards the steps he saw the men from the dockyard lining the top together and, on the edge of the green, the shopkeepers and the ladies from Sunday school where Bernadette had helped with the classes. They all swam before him, blurred.

He felt Kathleen's hand in the small of his back, pressing gently as she stood behind him.

'C'mon, lad,' she whispered, 'one foot in front of the other, steady now, you have the babe.'

And as she nodded to Mr Clegg, the funeral director, who signalled to the horsemen, the wooden carriage wheels slowly inched forward, lurching to the left slightly, lifting from a groove in the cobbles and settling into the next, then lifting again, until the horses increased their speed to allow the wheels to glide over the top.

As they moved down the street, the sobbing of the women could be heard, following them in waves, the slow repetitive peal of the death bells ushering them along.

Jerry had used the money saved for their future to buy his love a wicker casket and to use Clegg's best horses and carriage.

Bernadette had exchanged her silver heels for silver wheels.

As the procession slowly moved towards the end of the street, those who were attending the requiem mass got up from the chairs and fell into a regimental order behind Jerry and his family. The sound of their footsteps took on the rhythm of an army of mourning soldiers, as they marched in time, as methodically as the horses' funeral walk.

Those still in their headscarves and nightdresses, battling to keep out the cold with their overcoats, watched as the last black mantilla turned the corner. And then silently, they watched some more, before, with heavy hearts, they took the chairs back inside.

Jerry handed Nellie to Kathleen as he and Tommy moved towards the carriage. And now their friends would support him. The men he lived alongside and worked with every day of his life were about to help him to carry Bernadette in love and duty, and he needed them, as the tears poured down his face so hard he could barely see where he was going.

'Hold up, mate,' said Tommy, as he steered Jerry to the foot of the hearse. 'We need to unload her.'

Tommy used the language of the docks, as though the hearse were a ship. He was worried about Jerry's ability to walk straight, having never seen a man cry like this before. None of them had. Jerry seemed to have lost all composure.

'Me and Jerry will lift from the front, Seamus and Tommy Mac, get the end, Paddy and Kevin, move into the middle and bear the weight even. Now, steady, after three.' Tommy was taking charge, his way of coping.

Jerry began to shake. At first it was just his hands but as soon as he had handed Nellie over to his mother the shaking seized his whole body. When the men slipped the coffin along the waxed wooden runners, the shaking became violent, as he and Tommy lifted Bernadette up onto their shoulders, in unison and with the same control that they lifted heavy weights every day of their lives.

He felt Tommy's arm slap across his back, grab him firmly and rest on his shoulder, hugging him as close as possible. The men were carrying Jerry, a human wreck, as much as they were Bernadette. Their footsteps shuffled, haltingly at first, and then fell into time as they slowly marched up the path and in through the church doors.

At the moment the large wooden doors of St Mary's church closed, the bell above the door of the bakery tinkled as Mr Shaw returned from the green and let in a customer who had stood outside, patiently waiting. Life on the streets had already begun to move on.

The men who were returning to their work on the dock-yard slowly replaced their caps and turned to walk back down towards the river in groups of two and three. Within minutes they began to discuss the Everton away match on Saturday.

The children began to filter into the entry one at a time. Everyone began helping the older residents to put away their chairs before they made haste to check the babies and little ones they had been allocated for the morning so that the younger neighbours closest to Bernadette could attend the mass together.

They had all been too solemn, preoccupied and tearful to notice the thin young woman who had arrived at the top of the street and now stood at a distance.

She hugged the wall of the corner house, more to remain discreet than to shelter from the wind. She was dressed in a sage-green coat, fastened with a belt, and a matching green Napoleon hat with the front flap held up by three fashionable brass buttons.

She had a thin face, pale and pinched except for her nose, which appeared unusually large for her narrow face. Wisps of shoulder-length fine dark hair escaped from her hat to blow around her face.

Unemotionally, with small, dry, hazel eyes, she observed every second of the scene before her. She scanned the houses, all with curtains drawn both upstairs and down, and noticed, as the carriage had arrived in the street, a flurry of small faces dip under the upstairs curtains as, in one house after another, little noses pressed against the glass to view the horses.

She gave an involuntary shudder. She had the same distaste for children as she did for vermin.

She observed, with interest, that one of the women mourners appeared to be more distraught than the others. As she raised her hand, kept warm in her brown leather gloves, to tuck back an errant wisp of hair, she made a mental note of which house the woman had come out of.

As the mourners dispersed and went about their business, she moved away to catch the bus back into town. She was the only person that day who entered the four streets and smiled.

Most of the inhabitants, especially Jerry, felt as though they would never smile again.

# Chapter Four

WHEN THE LAST of the mourners had left the house, Jerry's daddy, Joe, managed to get the best part of a bottle of whiskey into Jerry with the sole intention of knocking him out. It worked.

Once Kathleen and Joe had him undressed and tucked safely into his bed, they tiptoed down the stairs and closed the door at the bottom behind them, just as they had done when he was a young and vulnerable boy. They looked at each other and breathed a sigh of deep relief.

'We haven't put him to bed in years,' said Kathleen, tears quietly trickling down her cheeks for the very first time.

Joe put his arm round her shoulder for comfort, struggling to contain his own worry and grief. The way Jerry had cried over the last week had torn at his father's heart.

'He's hardly put the baby down and he's going mad with no sleep,' she said, as she pulled her hankie out of her apron pocket to wipe her eyes. Kathleen was a strong woman and unused to crying. Joe had known the whiskey would push Jerry off the cliff. He knew how strong his son was, but he also knew no man could last a week with hardly any sleep.

'A night's sleep and all will be different in the morning, you wait and see. He will be stronger and we can all move on a bit,' he said reassuringly.

They had to return to the farm and their younger boys soon. Kathleen hoped Joe was right.

At five-thirty the following morning, Kathleen placed Nellie in the pram Bernadette had chosen, covered the hood with netting, to keep out the flies, and placed her in the backyard to sleep after her morning feed. It was the only day she had been able to get her hands on the baby for more than a couple of minutes, since she had carried her out of the hospital, five days ago.

Kathleen looked through the kitchen window, at the pram stood against the brick wall in the grey morning light, and whispered to no one other than herself, 'Thank God for Maura.'

Maura had offered to have Nellie when Jerry went back to work, which would have to be within the next few days. Kathleen knew, with such good friends and neighbours, Jerry and Nellie would survive.

Jerry slept for fourteen hours and, for the first time in a week, woke with dry cheeks. Alarmed, he fell down the stairs and into the kitchen, frantically looking around him.

'Where's the babby, where's Nellie?' he almost yelled at Kathleen, who calmly nodded towards the window and the pram outside.

'She's been fed and changed twice and is doing what all babbies should do, sleeping in the fresh air,' she said gently.

'Now, sit down, lad. We've buried Bernadette, it's time for you to eat a proper breakfast and for us to talk about the future.'

\*

For the next few days, Jerry learnt from Kathleen most of what he needed to know about running a house, and what he didn't know once she went back home, he was assured Maura would fill in.

Over the following weeks, absorbing himself in the challenge of being a single father, running a house and keeping down a manual job brought him back onto the path of sanity and exhausted him to such an extent that he was able to keep all thoughts of Bernadette at bay. He pushed her deep down into a room in his heart and locked the door, whilst he focused on rearing their daughter in the way they had both planned. Bernadette's memory constantly banged at the door to be set free, but it remained firmly locked. He knew this was the only way he could survive. But there were days when she burst out and took him by surprise. When she overwhelmed him and flooded his mind with her image he found it painful to get out of bed. To shave, to eat, to walk, to work, to pick up Nellie. These were the days when the pain in his chest made him bend over double. With all the will in the world and all his strength, on those days, he couldn't stop her.

Exactly a week after the funeral, when Kathleen and Joe were at mass, there came a knock on Jerry's door. Haggard and exhausted, dressed only in his vest and trousers, he almost left it unanswered. He had been worried about possibly getting a visit from the council, telling him he couldn't bring up a child on his own and that they would be coming to take Nellie away. That fear kept him awake and was the basis of all the discussions with his parents. He was terrified that his visitor was from the council and he might be about to lose his baby. His tiny Bernadette.

He opened the door, holding Nellie protectively in his arms, and stared at the woman standing on his doorstep. She was smartly dressed and holding a parcel wrapped in a muslin cloth.

He looked across the road and saw that every net curtain was twitching. Some of the women were standing on their steps, arms folded, watching the house. A visitor knocking on any front door was an event in a street that was a stranger to surprises.

'Good afternoon,' said the visitor confidently. 'My name is Alice. I used to work with your late wife, Bernadette, and I have come on behalf of the hotel to pay my respects.'

When it dawned on Jerry that his visitor had been someone who knew Bernadette, he was so relieved that he immediately invited her in for a cup of tea. Today was one of those days when he wanted to talk about Bernadette to anyone who would listen. This woman looked as if she wanted to talk about her too.

'Forgive the mess,' said Jerry. 'I have me own mammy and daddy here and I'm sleeping down here for the while whilst they have me bed.'

Jerry didn't follow through with the information that he was relieved by this arrangement. Getting into his own bed was something he hadn't done willingly since the day Bernadette had died, preferring to sleep on the sofa when Kathleen let him. This way he never truly gave in to sleep, using the excuse that he could keep the baby warm in the kitchen. Having to sleep alone in his bed, without his angel to pull into his arms, was more than he could face right now. Physically walking up the stairs and getting into bed was normality. He wasn't ready to cross that line and accept that life without her was now the new normal.

'Did ye know Bernadette well?' he asked.

He was completely ignorant as to who Alice might be and was racking his brains to try and remember whether she was one of the girls from the hotel who had come to their wedding. But they had all been Irish lasses and this lady was definitely English. She had an air of stuck-up-ness about her which no one from Ireland ever had.

Nellie stirred and, suddenly, it was as if Alice wasn't even there, while he turned his full attention to the babe in his arms.

'Shush, now, Nellie, don't fret ye little self, shush,' he whispered tenderly, as he rocked her up and down.

Alice looked at them both with a curiously expressionless face, clearly untouched by the scene in front of her and regarding it with, at best, mild curiosity.

'Here, let me make you some tea, you look worn out,' she said, and walked over to the kettle, making herself slightly too much at home, although Jerry seemed not to notice as he laid Nellie down in her basket.

Stiffly, almost reluctantly, Alice walked over to the basket and leant over. 'Goodness me, she is a beautiful little thing, isn't she, and with such a look of Bernadette about her,' she said with a false brightness.

'Aye, she has that,' said Jerry, whose eyes didn't leave Nellie as he straightened up. 'I'm overrun with cake, so would ye like a slice with ye tea?' he asked politely. He didn't really know what to say to this very proper and posh stranger, but the Irish gift of welcoming friendliness automatically kicked in.

'Oh, yes please,' said Alice as she handed him her muslin-wrapped gift. She seemed embarrassed as he opened it to reveal a cake and for the first time he looked at her and smiled.

'Oh, I am sorry, I didn't realize, I am such an eejit, thank you so much,' he said. 'I will be the size of a tram by the time I have eaten all this cake but it is all very welcome, I can tell ye.'

They sat down and Jerry sliced the cake. The conversation was slightly awkward, but she managed to keep it going while they drank their tea. Although he couldn't have said why, Alice made Jerry feel slightly uneasy. She spoke in a clipped, accentless tone and her smart clothes made him feel inferior. He found himself gabbling.

Fear of ruthless British dominance runs deep into Irish roots and Jerry had no idea that, from this inbuilt default position, he was already losing.

When it came time for Alice to leave, Jerry politely showed her to the door. He hardly took in her promise to return soon to see if he was getting on all right. As he turned back to

Nellie in her basket, he was already dismissing from his mind the whole strange episode and the unexpected visitor.

From behind her nets, Maura watched Alice leave. She had been standing at the bedroom window since the moment Alice arrived and she saw Alice smile, rather smugly, as she walked away. This disturbed Maura so much that she crossed herself.

'That one's up to no good, you can be sure about that, it's written all over her face. Holy Mary, Mother of God, I've a bad feeling about this, so,' she wailed to Kitty, who had brought them both a cup of tea sent up by Tommy and was hiding behind the curtains with her. As Kitty was growing older, she was becoming her mammy's best friend as well as her little helper. Maura gave a dramatic shudder.

'Jaysus, Kitty, someone has just walked over me grave, so they have.'

Maura went in search of Tommy to give him the news. As she passed through the kitchen door, she picked up her rosary, hanging off the big toe of the plaster cast of Jesus mounted on the wall, and thrust it into her front apron pocket where she stuffed both of her hands. A stranger on the street at any time was big news. A stranger arriving a week after Bernadette's death, who had been hovering around on the day of the funeral with a smirk on her face, was worrying news.

'Tommy, a strange woman has turned up twice this week, looking as though she has a stick up her arse, when Bernadette's still warm in her grave. She's giving me the creeps. You find out from Jerry who she is, now, or I'll be givin' out to you.'

'Calm down, Queen, it'll just be a mate of theirs,' said Tommy, trying to return to his newspaper.

'Are ye mad?' she yelled at him. 'You stupid man. What mate? I knew Bernadette better than anyone, I've known her all me blessed life, longer than Jerry even, and this woman is no mate, or I'd have known for sure. There's something bad about her, so there is, I can feel it in me water.'

'You and your feckin water,' snapped Tommy. 'Can ye water tell me what's going to win at Aintree today, am I right on the two-thirty with Danny Boy, eh?'

Tommy didn't see what hit him smack on the side of his head. It was Maura's knitting bag, the first thing to come to her hand, as she went to chase him out of the kitchen. Maura had a dreadful feeling. She had felt it before on the day of the funeral, when looking up the street she had seen that sly-looking woman, and she knew all was not right.

Distracted by her thoughts, Maura went into the yard to take in her washing before the damp air set in. The other women were still in groups of twos and threes standing outside their front doors. This was like an afternoon matinee at the cinema. No one was going inside until Alice had left and they'd all had a good look at her. Now silence settled over the chattering groups, while each woman stared at Alice and took in every detail from the shoes on her feet to her smug smile and purposeful stride as her shoes clicked and her hat bobbed down the street.

'So, she's up to no good, that one,' said Peggy.

'I've never seen a woman smiling, coming out of a house of death before,' said Mrs Keating.

'Aye, looks like she has her eye set on being the new Bernadette if you ask me, that high and mighty one,' said Mrs O'Prey, as she dropped her ciggie on the pavement and stubbed it out with the toe of her slipper, scorching the sole with a reek of burning rubber.

Nothing would get past the women on the street. They might not have been endowed with academic brilliance or good looks, standing there in their housewife's uniform of curlers, headscarves, wraparound aprons and baggy cardigans, but their emotional intelligence was as sharp as a new razor.

'Aye, so it does,' said Peggy, as Mrs O'Prey's words sank in. Peggy was always the last to catch on. 'My God, the brass neck of the woman. She's as brazen as yer like and, mark my words, I bet we will see her back here soon enough, Jaysus, would yer so believe it not?'

It was often hard to understand what Peggy was on about, even for her neighbours, but they all got the gist and never questioned her.

They carried on watching Alice, walking with a pert step back up the street towards the bus stop, and gave each other a knowing nod and a smile. Peggy put her hands on her hips and began to wiggle, imitating Alice's walk behind her back. They all began to laugh. Peggy always made them laugh.

On the bus back to the hotel, Alice knew she was going to have to play a long game. A thrill of excitement shot through her stomach as she thought about what she had set out to do. The first step had been easier than she had imagined it would be, although her nerve had almost failed her as she walked down the street towards Jerry's house, carrying the fruit cake she had paid the chef in the hotel to make. All of her brave thoughts over the last few days had deserted her. The plans she had made in her head did not seem so attractive in the cold light of day as she attempted to put them into action. It was the children on the street staring at her that finally drove her the last few steps to Jerry's door.

She noticed that front doors on the street were beginning to open and women were gathering in twos and threes, folding their arms and staring at her, as bold as brass. They intimidated her and left her in no doubt that it was her they were talking about. Her heart was pounding in her chest and her throat was so dry it had all but closed up. It had taken all her courage to knock on the door.

'The nerve of me,' she said quietly to herself, as she took her seat on the bus. She almost laughed out loud and looked around to see if anyone had overheard.

There was no doubt in her mind what she wanted, but it wouldn't be fitting for anyone to guess that yet. She wanted Jerry. It wasn't that crazy. The feelings she had nurtured for him over the years were so intense, he would surely feel and share them once he got to know her.

For years, Alice had been obsessed with Jerry. The man who had raised his cap to her. Who had looked into her eyes as he greeted her. The man who had once smiled at her in a way that made her stomach churn like it never had before or since. It was only Jerry who had entered Alice's thoughts over the last few years. Bernadette had been barred. Jerry was important; he mattered, Bernadette did not.

Alice had first met Bernadette when, as a new chambermaid fresh from the bogs, Bernadette had reported for her first day at the hotel. She had immediately caught Alice's attention. Not only was she not scared stiff and whimpering, she was positively bursting with energy, had bright shining eyes and was eager to start work.

Alice managed to remain hostile and distant with the impetuous, bubbly new arrival, who settled into hotel life very quickly.

Bernadette spoke and interrupted Alice so often, she felt her face burning with anger. However, it was impossible to shut up this girl who, even when chastised for talking, appeared never to take offence. Nothing, not even the worst telling-off Alice had ever given to anyone, using the harshest words, seemed to penetrate her happiness.

Alice was fascinated by Bernadette. By her hair, her accent, the way she smiled, the blueness of her eyes. She stared at the freckles on Bernadette's arms, the shape of her teeth, and she was transfixed by every word that came out of her mouth. She felt that if she was an oddity, so was Bernadette, just in a different way. But Alice didn't bond with Bernadette. She didn't like her.

The same couldn't be said of the young man who met Bernadette at the end of each shift every day. That young man did stir feelings in Alice and she was as obsessed with him as she was by Bernadette, but for very different reasons.

Alice had never before seen a man kiss a woman the way she saw Bernadette being kissed. It happened by accident, late one night, just as Alice was closing the blind in her attic room at the back of the hotel. She heard Bernadette's incessant laugh as she turned in to the back gate and watched as, bold as you please, she put her hands on either side of the man's face and kissed him. And then he kissed her back. Alice held her breath, stunned. She felt a thrill of intense excitement run through her entire body, something she had never experienced before. Rooted to the spot, she stared, open-mouthed, and watched them.

And this she did from the very same place, on every night Bernadette went out. Alice lived her life through a pane of glass and in secrecy.

One evening, just as she knew Bernadette was about to leave work to meet her mystery man at the gates, Alice sent her off on an errand whilst she herself slipped outside, under the pretence of dropping a note to the gatekeeper. She wanted to see his face, to look at Bernadette's man close up. She wanted to hear his voice and get close enough to smell him.

As she crossed the yard, with her keys jangling against her long black skirt, she tried not to stare, but it was impossible. She suddenly felt stupid in her housekeeper's long apron. Bernadette's beau was the most beautiful man she had ever seen.

He obviously felt her eyes on his face because he turned, delighted, and chuckled, raising his cap in polite, almost extravagant acknowledgment, and shouted, 'Top of the evening to you!' as she walked past. It was the nicest, warmest smile she had ever received from anyone.

She noticed his hair was almost jet black, curly and slightly too long. Alice felt as though she had had an electric shock.

'Good evening,' she managed to reply primly, but she felt as though she was trying to talk with a mouth stuffed full of knitting.

He was wearing a long dark overcoat and a sombre checked scarf, but she could see that this made his eyes shine even brighter and show off his face, which was tanned, not pale like her own and that of most of the men who worked at the hotel.

Alice felt her cheeks burn red and her heart beat fast. The blood rushed to her ears and she couldn't tell what she was saying to the gatekeeper, who was looking at her oddly. Her heart was pounding and her breath came short from rushing. Her eyes were gleaming at her own audacity. She had done it. She now knew his face. That was all she had wanted. For now.

Every day that Bernadette worked at the hotel, Alice watched her being met and dropped off by her man. She waited, like a voyeur, to see every goodnight kiss at the back gate. She closed her eyes and imagined it was she, not Bernadette, being kissed by the tall handsome Irishman with the gentle smile and laughing eyes who let his hands roam over her buttocks. It was she, not Bernadette, who lifted those hands off and playfully chastised him.

One Saturday morning, there was a knock on Alice's office door, and Bernadette burst in.

'Oh, Alice, I have the most fantastic news!' she announced, bouncing up and down. Bernadette was totally unaware that Alice didn't like her. It was not something she had ever experienced before and she didn't recognize hostility.

'I'm to be married and I would like to give you my week's notice. I'm to become a lady of leisure,' she trilled, as she turned round and round on the spot, her arms open wide to include the entire office in her exuberant embrace. 'Or more likely,' she enthused, not giving Alice time to answer, 'a hard-working housewife.'

Her laughter escaped through the open door and bolted off down the staff corridor, where the chambermaids looked up and smiled at each other, already knowing Bernadette's news.

Alice felt the blood drain from her face. Jerry was about to exit her life. She would no longer be able to see his face every day and imagine he was meeting and courting her, not Bernadette. She nodded in acknowledgment and told Bernadette she would leave a letter in her pigeon hole with her stamp card and a reference for the following Friday. She didn't wish her well, because she felt no such goodwill. She couldn't get her out of the office fast enough. Bernadette was so high on her own happiness, she didn't even notice.

From that Friday onwards, Alice never saw Bernadette again, but she never forgot Jerry. She thought of him every single day. When she slept at night, she dreamt of him. Vivid, detailed, dreams. Once she had seen his face and known his voice, he dominated her waking thoughts and, somewhere in her head, she lived in an imaginary world. One where he was collecting her, waiting for her, kissing her. One in which he was hers and whisking her away to a life in a comfortable house, where she could make a world of her own. A life void of Bernadette.

When years had passed and Alice read the announcement of Bernadette's death in the *Liverpool Echo*, she was breathless with excitement. All those dreams seemed suddenly within her reach. Jerry was alone.

The bus driver approached Alice for the money for her ticket. 'Lime Street station,' she said, as she handed over the money without removing her long gloves, of brown kid leather with six buttons. Alice hadn't bought them; she might have been the housekeeper, but her wages took into account that she was provided with board and food. She certainly couldn't afford gloves as fancy as this herself. They had been left behind by a guest, placed in Alice's lost property box and never claimed.

The bus driver raised his eyebrows. Fingerless knitted mittens were the best he ever saw on a cold day on his bus. Alice saw his look and loved it. Her plan had been developing in her mind by the minute. She wanted Jerry, but not his circumstances. She was not going to live a docker's life. She wanted better than that. That was what happened to the Irish girls at the hotel. She would have to work on Jerry to leave the four streets and use what little money she had to get them away. Alice had worked amongst guests who were travelling on from the Grand to America. She had overheard their conversations and read the letters and leaflets they had left behind in their hotel bedrooms. Alice was taken with the idea of America. New York sounded like the most amazing place in the world.

In a few short minutes she had transformed an idea into a certainty.

The only dent in her pleasure was the unwelcome news that Jerry had been left with a daughter. The wording in the newspaper announcement had repelled her: 'A beloved baby daughter left with a broken heart.' Alice loathed children and in Jerry's kitchen it had taken every ounce of resolve and determination she had to walk over to the basket and make the ridiculous sounds she had heard other women make when they saw a baby. Seeing Jerry's obvious love for Nellie roused no answering tenderness in Alice; she was more curious as to why a man would want to hold a baby and not look displeased. She knew this was something that made her different from other people, and she must disguise it.

It was not entirely Alice's fault that she felt this way. As a child herself, she had been so unloved and neglected that normal emotions were now almost impossible for her. From the age of three, she had known that her parents neither loved nor wanted her. Sitting in the doctor's surgery, suffering miserably with a nasty case of chickenpox, Alice had looked around at the other children, cuddled on their mothers' laps, while she shivered on a hard chair by herself. Her mother sat in the chair next to her, staring straight ahead with a rigid back, managing to look at no one, ignoring the reproachful stares of the other women. Alice leant back against the chair, wondering what it would be like to be touched and kissed like the other children. Alice was never touched at all.

Neither of Alice's parents had wanted children. From the

day she was born neither of them took to her. Her conception had been an 'accident'. One they had learnt from, because they never had sex again. The consequence of sex, Alice, scarred them for the rest of their married life.

Alice's father was a clerk at a solicitor's in town. The couple were just about comfortable, one and a little bit above poor. Alice's mother was a hypochondriac who invented a new illness each week, and her father worked hard to pay the doctor's bills. He was a suppressed, quiet man who accepted his lot in life, did everything he was instructed to do and never complained. Alice sometimes thought he would like to talk to her, that he wanted to be kind, but that he knew it wouldn't be approved of. Only one female in the house was allowed any attention from her father and it wasn't Alice.

As the years passed, Alice became almost invisible. You could walk past her in the street and be totally unaware you had done so, so slight was her presence. Her parents didn't talk to the neighbours and she had no friends to speak of, because she wasn't allowed to play with the other kids in the neighbourhood. She spent a great deal of time at her bedroom window, watching as other children wheeled push-bikes in and out of the houses up and down the street, sometimes pointing up to the window and laughing at her if she didn't move away in time.

'Oi, Miss Havisham,' shouted the boy from across the street to her, one afternoon when she had spent a particularly long time at the window, 'come out and play.' She ducked and hid behind her curtains and didn't go back to the window for days.

When she was about seven years old, she saw a small child and her father walking hand in hand past her window. No one had ever held Alice's hand. She watched intently, unable to look away as the little girl and her father passed by. She stared at their hands, clasped together, at the father striding on ahead laughing, his head bent forward against the wind to prevent his grey trilby hat from blowing away, and the flaps of his long dark grey overcoat kicking out in front as he strode purposefully forwards. Her eyes fixed upon the little girl, giggling, tripping along behind like a balloon bobbing around in the wind, about to break free and take off. She had to resist the urge to run out into the street to follow them and see what they did next.

What is he doing holding onto her hand? she asked herself. She sat for hours, replaying the image over and over in her mind. No matter how long she pondered, it made no sense to her and added to the confusing questions that were growing in her mind about her life.

It wasn't as though she was entirely short of physical contact. The impaired hearing in her left ear was surely due to the fact that whenever she did something wrong, apparently often, her mother hit her with such force across the side of her head that her ear blew up like a cauliflower for well over a week. During this time she couldn't eat properly or close her jaw fully until the swelling had subsided.

And that was about it. There was never any talk other than what was essential. No affection. No interest. She could never remember a meal with her parents, although every night it was her job to lay the table and then to clear the dirty dishes away, when her parents signalled to her that they had finished. She ate her bread and dripping each morning in the scullery, alone, whilst her parents sat at the kitchen table. She was never allowed to join them.

'Don't make any noise when washing up, Alice,' her mother would bark, as they left the room. When Alice made a noise, she reminded them she was there. Noise pricked their collective guilty conscience.

One evening when she was fifteen, while she was washing the supper dishes at the kitchen sink, her mother made a rare appearance and picked up a cloth to wipe down the table. Alice knew straight away that something must be wrong and nervously took her hands out of the dishwater.

'Your father has found you a job,' her mother said to her, without any preamble or niceties. 'On Monday you will start work as a chambermaid at the Grand hotel in town. You will live in at the hotel and earn your own keep. You can pack your bag over the weekend.'

With that, she put down the cloth and left the kitchen. Alice stared at her back as her mother walked out of the door.

The following Monday, Alice stood at the staff entrance to the Grand with her small suitcase at her feet, watching her father walk away without a backward glance. In her pocket was a bag of barley sugars – the first, and last, sweets her father had ever bought her, perhaps in response to the unspoken distress in her eyes.

She never saw either of her parents again. Within a year, they were both killed in a tram accident, having never written to her or visited her since the day she left. Alice inherited just enough money to bury them, and their furniture, which the hotel manager kindly allowed her to store in the hotel basement. Alice received the news of their death with composure and dry eyes. She was swamped by a feeling of relief. No one would hit her, ever again. There may have been no money, but she suddenly had possessions and had lost the people who inflicted so much pain upon her. Alice felt rich and, for the first time in her life, moderately content.

However, this contentment was destined not to last.

The bus pulled up outside the gates of St Mary's and through the window, in the graveyard, Alice saw the freshly dug mound of earth laid over Bernadette's grave like a quilt. It was covered in home-made wreaths and bunches of pink and white flowers. Alice smiled to herself. My turn now, Bernadette, she thought to herself. My turn.

What happened next was a mystery. There was a wire running along the roof of the bus for people to pull to ring the bell in the driver's cab, should they want to alight. As the bus pulled away from the church the bell rang, seemingly of its own accord, and the driver slammed his foot on the brake. He thought something must have been very wrong for the bell to ring as he was pulling away. The conductor, standing in the aisle, suddenly lurched forward and his ticket machine slammed into the side of Alice's head.

'Bloody hell!' he shouted as he grabbed the chrome rails on the back of the seat to steady himself. 'What the flamin' hell are you doin'?' he roared at the driver in his cab behind a screen of glass. Turning his attention to Alice, concerned, he enquired, 'Are you all right, luv?'

Alice was pale and still. She hadn't even flinched. Turning towards the conductor, she smiled as a trickle of blood ran down the side of her face.

'I'm very well, thank you,' she replied as she held her handkerchief to her cheek. 'Very well indeed.'

'As long as you are sure,' said the conductor as he walked away. When he reached the platform at the front of the bus, he turned and noticed Alice look out of the window, talking to herself.

'Nice try, Bernadette,' Alice had whispered.

As the bus approached Lime Street, Alice pulled the cord and stood up. She stepped off the bus and swept in through the staff entrance of the Grand. She made her way up to her own room, acknowledging the curtseys and bows of the other staff with a stiff little nod. Entering her bedroom, she shut the door behind her and looked around her at the room she had occupied ever since she had become housekeeper. Although vastly better than the rest of the staff accommodation at the hotel, it still was not much to show for her years of service. A single sterile room at the top of a hotel with an iron bedstead and a sink. She had a little money put by, but not enough to give her any degree of comfort, come the day she had to leave the hotel. Not enough to buy her a house or to pay for a lifetime of rent somewhere respectable. And Alice knew that, once she reached a certain age, the end would come for her at the Grand.

She had seen it happen to the previous housekeeper, Miss Griffiths, who had been forced out by rheumatoid arthritis at the age of forty-two. Not long after Miss Griffiths left and Alice was promoted to take her place, the hotel manager asked Alice to take a letter and some personal belongings around to Miss Griffiths' forwarding address. What she found there shocked Alice into a fear that was never to leave her. This fear had occupied her thoughts after she turned off her light at night, keeping her awake into the small hours, and was now propelling her into action.

According to the address on the envelope given to her by the hotel manager, Miss Griffiths lived in a large terraced house on Upper Parliament Street, in the not-so-salubrious part of Liverpool. When Alice knocked at the door, she could smell the stench wafting from within.

A young woman, no more than eighteen years old and only half dressed, had answered after the fourth knock.

'What d'ya fuckin' want at this time?' she screeched as she yanked open the door. It was two in the afternoon. She had the grace to say, 'Oh sorry, luv, thought it was one of me customers who couldn't fuckin' wait.'

'I am looking for Miss Griffiths. I believe she lives in flat number two,' said Alice once she had got over her shock.

'The spinster? Is that her name? Yer, luv, she's down the 'all. Close the door after youse, will yer, it's fuckin' freezing,' said the girl, leaving Alice standing on the doorstep. She almost fell back up the stairs, where Alice could hear a baby screaming its lungs out.

Alice stepped inside, reluctant to close the door, as there was no window. A dark brown wire hung from the ceiling but with no bulb attached. The floorboards were bare and filthier than any Alice had ever seen in her life. Rubbish was piled up against the wall in an open wooden box that obviously contained the remains of stale food, even though there was a metal bin outside. The smell of rotting food competed for dominance with that of cat pee, which was definitely winning. Next to the box was the shabbiest pram, with barely any rubber on the wheels, and two skinny, flea-bitten cats asleep inside. She could hear the noise of a man and a woman arguing, and the baby's crying hadn't stopped. It was relentless.

As Alice tentatively clicked the door shut behind her, she was suddenly plunged into darkness and stood still for a few moments to let her eyes adjust. Within seconds, she heard the sound of rustling coming from the box on the floor and realized she was probably sharing her air with rats or goodness knows what other vermin or wildlife.

'Don't panic, just breathe,' she told herself, as she placed her scarf over her mouth to reduce the stench of cat pee and whatever else was making her gag. She heard muffled music coming from down the hall and then saw a faint light struggle to penetrate the darkness from under a door. Alice gingerly made her way towards the thin strip of light, step by step, one hand holding her scarf against her mouth and the other flat on the wall to feel her way along the hall corridor. Suddenly she stood on something that moved so swiftly from under her feet, it made her lose her balance. She put both her hands out to save herself, but to no avail, ending up face down in a new musky smell she recognized. Shaken and shocked, she picked herself up as the door tentatively opened and, to Alice's huge relief, flooded the narrow hallway with light.

'Hello, Alice,' said Miss Griffiths, 'My poor girl, I am so sorry, are you all right? Can I help you up? How lovely to see you, please come in.'

Alice looked down at herself. She was covered in black dust, having fallen over a pile of coal outside the door. She took a handkerchief out of her handbag and began to furiously brush herself down.

'It is my fault,' she said, seeing how much worse the rheumatics had made Miss Griffiths and how gnarled her hands were. 'I will just put this back.' She bent down and retrieved the coal scattered around the hallway.

'I am relieved to see it's you,' said Miss Griffiths. 'Some of my coal is stolen every day and I don't ever get to the door in time to see who it is.'

Alice wanted to ask why it was kept on the floor outside the door but the answer awaited her as she stepped inside.

The room was hardly big enough for one person and Alice noticed that it was not as clean as Mrs Griffiths had kept her room at the hotel. Her housekeeper's eye took in the dirt on the floor around her fireplace and the smoky grime on the mirror hung on the wall. Alice wondered how Miss Griffiths managed to cope as she noticed her hands were so bad that her fingers appeared to have closed over on themselves. A badly made bed occupied one corner; at its foot was a table with a pot, bowl and a matching jug. Another small table stood against a wall with wooden chairs on either side, the seat pads covered in green leather. On this table stood a radio playing classical music, a bowl of sugar, a brown teapot, a milk jug and a cup and saucer. Two red velvet armchairs flanked the small range in which a pathetic fire with the remains from a handful of coal smouldered. Against the opposite wall was a cupboard that obviously contained food. A chest of drawers stood to the side of the door and above it hung a picture that Alice thought she had once seen in one of the hotel bedrooms before it had been redecorated. The cold from outside had seeped into the room and the dwindling fire had allowed the damp to take hold. On a diminutive rug in front of the fire slept a ginger tomcat with a battle-chewed and bloody ear.

Alice didn't like being here. Miss Griffiths had been her superior. Never a personal word had passed between them. Their past conversations had been about bathrooms, sheets and chambermaids. Alice knew nothing about Miss Griffiths but, over a short period of time, she had watched the older woman's hands turn out sideways to resemble a pair of fans and her back hunched, until she was so debilitated that she could no longer work.

'Would you like a cup of tea for your trouble?' asked Miss Griffiths, as she struggled to take the envelope and the bag from Alice.

If Alice felt awkward, Miss Griffiths felt diminished and embarrassed by Alice seeing her in this condition. Her job had been her world and she had been very professional, running a tight ship and managing the chambermaids as though she were a strict hospital matron. If only she had known, she was friendliness itself compared with Alice.

'Er, no, thank you,' said Alice. 'I had better be getting the bus back now. We have a new girl arriving off the boat from the bogs this afternoon and, as you know, I need to be there to sort her out.'

She had no idea what to say and took her leave within minutes, not noticing the look of acute disappointment in Miss Griffiths' eyes. It would never have occurred to Alice that she was the only visitor Miss Griffiths had received in many months. It never crossed her mind to offer to carry in some coal, or ask if there was anything she could help with. It was now almost impossible for Miss Griffiths to pick up a cup and saucer, but she would never let anyone know that.

Those thoughts still didn't cross Alice's mind when she heard three months later that Miss Griffiths had been found dead in her armchair, having died of dehydration and hypothermia. It was the constant wailing of the cat and the lack of coal to steal that had attracted the neighbour's attention.

Alice knew that if she didn't act quickly, this could be her fate. She would become the next Miss Griffiths. She was prepared to do whatever it took to make sure that never happened to her. Come hell or high water, her future would be secure.

Later that afternoon, at the end of their shift, the crew from the bus enjoyed their mug of tea in the Crosville hut down at the Pier Head. The conductor filled in his accident book and noted what had happened for his supervisor.

'She was a fucking loony,' said the conductor to the driver. 'Posh gloves, but away with the fucking fairies, if you ask me, talking to herself out of the window. Not even so much as a flinch when the ticket machine caught her in the face.'

'You're the nutter,' said the driver, 'pulling the bleeding cord and then saying you didn't.'

They finished their break in an acrimonious silence, the conductor not wanting to mention the woman with long red hair that he thought he had seen jump onto the bus just before the bell rang, but was nowhere to be found afterwards.

# Chapter Five

OVER THE NEXT year and a half, Alice put her plan into action with great skill and single-minded determination. She was living a lie but she was excited and fired up by the fact that it was no effort whatsoever, and she could very easily see the results of her scheming slowly and steadily becoming her reward.

She had hoped that the baby would travel back to Ireland with her grandparents or maybe even be popped into a convent. To her huge disappointment, she discovered on one of her first visits that the baby was going nowhere. It was a blow, but Alice even had a plan as to how to cope with Nellie. Week by week, she eased herself a little more into Jerry's life and each week made it a little harder for him to manage without her help. Without his even realizing it, Jerry was slowly becoming dependent upon Alice.

Alice was as cunning as she was cold. She paid her second visit almost a month after the first and then the next three weeks later. Each time she came with something delicious to leave behind and, by the third visit, she had begun to help with little things, like the ironing, or making a pie, with food she had taken from the hotel kitchen. This food was divided out amongst staff who worked at the hotel. For the lower grades, it was the leftovers from the table service; but for the more senior staff, it was a cut from the butcher's and a share from the fresh fruit and veg delivery.

Alice had never previously taken any, but now she pulled rank. She brought fresh beef and chicken to Jerry's house and, having taken lessons from the hotel chef, could cook a decent stew. The chef made her the odd pie with buttery hand-rolled puff pastry and steaming gravy, which, delivered in a wicker basket wrapped up in a tea towel, lasted Jerry a few days. In return, Alice supplied the kitchen staff with bedding, blankets and pillows. The hotel trade was doing well in Liverpool and everyone had their cut.

After the first six months, Jerry would arrive home some nights to find Alice in the kitchen cooking a meal. She always left straight away, insisting she didn't want to encroach upon his time. This made him feel bad and he implored her to stay and eat with him. He had never invited her to the house, but she quickly worked out that the back door was never locked and took the daring step one day to let herself in.

For Jerry, the pleasure of coming home to a clean house, with the range lit and a meal cooked, quickly surpassed his shock at finding a near stranger in his kitchen.

One day, when Jerry and Tommy were sitting on the dock wall having a ciggie break after unloading a hull, they began to talk about Alice.

'She is a strange thing, this Alice,' Jerry said to Tommy. 'She seems to like helping out and I can't work out what she wants in return because she won't let me pay her nowt.'

Eejit, thought Tommy, but kept his thoughts to himself. He wasn't going to start a row with his best mate. He also wasn't going to repeat to Maura what Jerry had just said, because she would kick off. Instead, Tommy made a few enquiries of his own.

'Was she a friend of Bernadette, then?' he asked, as subtly as a brick. 'It's just that I was wondering, like, why I never saw her before Bernadette passed away and, the thing is, I don't remember her from the wedding, either.'

'She was nursing her sick aunt in Macclesfield,' said Jerry, who had already asked this question of Alice during one of their first meetings. He had tried to place her in his mind and tried to remember meeting her. He couldn't. It was a mystery. He knew the name, he had heard Bernadette mention an Alice, but in what context he had no recollection. But he didn't have time to dwell on it and, anyway, she was obviously just kind and trying to help.

'I do feel a bit uncomfortable, so I do, just sometimes,' said Jerry. 'I mean, what would Bernadette say? But, Tommy, I swear to God, it's nothing like that, I never so much as touched her or had a thought like that cross me mind. Anyway, as soon as I gets in, she leaves.'

'Aye,' said Tommy, nodding. Maura had mentioned that. 'You know what I think, Jerry? I think she's broody and it's all about the babby. She has none of her own and I reckon she's hanging around 'cause she has a nature for Nellie. Not having had a baby of their own by the time they are twenty-one does strange things to a woman's brain, so it does, and the more time goes on the worse it gets. I don't know how Bernadette stayed so normal, I don't. Best thing to do is bang 'em up as much as ye can and as soon as possible and then ye can't go wrong. It's natural.'

Having both spoken enough for working men, they sat on the wall in silence, looking down at their boots while they finished their ciggies. Jerry was lost in thought as to how things would have been different if he had led his life according to Tommy's simple rules.

One day, Jerry invited Alice to stop, spend the evening and eat with him and Nellie. He felt bad that she had arrived with a meal and wouldn't take a penny off him.

His mornings were always rushed. On his way to work he took Nellie down to Maura's, with a basket full of nappies, and collected her on his way home. He often left the kitchen in a mess and felt horribly guilty at how much this nice, kind woman, who wouldn't stay longer than five minutes once he and Nellie got in, did to help them. He felt he should do something in return. Initially, she refused every single time but then slowly she began to accept the occasional invitation, always manufacturing reasons as to why she couldn't accept most times he asked.

Over time, although he had never so much as touched her, Jerry realized that Alice was becoming a fixture in his life and that others would regard her as more than a friend. Alice was odd, he recognized that.

Maura remembered the stories Bernadette had told her about Alice. Maura hated Alice, which made things difficult. Every time Jerry dropped Nellie off at Maura's, he was assailed by a storm of questions. He assumed that Alice didn't relate very well to Nellie because she didn't want to step on Maura's toes. Even he was aware that when Maura came into his house and Alice was there, the hostility between them froze the air within seconds. However, he knew that when Alice wasn't around, life was just that bit harder.

After about a year, he began to invite Alice to go with him to the Irish centre on a Saturday night, and on Sunday afternoons she would occasionally meet up with him, as he pushed Nellie around in her pram for a change of scenery. Jerry would do anything to keep moving and to blot Bernadette out of his mind. Thinking about her wasn't the source of comfort he once thought it would be; it was torturous and painful.

As Alice became a regular feature at the house, Maura grew spitting mad. If she could have poisoned Alice and got away with it, she would have. One day, when Jerry wasn't around, Maura decided to meet Alice on her own terms. When she saw Alice enter Jerry's house via the entry, she followed her into the house and pretended to be shocked when she found Alice in the kitchen. Alice was so much at home that there wasn't much acting involved in Maura's being stunned.

'Can I help ye?' she said. 'Are ye here for anything special? Only Jerry didn't mention youse was comin'.'

Alice knew she would have to deal with this one carefully. Maura might be bog Irish, but she could tell she was sharp.

'He doesn't know,' she responded, without a hint of friendliness in her voice. 'I finished early at the hotel and thought I would pop down to help him out.'

'Did you now,' said Maura, instantly affronted and her temper rising. 'Well, let me tell ye, miss, there are plenty of us here on this street to help out. Jerry doesn't need a stranger to do it for him.'

'Oh, I'm no stranger, Maura,' said Alice tartly. 'In fact, Jerry is taking me to the Irish centre on Saturday night. So I am sure we can chat there, but for now, if you don't mind, I have a meal to make.'

Maura stared with envy at the meat Alice had unpacked from her basket. A dark piece of brisket sat on the table covered in a dark-veined, deep-yellow fat. Maura could never afford meat like that in her house. The two women looked each other in the eye. Maura had met her match. As she retreated from the kitchen, Maura spotted the statue of the Virgin Mary on the mantelpiece, facing the wall, as if in disgust. She immediately thought Alice had done it.

In an act of defiance and with a determination somehow to leave her mark on the kitchen before she exited, Maura stormed over to the range and reached up to the mantelpiece.

'The Virgin Mother doesn't put her back on us,' said Maura, as she turned the statue round. 'She keeps an eye on what we're up to.' Then she flounced out of the kitchen.

Confused, Alice looked up at the statue and at the door

Maura had just slammed behind her. It is true, she thought somewhat ironically, the Irish are mad.

It was after a particularly bad second winter alone, with Nellie now toddling around the house, that Jerry asked Alice to marry him. He hadn't planned to and for days afterwards he regretted what he had done, but there was no way out of it. He had committed a mortal sin. He had made his bed and now he had to lie in it.

Two weeks earlier, measles had swept the streets and Nellie had been ill for the entire time. Jerry had barely coped. Maura was at her wits' end, with her own seven children all down with the same illness, including Kitty, who was usually like a second mother and a second pair of hands for Maura.

It was the first time Nellie had been ill and despite Maura's protestations that she could handle one more sick child, Jerry wanted his Nellie to have all of his attention. He took the whole week off work and didn't go down to the docks once. It was Tommy who kept both houses fed that week.

Jerry hadn't seen much of Alice while Nellie was ill, although it was the one time he could really have done with her help. He wondered where she was and why she hadn't called in, but he was too busy nursing Nellie to think too much about anything, other than keeping her temperature and her food down.

It had never once occurred to him to ask Alice to marry him. He didn't think about it even for a second, not even when he hit his lowest point, boiling Nellie's vomit-soaked sheets in the copper boiler in the yard, with the cold rain pouring down the back of his neck and the steam from the boiler scalding his face. Not even when he cried again and his tears ran into the trickles of steam on his cheeks.

Definitely not then, because that was when he thought he heard Bernadette say his name. As he looked up, he saw her through the steam at the kitchen window, like he used to. She was standing at the sink, smiling out at him. Definitely not then, because that was one of the few moments he felt Bernadette was somewhere near, when he needed her, when he knew he wasn't alone. One of the very few moments he allowed himself to think about who and what he had lost and lived without, when he let her memory roam free. And he was filled with shame at how angry those moments made him feel, the fury rising like acid in his throat.

It happened on a Saturday night. Jerry had invited Alice to the Irish centre, something he now did on a regular basis as a way of saying thank you. He didn't really know what else to do. Even though he'd worked out she didn't have much of a social life, he told himself that she appeared to enjoy herself and the odd glass of Guinness, so it usually turned out well enough.

The dockers worked hard, their wives struggled to manage every day, but it was all made bearable by the fun they had down the club on a Saturday night. They spent the first half of their week talking about the previous Saturday and the second looking forward to the next. So special were Saturday nights that it was the only night of the week the headscarves came off, the curlers came out and the Coty cherry-red lipstick was taken off the top of the mantelpiece, where it stood all week like an ornament, and was applied carefully in front of the mirror that hung above. Lipstick cost money. Nothing that cost money was hidden away. A lipstick was a possession to be admired and it remained on parade, ready to hand, to apply at a moment's notice. Maura dusted her lipstick, along with the pot dogs. The family lived hard during the week but there was no better fun to be had than in the Irish centre, or in the Grafton rooms on a Saturday night.

There was a comedian over from Dublin that night to do a turn and a band from Sligo playing afterwards, which everyone on the docks had been talking about for weeks. Jerry knew the craic would be good and he would be able to have a few drinks himself and relax, not something he did often. It didn't really worry him that Alice was intense and slow to laugh, that she never spoke to Nellie, that she avoided any intimate contact with him and was the coldest fish he had ever met. He didn't care. He just liked to have the company. Another human being to relate to. Someone to keep him talking about little things and stop him thinking and remembering.

The women in the street reminded him every day. They knocked on his window as they walked past and shouted to him, 'On me way to mass, Jerry, and I'll light a candle for the angel Bernadette when I'm there, so I will.'

He would stand and look through the nets as the women's shadows passed by, and feel nothing. He hadn't been to mass since the day of the funeral. He never opened the door to the priest and he hadn't prayed a word since the day Bernadette died.

The women on the street mentioned Bernadette every single time they saw him. They spoke to him with manufactured expressions of acute pain etched on their faces.

'Oh God, ye look like a man broken with tears,' said Molly Barrett, as he bumped into her in the entry. He had no words to reply with, as she dragged on her ciggie and went on her way. He knew she meant well.

Mrs McGinty would touch his forearm and look at the floor as though suffering an attack of acute colic before squeezing out a tear and saying, 'God, I imagine the pain, Jerry, is more than ye can bear, Jer, ye must weep ye'self to sleep every night, ye poor, poor man, and how is the poor wee motherless babby?'

The past two weeks had been tough. He was haunted by the fact that people kept telling him he couldn't manage, that he needed help, that he shouldn't have to cope. He knew people frowned at the thought of him bringing up Nellie on his own. As he walked out of a shop one day with Nellie in his arms, struggling to carry his bag, he heard the greengrocer whisper to the next customer, who nodded in agreement, 'It's unnatural, so it is, he won't keep that up for long.'

He realized he needed Alice's help. Alice never mentioned his pain. She never spoke of Bernadette, ever. He had heard her mention Bernadette's name only on her first visit. With Alice, he hid. She was a life after death.

He drank too much that night. Alice didn't like to socialize and, although she hadn't ever said so to him, she made it known. It wasn't that she was rude to people, she was just quiet. She never asked a question and never fully answered one, either. And she was asked a lot of questions. No one on the four streets knew where Alice had sprung from. Some of the women, especially Maura, knew what her game was, but there was nothing they could do. Alice gave them no ammunition to use against her. She didn't engage or converse. She knew their game, too.

Jerry had to sit on a table for two with Alice, not on a big circular table for twenty as he had with his Bernadette. The nights at the Irish centre with Bernadette had been some of the best in his life, full of dancing and laughter. Bernadette would often run down to the centre first when he was getting changed after work, or watching the footie, and he often tried to stop her.

'Jerry,' she would protest, 'we have no babbies, we aren't as busy as the others. I like to keep a seat for everyone at the big table.' And that is what she did and everyone knew she would.

'Keep me seat on Sat'dy night, our Bernadette,' neighbours would shout to her, during the week. 'We'll be counting on ye, Bernadette, me corns won't take the pressure stood.'

It was just one of the little things she used to do that made her, a new wife, one of the community, from the day she arrived on the four streets.

Alice had no intention of saving seats for anyone. God, how she hated the Irish centre and everyone in it. She hid it well, but not enough to join in.

'Are ye not good enough to sit with us then, ye two?' the odd person would say, as they passed by their table.

People were trying to be welcoming and willing to have Alice on their table for Jerry's sake. Jerry hadn't told them that Alice was a Proddie, but they had all guessed. Everyone had wondered whether she was part of an Orange Lodge and would be out on the march in July. But, as it was, they saw her going into Jerry's house just as the big march was taking two hours to pass through the city and so they knew Jerry was safe on that score. It was the nineteen-fifties, but in Liverpool it was as if the battle of the Boyne was only last week.

Some of Jerry's friends would be more insistent, trying to get them to bring their drinks over and join them on their table. Jerry wanted nothing more. But always, the answer was no. Alice would shake her head, look down into her Guinness, smile sweetly and appear shy.

She wanted to reply, 'No, you aren't good enough to sit with us, never mind us with you.'

God, how she hated Guinness too. Alice looked around the club on this particular Saturday and tried to hide her discomfort at the cigarette smoke stinging her eyes. When would he realize he needed her? When could she stop pretending to like this foul drink?

Alice had reached a wall. She had no experience of romance and no idea of what to do to take her plan to another level. For the first time since she had left home, she was lost for ideas.

Alice was the only person in the club who didn't laugh at the comedian. The only woman not to dance to the band.

Jerry, a fun-lover, who had spent most of his life laughing, recognized that he wasn't enjoying himself. In fact, he didn't even feel comfortable. He and Alice had run out of things to say half an hour ago. He had managed through the measles without help and, sure, hadn't he come out of the other side all right? The house might be a mess today, but Nellie was better and had wanted for nothing. Measles killed toddlers, but not his Nellie. He had passed the biggest test of a single father, one many women struggled with.

Time to stop this, he thought to himself. I will not ask Alice to come any more and in future will come here on my own and sit with the others.

Jerry was feeling stronger. It was almost two years since Bernadette had died. He could do this alone now. He took a deep sigh. He had just taken the first decision of his own in two years and he felt good. Empowered. He was going to get a grip, take control of his own life and look forwards for him and Nellie. It was time to make a visit home and take Nellie to see her family and the farm he grew up on. His mammy had written to say Joe had been ill, and Jerry was keen to visit him. He would arrange that tomorrow.

He looked at Alice, knowing she was about to become a thing of the past, and he felt lighter at that thought. No sense of loss, just relief.

A minute later, Alice took a very huge risk and slipped her hand on top of Jerry's while he sat and laughed at the comedian. As she lifted her own to put it on top of his, it shook. Her mouth was dry, and she was breathless. This was the most daring thing she had ever done in her life. The comedian sounded louder than he actually was and as she looked around, no one was looking at them. Everyone was laughing loudly and hysterically. It was a good moment.

She had no idea what he would do in response. She was terrified, but knew that, as he had already drunk a fair quantity of Guinness, now was as good a time as any. She had seen the look on his face, the expression in his eye when he had looked at her a moment ago. It was as though he had stepped back. She saw in his eyes the slight flicker of a decision and his body language spoke volumes, as he leant back in his chair and sighed. For the first time, she felt as though she was losing control. She had slipped backwards in the flash of a second and she knew that she had nothing to offer that couldn't easily be supplied by any other woman. A woman he could easily pay a few bob a week to and who would look after Nellie in her own home. Her capital was shrinking. His gratitude diminishing. She had to think fast.

She didn't look at him, as she felt the dark hair on the back of his hand bristle against her palm. Her heart was beating too fast; she couldn't catch her breath and she didn't dare look up.

She heard him say, 'Alice,' but she still couldn't look.

He said her name again. 'Alice, Queen.' This time she made herself look him straight in the eye with a bold stare.

'Would ye like another drink?' he asked, not knowing what else to say. He thought initially her hand on the back of his was to catch his attention above the noise. It was only when he saw the look in her eye that he realized he was wrong. Something else was going on with Alice.

She felt a small self-satisfied warmth with the sense that she had just taken a gigantic step. Emboldened, she radiated a new self-confidence.

The Guinness and Alice's hand on his were confusing Jerry. He was a sucker for human contact and had missed that a great deal over the last two years. When he looked at Alice, she smiled sweetly. That was hard for Jerry. He was still vulnerable and loved a woman's company. It was so long since he had had sex, he couldn't remember what it would be like to have a woman in bed next to him.

Hand on hand ... skin on skin ... limb on limb.

The thought of moving on from Alice to a future on his own flitted away, as quickly as it had arrived.

He turned over Alice's hand and laid his strong, brown docker's palm on top of hers. Her pale white fingers and delicate nails were almost half the size of his. He gently lifted both their hands to face upwards, still joined, palm to palm, as if in prayer, as he stared at them both. Jerry was lost in the moment of fusion. It had been so long.

There was no real beauty in Alice, no vibrancy, no passion. He couldn't compare her to Bernadette. Chalk and cheese. It was futile to compare any woman to Bernadette; she would fail miserably. After Bernadette, one woman was as good or as bad as another but only one woman was cooking his meals, cleaning his house from time to time and had her hand on his.

The band would play until two in the morning but it was now midnight and, much to Alice's relief, Jerry stood to leave.

'Come on, Queen,' he said, 'let's go.'

He had no thought other than that this was a new and strange situation, and he didn't for one moment want Maura or anyone else for that matter to see him and Alice holding hands. They would want to know what was going on and he had no idea himself. Five minutes ago he had decided it was time to move on from Alice, now here he was holding her hand. How had that happened?

Halfway to the bus stop, Alice slipped her hand into his again and held it.

'Jerry, can we go back to the house tonight for a drink?' she whispered. She did her very best to appear seductive although this was so new to her that she had never even been kissed.

Jerry was thrown. They had not done this before. Through the fog of Guinness he tried to recall what time the last bus was and whether she would make it home if they went to his house first. Nellie was sleeping at Maura and Tommy's where all the children were being looked after by Mrs Keating's daughter, so he had no reason not to leave the house later and walk her to the bus stop.

'Sure, but the last bus goes in an hour,' said Jerry.

She kept her hand in his and turned to walk back towards the house, pulling him round to follow her. There had been no conversation as to what was to happen – there never was much conversation between them – but Jerry didn't argue with the fact that they were deviating from their normal routine. He was too far gone. It was the Guinness holding Alice's hand, not Jerry.

She thought she knew what was coming. They would sit down and have a cup of tea and chat about how difficult Jerry was finding things. He would tell her that she had become the centre of his universe and that he couldn't manage without her, he needed her. That he was beginning to love the times she came round, their walks and occasional evenings out. He would tell her he loved her more than anything in the world. That he admired her cultured ways and wanted to move away from the docks, to make a fresh start together in America or somewhere better than the four streets. Maybe he thought about New York where Alice had always dreamt of living, amongst more ambitious people.

Alice had talked to Jerry about going into insurance and she was sure he was clever enough to get a job at the Royal Liverpool. They had been advertising this week and Jerry had a nice hand for writing. He would tell her he was going to take her advice and apply for jobs, and he would finish his little speech by getting down on one knee and asking her, would she marry him? This was in the world according to Alice. This was her plan.

Alice knew she might have to try to seduce Jerry. This was something she had only ever imagined, but it didn't matter, she would manage. She had overheard enough conversations amongst chambermaids to know what they got up to and wasn't she better than any of them? There were ways to avoid getting pregnant and she would use them. She might have to do this thing with Jerry to get him to propose. She had worked hard to get to this point and she wasn't going to let the time pass any longer. He was an honourable man. Once he had laid with her, he would propose. It couldn't go wrong and if an Irish slut from the bogs like Bernadette could manage it, then so could she.

Jerry's ideas were different. He had two bottles of Guinness in his free hand. He thought they would have a drink, and then he would take her for the bus or if they had missed the last one, he would walk with her down towards town to hail a cab. Then he would be up, bright and early, to play the ritual Sunday game of footie with Tommy and the other men and lads on the green, whilst Kitty looked after Nellie. He would then go to Maura's house for the usual big Sunday roast. Nellie loved nothing more than sitting in Maura's kitchen, eating her dinner in the company of seven other children. It was the one meal of the week when they pushed the boat out. Jerry always gave Maura money to contribute. He and Tommy earned the same wage. Jerry's had to keep two people. Tommy's had to stretch to nine, and it wasn't easy.

As they went in through the back door, Alice took off her coat. She was wearing a dress that evening that she had bought in town that day. It was cut lower than she would have ever dared wear before and she was self-conscious about the fact that she was displaying too much cleavage. All evening she had wished there was spare material she could pull over her breasts and she regretted not wearing a cardigan. She had spent the entire night trying to draw the neck of the dress closed. She had bought the dress only because she remembered Bernadette's beautiful figure and how the hotel porters used to comment about it when they thought she was out of earshot.

Whilst Jerry hung up her coat, she took another huge leap. She put her hand inside her dress and lifted each breast up and out to make it more prominent, pushing the material aside to display more cleavage. She took a deep breath. She had no idea what came next but hoped something would give her a clue. She wanted him to look at her breasts, which she had boldly presented, and then kiss her. That must be how it went.

Alice hadn't been round to the house for a couple of weeks, because she knew Nellie had been sick. Any child was bad enough, but a sick child was intolerable. She realized that while Jerry was trapped in the house with Nellie, Alice was safe and no other papist whore would be getting her nose in. She calculated that to stay away would be a good thing. It would make him see how useful she had been over the last two years and how much her involvement in Jerry's life made sense.

She was wrong.

She had almost overplayed her hand.

As Jerry switched the lights on, she looked around at the kitchen. The floor was disgustingly dirty. She shuddered. Filthy dishes met her eye, and mouldy remains of dried egg and fat clung to the greasy oilcloth on the table. It looked as if it hadn't been wiped once in the two weeks since she was last there. Jerry's and Nellie's dirty clothes were piled up on the corner of the kitchen floor, not even in a basket or a box. Jerry had spent all day washing the sheets and hadn't got round to the clothes.

A white enamel bucket of cold, pungent, dark-brown

water sat under the sink, full of Nellie's soaking dirty nappies. In the dim light from the overhead bulb, the indoor washing line had been pulled out across the top of the range, on which were pegged the few nappies Jerry had managed to wash out that day, now filling the room with steam. Its smell, and that of the enamel nappy bucket, mingled with that of Jerry's sweat-soaked work clothes and made Alice's stomach heave. She just about hid her revulsion.

Pull yourself together, you are nearly there, she told herself, as she forced another smile and looked Jerry straight in the eye. She wanted to leave the service of the hotel and begin planning a new life with the man she hadn't stopped thinking about since the day she first saw him. Having seen him treat another woman and even his repulsive child with so much kindness, she was determined to have him for herself.

Jerry opened the bottles and drank deeply from one. He looked at Alice as, without a word, he handed her hers. Alice took it from him before picking up his free hand and placing it on her breast. Jerry was stunned. Repelled. No. He didn't want this at all.

He could feel that Alice was shaking, as abruptly she moved his hand down and onto her abdomen and then slid it between her legs. This is what she had seen the girls do at the back gate with the men who walked them home to the back of the hotel. They didn't know Alice watched them every night. She had seen them put their hands down men's trousers and undo the buttons as they got down onto their knees, or sometimes if the men were in a hurry they raised the girls' skirts and almost lifted them off the floor as they pinned them against the wall and took them quickly.

They always reminded Alice of animals. Of the roaming dogs she had watched in the street when she was a girl. She had seen neighbours run out with buckets of cold water to throw over those that were locked together, howling and snapping, stuck in mid-copulation. She had only to step away from the window to remove herself but she never did. She had watched every chambermaid who had been taken at the back gate since Bernadette had left. Voyeurism had been Alice's life.

In those few seconds, whilst she moved Jerry's hand between her legs, a switch flicked on in Jerry that had been shut down for a long time. Suddenly, in the passing of a single second, he knew what he was about to do. He pulled away from her abruptly and staggered from the door with his back to the range. He stood looking at this plain, skinny woman, whom he didn't really know. Was this really about to happen?

He realized he had no idea how this situation had come about. He was deviating from his path of strict emotional control, a path he had walked in a steady line for two years. Now that he had stepped off he was beyond help. At that moment, his love for Bernadette turned to hatred. His anger at her leaving him bubbled to the surface for the first time since she had died.

He had drunk too much to control his fury. He felt hatred for God, the world, the priests, his neighbours who pitied him, for his parents for being elderly, for the life he had inherited and for the impossible job of being a father. He felt hatred for this scheming devil woman who was not the shy and proper Alice he knew. He hated himself. He hated everyone and everything and he was about to explode with anger.

'Come here,' he said roughly as he moved away from the range and towards her.

Alice stood frozen to the spot. If she did move towards him, she didn't know what to do.

'Come here,' he said again, only louder, with impatience and irritation.

For a second this shocked Alice, terrifying her into silence. This was the opposite of kindness, this was not what she had planned. This was not the fumbling she had seen at the back gate of the hotel. She was rooted to the spot, as he took the few remaining steps to stand in front of her. Without even kissing or touching her, he roughly pulled her dress up to her waist and her panties down over her suspenders and stockings. He took the bottle out of her hand, and placed it on the draining board. Jerry was an Irishman. He might have been about to have sex for the first time in almost two years, he might have been angry and have lost all reason, but he wasn't going to spill the Guinness.

Afterwards there were very few things Jerry remembered about that night. It would take too much time to go through the niceties and get Alice to bed, so he took her over the kitchen table.

He couldn't make love to her and look at her face at the same time, and so he turned her over. He could do this only if he couldn't see her eyes. He couldn't kiss her. Kissing her was the last thing he wanted to do. He wanted only sex, not affection. He wanted to punish her, badly. He remembered holding the back of her hair and accidentally pressing her face into the table without meaning to. His instincts were basic and animalistic, and if Alice hadn't deliberately engineered this, his lovemaking would have bordered on rape.

Making love to Bernadette had been nothing like this but that was what he wanted right now. No affection, no loving conversation, no kissing, no laughter. He wanted nothing to be like it was with him and Bernadette. Nothing. His anger with Bernadette for leaving him with a child and his intense hatred for life spilt out of him and into Alice as he pounded and punished her. And she didn't make a sound.

So angry was he and so consumed with loathing, he didn't notice the tears he cried all the way through. He didn't hear his own sobs.

She was relieved when he finished, staggered backwards against the range and picked up his bottle again.

'Oh God, for feck's sake,' he said, as he wiped his mouth with his hand.

Was that a good thing for him to say, she wondered? Did that mean he enjoyed it? She had never imagined she would lose her virginity, ever. But when she had, she had not imagined it would be like this. She was horrified and in shock, but she was tough. She was repelled by the surroundings and the smell, by the fact that nothing tonight seemed to be going to her plan. She knew what she was aiming for and if this was how to get there, so be it. She saw the tears pouring down his face, but pretended she hadn't.

Alice felt physically sick. She felt worthless and abused. She had thought that Jerry would at least kiss her the way she had seen him kiss Bernadette, night after night, from her bedroom window. That her first time would be less brutal than this. Tears pricked at the back of her own eyes and she willed them to stay where they were. If this was what she had to do to get his ring on her finger, she would go through it in silence. If it took her one step away from her single room in a hotel attic, if she had to endure this night, she would do it.

Pushing down on the table with her hands, she levered herself up from where he had left her. Her dress was around her waist and she frantically pushed it back down.

She turned round and looked at him. So acute was her embarrassment that it was one of the hardest things she had ever done in her life. He wouldn't meet her gaze, as he wiped his tears away with the back of his hand. Not looking at her was, in a way, a relief as he drank from the bottle.

'Get undressed, Alice,' he said as he undid his belt. 'Get all your clothes off now.'

For a second, with horror, she thought he was going to beat her with the belt but realized it was to further loosen his trousers. She had walked into enough hotel bedrooms and seen enough men naked not to be shocked, but she knew he would never have spoken to Bernadette in that way. Alice was jealous of a ghost.

'Get on your hands and knees on the floor,' Jerry said and Alice didn't recognize his voice. It was guttural and thick from the tears choking his throat.

She shook like a leaf and felt humiliated as, naked and

cold, she obeyed awkwardly. Her face was feet away from the stinking pile of washing. Stale remnants of breadcrumbs and food dug into her palms and knees, stabbing into her skin like sharp tiny pins. As he pounded her repeatedly, this time for much longer, it took all her strength to keep her arms rigid to support herself. The buckle from his belt pierced the skin on the back of her thigh almost causing her to scream out in pain. She could not withstand his weight and when he finally came, her arms collapsed and her entire body crashed forward onto the floor with Jerry laid fully across her back. A virgin no more. She was at one with cold, dirty concrete. Her face was pressed downwards and she smelt urine where, earlier in the day, Nellie had had an accident while she toddled around.

'Oh God, I'm sorry.' Jerry sobbed and sobbed and, for the second time that night, Alice did not know what to do.

She lay perfectly still and waited for the sobbing to subside. What had she done wrong?

When Jerry finally stood up, he staggered up the stairs to his bed, saying nothing to Alice. She heard him crying, so loudly and painfully that she knew the emotion locked her out of the room. She gathered herself together, snatched up her clothes, holding them tightly in front of her, and collapsed onto the small sofa against the wall. She was scared he would come back down the stairs and demand more, but after half an hour or so, she heard the sobbing subside and knew he had fallen asleep.

Even though she hated the stuff, Alice went over to the Guinness and gulped the rest to calm her nerves and, even though she didn't smoke, she lit one of Jerry's cigarettes. She was in shock. But that was all. It was done now. She was no longer a virgin.

There was now something she knew she had to do. She took out of her bag the potion she had bought at the chemist's and put the kettle on the kitchen range. She might have got what she wanted, but she wasn't going to get more than she had asked for.

*

Of the two of them, only Jerry knew that there were sailors taking whores up against the dock walls with more feeling than he had felt before or after sex, with Alice in his own home. Alice had no idea that what had just taken place had nothing to do with her. That she could have been anyone.

Now she was occupying the bed he had shared with Bernadette. He had woken up in the middle of the night and become aware Alice was there, lying next to him but as far away as she could be. He felt worse with Alice in his bed than if he had been alone.

When he had been on his own, he would place his hand flat onto the mattress and slowly pass it over the bed. It didn't always happen, but sometimes it would stop as it came up against her form. He would close his eyes and, as he breathed deeply, he would move his arm up and onto the milky-soft skin of her abdomen, which he knew as well as his own. He would run his hand up and across her breasts, over her face and into her wild hair. In the moonlight streaming in through the window he would see her eyes twinkle at him. And, just like that, he would lie and talk to her about Nellie and work, Maura and Tommy, and would fall asleep with her breath on his hand.

He knew now that would never happen again. He had never talked to Bernadette about Alice and here Alice was, lying in her place.

At first light, Alice slipped out to the outhouse to clean herself up. The sticky mess, which had spread across her thighs, had made her legs itch all night. She couldn't get it off her skin quickly enough as she scrubbed and scrubbed until her legs were red raw.

Whilst Jerry still slept, she cleaned the kitchen and put the nappies into the boiler. When he came down the stairs, smelt the frying bacon and potatoes and saw the clean kitchen, he was grateful. He knew what had happened the night before and he knew his duty.

He was ashamed. He knew he had behaved like an animal. Catholic guilt swamped him. His emotions had been primeval. It hadn't mattered that it was Alice, who had been good to him. He felt as though he had been possessed by something bad and vowed to himself that, as long as he lived, he would never behave like that again.

The previous night had been a passage back into the real world. He had vented his anger, which had bordered on loathing, at his Bernadette. His anger and venom extended to the hospital, the midwife and everyone else he had blamed for her death and for leaving him with the life he now had.

He had been consumed by an evil rage that had been locked deep down inside him since the moment Bernadette had died and last night it had erupted with a Vesuvian ferocity.

He had taken it out on Alice. He had abused her. He had punished Alice for things that had nothing to do with her. Jerry had heard men talking at the docks who had treated a whore better than he had treated Alice last night. As he woke his first thought had been, Oh God, what have I done?

He was worried about facing Alice, but that was secondary to the realization that he knew what he had to do and what his responsibility now was.

'Morning, Queen,' he said nervously, as he came downstairs.

As he looked at the clean kitchen, it occurred to him that it really didn't matter who took the role of a wife and a mother in his house. He didn't love Alice but he needed routine and order back in his life, and this woman could give him that. He needed someone to share rearing Nellie with him. The women were right. It was near impossible for a man to bring up a daughter on his own. It wasn't the proper thing to do. He owed it to Nellie to find her a mother.

Before he sat at the table she had scrubbed, the table on which she had lost her virginity, he walked over to the range where she was leaning over the pan, frying his breakfast.

'Alice, will ye marry me?'

He said it too quickly. It was too complete a statement; he left no room for ambiguity. The hangover from the Guinness blended with Catholic guilt and a misplaced sense of duty. Prompted by loneliness and despair, he had proposed to a woman who was as far from Bernadette as it was possible to be.

Alice smiled. She had got there. Not in the way she had thought, but she had achieved her goal. Neither of them had wanted emotional contact; only one had wanted sex, as a means to an end; and she had got there. Just as she had surmised, he felt duty bound, out of decency and honour, to propose once he had slept with her.

Now she had to leave the house quickly, before any of the neighbours realized she had spent the night. If they saw her leave, they would also know the truth: that Alice had won.

She sat on the bus back to the Grand, looking out of the window. The seats were made of green leather and the windows were so dirty she could barely see outside. She rubbed the condensation from the inside window with her gloved hand and stared through the circle she had made at the passing houses, at smoke billowing out of chimneys, at the warehouses, pump rooms and workshops.

She was sore. Walking to the bus stop had been painful. She felt as though the back and inside of her thighs were bruised. When she had gone to the outhouse, her urine had stung, and her scalp hurt, where Jerry had pulled her hair. She felt as though every breath she had taken since last night had been a shallow one.

She was tense and confused but, as always, acting and hiding it well. When she closed her eyes, she could see and smell the hard dried egg and grease on the kitchen table into which Jerry had pushed her face, as he had forced his way into her. But it was over now. She was betrothed. It had all been worth it. And here she was, thirty- two, smelling of sex and had still never been kissed.

# Chapter Six

JERRY AND ALICE married less than a month later. Alice wore a very expensive outfit that had fortuitously been left hanging in one of the hotel rooms by a guest travelling on to America. It fitted Alice's short and skinny frame well. The label said Moda Paris, London and New York. Alice had read the label over and over again, when she realized the outfit was going to remain unclaimed. This was now hers. Her wedding outfit.

'How many women from the docks have married in anything as grand as this,' she said to the head porter, who was disappointed that Alice was keeping the outfit. As Alice was head housekeeper, all unclaimed property was hers to do with as she wished. As head porter, he would have become the beneficiary of anything Alice didn't want for herself.

The wedding was to be held in the register office and Alice had decided that Jerry needed a suit, something there wasn't much call for on the docks. Jerry was puzzled by this and his first inclination was to pay a visit to Eric Berry, the pawnbroker's. Not only had he never owned a suit, he didn't know anyone else who had one either. On the day he had married Bernadette, he had worn one of his uncle's, which his auntie had kept in the wardrobe since the day her husband had died. It had originally been bought in from Berry's shop for his uncle's own wedding, which Jerry remembered attending as a child. Since the day Jerry had married Bernadette, it had hung in the same wardrobe as always, with a calico cloth draped over it to protect it from the moths and dust.

When he brought the suit downstairs to show her, Jerry found Alice's indignation hard to understand. Was it because he had worn it when he had married Bernadette? He couldn't have been less bothered about that; for all he cared, a suit was a suit. He hadn't enjoyed wearing it on the day he had married Bernadette and he was sure it would be equally uncomfortable this time around. Jerry had no emotional attachment whatsoever to a suit, which rubbed his neck and made him feel as though he had a wooden coat-hanger stuck down his back. One reason for dragging Bernadette away from their wedding so quickly hadn't just been about ripping her clothes off as fast as possible; it had been about getting out of his own too. His suit hadn't made it as far as the bedroom and he remembered it had been strewn on the stairs along with Bernadette's dress.

'That suit can go on the rag and bone man's cart in the morning,' said Alice, her nose and lips visibly turned upwards, 'and we will go into town, when you finish work, to have you measured for a new one.'

Jerry was in shock; this took some digesting.

'I know exactly where to go,' continued Alice. 'Some of

the guests who stayed at the hotel often needed to have a suit run up quickly. The concierge knows a Jewish tailor on Bold Street who would run one up in forty-eight hours. I will get a good price for it too.'

She didn't even look at him for his approval. As far as Alice was concerned, she had spoken. It was done. Jerry's expression was the same as if he had been told the following afternoon's football match had been cancelled.

'I don't have the money for new suits, Alice,' he replied very quietly and firmly.

An extravagance like that was not in his scheme of things. Jerry liked to live within his means. He saved half a crown every week and always had, but that money wasn't for him, or to be thrown away on suits. Even in the weeks he never quite made half a crown, he always managed to put something by.

Alice had found a new confidence since losing her virginity and receiving a marriage proposal, a confidence that was not to be challenged. 'I have some money saved, Jerry, and we will use it to buy the suit,' she said with an air of finality. 'I won't be embarrassed by either of us not dressing for the occasion.'

Was Alice, a woman, proposing to buy him a suit? Jerry was bombarded by a new set of uncomfortable emotions that he had never before experienced. He felt torn between wanting to keep Alice happy and being affronted at her telling him what to do. He and Bernadette had never operated like that. Throughout their daily lives, every decision had been taken by mutual agreement. Or so Jerry had thought. For the last couple of years, he had made every decision alone. Some had been challenging and far more difficult than others but he had grown used to that.

He looked at Alice and silently, almost submissively, nodded. This was all very new and for now, he decided to avoid a scene. Alice smiled briefly as she folded up the old suit and laid the bundle by the back door, ready to be thrown to the rag and bone man when he came down the entry the following morning. As she flung the suit down, she shuddered and walked over to the sink to wash her hands.

Jerry looked at the garment he had never before much liked. He now wanted to grab it off the floor and smell it. He wanted to hold it to his face and breathe in deeply the happiness of weddings past. Instead he lit a cigarette. Five minutes ago he hadn't given a fig for the suit; now he was fighting to overcome an almost overwhelming desire to rescue it from the rag and bone man and tell Alice it was this suit or none. Deceitful notions were dancing in his brain: of pretending he had thrown it out and hiding it in Tommy's house. Jerry dragged deeply on his cigarette. These new feelings were confusing and he had no idea what to do with them.

'Jeez, I'm just a bloke, what do I know,' he said as he shrugged his shoulders. He had given in. Alice had shifted herself into position.

He wore the new suit for the first time on the morning he and Alice were married. He had never felt more uncomfortable in his life.

'I'm trussed up like a bleedin' turkey,' he confided in Tommy with a hint of anger. 'Why would she be wanting to spend so much money on a suit for a register office?'

'Aye, yer look like one too,' responded Tommy, which made Jerry feel no better. Jerry and Nellie had arrived at Tommy and Maura's house for breakfast, before they left to go into town for the not-so-big day.

Alice was taking a cab from the hotel, an extravagance Jerry failed to understand. The register office was a ten-minute walk down Church Street. It would never enter his mind to take a cab if the destination was within walking distance, or if you could jump on the bus.

Tommy had more to say about the suit, without being asked. Maura had taught him well.

'Look on the bright side, ye will never be stuck for money again. Ye could always get a few bob for that suit, when it runs in and out of the pawnshop, and ye could always sell it, if times were tough. After all, ye can't eat a suit now, can ye? Alice is buying an investment, as well as summat to wear, though I'd never let no woman buy me a suit and that's for sure.'

Jerry looked at himself in the long dressing mirror in Tommy's bedroom. He didn't look or feel right and Tommy's comment, brutally honest as it was, niggled him. There was nothing he could say or do now. The die was cast.

Tommy and Jerry left the house to carry Nellie down the road to the green to play with Kitty. She was already looking after the twins and Angela and would be taking care of Nellie for the day. Jerry and Tommy were quieter and more subdued than they would have been on a cold morning heading off to work.

'Good luck, Uncle Jerry!' shouted Kitty as she ran to greet him and threw her arms round his waist.

Jerry loved Kitty and even he knew it was because she had been Bernadette's favourite. Quite often, right up until she died, when Kitty was still a little tot Bernadette would bring Kitty home from Tommy and Maura's house to stay with them for the night and play mothers and daughters. Each year since Kitty had been born, Maura had delivered a new set of twins and two new sisters, making a grand total of seven children in five years. It was a huge treat for Kitty to be in a house that was quiet and tidy and not full of smaller children expecting her to do things for them. Bernadette would fuss over her, paint her tiny nails in bright-red nail varnish and buy her special treats for the night. Kitty had cried a lot when her Auntie Bernadette had died. She was only little and had no idea what death meant, but she sensed it was a tragedy.

'You're getting married today,' Kitty sang, and all the little ones followed her lead and began laughing and singing. 'You're going to get married today, you're going to get married today,' they chanted, as they jumped up and down on the spot around Jerry and Tommy.

Tommy laughed at the kids, as Jerry watched his Nellie grab hold of Kitty's hand and try to copy the other children, by taking her thumb out of her mouth to jump up and down and sing. She did so with both feet on the ground, bobbing around, trying to jump, although all she achieved was to bend and straighten her knees. Nellie had no idea what she was singing about, but she grinned from ear to ear, looking from her da to her heroine, Kitty. It was the first time Jerry had smiled all morning, seeing his Nellie infected by the excitement.

'Thanks, Kitty, ye are a grand lass,' shouted Jerry, as he and Tommy walked away to collect Maura. 'Thanks, kids,' he shouted and waved his hand above his head. They all crowded round to wave goodbye.

'Who's he marrying?' asked Kitty's brother, Harry.

'Mammy says it's a witch,' replied Kitty, watching her da and Jerry walking away.

All the children stopped laughing and running about. This was big news. Jerry was marrying a witch? A witch was coming to live on their street? In unison, they all looked first towards Jerry's house and then at Nellie, who followed their lead, looking at the house and then seeing their reactions. She put her thumb back in her mouth. Something was up.

'Poor Nellie,' said Harry. 'What will happen to her?'

'I dunno, but it's strange, so it is,' replied Kitty.

'Never mind, Nellie,' said Harry, as he took hold of Nellie's hand. 'I will look after ye and save ye from the witch.'

Harry was only two years older than Nellie. Nellie took her thumb back out of her mouth and grinned up at him appreciatively. Nellie already truly loved Harry, who always looked out for her. As Harry took Nellie's hand, his hair gently ruffled and blew in the breeze, a soft kiss landed tenderly on his head and a warm cloak of protectiveness wrapped itself around his shoulders. Harry didn't feel a thing, but Nellie did and smiled.

Jerry and Alice had struggled to find witnesses for the day. Alice had no friends. Jerry didn't know a single person in Liverpool who wasn't an Irish Catholic and for a while they thought they might have to ask two strangers on the street to come in and stand for them. No God-fearing Irish man or woman would attend a wedding that wasn't a nuptial mass, held in a church and witnessed in the eyes of God and every saint that a day had been named after.

When Father James from St Mary's got wind of what was happening, he had called round to the house and given Jerry hell, without him having had to live a life and die for it. The women on the street could hear the priest's voice booming out of the front-room window and bouncing off the cobbles, and slowly they began to gather round. Within an hour, everyone in every house on all four streets knew every word of the conversation.

'The windows rattled and shook with such a force they almost broke with the sound of his voice,' said Peggy, which of course wasn't true, but this was Liverpool; no story was worth telling without a good dollop of exaggeration.

In the end, Maura and Tommy had agreed to stand witness, Maura for no other reason than she wanted to know exactly what was occurring and wanted, self-importantly, to relay back to the other women every detail of the event. Knowledge was king and, with it, she would be queen of the streets, if only for a day. Tommy agreed, because he was a decent man who would do anything for his mate and, once Maura had decided, he would also do anything for a quiet life.

Jerry, Maura and Tommy took the overhead railway, known as the Dockers' Umbrella, into town to meet Alice. It ran along the full length of the docks, looking down on a panorama of containers, crates and cranes, with stack upon stack of timber strapped together, waiting to be collected and dispersed to timber yards across the country. The murky horizon was sharply broken by the sight of billowing red ensigns, the merchant navy flags on the docked ships that were having their loads lightened and on the ships sat out at the bar, patiently waiting for the pilots to guide them in.

For the first time since setting foot on Liverpool's soil, Jerry longed deep down inside to return home to Ireland. It was a longing that had crept into his chest earlier that morning and had now settled in for the day.

His view from the window of the overhead railway made him feel low and depressed. A mist was rolling up the Mersey like a bolt of grey chiffon being randomly unfurled above the surface of the water and there was not a blade of grass in sight. As they passed by large areas of wasteland and rubble, interspersed by rows of blackened brick-terraced houses, much of the area looked as though the bombs had dropped only yesterday. The bleakness was made vaguely opaque and eerie by the combination of the grey mist and yellow smoke spewing from the chimneys of the factories, workshops and pump rooms, as well as those homes that could afford to keep a fire lit all day.

Since Jerry had vented his anger that fateful night, he had thought about Bernadette daily. He could remember everything as though it were yesterday. He knew now that he could let her in and dwell on his memories, and that afterwards he would still be whole in body and mind. He could think about her and not go insane. He wouldn't fall apart.

As the train moved slowly on past each dock, Maura and Tommy chattered away. Jerry imagined what the small farm his parents owned would look like this morning. He leant his head against the window and closed his eyes for a minute. The jolting of the train made his head loll backwards and forwards against the glass, but he went with it and didn't move or open his eyes. Within his own dark world, he could replace the smell of dirt and damp and cold steel with the rich, wet grass and peat of Ballymara.

The contrast between the view from the railway carriage and the image of home was intoxicating and dragging him in. He could see his father returning from the milking shed, with his faithful cows on their way back to the field. The cap on his head that he had worn for the last thirty years, a stick in his hand, the crazy dogs barking at his heels and the sun rising behind him, making the same journey he had every single morning of Jerry's life. The gentle rain was falling in the sunshine but, as always, it fell soft and pure as only Irish rain did.

He could hear the Moorhaun River tripping over the pebbles as it skirted Bangornevin and passed round the back of the farmhouse, which stood only two hundred yards from the banks. He heard the plopping of the salmon, jumping as they made their way upstream. And his heart clenched, as the sadness in the pit of his belly deepened.

In his longing thoughts of home, Bernadette drifted in. How different would their life have been if he had met and married his Bernadette back in Ireland, instead of in Liverpool? The farm wasn't big enough to feed two families and, for sure, there were plenty of siblings, as well as Jerry, to feed. But he liked to imagine that he could have found a way to have reared his Nellie in Mayo. To have lived with his Bernadette on the farm. To be living a very different life from the one he was today. For the last four weeks, each time Jerry felt low or down, he had escaped to an imaginary other past, full of Bernadette and Nellie. He knew such thoughts were crazy just when he was about to wed another.

Tommy suddenly nudged him in the ribs. 'Ready, Jerry, we're here.'

Jerry dragged himself back from the farm and Ballymara. He left his da locking the gate to the field and his mother walking up the path, carrying a pail of unpasteurized milk, straight from the milking shed into the house, battling the midges and wafting them away from her face with her free hand. He left his brothers in the kitchen, making plans for the day and finishing their bacon and tatties; the youngest carrying a large bucket full of brown bricks of roughly cut peat into the kitchen to stack by the fire for the day's baking.

He left Jacko, the donkey he had ridden when he was a lad, who was still alive today and up to his usual tricks. Jerry took himself up the hill directly opposite the front of the farmhouse and looked down across the fields to find

Jacko as he had so many times before, and there he was, two ears stuck up in the field of oats, the rest of his body hidden.

And there was his Bernadette, in her red dress. He had been looking for her and there she was, sitting on the long five-bar gate to the farmyard, the gate she had sat and swung on every time they went back home. It disturbed him that she looked so sad. Sadder than she ever had when she was alive. He closed his eyes and attempted to draw her smiling image back into his mind, to look into her eyes – as he often did now. Today, she refused to be drawn.

Tommy nudged him again. 'Come on, off, now!' he said with a sense of urgency.

Tommy was worried. Never before had he seen a man less enthusiastic to attend his own wedding. Maura linked Tommy's arm in hers as they walked up into town and tried to make happy chatter. They were meeting Alice at the register office doors in fifteen minutes.

'Have we time for a quick one?' whispered Tommy to Maura. 'We need to put a smile on yer man's face afore she sees him or we'll be taking the blame for making him look like he's going to a feckin' funeral.'

'Don't talk about funerals, or ye'll set me off, and sure if I start, I won't stop,' replied Maura, as they both turned sharp left and up the steps of the Grapes pub. Jerry silently tripped along in their wake, deep in thought and looking for all the world like a man heading to the gallows.

Alice had tucked herself away at the bottom corner of the square, with the doors of the register office in sight, giving herself good warning of when the others entered the square from Water Street. She did not want to be standing alone outside. She knew she looked conspicuous in her wedding attire and couldn't help wondering how many women had stood in this same spot, dressed for the biggest day in their life, only to be humiliated in public as office workers looked out of their windows and saw them walk away, alone. She was far from sure that Jerry would turn up. This was her final concern. She was quite convinced that Maura and Tommy would do anything in their power to persuade him that he was making a mistake.

Alice had spent her life as a bystander, observing the lives of others, and today was no exception. She felt a familiar sense of continuity as she watched shoppers, office staff, sailors and businessmen bustle across the square. Here she was, ironically, on the day her life was to change, doing something that was second nature, watching others. The knowledge didn't make her feel as good as it could. Narrowing her eyes, she peered into the distance as she pulled herself back from the edge of her reverie, aware that time was ticking by. Her heart was beating so fast, she could feel it thumping against her ribs and her mouth was abnormally dry. Had Jerry stood her up? They were due to be married in six minutes and she still couldn't pick him out across the square.

Suddenly, she felt her anger rise inside her like vomit, as they came into sight and she saw the three of them together, Maura in the middle and Tommy and Jerry each holding one of her hands, running up the ginnel that fed onto the square. The ginnel was dark, deprived of light by the tall buildings on each side. At first Alice couldn't believe it was them but there they were, suddenly bathed in light, as they broke cover and ran into the open square. If she hadn't seen them with her own eyes, she wouldn't have believed it. All three were running as if the wind were chasing them, with Maura squealing and laughing loudly as she tried to shake Jerry and Tommy's hands out of her own so that she could slow down to a walk and catch her breath.

'How dare they run up here at the last minute and forget about me,' muttered Alice to herself. As she took a step forward, she realized they were about to run through the doors of the register office. They had obviously assumed she was inside, waiting for them.

'Well, there's a mistake and make no mistake,' said Alice, as she began to walk purposefully across the square towards the building. She was attracting the attention of office staff leaving for their lunch hour. For a few moments, Alice had forgotten she wasn't looking in on the lives of others from behind a pane of glass; this was for real. This was her life.

The others first spotted her just as she reached the oak and glass revolving door to the lobby. They had been looking for her inside. Jerry immediately noticed something different about her face. It was cold and hostile, shrouded in anger.

Has she changed her mind? he wondered. Is that what she's coming through that door to tell me? Is that why she isn't already in here? Am I to be let off? Relief hovered expectantly.

The revolving door ejected Alice into the lobby. The hostility fell from Alice's face as she gave Maura a tight and brittle smile in response to her overly effusive greeting.

'Good morning, Alice, that's a beautiful outfit ye are wearing and would ye look at them gloves, go on now, let me take a closer look.'

The three of them smelt of the two hot rum toddies they had each just downed in the Grapes. Maura was nervous, talking too much and too fast. Alice knew that she could possibly risk everything if she remonstrated with Jerry for smelling of alcohol. He looked less than happy.

As Alice turned to show Maura the gloves, which Maura was by now just about peeling off her arm, Jerry realized that it was over. All done. The wedding would be going ahead. He was still in his twenties and the best of his life was already behind him.

They called into the Lyons Corner Tea Rooms for lunch afterwards, where they had shepherd's pie followed by apple crumble and custard with two large pots of tea. Most of it was eaten in silence although Maura did her best to keep the conversation alive, in order to find out as much as she could about Alice, the Protestant cuckoo who had forced herself into their Catholic nest. Tommy smoked more cigarettes than usual. A man unused to social niceties, he found the whole day extremely uncomfortable. If he had a Cappie in his mouth, no one would ask him a question, or expect him to talk.

As the waitresses bustled around them in their black uniforms, they would never have guessed that the very quiet party on the table in the corner had just been to a wedding.

When lunch was over, they took the Dockers' Umbrella back

to the four streets. As they entered their own houses, Jerry, Tommy and Maura closed their doors on each other and their shared past. No longer would Jerry be able to raise in conversation some of the fun nights they had shared together. Maura wouldn't call round with her letters from Killhooney Bay and news of her own and Bernadette's family. That was the past; a new future was about to begin.

'You would have thought she'd have been grateful to have me standing for her and not be so snooty with it,' said Maura to Tommy, in indignation, as they walked into their house.

'Ah, let it go now,' said Tommy. 'We've done our duty, so we have, we can sleep easy tonight. Not that yer man will be doing much sleeping, I shouldn't think!'

Maura grinned and slapped him on the leg. She was thankful she had her Tommy. They might not have had the most exciting life, but they were secure, emotionally stable and, for what little they had, always grateful.

Within thirty minutes of arriving home, Maura had curlers back in her hair, her floral overdress apron on, and was away next door to Peggy, to recount the activities of the day.

'Quick as yer like, I'll put the kettle on,' shouted Peggy, out of the open kitchen window, as she heard the latch rise on the back gate and saw Maura walk up the path.

She picked up her mop, which was leaning against the wall, and ran with urgency back into the kitchen, where she used the end to bang hard three times on her kitchen wall adjoining the house next door. This was to alert Annie to hurry away in; it was the code that Maura was back with news.

'Get ye away here now, quick, missus, O!' shouted Peggy at the wall, when she finished banging, and was reassured to hear her neighbour's back door slam shut in acknowledgment, as Annie rushed down her path to join them. But not before she had used her own mop to bang on the kitchen wall to alert Sheila, who in turn used hers.

In the absence of telephones, it was an efficient system. Within five minutes, six women were sitting round Peggy's wooden kitchen table, in front of the range where a tiny fire burnt, just enough to boil the kettle slowly.

Peggy had nine children. Every penny and every lump of coal was counted. She was as sharp as a box of knives and God help the coalman if he tried to short-change her weekly hundredweight of coal. If she caught him in time, she made him wait whilst she inspected the sack to see if it was full to the top. A short-weight sack was a day's warmth and, in winter, that mattered. Between her nine children there were five pairs of shoes. Whoever's turn it was for the shoes would play outside, or go to school that day.

Peggy and Paddy lived an entirely different life from that of Bernadette and Jerry. Bernadette, who bought the occasional new dress, but never without giving away to someone else something she already had, had been the glamour in their lives. No one had ever seen Bernadette outdoors with her curlers in. Today wasn't just a day to gossip about Alice, it was a day to talk about their Bernadette too.

Sheila, who was only twenty and as yet had just two children, walked through the door with a shovel of coal in one hand, a baby in the other arm resting on her hip, and a two-year-old holding onto the end of her long apron trotting along behind her. Before she sat at the table, she threw the heaped shovel of coal on Peggy's fire and no one questioned it or batted an eyelid. She wanted to stay and hear every word of the gossip rather than be driven out by the cold and, besides, they would need the range.

'A lot of tea will be drunk this afternoon, so it will,' Sheila announced, as she closed the range doors to let her shovelful of coal catch.

This morning was one of those days when something had happened to lift the daily monotony and the relentless grind to pay the rent and feed a family. It required a sense of occasion and urgency. The air in the kitchen as they all settled down was tight with expectancy. Everyone needed to concentrate on Maura's every word, each being too important to miss.

Whilst Maura had been at the register office, Annie had made oat biscuits, with syrup that had found its way from a ship into Annie's kitchen en route to the Lyons factory. Peggy and Annie had given all the children a delicious, chewy biscuit and sent them into the front room, or out to play. This morning wasn't about changing nappies, scrubbing floors, washing nets or making bread. The tea and biscuits around the table powwow were as important to the women on the streets as a meeting of world leaders was to global security.

Maura sat and waited for everyone to settle down, for the tea to be poured and babies calmed, before she commenced. This was her moment. She was queen of the news – and what news she had to impart! She began with the gloves and ploughed on straight through the oohs and aahs to the ceremony itself.

'It will all end in tears, such as every ungodly marriage does, so it will,' said Peggy with absolute authority.

This seemed to be the general opinion when discussing Jerry and Alice on any day, not just their wedding day, and no one present had talked about much else since Alice had arrived on the street. It was true that no one could find anyone who had taken to Alice, or had a word to say in her defence. She gave people good reason to distrust and dislike her.

'That Alice, she's no better than she thinks she is,' said Peggy.

Everyone looked at her for a moment trying to fathom what it was she meant and then, giving up, moved on.

'Alice is a Protestant; she has probably been in the Orange Lodge. What in God's name was Jerry thinking of, marrying such a woman and bringing her amongst us?' said Sheila, if for no other reason than to make her own contribution.

As different from every one of her neighbours as it was possible to be on a practical level, Alice just wasn't the same as any other woman; she was slightly unusual, odd even. Alice would never belong. That much had been decided from almost the first time the women on the street had been aware of her existence. Each one round the table knew exactly what Alice was up to. They had all seen right through the game of the plain spinster preying on a grieving man.

'God help me, it was so hard,' said Maura, putting one hand onto her left breast and the other to her brow for effect.

'I had to get meself half piddled in the Grapes with a couple of rum toddies, which went straight into me blood, so it did.'

All the women gasped. Not one of them had ever before drunk a rum toddy during the day, let alone in the morning.

'It hasn't even been two years since our own Bernadette was sitting round this very table with us, before she was taken,' said Maura.

They all looked to the floor and crossed themselves simultaneously, muttering a chorus of, 'God rest her soul,' and then for a moment lost themselves in their own thoughts of remembrance. Bernadette, who had made them all laugh within seconds of walking in the room. Who never arrived without a plate of food she had made, for them and any little ones around. Bernadette, who had amazed them all with her ability to control her own reproductive organs, whilst unable to control her wild red hair. She had become pregnant only when she decided it was time to, thereby keeping her richer and more beautiful, and, sure, who would have denied her that?

Her soul had been as beautiful as she was. Bernadette, who if the women in the streets had their way would by now be canonized. Even if Bernadette had been a demon, she would have seemed a saint compared with Alice.

The gossip continued for well over two hours and the women savoured every minute. Grand events like this didn't happen every day and this one would be relished for a long time to come.

When Jerry and Alice walked into their kitchen for the first time as a married couple, Alice announced that she would like her own furniture to be moved out of storage at the hotel and into the house.

'It's the very best quality and I've cared for it well. It will improve the place no end,' she said to Jerry, walking over to the range to put the kettle on.

Jerry was taken aback. The house was how Bernadette had wanted it to be. She had lovingly invested herself in every little detail. He wanted to keep it that way. The realization swept over him afresh: marrying Alice was going to be about more than he had bargained for.

'That's fine,' he replied, with a smile he didn't feel. 'I'll borrow the coal wagon from Declan, after he's finished his drop-offs on Wednesday, and get yer man Tommy to help me.'

Alice looked at Jerry without a hint of softness. 'I want better than a coal wagon for my belongings, Jerry. I want a proper van.'

Jerry decided it was time to tell Alice a few home truths about how much he earned and how much life cost. She had been protected by having full board in her hotel accommodation and free food, and probably felt more secure than she should do with the small nest egg she had saved. She had left the Grand only yesterday and now wouldn't be returning except for her belongings, so it was time to talk facts.

The row about the housekeeping budget began when they had been married for less than four hours, and the row about Jerry having no intention of ever leaving the four streets or the docks to emigrate to America began after five.

In his effort to put right a night of shame, haste had taken over from common sense and he had never considered the practical issues of their living together. He had just assumed that life would become easier, with a housewife at home. Alice had been very keen to leave the hotel as soon as possible. And here they were, on their wedding day, arguing. The contrast between Jerry's two weddings could not have been greater.

The row about Nellie was the third and last on their wedding day. Nellie had blossomed over the last two years, her days spent in the midst of the hullabaloo at the Doherty house, her evenings and weekends basking in the one-to-one devotion of her father. Her hair was short, strawberry blonde and curly, but was already showing signs of darkening and taking on her mother's wild untameable redness. She was described by everyone as a little cherub, because that was just how she looked, like a tiny angel, and she brought out the protective instinct in everyone who met her. Nellie had never carried her father's sadness. She had never known a mother's love, other than the next best thing, which had come from Maura. But Jerry had done more than his utmost to compensate. It was the next to best life for an only child, but all that was about to change.

As Alice was preparing their supper, she announced that she would like to eat at separate times from Nellie.

'I also think it would be a good idea, Jerry, if just the two of us eat at my table. You could get something for Nellie to sit at. Maybe turn one of the tea chests in the backyard upside down and put an oilcloth on it?'

Alice had completely misjudged Jerry. Like a lion, he

roared, 'We will not, she eats with us, so she does, she's not a dog being sent to eat in a kennel!'

Nellie, who at two years old joined in the rough and tumble at the Doherty house and had been brought home by a very grown-up, seven-year-old Kitty, knew full well that this argument was about her. Putting her thumb straight in her mouth, she began to cry. All was not good. Everything was different and she had no idea why. Alice was here again but this wasn't the normal routine; she was usually gone by now, much to Nellie's relief. Nellie knew Alice didn't like her, but she didn't have the words she needed to communicate this to Jerry.

The row about her raged over Nellie's head. She had never seen her da angry before, but she wasn't frightened when he scooped her up into his arms and held her tight, as he gave out to Alice. Nellie didn't know why, but she understood enough to know that her da was fighting her corner. She put her arm around his neck and placed her head on his shoulder. Her fingers twiddled the hair at the nape of his neck round and round between her fingers, as the shouting continued.

She looked at the statue of the Virgin Mary on the mantel-shelf above the fire, which, now that she was in her da's arms, was directly at her eye level. Nellie had often stared at the statue. When she was laid in her crib in the kitchen as a baby. As a toddler sitting in her wooden playpen, and often when she was in her da's arms, as he sang her to sleep. Now Nellie stared intently at the statue and was rewarded as, through the tears swimming in her eyes, it smiled. Nellie grinned back and hugged her da tighter. It had happened so many times before.

That night, Jerry and Alice lay next to each other in a hostile silence. Alice lay, waiting to be assaulted, but hoping the row had been enough to deter Jerry from lovemaking. They hadn't had sex since the night she had lost her virginity and although doing the deed had got her here, where she wanted to be, it was not something she relished doing again.

Jerry, lying on his back looking at the ceiling, decided that they couldn't go on like this. He had to do something. It was time to perform his wedding-night duty and get it over with. They had to put behind them an awful day. This time he kissed Alice. He had kissed her a number of times since the night they had crossed the line and it had never been unpleasant. Kissing Alice didn't stir him in the way kissing Bernadette had, but, as the sailors said, any port in a storm. Maybe having regular sex would make him feel happier in himself.

This time he tried to be as gentle as he had once been rough, he really tried. He tried to make it responsive and special. Alice didn't. It was over in five minutes. When he said goodnight, Alice didn't respond. She hadn't made a sound or moved a muscle from beginning to end. Five minutes later, as he began to drift into sleep, he heard the latch of the bedroom door lift as Alice left the room.

Jerry lifted himself up onto one elbow and lit a cigarette. He looked out through the bedroom window at the stars illuminating the inky-black sky. There was a full moon and he could hear a tug out on the river and a tomcat fighting in the street, screeching like a baby. As he blew out smoke, he lay back on his pillow and felt lonelier than he had ever done in his life. His eyes filled with tears brought on by the familiar pain of loss, enhanced tonight by guilt and shame, as he gazed up at the sky and whispered, 'I'm sorry, angel, I'm so sorry.'

# Chapter Seven

MAURA KNEW IT would be just a matter of time before Father James called round to the house to ascertain for himself the details of the wedding. He wouldn't want to hear it in bite-sized chunks, from women who he knew were exaggerating their own sense of importance in the situation and embellishing their second-hand knowledge. At the six o'clock mass, some of the women had tried to engage him in gossip and ask him what he thought.

'I have no opinion now,' he replied sternly, brusquely dismissing the invitation to gossip, 'until I hear it from the horse's mouth meself.'

'Well, they are legally married in the law, so they are, Father, and that's a fact,' said Peggy indignantly, affronted at being put down so abruptly in front of the other women. Peggy was never quite as deferential to the priests as the other inhabitants on the streets.

Father James shook his head in disbelief and boomed, 'The only marriage that matters, Peggy, is a marriage made before the eyes of God.'

He was as keen as the women to know what had happened. He also knew the best place to find out was to get himself to number nineteen as quickly as possible and inveigle Maura into giving him the unfiltered version.

\*

Maura had missed the six o'clock mass and was in the process of wiping the dust from her windowsills for the second time that day. Cleanliness was next to godliness. She felt guilty at having attended a Protestant wedding and missing mass. She knew that Father James wouldn't be able to keep away and that she would see him walking through her back door at any minute, now that evening prayers were over.

The Father often liked to visit Maura's house, which annoyed Tommy.

'Jaysus, Maura, we get more visits from the Father than the whorehouse gets from a sailor,' he liked to complain. 'Everyone will be thinking we are the biggest sinners in Liverpool.'

'Go wash yer mouth, ye heathen, ye,' she would shout, as she flicked him with a rolled-up tea towel.

Tommy had learnt from bitter experience not to say a word against Father James. The tea towel hurt. As he walked out of the house, sulking, he shouted over his shoulder, 'I'm away to the outhouse for a shite. Maybe ye can leave me be in peace in there, eh?'

Tommy didn't get it. He didn't understand the prestige or the feeling of self-worth and status that being popular with the priest gave Maura. She liked the fact that the others saw him tripping in and out of her back door; it made them jealous, so she thought. Maura wouldn't have a word said against Father James. It was her dream that one day Harry would become a priest or Kitty enter the convent.

Father James was a disciplinarian who brooked no dissent from his flock. Jerry's marriage in a register office to a Protestant had been undertaken in defiance of the Church and God. The Father had a sinner in the midst of his flock and he wasn't happy. It was the first step on a road that could lead a community into ruin and it had to be stopped in its tracks.

Sure enough, an hour later, as Maura was washing the dishes, after what felt like the feeding of the five thousand in her kitchen, she heard the click of the gate latch and through the window saw Father James's hat, darker than the night sky, loom towards her up the back path.

'Come along in, Father,' said Maura, 'and have some tea. Tommy,' she shouted upstairs, 'Father James is here.'

As he took off his cape and placed it over the back of the kitchen chair, Maura noted that, yet again, the Father's cassock was dirty with what looked like soup stains down his front and he never looked as though he had managed to shave as well as he should have, with clumps of whiskers around his mouth clinging onto the remnants of food he had eaten that day. He always left on his ostentatious hat. Father James thought it gave him an air of authority, especially with the children.

Tommy was tucking in Harry, who hadn't been sleeping so well. His asthma had been worse than usual that evening, as it always was when there was an unloading of stone on the Herculaneum dock.

'Night, night, little fella,' said Tommy, as Harry finally closed his eyes and Tommy could creep down the stairs.

'Jaysus, Maura, it took me half an hour to get him off, what are ye doing shouting like the foghorn up the stairs?' said Tommy, as he entered the kitchen, closing the door behind him. Maura gave him a look that told Tommy to shut up quickly, just as he saw Father James out of the corner of his eye, standing by the back door.

'Oh hello, Father, how are ye, 'tis a pleasure as always, are ye staying for a cuppa tea?' Despite the resentment Tommy felt at once again finding the priest in his kitchen, no one observing would have guessed that Father James wasn't Tommy's favourite person.

Everyone had to be courteous and grateful to the Fathers. They were the community pillars of truth, morality and discipline. When times were desperate, they provided food from the sisters, or sometimes clothes from a big house in town. Almost every family in the street had, at one time or another, found itself knocking on the Priory door on a dark and cold winter's night, looking for help in the form of food or coal. The Fathers and their housekeeper were the last port in a sea of poverty. Their authority came from God, not the City Corporation offices or the government. They were the mortal representatives of God's voice on earth and no other office could match that.

'I am indeed, Tommy; I have come by, though, to hear about how the sinful service that calls itself a wedding went today and which you yourself and Maura took part in.'

Maura wasn't expecting that and looked quite crestfallen.

Tommy left Maura and Father James to it as they took a tray of tea and fruit loaf into the front room. He made his excuses and sat at the kitchen table to do his pools and read the *Liverpool Echo*. He lit his Capstan Full Strength ciggie, put on the radio, stoked the fire and poured his own tea. He grinned as he cut himself a slice of fruit loaf; Maura had made it that morning by soaking overnight in cold sweet tea a large pocketful of sultanas that had been Tommy's share from a chest that had split the day before. Tommy often joked that he could fit a small baby into one of his jacket pockets, but promised he never would.

Just the one tall lamp, with a large red lampshade, was lit in the corner by the table. It had seen better days but despite its shabbiness, along with the glow from the fire, it bathed the kitchen in a warm light. Tommy inhaled deeply on his cigarette. Everything was all right in his world. Wasn't this just the best bit of the day? His family were well and asleep on full bellies, a blessing in itself and not something that could be said for every child on the four streets. Each one tucked up in their beds, dreaming their own dreams. He looked down at his paper and heard the murmur of Maura's and the priest's voices.

Father James was the only person who was ever taken into the front room. In Maura's eyes, the kitchen wasn't good enough for someone of Father James's standing and importance. Father James was the 'other man' in Maura's life, the only person towards whom Tommy felt any resentment. It was a sin he couldn't take to confession and so it festered and rotted in his gut.

He knew that the Father and Maura talked about the oldest twins becoming altar boys and entering the priesthood, and that they did it behind his back. As God was Tommy's judge, that would never happen. Maura would witness the wrong side of Tommy's temper if she ever tried to overstep her matriarchal mark to pull that one off. Being the mother of a priest brought with it a sense of pride and an elevated standing in the community. Tommy knew this was something Maura craved and would seek through the advancement of at least one of their sons to the priesthood.

'Even a worm can turn,' whispered Tommy to himself. He had rehearsed the words in his head ready for the argument that would come one day soon. He knew everyone thought he was a pushover but he also knew the boundaries he would allow himself to be pushed to. Even a worm can turn.

He sighed and leant back in the kitchen chair as Maura walked into the kitchen. Tommy looked up with an element of surprise and, thinking he might have left via the front door, asked, 'Has the Father gone?'

'Not yet,' said Maura. 'He's gone up the stairs to bless the kids whilst they are sleeping. He's a bit mad that none of them were at mass this weekend. I asked you not to stop them going, Tommy,' she half hissed.

'Aye, well, did ye tell him that football's a religion too, so it is?' said Tommy, through his chuckles. He had beaten the priest. One up to Tommy.

'Hush yer mouth,' she hissed. 'He may hear ye.'

Tommy leant over and turned up the volume on the radio and, as he did so, winked at Maura and they both giggled. She moved over to the sink where the bowl of cold greasy water awaited her with a knitted dishcloth floating on the top. It would have never entered Tommy's mind to wash the dishes. That was women's work and the dividing line was strong and well understood. Maura plunged her red, weather-chapped hands into the bowl and carried on where she had left off with the dishes. Whilst she waited for Father James to come back down the stairs and into the kitchen, she and Tommy chatted in the same relaxed way about the travails of their family life, as they had every night since the day they had married.

*

Kitty was exhausted and had fallen asleep as soon as her head had hit the pillow. She shared a large bed with her sister, Angela. The boys were behind the curtain and also shared a bed. She had heard her da comforting Harry and sitting with him, having put a towel over Harry's head and made him breathe over a bowl of steaming, medicinal-smelling water, and then that was it; she went out like a light. She sometimes thought that being the eldest, and a girl, was a curse. She had spent the day looking after her four younger brothers and her younger sister, and she had looked after Nellie too. But she hadn't minded looking after Nellie.

'Sure, Mammy, Nellie was a dream altogether,' she had told Maura when her parents returned from their exciting excursion into town.

Nellie was a good kid who did everything she was asked as soon as Kitty asked it. She never cried or whined, unlike

Kitty's younger sister. Kitty would rather have a dozen Nellies than one crying, whinging Angela, any day. Since she had been able, Kitty had helped her mother with childcare as soon as she was big enough to carry a child on her own small hip. She accepted that she was the working, practical appendage to her mother's ever-productive womb and that was her lot in life. At such a young age, she not only knew what her future would hold, she was already an expert at it.

When she looked back, she couldn't remember how it had begun. She didn't know what had woken her. Was it a noise or simply a sense that there was an alien presence in the room? She turned over onto her side to make herself more comfortable and to move their Angela's feet out of her back. Even when she was asleep, Angela could be difficult. Kitty had to put Angela next to the wall to sleep. She cried if she was on the outside because she was scared, and would lie next to Kitty and spend her nights kicking, or crying out and waking up the others.

Kitty opened her eyes slowly, taking in the familiar shadows in the room but aware something wasn't quite right. She froze as she saw black skirts swish across in front of her face and then let out a startled gasp. He very swiftly clamped his hand firmly over her mouth.

'Hush now, Kitty, 'tis only I. Don't make a noise and wake the others.'

As he moved his hand away from her mouth, Kitty realized she couldn't make a sound. She had been about to say sorry after she had gasped, but there was something unnatural about how hard his hand had pressed on her mouth.

She could smell the stale tobacco on his stained fingers and an acrid aroma of unwashedness that had rubbed off his hand onto the skin under her nose. She could taste blood on her inner lip where his hand had so suddenly slammed on her mouth. Her heart was banging against her chest wall so loud she could hear it. Could Angela hear it?

She had known Father James all her life. He had christened her and taken her first Holy Communion, but he had never before touched her, other than to lay his hand on top of her head. She was confused and afraid. Waking up to find him standing by her bed was not a normal occurrence. She could hear music from the radio and her parents laughing downstairs. If Father James was in her bedroom, her parents must surely know. Why weren't they in here too? Why was Father James alone? Why had he banged her on her mouth and nearly stopped her breathing? What was she supposed to say or do?

Questions chased each other and, trapped, ran wild in her head. But she didn't speak or move. He had told her not to make a noise. Kitty did as she was told. Father James was an authority that even her parents obeyed; she wouldn't dare make a noise.

She lay with her eyes wide open, looking at his face and wondering what on earth she should say. She had no idea how old he was. Much older, she guessed, than her parents. His hair was grey all around the sides, and she knew, from the increasingly rare occasions he took his hat off, that he was bald on top. She hated his scary hat, which made him look like the pictures she had seen in school of Guy Fawkes. She could see the dark hairs erupting out of the end of his nose and protruding in huge bushes from both of his ears as though they were trying to escape, screaming in terror, from the unnatural thoughts inside his brain. His skin was pale, with a dark shadow where he had shaved, and the wide brim of his hat meant that when his head was bent down, as it was now, his face was in total darkness. She couldn't see anything of his expression, except the gleaming whites of his eyes.

There was silence while he stood leaning slightly over her, staring intently at the outline of her thin body under the pink cotton candlewick bedspread. She noticed that he seemed agitated, pressing his knees into the side of the mattress, pushing his weight onto the bed and grabbing hold of the headboard with one hand to steady himself. He thrust his hand through a fold in his black skirt and Kitty immediately screwed her eyes shut. This was very out of the ordinary. The black material of his skirt was brushing against her arm and she wanted to lash out and knock it away. His knees, pressing into her mattress, were less than a finger's width from pinning down her arm. He hadn't told her not to look, but she knew she didn't want to see what he was doing right now.

What was wrong? Why was he here? Why had her parents sent him upstairs to her? Did they think something was wrong? What were her parents doing laughing whilst he was here scaring the life half out of her? She wanted to shout loudly, 'Mammy, Daddy!'

She had never wanted to be close to them as much as she did right now, not even on the odd occasion when she had awoken in the night with a high temperature, shivering and shaking, feeling so ill that she couldn't stay in her bed and needed to be with her mammy. On those nights she would wander into the kitchen half crying and flushed with sickness. Within seconds Tommy would scoop her onto his knee and hug her, making soothing sounds, whilst Maura fetched a bowl of tepid water and a flannel, and sponged down her limbs with long strokes. Both of her parents concerned, both flapping, emitting soothing noises until the temperature finally subsided. She would spend the rest of the night fitfully sleeping, watched over by one or the other, no more than a hand's reach away. She wanted her mammy desperately now, in the same needy way, even though she wasn't sick.

But she knew that if she woke the kids for nothing, she would probably be in trouble. She lay with her eyes squeezed tight shut as she heard his breathing become rasping and rapid.

'Hush now, Kitty, you good child,' he said breathlessly and gratefully.

She hadn't spoken or made a sound, she had nothing to say. Why was he hushing her? She lay deathly still and didn't move a muscle. She heard the muffled friction of his vestments rhythmically moving and she could feel the mattress slightly shifting under her. What in God's name was he doing? He would wake Angela and the boys. Why was he making that noise?

She opened her eyes, to tell him in a whisper that he would disturb the others because the mattress was shaking, and to ask him to stop doing whatever it was he was doing. She was ready to call her mammy right now. In her role of junior carer of the little ones, she had the confidence to call for help. Not because she was frightened, or because she felt as though the precious space of their bedroom was invaded and no longer safe. Not because the inside of her lip was bleeding, or because she felt scared and violated, but because this was now breaking their carefully managed routine of domesticity. The little ones were her responsibility and were about to have their sleep disturbed, and that now gave her the confidence to shout for her mammy in the presence of the priest. They wouldn't tell her off, because she was just doing her job in looking out for the others. Father James didn't have children, he didn't understand. Her parents would know she wasn't being disrespectful to the priest.

As she opened her eyes and turned her head to shout for her mammy and daddy, his ejaculation left him, like an opaque milky fountain, and hit her full in the face.

And then again. And again. Again.

He was still holding onto the headboard as he slumped forward and let out a low groan. She gasped in horror. The bitter smell of his close proximity robbed her of her ability to inhale. He was leaning so far over the bed that he was less than six inches away from her face. She stared in transfixed terror, her mind screaming a rejection of what she was seeing, as the final flow of his exudate slowly oozed out onto the end of his langer and formed into a threatening drop. Her fingers clenched the bedsheets tightly. She was too terrified to raise her hand to her face.

He gave a last irregular gasp and spat out the word, 'Feck,' as, spent, he leant more heavily on his knees into the mattress. Less than an inch from her face, the last milky drop dribbled slowly and clumsily, still attached by a thread of slime, onto her chin and slithered down onto her neck. She screwed her eyes tightly shut and swallowed her breath in gulps, as she fought off the instinct to scream repeatedly and loudly, and to prevent the contents of her stomach from discharging themselves onto the bed.

She couldn't scream. She had to protect the others from the badness in the room. They were safe whilst they were asleep.

She could feel his sperm, now cold, slowly crawling down her nose and cheek. She felt her fringe, wet and sticky, clinging to her forehead. Her stomach leapt in revulsion as a puddle halted its downward journey and settled in the dipped valley of her cushioned, clenched lips. She could faintly taste salt, seeping through her teeth and onto her tongue.

Helpless, trapped, terrified, she felt as though she was about to choke. She could not breathe and although she would rather die than open her lips, a low cry, beyond her control, escaped her. Shocked, at first she wondered whether the sound had come from him, then recognized it was coming from somewhere within herself. She fought to stop, but was driven by fear. Surely she was ensnared in a nightmare; this couldn't be happening. She was terrified he would now ask her a question and she would have to open her mouth to speak. All she could think, as she cried, was, Oh God, please let this end and take him away.

She longed for Angela to let out one of the noisy, tortured cries she sometimes did in the night, as though she had been poked unexpectedly with a sharp stick. This quite often brought her mammy running up the stairs to check she was all right. The boys were so used to Angela's noises that they slept through, but Angela always woke Kitty or her mother, and either one or the other went to her side, checking her to make sure she hadn't woken herself. Please scream now, Angela, Kitty silently begged.

She kept her eyes firmly shut and played dead. Every muscle in her body was rigid and tightly sprung, ready to do battle if he touched her again. He didn't say a word. She almost lashed out in terror at the pressure of his leg and let her breath out suddenly with shock as his hand came down to wipe her face and rub and rub at her skin, with what she assumed was his skirt, or maybe a handkerchief he kept somewhere in there, just for this occasion. She was pathetically grateful to him. Removing the slime was a huge relief.

'Stay quiet now, Kitty, there's a good girl,' he whispered in a thick voice, as his breathing returned to normal. 'Mammy and Daddy will be very angry with ye if ye say anything about this to anyone, even to them. They don't want to hear a word of this, do ye understand what I'm sayin', child?'

He knew she was a child.

'God will be very angry, and throw you into the fire and flames of hell and eternal damnation if ye so much as let the words pass ye lips and upset ye mammy and daddy. Do ye understand, Kitty?'

She nodded. She still hadn't opened her eyes.

'What ye have just done, Kitty, was very bad, a bad sin, ye have been a very bad girl.'

She thought she had always been good. She strove to be a good girl. Why had she been bad? What had she done wrong?

He had stopped talking. He was quiet, but he was still there, and although she could now hardly hear his breathing, she could sense him. She still didn't open her eyes. And then she heard him whisper, asking God to forgive her for her sins and save her from the fire, and then, with a flourish of his vestments, he was gone.

'I will be away now,' shouted Father James, as he strode through the kitchen purposefully, on his way to the back door, his black cape billowing out behind him.

'Ah, thank ye, Father, for blessing the kids,' said Maura. 'It is so kind of ye. I know they don't always go to mass, but they are all good kids.'

'Aye, they are that,' he replied. 'Don't fret, Maura; if they miss a week I will always pop in. It's no trouble, but they must make confession and communion now.'

'Yes, Father, they will that,' promised Maura to his departing back, as the door closed. She turned to Tommy. 'Sure he was in a hurry tonight.'

Tommy wasn't listening, he was somewhere else. He put his hand out to Maura to hold hers and pulled her down onto his knee.

'Ye know, Maura, as you and the Father were talking tonight, I was sat here, counting me blessings and thinking how lucky we are, ye know. Maybe seeing Jerry's fall in fortune has made me think, but there was once a time, I am ashamed to say it, when I envied him, as he always had much more than we did. We are always struggling, but look at us now, eh? We are warm, I've good work, the kids are fed and all safe and asleep in their beds, and they've even been blessed tonight. Life can't get much better than that, now, can it?'

Maura cupped her man's face and they kissed tenderly. They were united in their love for each other and for their children, whom they adored and who were their pride and joy. They had little else, but it was enough.

The room smelt funny. Kitty thought to herself that this wasn't the first time the room had smelt like this. She had woken up on a number of occasions, feeling something sticky and itchy on her skin and smelling this smell. She had thought it was snot. She remembered waking with the itchiness and wiping it away with the back of her hand and the corner of the pillowcase.

Kitty began to cry, quietly. She didn't know why. She didn't know what had happened. She just knew it was something bad. With brothers to look after, she knew exactly what a langer looked like, but she had never seen a grown man's before. Tommy was very careful to maintain dignity within the family and none of his children had ever seen him undressed. Something she had never before seen or encountered had been violently thrust upon her and rent her childhood apart.

Father James, God's voice on earth, had told her she would be thrown into the eternal flames if she told anyone what had just happened, but she wanted her mammy so badly. She could hear her parents laughing downstairs, all the familiar sounds of family. Security and safety in love. She wanted to run down the few stairs that separated them, the few yards of distance between her bed and the kitchen table. To be in the same warm, brightly lit, protected space they were. She wanted to wash the lingering smell from her cheek at the kitchen sink with the distinctive clean and antiseptic smell of the Wright's Coal Tar soap, which lived in a broken grey saucer on the windowsill. She sobbed quietly until, once again, exhaustion claimed her.

She didn't open her eyes again until the next morning, when an unexplained feeling of badness and shame was quickly drowned by the calls of siblings asking for her help. She could tell no one. No one knew about the evil that had crept uninvited into her room. When she washed at the sink, she plunged her face into the bowl of water with a force that made Maura shout out at her for splashing the floor. Finally, Kitty got to hug her mother. She flung her arms round her waist and buried her head in her chest. Maura kissed the top of her head and rubbed her shoulders, too busy with the morning routines and the chores of daily existence for procrastination.

What Kitty had suffered that night was the by-product of being poor. It wasn't the outward signs of poverty or the lack of shoes and clothes that defined a poorer child and brought the deepest lasting misery. It wasn't even the hidden hunger pains, pale skin and pinched cheeks, an unheated house or broken furniture. It wasn't having to share a bed with springs protruding from a stained mattress or having to walk on cold, bare, splintered floorboards. What often defined a poor child was shame. Shame not just from being without, but from having encountered something dark that roamed the streets and homes of the vulnerable. An evil that did a greater damage and left a deeper mark than an empty belly. Hunger could be fed, a numbed body could be clothed, but a damaged soul could not be seen or healed. Poverty, gratitude, a sense of inferiority and insecurity made children prey to the things that were invisible and were never spoken of.

# Chapter Eight

TIME ROLLED BY and life on the four streets altered very little. People still existed rather than lived, and Alice, wallowing in the residual memory of a dream, withdrew into her familiar pattern of isolation.

She had given up any pretence of enjoying Saturday nights at the Irish centre and had no interest in the new band, the Beatles, that Jerry and the others had been raving about since they had played at the pub.

Through her window, Alice watched life on the four streets. She was the first to see Peggy, an unsuspecting follower of fashion, walking down the street with no curlers in and her hair piled up on top of her head like a beehive. Alice thought she looked ridiculous, but she didn't say that to anyone other than Jerry, because she didn't communicate with anyone on the street. Instead, she preferred to stand at her window and watch as the world around her went on with its business through a pane of glass, just as she always had.

Alice had been unable to make the leap from her past into her future. She had worked hard and put everything in place for the life she wanted, but she never once accounted for her own social inadequacy or her history to date. Observing life was very different from living it.

She struggled most with Nellie and for much of the time made sure the child was out of the way. She couldn't touch her and never spoke to her. Throughout her upbringing no one had ever spoken to Alice. She didn't know how a normal family worked.

When deep in thoughts of regret, Jerry often pondered on how he had ended up where he was. He now recognized that he hadn't been given much of a chance. How was he supposed to have known what was going on when Alice had arrived at his house only a week after the funeral? But now he knew he ought to have done. He had at last realized that, even at the time, her knock on the front door had created a stir on the street.

The only person who had ever knocked on his front door before that day was the man from the Pru, who collected the sixpence club money every Friday night. The man from the Pru knocked on everyone's front door. It was an act of significance that highlighted his status and degree of importance in their lives. Most of the people in the street handed over the sixpence without question. The money would pay for a burial when it was needed. This was a big deal. For Catholics there was a stigma attached to being buried in a pauper's grave, an end met by many in years gone by.

But no matter how much thought Jerry gave to his predicament, the fact was he couldn't get out of it. And in truth, he and Nellie were finding their level; they were managing, with the help of people he would be grateful to all his life, especially Maura, who constantly gave out to him about Alice.

*

Nellie never got the chance to talk at home, when her da was out at work. That was why, whenever she found herself in the company of others, she never stopped talking. It was as if all the words she hadn't spoken in her own house and all the thoughts in her head, unvoiced and unheard, came pouring out. It was impossible to stem her enthusiasm, or to stop her asking questions and laughing. Nellie saved up everything she had to say. She was irrepressible. She was beside herself with happiness in the company of Maura's noisy family from up the street, and if she didn't have her da at home, she would have happily lived at number nineteen. Over time, she ended up spending more hours at the Dohertys' than in her own home.

But now, at five years of age, even Nellie was beginning to sense that Alice was different. Nellie desperately wanted Alice to like her. She wanted to make Alice smile or get out of bed in the mornings. Or to stop Alice snarling and being grumpy to her da. She wanted not to be scared of Alice and for her to be nice, like Maura.

Maura and Tommy often discussed the 'Alice' situation. Sometimes it felt as though they discussed nothing else. Maura was concerned by Alice's behaviour. Even though there were net curtains on the upstairs window, Maura could often make Alice out, a ghost behind the nets, staring down at the street. Neither of them knew what to make of such very odd behaviour.

Over the last few years Alice had retreated into a place Jerry couldn't recognize. She often didn't get up in the mornings and, more often than not, he had to see to himself and Nellie before he left for work. Alice did the basics, the washing and cleaning, and there was a meal ready each night when he got home. But she wouldn't go outdoors any more, so all the shopping fell on Jerry. The last time he suggested that they go into town, to buy Nellie a new coat at C&A, his request had been met with recriminations and tears.

'Why are you asking me to do that, Jerry, why? You know I don't like to go out.'

'For feck's sake, Alice, why won't ye go outside the front door?' shouted Jerry, more in exasperation than anger.

'Because no one round here likes me and I don't want to be seen. I never wanted to live here, I wanted us to be better than this and for you to get a better job, so we could travel to America or somewhere more civilized than these dirty streets.'

Alice wasn't budging but she also wasn't being truthful. Stepping outside the front door was something she had found difficult since the day she moved in.

'I never said I was going to leave either my house or my job when we married, Alice. There was no discussion along those lines and there never will be. If I don't end my life here, I will do it back home in Ireland, but I am not moving away from the people who have looked after me and Nellie so well!' By this point Jerry was roaring in anger, hurt by what he saw as an attack on the home he and Bernadette had made. 'They are like me family and if I live to be a hundred years old I will never find enough ways to thank them.'

'Thank them, thank them?' screamed Alice. 'What about me, what about the sacrifices I have made? I gave up my job to look after you and your snotty kid.'

Jerry stormed out of the door before he did something he regretted.

*

The women on the street had now, by and large, forgiven Jerry for marrying Alice. Things had moved on. Everyone had accepted that Jerry had to remarry, and quickly, and he was an attractive option for any woman. There was no man in Liverpool as good-looking or as good-natured as Jerry. What had upset them had been the shock of a woman getting her feet under his table and the eejit not being able to see what was going on. Their worst fears had been realized. He would never have sought out a wife and a mother for Nellie, and so one found him.

It was not so easy for Maura. Although she struggled hard to keep on an even keel with Alice, Maura would never accept her. From the moment she had first witnessed Alice's arrival in Jerry and Nellie's life, Maura had known it was bad news.

One early morning, she said to Tommy, as she had a hundred times before, 'That Alice is a Protestant whore, coming to Jerry's house with her brass neck, Bernadette not yet cold in her grave, and her banging on the door, trying to get into her bed, and him so torn with grief he couldn't see through her.'

Tommy could not for a second see what the problem was now. They were years into the marriage already, so surely it was time for Maura to move on and change the tune? But always aware of the need to dodge the wrong side of Maura's tongue, he didn't dare say it. Anything for an easy life.

Alice had pulled the rug right out from under them and usurped the places of both Maura and everyone back home in Ireland, and to her dying day Maura would never forgive her.

'Between us, Tommy, after a decent passage of time, we would have found a good Irish Catholic girl for Jerry,' she insisted. 'God knows, there's enough of them to pick from.'

Tommy, as usual, wasn't listening. Instead he was worrying about Kitty, who was becoming more and more withdrawn with every day that passed.

'What's up with our Kitty?' he asked Maura, as Kitty passed through the kitchen, without a word or a glance in his direction.

'I think she's about to start, but she's too young really she is,' Maura replied in hushed tones. Tommy understood, without her having to spell it out, that Kitty's period was about to begin. 'She's so sour and miserable, so she is, I can't get a word out of her.'

'No, nor can I,' replied Tommy, who was more worried than he was letting on.

He and his Kitty had a special bond. Sure, he loved his twins. Not many men could boast two sets of twin boys, surely a testament to his virility. There was no better joy than playing footie with his lads on a Sunday morning on the green, or going up to Everton on a Saturday afternoon to watch a home game. He always walked the distance to the match with one of them perched on his shoulders on the way, singing footie songs and hooking up with other match-goers. But it was different with him and Kitty. She was his first-born and they had a great rapport with each other.

Kitty was clever and liked to talk about everything she had heard on the radio, or read in a book. Her mind was inquisitive and probing, though Tommy had no answers for any of her questions.

'Da!' Kitty would squeal in exasperation. 'Why don't ye know about Africa? I want to know who lives there. I heard the man say on the radio that there was summat called apartheid in South Africa, tell me, da.'

Kitty would playfully shake her da's shoulders, as though she could shake the knowledge out of him. But instead of feeling inadequate, Tommy burst out laughing.

'Kitty!' he would splutter out through his laughter. 'I can't even say it, Queen, never mind know what it is, for God's sake.'

Kitty would laugh too and stamp her feet in exasperation, often pulling a face, which told Tommy she thought he was useless, but she loved him anyway.

Tommy was relieved to take on board Maura's explanation that the way Kitty was changing was to do with her monthlies. There was none of that with the lads, thank goodness, and he reflected on the fact that with Maura, Kitty,

171

Angela, and now Niamh, one day he would be living in a house where at least one woman, out of his wife and daughters, would be out to murder him as soon as look at him.

Telling this to Jerry one day, he told him how lucky he was. 'Can ye imagine anything worse, four of them all out to kill me? You should think yeself lucky, mate, you only have Alice and little Nellie.'

Jerry smiled. He had confided in Tommy many a time that he would now like another child. He thought it might be what Alice needed, to bring herself out of her shell.

Tommy, in turn, confided in Jerry about Kitty.

'Ye expect Angela to be miserable, she's been fucking miserable since the day she was born. If Angela had been the first, we would have dreaded the second, but our Kitty is different and I'd hate to see her good nature disappear.' His face creased into a worried frown. 'When I came down this morning to light the fire, she was already sitting at the kitchen table, crying. She wouldn't tell me what was the matter and I must have asked her ten times. All she made me do was promise that I wouldn't tell Maura. Why would she ask me that, eh, Jerry? Why wouldn't she want her mammy to know she was upset?'

'Women,' replied Jerry. And that was it. Neither knew what to say. Women were as unfathomable as the ocean itself. They hadn't got a clue.

Tommy had no idea how to deal with the problem of Kitty, or how to make it better. He had promised he wouldn't tell Maura. Kitty was the one child he wouldn't betray in that promise. He put to the back of his mind the sight of her crying quietly to herself at the kitchen table and got on with the routine of his life. Almost.

Kitty felt as if she was dying inside. As though each day a part of her crumbled away. Father James had taken to coming upstairs to 'bless the children whilst they be in innocent sleep' about once a month. Whereas once she was the first to fall asleep, now Kitty lay awake every night, until she heard her parents switch off the kitchen light and rake down the fire. That blessed sound, that familiar click, the sound of her mother washing their cups in the sink and her father closing the outhouse door, before he came up the stairs to bed: all those familiar bedtime noises told her that now she was safe for the night and she could sleep.

Kitty was reaching adolescence and the first sprouting of tiny breasts had begun to appear. Embarrassed and bemused, she had been shocked when they appeared almost overnight. Maura noticed them too and assumed the physical signs of womanhood were the source of her moodiness.

Maura wasn't the only person to have noticed the changes in Kitty's body.

She always pretended to be asleep when he came into the room. He had begun fumbling around under the bedclothes to feel her breasts. When his hand found one, it didn't move, just rested there for a while, deadly still, before he removed it and began his fumbling. His jerking and panting and gasping.

As the years moved on, she had learnt to roll over, pretending to be asleep with her head buried in the pillow, and thankfully she had never again had to endure him wiping her face. Even if she were lying on her front when he came into the room, he would still push his hand under her slight frame to find her breast. He couldn't risk being heard trying to wake her up.

Kitty screamed, not only in her head, but in every nerve of her body. But she lay there rigid, not moving a muscle until she heard him rush down the stairs. Then she could cry her silent sobs into the dark and to no one else.

What could she say? What could she tell anyone? No one would believe her. They would think she was away with the fairies. They would call her mad Kitty and send her to the mission, where the old people who had lost their minds and who had no family went to be looked after by the nuns. Father James was the most important man in the whole of Liverpool, wasn't he? Even the head nun in her school, Sister Evangelista, had him come in every week to take prayers at the assembly.

Only last week, Kitty had been putting out books for the geography lesson to help the teacher when Sister came into her classroom.

'Kitty, Father James has asked especially that you make his cuppa tea and take it to him in my office,' said Sister Evangelista.

Kitty froze to the spot.

Sister Evangelista began talking to Kitty's teacher. 'The Father's a saint, he's so many families to look after he must work all the hours God sends,' she said.

Sister Evangelista thought Father James was a saint?

Kitty felt as though she lived on a different planet from everyone else in the world. She was remote from everyone and everything that made any sense.

'Father James is going to stay after prayers and help with teaching the Bible to the little ones in the infant section. I'm sure they could have no better teacher. He's so devoted to the Word.'

'Aye, that he is,' said Kitty's teacher. 'He lives and breathes "suffer the little children"; he sits each child on his lap when he is reading the Bible to them, such a loving Father.'

They were both teachers, both women Kitty looked up to and respected. Kitty knew that some of the girls didn't like Sister Evangelista, but Kitty did. Both women, just like her own mother, revered, respected and adored Father James. Father James was untouchable. Kitty was lost.

There was no one and nowhere she could go to for help with this blight on her life. This miserable torment, which robbed her of her sleep, her peace and her innocence, was something she would have to bear and could not share. This shame that made her feel disgusting, dirty and unwhole was hers alone. Kitty was quite sure that if she did confide in someone, they would think it was Kitty who was to blame, not the saintly Father James. She could not cope with that on top of what she had to bear now.

'Kitty!' shouted Sister Evangelista. 'What is up with ye, girl, get away with ye now and make Father James his tea, he is waiting for it in the office.'

'Yes, Sister,' said Kitty dutifully, as she made her way to the kitchen.

As she walked into the office, she did not look up. Her eyes were focused on the table in front of her, fixed on the dark wood grain of the desk. She didn't even know if he was there and listened for his breathing. He was there. He watched her carefully, as she moved towards the table where he was sitting, waiting, with the Bible in his hands open at the New Testament.

'Ah, Kitty. Thank ye for the tea. I just wanted a quick word. I wondered, was ye interested in stamp collecting?'

She didn't know how to reply. Even if she had known what to say, the fear in her stomach would have prevented her and stopped it coming out. How could he talk to her so normally? He was the man who did strange things over her, when she lay in her bed and her parents were downstairs. How could he talk as though none of that had happened? He had put his cold, smelly, wet, fish-like hand over her breast and felt it.

Her most difficult days of adolescence and embarrassment were being violated. Only this morning one of the twins, Declan, had burst back into the bedroom unannounced, as she was changing, which she now did when the others had gone downstairs. She closed the bedroom door, which was unusual, and dressed in private, such was her shyness around even her own sisters. Declan was curious as to why the door was closed and had satisfied his younger-brother nosiness.

Then he ran down the stairs yelling, 'Mammy, Mammy, Kitty's growing titties!'

From upstairs Kitty had heard the sharp slap and then Declan's screams, as had probably the whole street.

That was the first time she had ever known her mother hit Declan. She was protecting Kitty from her annoying little brother. Maybe she would protect her from the priest? That morning was the first time Kitty had considered the terrifying possibility of telling her mother. If Maura slapped Declan for peeping into her room, surely she would give out about the priest and what he did?

Father James noted her silence, but carried on anyway. 'I have a wonderful collection, Kitty, left to me by my own father, and I wondered if ye would like to drop by the Priory to have a look. Yer mammy tells me ye have a thirst for knowledge and different countries of the world, and when I suggested it to her, she thought it would be a grand idea.'

Kitty still could not speak. He was talking about her to her mother? Her own mother was colluding to send her to him in his house, where she would be unsafe. For the first time in her life, Kitty hated her mother.

She was flooded with a feeling of intense anger towards Maura, which gave her a courage she didn't know she had.

'I cannot come to the Priory, Father,' she replied. 'I have to help me mammy with the kids. It would be too selfish of me altogether to take time away; and Daddy would wonder why I had done it, as the arthritis is beginning to get into me mammy's knees, now making them very sore.'

She didn't know how she had found the strength to say the words and defy him. She had no idea that self-preservation was kicking in. She could have been fighting for her life.

Father James looked surprised but Kitty stared at him

defiantly. 'Be that as it may, Kitty, 'tis your choice. Maybe I'll ask yer mammy another day,' he replied very slowly.

Kitty closed the office door behind her. She stood with her back to the door with her arm behind her, holding tightly onto the brass knob. It was an involuntary attempt to keep the children safe from him and to keep him locked in the office. She stood there for a few seconds whilst she gathered her breath and then, feeling stronger for having thwarted his ploy to get her to the Priory, went back to her classroom.

Kitty had won one over on Father James. What she didn't know was that it had happened only because Father James was slightly afraid of Tommy, in whom he had always sensed a lack of respect. If it weren't for Tommy, if Kitty had a more compliant daddy, Father James would have called round to her house that night and told Maura to send Kitty to the Priory after evening prayers. But as it was, she was Tommy's daughter, so he would let it rest.

It was a warm May and Maura thought, sure, why not, when Kitty suggested throwing a party for the twins' birthday. Kitty was always looking for ways to make people happy, even though she wasn't too happy herself these days. She had become so miserable that Maura jumped at the chance to do something to please her.

Kitty's suggestion for the twins' party had been brought on by the arrival of a hessian sack of flour, which, as far as the children were concerned, had appeared out of nowhere in the corner of the living room. The children were often amazed at the things that turned up in the house during the night.

'It was a magic leprechaun,' Maura would reply if the children pushed for an explanation. A leprechaun was as good as they were ever going to get. Maura had morals.

The sack was eventually moved upstairs into Maura and Tommy's bedroom, because she simply couldn't keep the children from jumping on it and filling the room with a white powdery fog, which settled in a fine dust upon everything in its way.

'As though there wasn't enough dust to deal with from the docks, without it being created indoors as well,' Maura grumbled, helping Tommy negotiate the narrow stairwell as they dragged the sack up the stairs.

The sack of flour had fallen off the back of a ship in the docks, which Tommy had helped unload the previous night. Odd arrivals into the houses on the streets often happened at the end of a shift.

'Split it between Brian's, Paddy's and Seamus's missus' was Maura's only instruction, as Tommy bent backwards and let the sack fall with a thud from across his shoulders onto the floor in the corner of the room, letting out a cloud of white smoke.

It was a case of who wins, shares. Tommy had been working in a gang of four on the dock last night and as soon as they spotted the opportunity to lift the flour, they did so. It involved big Seamus lifting two bags at once from the hold of the ship, as though the weight were only one. Jerry took the bags at the gangway, but passed only one to Brian who, as quick as you like, ran to the entry gate where the security guard was fast asleep. When he raced back into line, Tommy then fell out and ran to the perimeter wall. The gate was closed, but not locked as it should have been. The guard had taken a mug of rum at midnight, once all the dockers were in through the gate to unload the latest arrival, and had fallen into a deep sleep, before relocking the gates.

Tommy had noticed the guard was asleep and pointed it out to the others with a nudge and the nod of his head in the direction of the guard's wooden hut. No words were spoken. Everyone knew the drill. At the first opportunity, a bag would be dropped. It was a high-risk strategy. There were twenty-five thousand dockers working on the Liverpool docks, mostly Irish Catholics, and although they were all part of the Irish Diaspora, the dock gateman was an Orange Lodge Protestant from Belfast who had no respect for or empathy with the Catholic dockers and navvies. He regarded them as papist left footers and could often be heard singing Lodge songs under his breath. He was a nark, but, thankfully, there weren't many who were. The casual nature of dock work, which meant you were only guaranteed that day's work, created a bond amongst fathers, sons and families who worked on the docks together.

The dockers might have had no long-term security, the Mersey Dock Company may have tried to keep wages low and conditions harsh, but try as they might they could never break the resourcefulness of the Liverpool Irish dockers, who made sure that if a load could be eaten or worn, some of it would end up in the bellies, or on the backs, of their own kids.

Tommy squatted down, took two corners of the hundredweight sack, hoisted it up onto his back and was running up towards the four streets in minutes. He deposited the sack in the living room, hared back down to the docks and slipped in through the gates, in line with his gang, with only seconds to spare before the night guard woke.

It was always much easier to take things that could fit inside pockets or the butty bag. A hundredweight sack was an operation, and operations happened on a regular basis, but it was the smaller gains that kept life ticking over on a day-to-day basis. Tommy regularly came home with his huge pocket full of currants or sugar. Sometimes, if they knew a molasses ship was due in, some of the men would take a bottle of cold tea to the dockside and, after they had drunk it, fill it with the molasses that 'leaked' out of the pipe pumping it from the ship into the tanker. It only took someone to make sure that the connection to the tanker wasn't quite tight enough when the pumping began.

With the flour, Tommy had provided the means for Maura to make a birthday cake for the twins and the party was decided.

'That'll be grand for the boxty bread, too,' said Maura, as Tommy went to slip out of the house, a moment of harmony growing between them.

'Aye, it will that, and no one can make it as well as ye,' said Tommy as he leant back in the door and kissed Maura briefly, before disappearing down the street into the early morning grey miasma. He hadn't even stopped for a mug of tea.

Maura knew that Tommy thought all the time about the well-being of herself and the kids. Knowing it was the twins' birthday coming up, he had kept his eye out for anything on the ships he could commandeer to make it a bit of a day for Harry and Declan, even if it meant a risk. Taking risks was what a lack of secure work forced you to do. Despite the Dock Workers Act of 1948 requiring the dock company to keep a register of workers, the dock company openly flouted the law and continued to keep the dockers keen, impoverished and waiting at the gates each morning.

The dockers knew how poor they were and what a struggle life was with so many children, but they were also aware of how much the world was changing around them. They were aspirational. They wanted more for their children than they had had growing up during the war years. They knew that they deserved better living standards, and that some of their working conditions were downright dangerous. Safety measures amounted to little more than the tweed caps they all wore religiously, in an attempt to protect themselves from a swinging crane or load. In such circumstances – all too frequent – the cap was useless, but it made the dockers feel less vulnerable.

On the day of the party, prams – each of which contained at least one sleeping baby and often two, laid head to toe – lined the entry wall on either side of the tall wooden gate leading into the yard. The prams were safe. The community didn't take from its own. Thieving was reserved for the contents of the ships, vans and trucks parked at the docks and, besides, who would steal a pram with a baby in it? Everyone had enough mouths to feed.

It was a warm and sunny day, and children ran in and out

of the yard, squealing with anticipation and spilling over into the entry. They were all dressed in the best they had, which might have been worn, third-hand, home-made or worse, but, on party day, clean. They were excited. A birthday party was a major event. It had been talked about for weeks and now it was here. Harry and Declan would even get a present wrapped up in paper to open in front of everyone.

Mothers sat in the wider part of the Dohertys' yard, just inside the gate, on wooden chairs they had wheeled down the street, balanced across the tops of prams. As it was a special day, they smoked Embassy cigarettes instead of roll-ups, and chatted about the new Hoover that could be bought in town from Blackler's if you had the money. No one on the four streets could afford to buy a machine to lift dirt off a floor. There were enough children to do that.

They had removed their aprons, which signified a special event. Aprons came off for mass, parties and Christmas Day. But none had taken the wire rollers and pins out of their hair, covered by headscarves. Even at mass, Jesus had to put up with those. The hair rollers indicated that something better might be round the corner. The enduring permanence of wire and pins pricking their scalps was the physical and material manifestation of hope, yelling loudly that every woman on the four streets was waiting for better days to come. One day there would be a reason to take them out and, when that day came, they would have had their hair done and would be at the ready.

In the narrow section of yard outside the back door, Maura now had Bernadette's bright yellow Formica kitchen table which had been set up and was laden with sandwiches, fairy cakes and jelly. The bread for the sandwiches had been lifted from the back of a bread van making a delivery in Bootle, just a mile or so away, at seven that morning, stolen to order by the O'Prey boys, heroes for the day. One wooden tray of soft rolls and one of barm cakes. The non-edible evidence of the theft had already been chopped up and placed in the wood store to be burnt under the copper wash boiler on Monday.

Early that morning, Maura had left her house, accompanied by her brood, to fetch Nellie to the party. As Kitty and the children ran up to the green, Maura had knocked on Jerry's door and told Alice, firmly, that she was taking Nellie with her. This was in accordance with instructions from Jerry, as given to Maura, when he had called for Tommy to leave for work at six that morning. He didn't want Nellie to miss the big event in the street. Alice was difficult and bloody-minded. It was better to collect Nellie in the morning than risk Alice saying no later in the day.

'I've come for the child,' said Maura when Alice opened the door after what seemed like an age. Maura felt very conspicuous, stood in her own street waiting for an answer. She felt as welcome as the rent man after a lean week.

Alice stared at her for a few long seconds, as though she was having trouble understanding what Maura said. 'Wait here a minute,' she replied in a monotone, and closed the front door in Maura's face.

'Jeez, have ye ever known the like,' hissed Maura to Peggy, who was stood at her door puffing on a ciggie and watching. The kids were already impatient and hopping around on the street, eager for Nellie to run about and play. 'A stranger in me own street, in a house I knew and cleaned, long afore she did.'

Maura's blood boiled. If Nellie hadn't been Bernadette's child she would have shouted through the letterbox, in a manner far from ladylike, 'Feck off with yer, ye haughty stuck-up Protestant bitch,' and stormed off into Peggy's to confer. If Nellie hadn't been Bernadette and Jerry's child, and therefore worth the effort, a street war would surely have broken out.

It took every ounce of Maura's willpower to hold her tongue and to keep her hands to herself, as, after what seemed an eternity, Alice opened the door and pushed Nellie out onto the street. Nellie looked dishevelled and as though she had been crying, but as soon as she saw Maura, her face lit up.

Maura knew there was no point in kicking up against Alice. She knew that if she did, she would force Jerry to take sides and he would have to side with Alice. Or 'his bitch of a Protestant wife' as Maura frequently called her.

'I know I'm a Catholic and I shouldn't say this,' Maura had confided to Peggy only the previous morning, 'but if Jerry told me he wanted to get a divorce, I would jump for joy, so I would.'

'Right ye are there,' replied Peggy, 'just don't go saying that in front of Father James now, or any of the nuns, or they'll have ye doing a penance.'

They both roared with laughter, because they knew Maura was joking.

'If my Tommy's words get any sharper, or his arse any fatter and lazier, I'll be divorcing meself,' spluttered Maura.

'Aye, away with ye,' said Peggy, 'yer Tommy's words are only sharp because he's always having to slip them in sideways, ye talk so much. Hush giving out about divorce, for Jerry or anyone, no one gets divorced around here.'

Both women laughed as they worked out how to make the Camp coffee that had appeared in the grocery shop that week. Peggy had been told that everyone was drinking it and it was all the rage, so she had bought a bottle for them to try for a change. They poured the brown glutinous liquid into two cups, added the hot sterilized milk and then drank it, pretending they both thought it was lovely.

They never touched it again.

Peggy and Maura went on their way, with Maura's anger towards Alice having dispersed. But it was a continuous battle to hold her tongue and one Maura knew she had to keep fighting, to make sure she kept true to the promise of her prayers and was able to keep a watchful eye over Nellie.

It was only because Maura had got the child into the church with Jerry's mammy Kathleen, for a quick baptism the day before the funeral, that Nellie was safe in the light. As Maura was her godmother, it was her job to ensure she stayed there and if that meant keeping on even terms with Alice, so be it.

Nellie was excited to see the Doherty children and Maura, whom she loved so much, and left the house without a backward glance, skipping along, towards the green at the top of the street. She chatted away to the children and

Maura all the way without stopping. Her long, strawberry-blonde curls had turned to a distinctive red and bounced up and down, freshly rubbed through with a hair lotion called Goldilocks that her da had bought from an American sailor on the Canada dock. He had applied it last thing the previous night, in preparation for today. Her blue eyes sparkled; she found it impossible to contain her anticipation. She had no idea what a birthday party was.

At the jumble sale at a church hall in Maghull, Maura had snapped up a dress and a hand-knitted pale-pink cardigan for Nellie, which she put on her as soon as they got back to her own house. The pink cardigan had faded from overwashing, but it didn't matter; Nellie still felt like a princess. Jerry had that morning given Maura the threepence the dress and cardigan had cost. He had no idea about clothes and he knew better than to ask Alice to take Nellie shopping.

He depended on Maura for almost everything to do with Nellie, who had found her way around Alice. She had even begun to do little things that she had watched Jerry do in their own home, and Kitty and Maura do in theirs. He laughed so much that he almost cried when he caught her in the kitchen one day, battling with the big broom and trying to sweep the kitchen floor.

When he told Maura, she added her own pearls of wisdom. 'Aye, well, it's because, even at her young age, she can feel the need for a mother in the house. She senses the absence of a caring woman, Jerry.'

Jerry didn't reply. He wished Maura wouldn't let on so about Alice all the time. He knew the mistake he had made, but it was his mistake and he would have to live with it. That would be much easier if people stopped reminding him of what he had done.

Sometimes Maura felt angry with Jerry, as if he had forgotten about Bernadette. She knew he never mentioned her name in the house, or to Nellie, and yet when Maura did so, she saw the lump in his throat and the tears in his eyes. Maura, too, welled up every time she thought of Bernadette. She often spoke of her to Nellie.

'She was a lovely woman, a saintly woman. God knows, why would he take a new mother and so young?' she would gasp, over-dramatically, as she clasped Nellie to her bosom.

Nellie had no idea what Maura was really talking about. She knew Alice wasn't her mother, because she called her Alice and everyone else had a mammy. She had never seen a photograph of her mammy, and yet she knew what she looked like, a lady with long red hair and a lovely smile. She was sure that she had seen her. She sometimes dreamt about her. She thought she had seen her sitting on her bed once, when she was half asleep, but when she sat up there was no one there.

The excitement in the Doherty house on the day of the twins' party was intense. All the kids helped to get the yard ready and move the furniture outside. By the time four o'clock arrived, the children began streaming in through the back gate in their Sunday best clothes, clutching either a bag of sweets or a plate of sandwiches or cakes. Everyone did their bit to contribute to the occasion.

Soon the party was in full swing, the children playing and the adults chatting away, with Maura filling up cups of tea whilst trying to pull apart the boys, who had decided to box each other's ears.

Nellie had eaten enough. Maura had loaded her plate, whispering, 'Fill yer boots, Queen,' as she had sat her down at the table. Now that the plate was empty, and with no one to tell her to get down and play, Nellie knew she should stay put until everyone else had gone home and her da arrived.

Nellie had spent hours yesterday at home alone with little to do and no one to talk to. Maura had been especially busy baking and getting ready for the party, and Jerry had felt too guilty to take Nellie across to Maura's house. Alice never addressed a word to Nellie, so it was hard for her to sit quietly in a yard full of social activity. She climbed up onto one of the kitchen chairs placed around the table to see over the heads of the other children.

All the adults were busy, chatting or attending to children. The sun was shining and the concrete yard floor had been washed clean of coal dust for the party. Nellie stood with her hands in front of her, smiling. With a full tummy and everyone around her chatting and laughing, she felt very happy and content.

Looking up, she spotted the rope washing line running across the yard above her head, strung between the two dark-red brick walls. She could just about reach it, so she raised her hands to the rope and held on. She then lifted her feet up and swung, backwards and forwards, before putting them back down onto the chair. No one had noticed.

She raised her hands and did it again, back and forth, back and forth.

Harry spotted her and thought it looked like a fun game. He climbed up onto the table to join her. Two years older, Harry was twice the weight of Nellie. They both swung together, giggling, until the rope snapped and gave way, dumping them both in a heap on the yard floor. They shrieked and laughed so much they were almost out of control. Then, suddenly, Nellie threw up all down the front of her pink cardigan.

As some of the mothers moved over to pick them up, the cry automatically went out: 'Where's her mammy?'

There was an awkward moment, as no answer came back, then Maura rushed forward. Scooping Nellie up, she said very firmly, 'I'm her mammy today, aren't I, Queen?' as she removed the jumble-sale cardigan and wiped Nellie's face.

Maura's neighbour of next door but one, Deirdra, a slovenly woman from Tipperary who had only arrived on the four streets two years ago, tutted and shook her head. 'You have enough with your own to look after, without one more to add to your troubles. Where's that Alice woman? Is she not interested in the child?'

Nellie heard this and a feeling of aching loneliness settled in the pit of her stomach. Maura sensed this and glared at Deirdra, hissing, 'Hush yer mouth, why don't ye, and look after yer own breed, before commenting on others people's.'

Suddenly, a lump came into Nellie's throat. She felt acutely alone. Different from everyone else. Why did everyone regard her with such pity in their eyes? Why did the other mothers look at her and then tut and whisper to each other? Why did she have no mammy to talk to about what she had done that day? She wanted someone to say about her, 'God, that child is driving me mad,' but all day no one spoke about Nellie. No one told her off for being naughty, or praised her for being good. In a confined space full of mothers and children, even as young as she was, she knew she was invisible.

With a pain in her heart and tightness in her chest, she missed the mammy whom she sometimes saw but had never known. She pressed her head tightly into Maura's shoulder. She didn't want Harry, who was staring at her intently, to see the tears that had suddenly sprung into her eyes and that she couldn't stop from pouring silently down her cheeks. For the first time since the day she was born, she cried for her mammy, Bernadette.

They heard the noise first: a wailing on the wind that began to filter through and fragment their conversations. It was an audible static that hurt their ears and sent the dogs yelping down the street. And then, rapidly, the wailing became a sudden fierce gale, rising from the surface of the Mersey and taking the water upwards with it, blasting in across the docks and up the steps. On its way it shifted cranes, rocked ships and knocked over piles of stacked-up timber. It scooped up the dust from the bombed-out wasteland that surrounded the four streets and, like a plague of small flies, the dust swarmed ferociously into the centre of the street.

It wrapped itself around the children playing in the yard, blowing into their ears and up their noses and sending them running to bury their heads in their mothers' aprons. It hit the eyes of the women and filled their mouths with dust, making them choke and splutter, and covered their bodies like a brown shroud. Dragging their children along with them, they abandoned the party and idle gossip to run inside and wash the dust out of their mouths and off their skin.

The storm carried on its crest a dead mother's heartache and whilst Maura rubbed Nellie's back and whispered gently into her hair, 'There, there, now,' it found its way between them both and mingled its tears with Nellie's own.

# Chapter Nine

T$_{HE}$ MORNING AFTER the party, Nellie woke and sat bolt upright in bed, worried, bleary-eyed, rigid. She did the same thing every morning. Her attention focused on the noises coming from the kitchen. She listened hard for the sound of ashes being riddled, or a shovel of coal being thrown into the range. If she awoke to silence, she would put her ear flat to the cold wall at the side of her bed, concentrating hard, in order to hear better. Once she heard the falling clatter of coal upon brick which let her know Jerry was downstairs, she threw herself back on the pillow and, with her arms straight by her sides, closed her eyes and breathed a loud sigh of deep relief.

'Thank you, Holy Mary, Mother of God,' she whispered, and crossed herself. Maura said she should do this, every morning, and Nellie had, as always, taken her words to heart.

After her morning prayer, she rubbed the sleep out of her eyes, then, with dramatic urgency, she cast aside the blankets, threw herself out of bed and pattered across the cold red linoleum of her bedroom floor. The lino was patterned with large bunches of white, pink and yellow roses, tied together with a green bow, which Nellie used to hop across like islands in a red sea.

When she was a baby, toddling across the lino one morning to Jerry, he had said, 'Quickly now, before Jack Frost gets ye.' Startled, she looked behind her to see what he meant. There was nothing and no one there. Nellie assumed Jack Frost must live under her bed, as she could see nowhere else for him to be.

She had never forgotten those words and since that day, every morning as her feet first touched the floor, she was done for. Now that she knew where he lived, there was no escaping him. Jack Frost would reach out from under the bed where he hid all night and seize her little feet, freezing her to the spot. He would wrap himself around her calves, making Nellie gasp as, just for a second, not satisfied with just her small limbs, he took her breath away too.

Grabbing her breath back, with a squeal that she tried hard to suppress, she flew lightfooted towards the bedroom door, scared to creak a floorboard or bang a door, thereby waking Alice. The thought of Alice spread icy tendrils up from her calves into the pit of her stomach. She mustn't wake Alice.

It was very important for Nellie to catch Jerry in the mornings. If Alice chose to stay in bed, she would forget about Nellie, who would then have to stay in her room, without food and with a rumbling, empty belly, until Alice fetched her, which sometimes could be very late in the day. This distressed Nellie as she needed the outhouse and often had to sneak out in fear of being heard or caught by Alice.

Home was a menacing place when Jerry wasn't there.

From the first day Alice had moved in, almost every minute that Jerry was out of the house was a minute Nellie spent in her room, alone. In the early months, she would be left in her bed all day. Alice would leave her with bread and a drink to feed herself with, and walk out. Sometimes Nellie would cry for hours, until her tears became a whimper. After a while, she learnt that crying was pointless. Crying achieved nothing. It made no difference whatsoever, other than to make her sick, and so she stopped and became quiet. At the end of each day, Alice would bring her down an hour before Jerry arrived home. She would change the soaked nappy and put her straight back into her nightdress, before bringing her downstairs, plonking her onto a kitchen chair with a crust of bread in her hand, just in time for her da to walk in through the door.

When Nellie started talking, Alice laid down the boundaries of behaviour she expected from her stepdaughter. One morning Alice squatted down on the kitchen floor, her face level with Nellie's, and said, 'I just want you to know, little madam, that when your father is out, you don't speak until you are spoken to. Don't ever speak to me first, unless I ask you to. Do you get that?'

Alice spat the words out with such venom that Nellie was speechless. The fire in the range was burning high behind Alice's back, the flames licking and dancing, an orange and yellow burst of light in the otherwise gloomy room. Nellie's imagination ran away with her. She knew she was in danger. The thought went through her mind that if she said the wrong thing Alice might throw her in the fire. She thought she would be all burnt up, like the potato peelings, and her da wouldn't know where she was or be able to find her.

Alice terrified her. She did exactly as she was told and spoke only when her da was in the room, but each and every time she did, she cast a sideways glance at Alice, just to make sure it was OK, and Alice was always, without fail, staring at Nellie with a blank face. Only her eyes carried any expression and they were saying a great deal to Nellie.

Sometimes, Jerry would leave for the docks and work through for a straight twenty-four hours. This was hard for Nellie, although it did mean that even though he was in bed, recovering the following day, her da was at home. His being in the house made an enormous difference, for Nellie lived two lives. The one her da and Auntie Maura knew about, and the one she had to keep secret.

Nellie never really surprised Jerry when she opened the kitchen door in the mornings. He always expected her, although he never woke her, preferring to wait until the fire was lit and the kitchen had warmed. For more months of the year than not, Jerry could see his own breath indoors. It appeared to him as though Nellie had some form of sixth sense, because every morning, just as the fire was lit and the crystallized icy flakes slowly began to melt away from the inside of the window-pane, Nellie would walk in through the door, eyes still full of night-time dreams, clutching her old teddy. Jerry had no idea what a punctual alarm clock his morning routine was. It made all the comforting morning sounds Nellie loved to hear. It never altered and provided her with a familiar morning song to wake up to.

One morning she had come down and he wasn't there, despite the fact that she had heard all the usual wake-up sounds. She hadn't known what to do. Disappointment washed over her, as tears began to flow and she began to sob. A morning without breakfast and a cuddle from her da was indeed miserable, as she might not eat again until the evening. Suddenly, the back door flew open and her da came in with the coal scuttle in his hand. As soon as he saw her, he placed it on the floor and ran over to her, lifting her up into his arms and hugging her.

'Shush now, princess, what is up with ye?' he soothed. She never replied and he never knew, but now, in the mornings if he went outside for coal, no matter how cold it was, he left the back door open so that she would know where he had gone.

This morning, as Nellie tiptoed down the landing, Jerry opened the first tap for running water, and she heard the cistern clank and the lead pipes play a tune that was more suited to a game of musical railway sidings than a domestic water supply. She stopped dead in her tracks, terrified that the sound would wake Alice and that she would be trapped outside her door. With a sharp inward gasp, she swiftly covered her mouth with her hand so that Alice couldn't hear her breathe. If Alice did wake, she mustn't know Nellie was there. She willed herself to be invisible as well as silent, believing this could be achieved by squeezing her eyes tight shut.

Once the water began to flow and the clanks subsided, Nellie opened her eyes and breathed again. She tiptoed stealthily down the wooden stairs, skipping the next to last one at the bottom, which always yelled out in protest as soon as it was stepped on.

As soon as she opened the kitchen door, her eyes alighted upon Jerry and she took her thumb out of her mouth, smiled her beaming smile and ran across the cold stone floor to hug him.

'Good morning, my beautiful colleen,' he said, swinging her up in his arms and lifting her above his head. 'One, two, three,' he shouted, and then threw her six inches into the air. 'By Jaysus,' he puffed, 'I won't be doing that for much longer, I'll be hitting the roof, so I will, and sending the tiles flying into Harrington Road, yer getting such a big girl.'

She hugged his neck, and he breathed in the scent of her hair, just the same as her mother's. He savoured the moment, as he closed his eyes, rocking her slowly from side to side, hugging her tight. Nellie closed her eyes too. They both remained quiet, locked in their special moment until they felt her join them, as she nearly always did. They both felt the intensity of the love that flowed and wrapped itself around them, holding them tightly together and lasting for just a minute. Then it was gone as quickly as it came. But it never failed them; it was always there.

After crashing the range doors once he had put his rashers of Irish bacon and sliced tatties in the oven, Jerry started dancing around the kitchen with Nellie, as he did almost every morning, holding one of her hands out to the side as if they were waltzing. Some mornings Nellie left after him for school, but her weekends were just like the early years with Alice had been, lonely.

Jerry sang at the top of his voice, accompanying Cliff Richard on the red and grey Roberts radio, as he swirled her around the kitchen, and she began to giggle. He never seemed to be in the slightest bit scared about waking Alice.

When they finished dancing, he filled a bowl with milk and water, dropped four or five cobs of bread into it with a sprinkling of sugar and popped it into the range oven with his rashers. If Nellie didn't have her breakfast and milk with her da in the morning, she might go all day without food, but she would never tell him that, because Alice had told her not to. She might also have a bit of bacon and tatties, if she hurried and finished her bowl first. She made sure she hurried.

Jerry took his breakfast and Nellie's 'pobs' from the range and placed them on the dark wooden table. Jerry had loved the yellow table he and Bernadette had saved for and bought together. Now, he and Nellie sat on Alice's very cumbersome oak chairs with dark brown leather seat pads. Jerry and Nellie called them chairs; Alice called them ladder-backs.

At least the bright yellow table had gone to Maura and Tommy, who had been delighted beyond words. They had too many children ever to be able to afford anything new in the way of furniture. Everything they owned was falling to bits. Maura had cried the day he and Tommy carried the table into their kitchen along with the four modern chairs, with spindle chrome legs and plastic seats and backs, covered in the same pattern as the Formica table. It was bright yellow with a design that looked as if someone had scattered a box of grey matches over the top. Maura wrote to her relatives in Mayo and told them it was time they came for a visit. She wanted them to report back to her relatives and friends in the village how prosperous Maura and Tommy were in England and how good the wages must be, if they could afford a Formica table.

Once Jerry and Nellie sat down to their breakfast together, the chatter began. Nellie's chatter, that is. Jerry could never get a word in edgeways. She talked and rambled non-stop. Sometimes she almost made him late, a disaster for a docker. Work was on a first come, first served basis and it was getting harder to be taken on each day.

This morning, the tide was out and Jerry had an extra half-hour. It was Sunday and there was no school for Nellie. From the upstairs window he could see out across the river. He knew, from having popped into the dock office the day before, which boats were expected in and he could see the tugs and pilots weren't moving out yet.

'Let's play a game, shall we,' he said to Nellie. He didn't often get time to romp about with her. There was no Alice up and making demands on his attention, so why not? Nellie was squealing and jumping up and down on the spot.

Eager to make her happy, Jerry remembered a game Nellie had played at Maura's at the weekend and said, 'I have an idea. Why don't we make a den?'

Nellie could not believe her ears and was beside herself

with excitement. Jerry took her into the living room and they pulled out the dark oak sideboard, which was normally flush with the wall, and put it across the corner of the room. Jerry lifted her over the top, so she was in the triangle-shaped space, and then pulled the sideboard away and squeezed in himself.

The sideboard was another of Alice's possessions. Again, it was too large for the room but it was her pride and joy and she polished it every day.

Nellie and her da played in the den, pretending that they were in a cave and that out in the living room were lots of wild animals they had to hide from. They both had to go into the kitchen to fetch essential supplies for the den, dodging the imaginary wild animals.

'Quick, let me in,' squealed Nellie, who did the first run to the kitchen to fetch water. 'The fish are chasing me.'

'The fish?' laughed Jerry. 'Why is ye worried about the fish? It's a big lion I can see chasing ye.'

Nellie squealed and both feet left the floor in shock, as she ran, spilling her water on the way. As she squeezed back in behind the sideboard, she screamed when Jerry once again pulled it across the corner, closing the little gap he had left for Nellie.

After they had been playing for a while, Jerry heard the tugs. 'I have to go, Queen,' he said to Nellie. 'You stay here and play with Alice, I will go and wake her.'

Nellie froze. She couldn't speak or move. Within seconds Jerry had moved the sideboard out, removed himself and easily pushed it back again. Jerry was a docker and his upper-body strength was immense. It was no effort for him.

He took his cap from the nail on the back of the kitchen door, along with his jacket, and shouted up the stairs to Alice, 'Come down and play with Nellie, she's waiting for ye. Alice, do you hear me?'

He waited for a 'yes' to come down the stairs and then he was off, out of the back door, down the entry, across the road and down the steps to the dock. He was standing at the dock gate, shouting greetings to the other men and laughing about the football prospects for the Everton team, just as Alice put her feet out of bed and onto the bedroom floor. Alice didn't like being woken. Alice wanted to hide in her bed under the blankets and be alone. She liked being shouted awake even less. What did Jerry mean, Nellie was waiting for her? If the child had any sense she would be back in her room, where she ought to be.

*

Nellie tried to move the sideboard to get out, but it was too heavy and she was trapped. She put her fingers onto the top and tried to scramble up. It was too high. Her feet had nothing to grip onto. Her toes pounded like a dog at the door scraping to come in, with no effect. She could hear Alice's footsteps upstairs and she knew she needed to get out. She lifted her hands higher and tried hard to pull herself up. She heaved her feet off the floor, pressing her knees into the back of the sideboard and the soles of her feet flat against the wall behind, to shimmy herself up, one last time. She gave it every ounce of strength she had. The sideboard rocked towards her as she tipped it slightly up off its front legs, just for a second, and then she heard the crash and froze.

As a terrified Nellie squatted behind the sideboard alone, where, only a few minutes ago, both she and her da had been laughing heartily, she heard Alice's footsteps slowly descend the stairs into the kitchen. Alice didn't say a word. She never did. She walked over to the radio and switched it off. Alice hated noise. She was slightly surprised that the kitchen looked exactly as it always did, and yet she knew something was different; she knew Nellie wasn't in her room. She could sense her, smell her, and she wanted to know what had made the loud crashing noise.

Alice put the kettle back on the range to boil, and then walked into the living room. She saw the sideboard moved from its usual place and she stared, with absolute horror, at her parents' precious ornament, a china dancing lady, smashed to smithereens on the floor.

Alice didn't shout. She never shouted. Hissing was more her style.

'So, this is it, this is the day it all changes, eh?' she spat quietly. She walked to the corner of the room and attempted to heave the sideboard back into its original place. Then she saw Nellie, huddled as far back against the wall as she could be, cowering and shaking. Nellie didn't say a word; she knew that was forbidden.

'You dirty, stinking, foul little bitch,' Alice hissed under her breath. 'Stand up.'

Nellie couldn't. She couldn't even breathe properly, let alone stand up. Her legs were shaking so much she couldn't move. Her throat had closed over and her mouth was so dry that, even if she had wanted to speak, she couldn't have.

'STAND UP!' Alice shouted. Nellie wished she could. She wished she could stand up and run out of the door and down to Maura's house, but she couldn't move a single limb.

'How dare you touch my furniture, how dare you touch my furniture, how dare you?' Alice hissed.

Nellie looked at Alice for the first time. Blotches of red had appeared on Alice's neck and were marching up towards her face. A dribble of spittle below her lip had flown out in anger and stood out bright white against the now very red chin. Alice wasn't looking at Nellie, she was talking to herself. Muttering about vermin and foul children, about her ruined life, ruined because of a brat. Even as she was moving the sideboard, she carried on talking to herself, looking over her shoulder to the door. She was in such a rage that she didn't care if Jerry walked in.

Alice's dark hair was tied back in a tight bun, but a section from the front, which would have been a fringe if Alice had ever had a style, suddenly flew out and bobbed backwards and forwards across her eyes like an overlarge windscreen wiper, distracting her. Alice tried to tuck it back, but the errant strand was adamant. As soon as Alice managed it, it flew straight back out, with such a flop it was as if ghostly fingers had pulled it out, and it landed again in front of her eyes. Nellie knew that piece of hair was saving her.

The sideboard was heavy, but Alice heaved and pulled until the gap between it and the wall was big enough for her to get inside.

'Come here, you little bitch,' she shouted, as she leant down and took hold of Nellie, who was tiny and frail by any measure, by the top of her hair, lifting her off her feet. The pain was excruciating, but still Nellie never made a sound. As her feet touched the ground again, she wet herself. She couldn't help it.

The pain in her head was searing and the amber liquid running down her legs stung. She had no time to register the extent of the pain, it was all happening so quickly. Alice let go of Nellie's hair and grabbed the top of her arm. She dug her fingers and her nails into Nellie's shoulder and arm so tightly that, despite herself, Nellie let out a stifled scream. She was as light as a feather and as Alice swung her through the doorway from the living room to the kitchen, her shins crashed against the door frame.

Nellie could smell Alice's acrid sweat. Alice was wearing a bottle-green jumper and she could see every stitch in every row as her face was rammed up against it. The smell was overpowering close up and caught the back of Nellie's throat, making her gag. Out of the corner of her eye, Nellie could see her 'pobs' bowl and her da's tea mug on the draining board. Suddenly, the sight of something that was her da's made her cry with lonely desperation. Seeing his mug accentuated the fact that her situation was hopeless; she needed him back now.

As they got closer to the range, Nellie began to breathe so fast she became dizzy. She was crying so hard she was beginning to panic. Her feet kept leaving the floor as Alice jerked her along, gripping the top of her arm tightly, lifting her up and swinging her through the air like a rag doll towards the kitchen. This was it, she knew. Finally, Alice was going to put her in the fire. She was going to burn in the flames of hell, like the priest in church said you did when you sinned. She had broken the dancing lady. She was a sinner. She knew was going to die, like her own mammy.

As they approached the range, Alice picked up the boiling kettle. She was still talking and hissing to herself; about her ruined life and having to change the bed sheets of dirty people no better than scumbags, and now she was expected to pander to a verminous brat. Still holding Nellie off the floor by the top of her arm, Alice poured the boiling water out of the kettle into the sink. Then suddenly, Nellie's arm was set free as she grabbed her hair again, jerking her head back.

Although it hurt her so much, Nellie was relieved. The pain in her arm had been so bad she had felt like it was going to snap. She didn't know that in a few more minutes, her shoulder would have dislocated and that Alice had let go just in the nick of time. Alice pulled her head so far back Nellie thought her neck was going to break. She let out another stifled scream and her breath came in short, fast gasps, as Alice brought the bottom of the boiling-hot, copper-bottomed kettle down close to Nellie's face. She stopped with only half an inch to go.

The heat of the kettle was burning into Nellie's nose and cheeks; paralysed with fear, she couldn't move. Her cheeks were burning with a raging heat and it felt as though silence had descended over the kitchen. She whimpered, 'Please don't hurt me,' each word followed by a tiny sob.

'See this?' screamed Alice. 'See this? Next time I won't stop, next time I will smash it down straight onto your ugly face. Do you get it, do you?'

Nellie tried to nod, but she couldn't move her head because Alice's grip on her hair was so tight.

'Do you?' Alice screamed, spit flying out of her mouth to sizzle where it hit the boiling-hot kettle.

The sudden loud smash of pottery on the concrete floor startled Alice. Nellie was vaguely aware of the noise as it happened somewhere in the kitchen, but it was a mere backdrop to the sound of the pain screaming in her ears.

Alice turned her concentration away from Nellie and looked down at the smashed statue of the Madonna, broken into a hundred tiny pieces, fanned out like broken eggshells across the kitchen floor. Alice slowly placed the copper kettle back onto the range. Turning away from Nellie, she stood and looked at the pieces on the floor and then at the mantelpiece above the range. She couldn't have done that, could she? Alice ran her hand along the shelf, feeling for a reason to explain how the Madonna had moved six inches to the edge and fallen off. For a moment she forgot about Nellie as, in utter confusion, she bent to pick up the larger broken pieces from the floor.

Nellie hadn't taken in what had happened. She could not see through her tears or feel through the pain searing across her scalp and throbbing in her arm. She was quietly sobbing and felt sick and dizzy. The hyperventilating from her fast breathing was having an effect and her legs felt weak, pins and needles pricking her whole body. And then, as violently as it had begun, it ended. Everything went black.

Nellie had fainted in blessed relief.

Just at that moment, Jerry moved to take a corner of the crate being unloaded from the back of a newly arrived merchant navy vessel. The other dockers called him Stanley Matthews after the great footballer because he always took the corner. Tommy leapt to take the other corner.

'How's the colleen this morning?' he shouted to Jerry, as with six others they carefully steered the crate away from the ship's gangway.

'Sure she's grand, never better,' Jerry shouted back.

They both knew they were talking about Nellie, not Alice. As he spoke, the image of Nellie, not half an hour since, came into his mind. The thought of her running through their imaginary jungle with a cup of water and squealing that she was being chased by fish, looking and sounding just like her mother, made him chuckle yet again. His heart was warm. When Nellie was excited or happy, he saw his Bernadette. It made a difference to his day. The glimpse would stay with him all day as he still thought about her, often.

His daydreaming was broken by the yells of warning from the men at the front. The side of the butter crate they were moving had come adrift and collapsed. Two hundred and fifty smaller wooden crates of New Zealand butter were spilling out of the side of the crate all over the dock floor. As Jerry heeded the warning and ran, two of the crates hit him hard, square on, one on the top of his arm just below his shoulder, the second on the top of his skull.

He didn't see them coming, which was rare. He was usually one of the fastest to jump out of the way of trouble, making him one of the few men on the docks who had never sustained an injury. Neither crates hurt him badly, but enough to make him scream out in pain.

'Shut yer feckin' moaning,' said Tommy, as he ripped open a lid of one of the smaller crates and started stuffing half-pound packets of butter into his pockets. 'Stop crying like a babby and fill yer fecking pockets, there'll be butter on the table fer weeks.'

Jerry did as he was told. He scooped up the smaller packets and, flinching, rubbed the top of his arm and his head. He felt the pain from the bruises for days afterwards.

An hour later Nellie woke, exactly where she had been thrown onto her bed. Her head was at the bottom where her feet should have been and she was shivering, on top of the blankets. As she lifted her head to look around the room and check she was alone, she felt a sharp pain in her arm and as though her scalp was raw. She lay back, face down, on the bed, eyes open, heart closed. She couldn't even sob. Her bed was wet and cold. She knew her room smelt and her legs stung. For hours she lay, staring at her fingers or at the door. The pain in her arm and head throbbed, and she felt so alone, so sorry for herself.

She cried quietly, as she listened to the sounds of Harry and the other children playing outside on the green while the light began to fade. The noise tormented her and emphasized her loneliness. She could pick out the individual children by their voices or their laugh. She thought she could hear them shouting, 'Nellie, where are you, come out and play.'

They weren't and never would. The kids in the street had got used to Nellie being kept inside, and Nellie's was the only house that the kids dare not run in and out of without knocking on the door first – and no one did that. Harry's mammy had said Alice was a witch, they had all heard her, so it must be true. The children were scared half to death of what would happen to them if they did knock on the door and she said, 'Come in.'

'If ye knock on Nellie's door,' said Harry, 'the witch will turn ye into a rat and then she'll tell Jerry, "There's a rat in the yard," and he will beat ye to death with the mop until ye was splattered all over the yard. Sure he would because he wouldn't know it was really ye.'

The others would clasp their hands over their mouths. They imagined all manner of horrors in Nellie's life: that she was locked in a crate in the yard, or that Alice turned her into a black cat and sometimes couldn't turn her back again, which was why they went days without seeing Nellie. The kids on the four streets gave Nellie's house a wide berth, sometimes staying in the centre of the road, for fear that Alice's hand would reach through the front door and pull them into the dark, never to be seen again. They all genuflected and crossed themselves as they walked past Nellie's door. And sometimes Nellie saw them.

Nellie knew she was different. She knew that all the children in the road lived the same life, but one that was nothing like her own. Nellie was odd.

Late that afternoon she tiptoed along the landing and sat on the top stair. She needed the toilet but didn't dare ask. The street lights came on and she heard the children being called in for their tea. She couldn't hear a sound in the house. There was no movement from downstairs. No light. The house could have been empty, but Nellie knew it wasn't. Alice never went out. She could sense Alice, sitting in her chair, staring vacantly into the fire, or standing in the dimness of the bedroom, staring out at the street.

Nellie went back to lie on her bed. She was cold and sore and despite a desperate need for the toilet, which had distended her tummy and made pain wash over her in waves, she still didn't dare ask.

Lost in her thoughts, she didn't hear Alice come into the room.

'Get up,' she barked, hovering in the doorway, reluctant to even step into the room that was Nellie's world. 'Go to the outhouse and then to the kitchen to eat, before your father comes home. Then you can get back into bed.'

Her ominous form disappeared from the frame of the doorway almost as soon as it had arrived. Nellie was so lonely that even the arrival of Alice at her bedroom door momentarily dispersed the sadness, if only to replace it with fear.

Nellie did as she was told. She couldn't object and, anyway, she was so desperate for the toilet, she flew down the stairs, terrified that she would soil herself. God alone knew what the consequence of that would be.

Before going, she looked back at the new yellow street light that had been erected directly outside, casting a warm and comforting glow into her room. It wasn't all bad. If she was in her bed when her da got home, she knew he would come in to say goodnight. She also knew she would be too scared to tell him about her beating. That she would hide the bruise on her arm away from him. That she would not be able to answer him when he asked her what she had done that day and, even at her young age, she would see the hurt and worry in his eyes when his questions were met with silence. Jerry had not the intuition to realize that if Nellie gabbled with enthusiasm on the days she spent at Maura's, there must be something badly wrong on the days she didn't speak at all.

That evening, Jerry paused outside his back door, reluctant to go in. No other man on the streets knew how Jerry lived. He was the only man who had a wife and yet got his own breakfast. Dockers worked long physical hours, while the women stayed at home and ran the house. That was the way it was. Jerry was thankful that he and Bernadette had only one child. How would he have managed with half a dozen? No other man would know how to begin to cook his own breakfast or dinner. No man on the four streets knew that was how it was for Jerry. To think that everyone once envied him for having the most beautiful, the most loving, the most perfect wife. And look at him now. If they knew how it had worked out for him, he would be a laughing stock. It wasn't only Nellie who lived a double life. Nellie and her father lived in the same house and shared a mutual love, but neither knew how the other existed for most of the day.

In the moments when Jerry allowed himself to dwell on the situation, he knew that a time would arrive when he would have to face facts and do something, but, more importantly, Alice would have to accept that something was seriously wrong. He had spent hours trying to find a way out, but there was none. He was trapped in a loveless marriage, forever. One drunken night of insanity and a lifetime to pay for it. He often reached the conclusion that it was no more than he deserved for having behaved so badly. But how much should a man have to pay for a mistake?

Alice's behaviour had become questionable from almost the minute they had married, although even he recognized it was getting much worse. She appeared to have huge difficulty in relating to Nellie, or to anyone, for that matter, other than Jerry. She had been different when they had first met, but not so much as to raise any real concern. Now, he felt her behaviour was deteriorating by the day. Still, on balance, he reassured himself, at least she was still managing to look after Nellie when she wasn't at Maura's. If he wasn't working, God knows what would happen to them.

When he reached this point, he always comforted himself with the thought that he couldn't have carried on the way he had been for much longer, struggling as a single father. If he had, someone would surely have reported him to the authorities.

Sometimes he thought that if he had managed to survive on his own until now, it might have become easier. Nellie was at school during the day. Her baby days were over, it was all so much easier now. Maura could have looked after Nellie after school and at weekends; he would have willingly paid her for that, if she had let him, and he could have paid Margaret O'Flynn in number eight to do a bit of cleaning. She had offered more than once. Why hadn't his head been clearer at the time? How had he let things get on top of him in the way they had? He had been swamped by grief. Unable to make a decision, or to think straight. What a mess.

Anyway, here they were now, him and his girl, and weren't they just getting on grand. He and his princess shared a lot of laughs and love, and that couldn't be bad.

When Jerry arrived home in the evenings, only Nellie knew that Alice was lying when she recounted Nellie's imaginary day to Jerry. He would often listen, in an absent-minded way, as he was removing his boots or having a wash-down at the kitchen sink. Sometimes Nellie's eyes would fill with tears and her bottom lip would tremble uncontrollably in relief at the sight of him. When that happened, Jerry would almost immediately notice. One evening, though, when he didn't notice Nellie's tears, he was taken by surprise.

He thought he had felt Nellie pull at his sleeve but when he looked, she was standing on the other side of the room by the door, looking at him with eyes about to spill over. He stared at his arm questioningly. He had felt a strong, firm tug on the cuff of his jacket; not once, but twice. Firm and decisive.

Once again, the temperature in the room had dropped. This was something that happened often, without reason.

The fire could be blazing hot and yet he would feel the warmth in the room evaporate as though it were icy outdoors, even on a warm and sunny day, and then rise again just as quickly.

Without hesitation, he walked over to Nellie and picked her up. Although she was getting bigger, he lifted her onto the draining board so that she could sit next to him and watch him, whilst he washed away the grime and dirt from a day's dusty hard labour. He didn't ask her why she had tears in her eyes. He didn't dare.

He knew someone had pulled his jacket cuff. He also knew no one else was anywhere near. This wasn't the first time it had happened. He knew it was Bernadette. He felt she had never left the house and that she was there, watching them both.

On a clear night, he would often leave Alice listening to the radio and step out into the yard. He would look up at the sky, pick out his star and talk to Bernadette.

'Hey now, she's OK ... I'm looking after her and she's gonna make ye really proud one day. We both miss you ... loads and, God knows, I still love you, only you.'

He managed to go on only because Bernadette could still be seen daily, twinkling in the navy sky, reflected in the street puddles and on the Mersey, flowing pink on heavy summer nights.

Jerry sighed heavily, and went indoors to Alice.

That night, Jerry went into Nellie's room and sat on the edge of her bed to say goodnight. Nellie rubbed the back of her da's hand with her finger and traced the blue veins that ran from his arm up to the base of his large stubby fingers. She pressed each thick, knobbly vein down with her finger and pushed the blood slowly out, watching it spring back and fill as she lifted her finger off. She picked up her da's hand and pressed his palm into her face, inhaling the smell of molasses, grain and jute.

Jerry studied her. She had no words for him, but absorbed and distracted herself with his hands. He noticed her bed was damp. He smelt something in the room he didn't like. Was it fear?

When he bent down to kiss her goodnight on the top of her head, she buried her face in his chest and clasped her hands tightly around his neck. She inhaled the smell of toil and labour, sweat and dust. He saw a scalp that, like his own, was red raw.

As Jerry left her room, he knew it was time to act. He was out of his depth. He had noticed her flinch as he tucked the blanket in around the top of her arms. She was too thin. As he held her, he could feel her ribs digging into him. Her eyes looked haunted and had great black shadows underneath them.

Something was seriously wrong.

It was time to put his pride on the back burner.

Later that night, when Alice had gone to bed, he sat down at the kitchen table with a paper and a pen and wrote to the only woman he knew who could help.

*Chapter Ten*

A WEEK LATER, while she was playing out on the green with Harry after school, Nellie stopped in her tracks. A lady walking down the street seemed to be looking over towards them. She looked familiar, but Nellie didn't know why. She was stout and well fed, which made her stand out; most of the women on the four streets were thin. Everyone Nellie knew in her life was right here, within fifty yards. The lady was wearing a black hat, with grey curls poking out, and a long black coat, with three buttons at the top and a velvet collar, that went almost all the way down to the floor and she carried a large bag. Nellie saw her stop and talk to Peggy and Sheila, who were chatting on the front step, then Peggy pointed straight at Nellie.

As the lady turned round, Nellie immediately knew she was kind; she could tell by her round rosy cheeks and the fact that she hadn't stopped smiling since Nellie and Harry had spotted her.

'Why is Auntie Peggy pointing at me, Harry?' said Nellie. Every parent on the street was known as auntie or uncle to all the children.

'I dunno, Nellie,' said Harry, who automatically walked over and took Nellie's hand. That was Harry's job in life, to protect Nellie. 'That's a big bag, maybe she has some sweets in it,' he said, his voice high with expectation. They both stared as the lady came straight over to the two of them. Harry squeezed Nellie's hand tightly.

'Hello, Nellie,' said the lady. 'I'm your Nana Kathleen and I've come over from Ireland to stay and help you and your daddy.'

Nellie grinned. In her little mind, this meant Alice would be going and she was very excited. Nellie didn't remember Kathleen from when she was a baby, but when they were having their breakfast Jerry always read out the blue airmail letters that arrived every couple of weeks. It was like having a new chapter of a book read, each time one arrived. Nellie dreamt of visiting Ireland. Of riding her daddy's donkey, Jacko, and of meeting her uncles and seeing the river her daddy and her Grandad Joe had poached the salmon from. She could see it all in her mind's eye and she knew she was in love with Ireland, before she had ever even been.

Sometimes, when he'd finished reading out the letter, her da would tell her about her grandad and her nana, and the people who lived on the farms and ran the pub and the shops. Some of the stories made her laugh so much that she made him tell them to her over and over again. She loved to hear how the priest had drunk so much Guinness in the village pub one Saturday night that the following Sunday morning he was found, fast asleep, propped up against a headstone in the graveyard. He was still so drunk, he couldn't take the mass. Cuddled up next to him was Mulligan's pig, which had also been lost and had stuck close to the priest for warmth.

'I'm not sure who smelt the worst,' said her da, 'the priest, from the Guinness, or the pig!'

The story never failed to make Nellie squeal with laughter. Even though she had never been to Bangornevin or Ballymara, she imagined the scene, just as it had happened.

Nellie threw her arms around Kathleen's legs and cried. Nana Kathleen had come. This was the happiest day of her little life.

Nellie hadn't managed to hide her bruises from Jerry. He had seen the fingerprint marks on the top of her arms and noticed that the skin on her bright-red scalp was now the same colour as her hair. It was not an unusual occurrence on the four streets for kids to be given a good hiding for misbehaving, and as a child Jerry had received many a whacking himself from his own da. But with a girl it was different, and Jerry knew Nellie hadn't a bad or naughty bone in her body. Whatever Alice had hit her for, it wouldn't have been deserved. He also shared Maura's concerns at how skinny she was.

'Jaysus, Jerry, I've seen more meat on Murphy's pencil!' she frequently said to him, and she was right. Jerry couldn't understand it, as he had always believed that Alice fed her well.

Jerry had taken Nellie to Maura's every day since the night she had silently traced the veins on the back of his hand and he had seen her angry red scalp as he bent to kiss the top of her head. He hadn't said anything to Nellie, but she didn't complain about being taken. In fact, when he told her at breakfast, she began to cry, but she was laughing at the same time. This disturbed him. Clearly, Nellie didn't want to be in the house alone with Alice. When she arrived home from school, she went back to Maura's with Kitty and he called to collect her.

Jerry had acknowledged that he was sinking.

'I'm just a simple man and I'm struggling here,' he had confided to Maura and Tommy in the past. But now, he had taken action and, when Jerry told Maura what he had done, she also laughed and cried together with relief.

Once Maura knew that Jerry had written to send for Kathleen, she waited 'til Jerry and Tommy had gone to work and the kids were packed off to school, then out came the mops banging like jungle drums on the kitchen walls up and down the street. The women ran like mice up the entry, carrying children in their arms, curlers bobbing under scarves, some in slippers and not yet even dressed, with ciggies thrust into coat or apron pockets, to gather in Maura's kitchen and hear the news and each drink a bucket of tea.

Once Kathleen appeared on the scene, Nellie quickly realized that Alice wasn't going anywhere, after all, but things in the house altered dramatically. Alice accepted Kathleen's arrival meekly, and soon became almost subservient to her. Kathleen had a way with her. It was of no consequence to Kathleen that Alice was a Protestant, or that she had been married in a register office.

'What's done can't be undone, Maura,' she said, when

Maura brought it up. 'I want to make progress, not dwell on the past.'

She quickly realized that there was something disturbingly wrong with Alice's basic character.

'God knows how he never saw it,' Kathleen wrote to her son back in Ireland, 'he must have been blinded with the grief.'

Kathleen was up for the battle. She had solved bigger problems than this.

One of the first things she did was to march Alice straight to Dr Brendan O'Cole. Surely there must be something he could do? Alice spent a while in with the doctor, who came out to chat to Kathleen afterwards. His own mammy and Kathleen had attended the same convent school back home.

'It's a personality problem, Kathleen, there's little medicine can do for that. But she's also suffering from anxiety, so I'm putting her on Valium, ten milligrams four times a day. You should see a great change altogether, but don't expect miracles. She wasn't brought up running free on the peat bogs, like we were. She had problems.'

'I thought as much, Doctor,' said Kathleen. She had actually changed Brendan's nappy when he was a baby, but felt it right and proper to award him the respect due to his position.

'Ye will cope, Kathleen, as my mammy would too. Ye will make a great difference to little Nellie's life by being here, I'm sure,' said Brendan, who felt about six years old when he was talking to Kathleen.

'Aye, I hope so. I've never been so wanted in all me life before, which leads me to believe something must have been very wrong.'

Alice left the doctor's surgery with a prescription for medication that meant she now spent much of the day staring peacefully into the fire, rather than standing at the bedroom window, glaring at the street. Every now and then, she even smiled.

*

Kathleen was relieved to have been sent for. What Jerry didn't know was that Maura had written to Kathleen often and pleaded with her to come back and visit, but Kathleen had always said no. Any request for help had to come from Jerry himself. He had to want Kathleen to be there.

On her first visit, she stayed for six weeks. Then she went home for three and came back again for another six. Jerry's daddy, Joe, had passed away a year since. Kathleen's sons had almost all married, and they and their wives managed the farm and the house while she was away.

Kathleen established a routine in the house, which even Alice managed to adapt to. Having Kathleen around taught Alice how a real mother behaved. It was the first time in Alice's life she had known normality. She still had no love for Nellie, which was obvious to Kathleen, but Kathleen also knew that Jerry had made his choice and it was now Kathleen's job to pick up the pieces. Alice was his wife, in God's eyes or not.

Nellie was in heaven. Kathleen brought everything into the home a mother should and, as time passed, Nellie loved the way that all the women now popped into their house for a chat and to have a fuss with Nana Kathleen. It was as if she was everyone's mammy. Alice never made a word of complaint; she knew she couldn't.

Maura never dreamt it would be possible for things to alter as much as they had. For the first time, Jerry's back door began to open and people walked in. Nellie noticed the women never spoke much to Alice. It was now definitely Nana Kathleen's house. The cuckoo in the nest had been put firmly in her place. But it really didn't matter; on forty milligrams of Valium a day, Alice couldn't have cared less.

'Writing to me mammy was the best thing I have ever done in me life,' Jerry said to Tommy, one day soon after Kathleen's arrival. 'Even Nellie is putting on the weight now. We all are.'

'What could I say to him?' said Tommy to Maura, when he got home that night. 'I wanted to say, aye, well, what's the use of Alice, why didn't you just send for Kathleen in the first place?'

'Because he's a man and he's proud,' said Maura, 'and, like with all men, pride comes before a fall.'

Kathleen's price for staying was for Jerry to trip down to the off-licence every Friday and Saturday night and bring her back two bottles of Guinness. She would put the poker into the fire and, when it was red hot, plunge it into the Guinness.

'That's me iron, Queen,' she would say to Nellie, who watched this ritual with fascination.

On Fridays, Kathleen went down to the bingo with all the other women and even took Alice with her once or twice. Kathleen was teaching Alice to knit; although she wouldn't touch baby clothes, she had been knitting Jerry a scarf for weeks.

Life settled down into a steady pace. The kitchen was like an advice surgery every morning and Nellie loved listening to the problems that everyone brought to Nana Kathleen.

One morning young Sheila came in, crying, with her newborn baby. She had four now and looked exhausted.

'Kathleen,' she cried, 'this babby hasn't slept a minute since it was born, what am I to do, I'm near at me wits' end.'

It took Kathleen mere seconds to diagnose the problem. 'A baby with cold feet never sleeps,' she said. 'Get some socks and some booties on its feet. Here, give him to me.'

Kathleen sat in front of the range with the baby on her lap and his bare feet facing the fire. She rubbed and warmed his feet between her hands and, slowly, the baby calmed. Within ten minutes, he was sleeping soundly. Nellie sat and grinned, feeling very important in having such a nice and clever nana.

Her life had been totally transformed. She now loved going to school and when she arrived home she ran in and out of the house with the other kids to play, rather than go straight to her room as Alice had made her. Her Nana Kathleen would be waiting for her with a mug of tea and a rock cake she had baked that afternoon, and often she and Harry would sit and eat it together before they ran outside. It was almost as though Alice didn't exist.

It transpired over the weeks that Kathleen was the only woman on the street who didn't have the time of day for Father James.

'He gives me the creeps, that man. Mind, I'll hold me tongue and say that to no one but you, Jerry, but he makes the hair on the back of me neck stand up when I see him walking up the street in his big fancy hat.'

Father James sensed Kathleen's reserve and kept his distance. He knew he had met his match. There was no charming Kathleen or pulling the wool over her eyes. She was polite enough at mass, but he knew not to chance a social visit.

Kathleen tried out her reservations on Maura one morning, when they saw Father James leaving Brigie's house down the road. Brigie had been blessed with eight daughters and not a single son.

'That man should be spending more time in his own church and less in other people's houses, if you ask me,' Kathleen said. 'Back home, the priest calls only for a birth, or the last rites. No other good reason for him to be dropping by all the time.'

Maura looked shocked. 'Kathleen,' she said in a pained voice, 'we are lucky to have the Father and grateful to him for sticking with us. He's so well thought of now, he could be in a cathedral, and Rome was wanting him to go to New York, but no, he stayed with us and we won't hear a bad word against him.'

Kathleen knew better than to argue, with no more than her suspicions to go on. Kathleen just knew. In her older years, she had learnt to size people up pretty quickly and Father James wasn't coming out well.

One day the Granada TV rental van arrived on the street

and soon almost all the houses had a TV set, with a grey sixpenny meter on the back, installed in pride of place in their front room. Once a week, the man from Granada would come round to empty the box. He would count all the sixpences on the floor in front of the TV and then write the amount down in a little black book.

He liked Nana Kathleen, who always gave him a cup of tea and a slice of freshly baked cake, while he told her the business of every house in the four streets. The Granada man was very observant; nothing got past him. It was through the TV man's visits that Nana Kathleen heard a lot more about Father James, and she didn't like much of what she heard. She also knew everything there was to know about every neighbour and what was occurring in every house. A cup of tea and a slice of cake paid enormous dividends.

With television, life altered overnight. Instead of listening to the voices coming out of the radio or staring into the fire, everyone sat and watched the telly. Times were changing. Jerry began to comb his hair like Elvis and in the mornings as he shaved he sang the Beatles song, 'Love, love me, do,' into the mirror above the sink. The Mersey beat was taking a grip and had filtered through onto the streets, where some of the houses were replacing their copper boilers and mangles with new, twin-tub washing machines. Nana Kathleen would not succumb. 'There's nowhere to store the ugly contraption, other than against the wall with a tablecloth thrown over to hide it. Why would I want to do that now? We have little enough room as it is,' she protested whenever the idea was brought up by a thoroughly modern Nellie. No one yet had a cooker, but they weren't far off, and nearly everyone now had a fridge.

On the day the letters arrived informing the residents that the four streets were to be added to a slum clearance list and they might be offered new houses, the jungle-drum mops went crazy. No one wanted to move and not a single letter was replied to. Everyone was happy to stay just where they were. One big happy family.

It was hard to believe that once things had been so bad and unhappy for Nellie and Jerry. That, not long ago, Nellie had been creeping down the stairs to avoid Alice and to sneak food from the cupboard, if she got the chance. Now she was woken by Nana Kathleen, shouting up the stairs, to tell her that her breakfast was ready.

'Skinny miss, get your lazy bones up and out of that bed now, before I send in ye da with a cold flannel!' she would shout, and Nellie loved it.

She was growing up and life had been constant and steady since Nana Kathleen had arrived. Thanks to Kathleen's luck at the bingo, Nellie had even been to Ireland for a holiday, visited her cousins and stayed at the farmhouse where she had become firm friends with her auntie Maeve and uncle Liam.

One Friday night, when she had been fast asleep, she had been woken by Nana Kathleen, sitting on her bed and singing. The landing light was on and Jerry was standing behind her, laughing.

'Come on, Ma,' he said, 'let's get ye into bed.'

'No, Jerry,' she protested, 'I have news for my Nellie. Tomorrow, Nellie, me and you, we is going on a holiday to Ireland, so we is. I've just won the jackpot on the bingo tonight and we are going home to celebrate.'

Nellie sat up in bed, hugging her knees, looking at her da. Could this really be true? Would she really see the church and the Moorhaun River?

'Will I see the salmon jumping, Nana?' she squealed, now wide awake.

'Oh sure ye will, that and more,' said Nana Kathleen as the Guinness took over and she collapsed onto Nellie's bed and was out like a light.

True to her word, the next morning, Nellie had all of her few clothes packed into Nana Kathleen's carpet bag and they took the boat to Dublin, the same boat Jerry and Bernadette had met on. Nellie felt like the luckiest girl in the world. She didn't know anyone else who had been on a holiday.

She was so happy she thought she would burst with sheer joy. Nana Kathleen was her angel.

A few weeks after they returned from Ireland, Nellie came down to overhear a conversation between her da and Kathleen that made her realize all was not well.

'I know the signs sure enough, Jerry, and only you will know if I'm right. I'd say she was about four months' gone.'

The blood left Jerry's face, as he sat down on the chair. 'For feck's sake, Mam, are ye sure?'

'I've seen enough, I'm sure all right,' said Kathleen. 'Alice is pregnant.'

Jerry couldn't help being delighted at the news, but he was also anxious. He had long ago given up hope of having another child and he wasn't at all sure how Alice would cope.

Very soon after the wedding, Jerry had decided that sex with Alice was cold and pointless. She would deploy any number of reasons to avoid it and after the rare occasions when it did happen, she would assiduously sit in the bath and douche herself, using a soft rubber hose and a solution she had bought from the pharmacist, for at least half an hour afterwards to ensure she wasn't pregnant. Jerry would lie in bed, smoking a cigarette and listening to the sound of his would-be babies being flushed down a tube. He would look through the window, listening to the distant tugs on the river, feeling bad and swearing that this would be the last time. He didn't know how Alice managed it, but each time they had sex, he felt more alone than he ever had before.

Whilst Alice slept, he often lay in bed, wide awake and looking at the stars, thinking of Bernadette. It was his way of keeping her in his sight. Bernadette was a star, one he could see each night and talk to. In the weeks following the funeral, he would take Nellie out into the yard, shuffle her up in his arms and turn her face to the night sky for Bernadette to see. Holding her in his large palms, he whispered to the twinkling inky night sky, 'Here she is, just look at her, she's putting on weight every day and just take a look at those big blue eyes, who do they belong to then, eh?'

He would frequently dwell on the issue of his own sanity. He felt as if Bernadette had never actually gone. The unexpected suddenness of her death had left him unable to grasp the reality. In the early days, he thought he could hear her running up the stairs, feel her breath, sense her sadness. At night, when he left Nellie's room, the hairs on his arms stood on end as though someone had swept in as he walked out, brushing close as they passed him. But he knew that was truly mad.

Kathleen stayed as long as she could, but she had to go back to Ireland ready for the birth of her third son's grandchild in her own house. She promised to return in time for the birth of Nellie's little brother or sister. Jerry knew that once Kathleen had left, Alice tried everything possible to rid herself of the baby. She soaked her soul in gin and took various concoctions of pills bought from a dodgy nurse on Scotland Road who looked after the girls who serviced the sailors whilst they were in port.

But the baby hung on in and slipped out, with the minimum of fuss, at four o'clock one cold and foggy morning, three weeks before he was due. An early morning star.

They had been woken from their sleep by the sound of Alice's waters breaking, like a champagne cork suddenly popping in the room. As soon as he realized things were happening fast, Jerry left Alice lying moaning in bed, and ran to the pub, the nearest place that had a phone he could use, to call the midwife. Alice had refused to attend a hospital.

Neighbours were well used to the odd hours people ran up and down their street to get to the pub for the phone. Births and deaths never happened conveniently during opening hours. As he ran, not a single set of dentures, soaking in pink Steradent, rattled in their glass on a bedside table. Nor did the sound of boots on cobbles disturb a stray ship's rat, raiding the bins. In the dead of the night, only the feral, hungry cats sitting on top of entry walls and bin lids looked curiously through the smog, with interest, at a man in his boots and pyjamas, frantically trying to knock down the pub door. Quietly.

When Noleen, the midwife, arrived at the house, she asked how Jerry was going to manage the new baby, with Kathleen back in Mayo. Noleen, who had made a few house visits, was fully aware of how much Kathleen carried the house and that there were problems with Alice. Work on the docks was thin and big men like Jerry who could get it were working every hour God sent, to make sure they kept their place in the gang. That way they got to keep their jobs.

'I have no idea, Noleen, but Mammy will be back as quick as she can,' he said as he lit the fire in the bedroom, which had been set ready for weeks, whilst Noleen set to work with calm and authoritative efficiency.

She knew she was chancing her luck when, once the baby was born and she had cut the cord, she lifted him without any warning and plopped him down onto his mother's chest. It was a risk, but she considered it worth a try. As she laid the baby down, his wide open eyes looked into his mother's and begged for acceptance.

'Would you look at him, all knowing,' said Noleen, with forced gaiety, grinning from ear to ear. Like all Irish Catholic midwives, she regarded each birth as a miracle and a gift. It never crossed her mind to wonder why such a good God gave poor women so many babies whose mouths they couldn't feed, and why he chose every now and then to make one of them bleed so much from forcing yet another child out of a tired and shot womb that they died in her arms before the ambulance arrived. Noleen was a kind woman and genuinely took a delight in every delivery she attended.

'Sure, he's been here before, that little fella, so he has,' she trilled.

For just a moment, a tiny moment, suspended in the warmth of a room imbued with the love and magical hope a new baby brings, there was a chance. Noleen's words had penetrated Alice's fog, and caught her up in the expectation heaped upon her. Alice thought she would dig deep inside and try to give motherly love a go. She met her newborn son's eyes, as Noleen and Jerry watched, holding their breath.

She tried. They could see she tried, for a second, but then, just when Jerry and Noleen looked at each other and dared to hope, Alice turned her head away and stared into the fire.

'Take him, will you,' she said to Jerry, 'and call him what you wish.'

This time Jerry's tears were not of joy, but of sorrow, as he knew with total certainty his prayers were unheard.

Jerry and Alice had been sleeping with a brown rubber sheet on the mattress for weeks, in case of this very eventuality, a sudden birth, and so it took the midwife only an hour to clean up mother and baby, change the bed and throw a shovel of coal from the bucket onto the fire, before she sat on a chair by the fire to write her notes.

Jerry woke Nellie, despite the fact that Alice begged him

not to, and told her the news. Her reaction to the new baby was something he couldn't predict. He had been too scared to discuss it with her before the event. He had wanted to share his joy with her but she was only a child. He needed to know as soon as possible how Nellie was going to take to the new arrival in the house.

Nellie, dressed in her long flannelette nightdress, rubbed her bleary eyes and, clutching her teddy, padded across the landing to her da's bedroom, her hand in his. His big palm felt hot but the lino was cold beneath her feet. It was the first time Nellie had ever seen the fireplace in her da's room with a roaring fire in the grate. Only a single bedside lamp was alight and the room was warm, filled with a golden glow. The reflection of the flames chased each other as they danced and crackled up the walls and across the ceiling.

Although she was now too big to carry, Jerry lifted Nellie into his arms. Her red curls, now grown past her shoulders, tickled his nose and face as, half asleep, she sucked her thumb, a habit she still couldn't break at night. Her other arm was hooked tightly around her father's neck, as he carried her round to the far side of the bed, to look into the crib. Noleen looked on and smiled at what was an intimate and special moment, when a little girl meets, for the first time, her brand-new baby brother.

Jerry felt sick and tearful with relief when he saw Nellie's face as her eyes alighted upon her baby brother. She took her thumb out of her mouth and lovingly grinned from ear to ear. She kissed her father's cheek hard and took away his tears with her lips, whilst her hand clasped his other cheek hard. His eyes shut tight while he suppressed the pain that had rushed unbidden out of his heart, as he remembered the moments of her birth.

Nellie, barely containing her excitement, squealed and wriggled in his arms, to get down and closer to the baby.

'Let's call him Joseph!' she exclaimed, clapping her hands together and feeling very clever. It was almost Christmas, and that day at school Father James had spoken at mass about what a great man Joseph had been to take on a pregnant single mother, Mary. With her wide eyes gleaming, she turned excitedly to Alice who was neither watching nor listening.

So, Joseph he became.

Alice was untouched by the endearing scene and continued to stare into the flames. She had given up trying to find within herself whatever other women had that enabled them to give a fig about their children. There had been years of arguing and grief from Jerry. Shame heaped upon her by the neighbours she watched from her window, acting like good mothers should. She had become the living proof that a Catholic man had committed a mortal sin when he married a Protestant woman. In the words she had heard Maura speak to Tommy on the day of their wedding: 'Surely, as God is anyone's judge, no good will come of it.'

She lay with both hands on her belly, as though nursing a wound. She was unreachable.

A few days later, once Jerry had returned to work, Nellie answered the front door, with Joseph in her arms. She had been kept off school for the week whilst they waited for Kathleen to return, and until Alice recovered a little from the shock of giving birth. Jerry had not explained this, but they both knew someone needed to be there to look after Alice, as much as Joseph. She knew that when she went back to school, if Nana Kathleen hadn't yet managed to return, Maura was going to come in to help feed and change the baby, even though Jerry hadn't managed to get Alice to agree to this yet. But even without Alice's agreement, Maura had already been in once this morning, as had Noleen the midwife. They had all given Nellie so many instructions that her head felt as if it was going to collapse and fall off her shoulders.

Julia, her classmate and friend from down the road, was going to pop in on the way home from school with her mammy, Brigie. Yesterday morning they had both arrived with a large, navy-blue, Silver Cross carriage pram, already made up with soft white flannel sheets and a net covering the opening of the hood.

'The pram is still warm from the baby in number four, who's been turned out into a pushchair to make way for Joseph,' joked Brigie. 'The little fella won't know where he is when he wakes up!'

There was a little hand-knitted teddy on the pillow, popped into the pram as it went down the street by one of the neighbours with a handwritten card. There were freshly baked scones in a bag with a little note from Mrs Keating and a hand-knitted white baby cardigan that Mrs O'Brien kept handy in the drawer for new arrivals on the four streets. Now that hers were all grown up and she had a bit more time on her hands, it was her job to knit the matinee coats. There was also a pile of pale-blue baby clothes and folded terry-towelling nappies, all of which had already been through a number of little boys in the street, washed and pressed ready for use, contributed to by almost every house.

Finally, there was a triangular paper packet full of tea leaves. The four streets were never short of tea. At all times, in one of the backyards, kept dry in a coal house, there was always a wooden tea chest full of leaves, courtesy of a dock gang catching it off the back of a hull.

A brown earthenware pot with the Pacific Steam Line logo embossed on the lid, wrapped up in newspaper, sat under the pram canopy. It was full of an Irish stew for the evening. There was also a loaf of bread and three sausage rolls, the pastry still hot, and three vanilla slices from the corner bakery.

The pram contained all that was needed for a new baby, plus a feast. Nellie wasn't aware of it, but there had been a collection of halfpennies down the road for the extra meat for the stew and the pastries. She certainly felt the weight of responsibility on her shoulders with the new baby, but she knew she wasn't on her own; there was an entire community to help and support her and her da.

Later in life, as a young woman living amongst those who became obsessed with the material value of their house, car or next holiday, Nellie often looked back in wonder at the resourcefulness, compassion and love that existed in such a poor community, which had nothing to call its own. It didn't often know how the next meal would arrive onto the table, but it took comfort and pride in knowing it had everything of any real value: family, good neighbourliness and friendship.

As she opened the front door, thinking it would be one of the neighbours and grateful with expectation, her heart sank to see Father James standing on the step. She noticed his hands were empty.

'Saints preserve and save us,' he exclaimed when he saw the child straining with the effort of holding a baby. 'Where's ye heathen mammy?'

Nellie had been told not to answer him, and so she didn't. The priest knew her father was at work and launched into a tirade of instructions for Nellie.

She caught bits about Alice needing to be 'churched'.

'The baby needs to be brought into the light and absolved of the original sin. Do ye hear me, Nellie? He needs to be brought up as a Catholic and not a Protestant, as your sinful self has been,' he spluttered.

Nellie didn't reply.

'Do ye not know your own mother would spin in her grave if she knew what the ways of your father have become, since the poor woman's passing?' he went on.

Nellie stood and stared. The hallway of the house was long, narrow and dark. Although tiny, the baby weighed heavily in her arms. She looked over her shoulder to the door of the kitchen and waited, expecting Alice to come through it and save her from this angry priest. But nothing happened.

She had struggled to open the door and not drop the precious baby, who needed her so badly. Closing it was easier. She shuffled forward and, without looking up at him, lifted her foot slightly and kicked the door shut in the priest's face. As the door swung to, his shouting became louder, as though he thought the increased volume would prevent its closure, and the baby began to cry.

Once the door had safely banged shut, she could see his shadow, still silhouetted through the two mottled sheets of opaque glass. His hat made his profile look more like that of a gangster than a priest. He wasn't going to give up that easily although the closed door muffled the noise. She wished hard that he would just go away. She shuffled over to the foot of the stairs and sat herself down on the bottom step, taking care not to trip over the long shawl her father had brought home – it never failed to surprise her how much fell off the back of a seagoing liner – and had left out to be wrapped around the baby to keep him warm.

As she lifted Joseph onto her knee and adjusted his position, he turned his head towards her chest, pecking frantically like a little bird in the nest looking for food. She had no idea what he was doing. Light and warmth flooded the hallway as Alice opened the kitchen door. Her footsteps sounded, slow and heavy, on the linoleum as she walked down the hallway.

She made no mention of the priest as she handed Nellie a bottle and said, 'Here, give him that. It will shut him up.' She turned on her heel and walked back into the kitchen and the warmth of its fire, closing the door behind her as she went.

The previous evening, Nellie had sat and helped her father feed the baby when he got home from work. She had watched him change the disgusting nappy, full of his black and dark green meconium. She had held the baby's head whilst her da splashed water on his bottom and she had shaken the Johnson's talcum powder over him, creating a cloud that made them both splutter and laugh. She helped to fasten the nappy pin, terrified she might put it through his wiggly bits. Her father showed her how to put the back of her hand on the inside of the nappy, flat against Joseph's abdomen, as a shield, to stop that happening. And Nellie had giggled as little Joseph decided, once again, to empty his bladder, which went straight into her father's face as he bent to fold the new nappy over his son.

How she wished her da was here now and not at work. How she wished Nana Kathleen would hurry back. She was still shaken from the priest's visit. He had finally moved away from the door. She nervously put the teat of the bottle into Joseph's tiny mouth. He helped her out by latching on immediately and suckled frantically while his wide-open eyes stared gratefully into hers.

She was overcome with love for him. She knew Alice's coldness better than anyone and that her job would be to protect him, whilst her da or Nana Kathleen couldn't be there. She shifted her arm under Joseph's back and brought her hand up to support his neck. As she cradled him in her arms, she whispered into the side of his face, 'Don't worry, Joseph, I will look after you.' Her tears fell from her cheeks onto the floor. Lonely and lost, she never felt the ghostly arms slip gently around her shoulders, or the tender kiss on her own cheek, but she did suddenly feel much better.

# Chapter Eleven

It was a normal morning on the street. As Nellie crossed the road to 'run a message' to the shop on the corner, she heard Peggy shouting at the school welfare officer.

'I have five feckin' pair of shoes and nine kids, would ye like to choose which feckin' kids stay at home, come on then, come on in, will ye, King Solomon, and choose.'

Peggy stood back and held the front door open, to usher the welfare officer into the house, at which point he banged his book shut and fled down the street. He was no stranger to being shouted at but Peggy scared him more than most.

'Do ye think I want four feckin' kids hangin' round me neck all day, eh? You don't come here, mister, and complain about my kids not being in school until you bring some feckin' shoes with you. Can you 'ear me?'

He was already gone, speeding away in his Morris Minor up the Vauxhall Road.

'There, he won't be back in a hurry,' said Peggy to no one in particular, before she went back inside and carried on shouting, this time at the kids.

He would be back, without the shoes. Peggy would shout at him, again. He would flee to his car, as always, and on it went, a well-rehearsed, recurring drama.

'Jeez, can you hear Peggy giving out,' said Maura to Kitty, who was on her way out of the door to school. 'She will be giving this street a bad name, the way she's carrying on, so she will. I'm going to ask Kathleen to talk to her.' Kathleen was back and settled into number forty-two. Her son Liam and his wife Maeve were running the farm back home so Kathleen had decided to stay put in Liverpool, until her job of bringing up Nellie was done.

Maura had made the same comment to Tommy the previous evening, although he didn't appear to be convinced it was a good idea.

'Why don't you have a chat with her yourself?' Tommy had said, thinking that it would surely be a useless exercise anyway. A letter from the Pope wouldn't stop Peggy shouting.

'Because I don't want to fall out with me next-door neighbour and she has respect for Kathleen, her being older and all that,' said Maura.

'Maura, me love, our street is on the list for slum clearance, how much worse a name can we get than that, I ask ye?' Tommy said reasonably.

Maura had muttered on under her breath, that the only way she would be taken out of her house would be in a box, but Tommy had stopped listening. He was studying the form of the horses for the three-thirty at Kempton, his newspaper laid out on the kitchen table. The children were growing and the sanctuary of the outhouse was no longer his; there would always be one or the other knocking on the door for him to get out.

Tommy didn't really mind. He had never raised his voice to any of his offspring and they all regarded him as a big softie, compared to every other da on the street, other than Jerry. Their peers often felt the belt or the slipper. All Maura's children knew how lucky they were to have such a gentle man as their da and he was adored by them all.

Tommy took the pencil from behind his ear, ready to draw a circle round the name of his favourite filly, and became aware that someone was standing next to him. He looked up to see Kitty by his side.

'Hello, Queen, where's your mother?' said Tommy, in sudden surprise.

'She's gone next door to see Kathleen,' said Kitty, as she pulled out a chair and sat down at the table next to him.

'Jaysus, thank God for that, I thought I'd gone deaf there for a minute, Kitty.'

He looked sideways at Kitty and they both burst out laughing, something they used to do all the time, but getting a laugh out of Kitty these days was much harder work than it ever had been when she was little.

Tommy folded the paper, a natural subconscious gesture, which he had no idea he was making, in order to show Kitty she had his full undivided attention.

'Is everything all right, Queen?' he asked.

'Aye, Da, not bad. I'm taking the kids out for a picnic to the Pier Head to see the ferry.'

Kitty always spoke in the same tone these days. No ups

or downs, no stream of chatter, interspersed with giggles. Tommy thought to himself that Kitty was like half the child she once was. A bright burning lamp turned down to dim. It was a long time now, years even, since he had seen the old Kitty.

'Grand,' said Tommy, 'but have ye been afflicted with a blindness, Kitty? Have ye not noticed, it's fecking freezing and there's snow on the ground? What kind of picnic is that?'

They laughed again as Kitty explained, 'Da, there's been snow for months. I'm going crazy being stuck indoors.'

Then she became sombre, as she came to the real reason she had sought out Tommy, just as soon as she could get him on her own.

'Da, will ye do me a favour?' she said, quietly, glancing nervously over her shoulder and out of the kitchen window to see if Maura was returning.

'Aye, Queen, what is it?' He had already reopened the paper, but now looked up and closed it again. He could sense Kitty was about to ask him something serious.

'I don't want to be confirmed, Da. I don't want to go to the Priory for me confirmation lessons and I'm too scared to tell me mam,' she said in a rush.

'Jaysus, Kitty,' spluttered Tommy. 'Why don't ye ask me to tell her ye is joining the circus, it'd be easier.'

'I know, Da, but I just don't want to and I know she will give out so much.'

Tommy smiled. This was the daughter Maura still hoped might one day become a nun. He was secretly pleased. It was the last thing he wanted for his precious Kitty.

For a man who only ever wanted a quiet life, breaking this bombshell to Maura was not something he would look forward to, but he wouldn't let his princess down.

'Come here and give yer da a hug. I'll find a way, Queen. I don't know how right now, but I will do me best.'

'Thanks, Da,' said Kitty as she hugged him tight. She closed her eyes and wished she could be honest with him, but the shame wouldn't let her.

*

Nellie had arrived at the corner shop.

'Two ounces of red cheese, please,' she said as she handed the money over to Sadie, the shopkeeper, to ring into the till.

'OK, Nellie love, here you go, and tell Nana Kathleen to grate it now, as it will go further. And don't forget to let her know I will be over on Saturday morning for me tea leaves now, will yer, Queen?'

Nellie loved the fact that everyone wanted to pass a message to Nana Kathleen, even the teachers at school. Nana Kathleen had become everything from a Sunday school teacher to a marriage guidance counsellor, and she was the fount of all knowledge. No one knew how she did it, but nothing got past Nana Kathleen and there wasn't one bit of gossip she didn't already know by the time she was told it. She wasn't a gossip herself, but the keeper of all secrets. Nana Kathleen's friendship with the Granada TV man was paying dividends. It was amazing the rewards she could reap, for nothing more than a cup of tea and a slice of cake.

Kathleen read the tea leaves and her reading day was on a Saturday. The house became like Lime Street station as every woman from miles around came to have their tea leaves read. She sat at the head of the kitchen table whilst Nellie and Kitty made cups of tea and the women went in and out all morning.

Her palm had to be crossed with silver, which meant everyone paid sixpence, and it was the sixpences that paid for the two bottles of Guinness. But if Nana Kathleen thought someone was stretched for the money, as they went to give her the sixpence, she would press an extra one back into their own palm so they came out sixpence up, as well as feeling better for hearing a bit of good news in the tea leaves.

'Kathleen's so good,' said Brigie to Peggy, one morning as, having left Kathleen's kitchen, they were walking down the entry to their own back doors. 'How could anyone have known I had a letter from America last week? I've told no one and it's been sat on the mantelpiece next to the telly since it arrived.'

'Sure, it's a mystery, so it is,' said Peggy, 'and no wonder she gives Father James short shrift, she wouldn't want him spoiling our fun, now would she.'

'I'm amazed Maura hasn't kicked up, her being so religious an' all that, but even she's getting her tea leaves read, can ye imagine and their Kitty's even making the tea!'

Both women roared with laughter on their way home, one thinking there was a windfall on its way, and another expecting a surprise visitor from overseas and a letter from a tall government building. No one ever questioned that there was never any bad news from Nana Kathleen on a Saturday morning. Bad news was as rare as Irish sunshine in Mayo on an April morning.

Kitty ran up to Nellie, as she left the shop.

'Nellie,' she called, 'let's collect up Joseph and the kids and walk them down to the Pier Head and watch the ferries, do ya fancy that?'

Nellie dashed back home with Kitty and began the process of packing Joseph into his pram for the trip. They were going to take Harry, but he had just fallen over on the entry cobbles and skinned the top of his knee. Maura was liberal with her brown iodine on cut knees and it smarted like nothing else.

'Blow, blow, BLOW!' they could hear her shouting, as far as three doors away, while she sloshed the pungent-smelling liquid onto Harry's knee. It stung like hell, as his screams ripped the morning air.

They collected Peggy's latest baby, to pop into the Silver Cross with Joseph, and sat a couple of toddlers on the navy-blue apron. Another was so desperate to join in, she lay on the wire shopping tray underneath. There were six little ones from various houses on the streets, holding onto various parts of the chrome frame and the handles, all trotting along beside Kitty and Nellie. They looked like travellers moving a caravan to a new destination.

Tucked down either side of the pillows to keep them warm were bottles of formula for the babies when they woke. Two empty glass pop bottles full of water were pushed down by the side of their legs for drinks for the other children during the day, along with a pack of Jacob's cream crackers, sandwiched together with jam and wrapped up in greaseproof paper. The closest Liverpool had to a delicacy.

They would be gone for only a few hours. The wind down at the Pier Head was biting, but Kitty didn't care. She had wanted to escape the four streets, to look out over the wide expanse of water. She felt for the first time in years as though she could escape the stress. Her da was going to stick up for her. She had been terrified at the thought of having to go to the priory for her confirmation lessons and being in the building alone with Father James. Her da was going to save her.

Maybe, if her ma was all right and didn't kick up a fuss, she could tell her parents about Father James and his visits to her bedroom. Even as she thought it, though, she knew she would never have the courage to take that step. She still couldn't risk not being believed, of having to justify what she was saying. She would have to live with the shame until she could get away altogether, but she was worried about Angela. Would he move on to Angela next?

The little ones had enjoyed the change of scene and the adventure, but were starting to tire. As they headed back, two of Peggy's boys began misbehaving, and getting home took much longer than reaching the pier. The snow had begun to fall again and Kitty and Nellie were relieved to turn the corner at the bottom of the street. If only they had turned the corner either two minutes later or two minutes earlier, if only they had done lots of things differently that day, then disaster might never have struck.

Callum O'Prey had brought the car round to the house to show off to his mammy. Callum had spent his life searching for things to show off about and impress his mammy with. He used to be the fastest runner in the street, and for that he had the privilege of robbing the bread vans every time there was a 'bit of a do'.

Callum could cater a party for twenty out of the back of a bread van making a delivery. He stole to order. The more he stole, the more respected he felt. The van driver never knew where his sausage rolls and custard tarts ended up.

The car was a shiny, brand-new, grey Ford Anglia. No one else on the street owned a car. Neither did Callum. It was stolen.

People like Callum didn't own cars. The idea of stealing one to keep was just too fanciful; he wouldn't have known what to do with it. He fully intended to take it back to Dale Street, where he'd found it. He didn't even have a driving licence. Callum wasn't that much of a rogue; he was just an underprivileged boy from a loving home in desperate need to be someone, even if just for one day.

He wanted to be a big man, one his mammy could brag about, like Mrs Keating from next door did about her lad, who had become a sergeant in the army. Callum had tried to sign up, but had failed the medical on account of his chronic asthma, made worse by the roll-ups he chain-smoked each day.

'Sure,' Callum had said to the friend who was walking with him as he stole the car, but who refused to get in, 'yer man is inviting me to take a spin, or why would he have left the keys in it now?'

He had driven a few bangers before around the wasteland at the back of the garage where his pal, Michael,
worked, and it had been easy. Callum was fascinated by cars
and engines but, in his world, people from the four streets
would never own a car. He wasn't very brave and hoped the
owner was having a very long lunch so he could get the car
back before anyone had noticed it had gone.

Today, he loved the smile on his mammy's face as he spun
her the line about how a man in town had asked him to run
a few messages in his car for him. He stayed just long enough
to drink a cup of tea with his mammy, eat a cheese sandwich
and have a show-off. He loved the fact that as he enjoyed his
fifteen minutes of fame, every child on the street was hanging
around the car, looking in through the windows and yelling
through the door of the house, 'Callum, is that car yours,
will ye give me a ride?'

'Oh, Callum,' his mammy trilled, 'fancy that, you driving
round in a smart car. Yer man must know ye to be a trustworthy person, brought up the right way.'

She was even bragging at the door, as she saw him off to
carry on with his errand, and shouted down the street to her
neighbours, 'Would ye look at our Callum now, would ye,'
her face flushed with pride and pleasure.

'Did ye not need lessons to drive that, Callum?' shouted
Peggy from across the road, having known Callum since the
day he was born.

'I can drive all right, Peggy, but I have to get back to yer
man now,' Callum called as he dived back into the driver's
seat, not wanting to answer any probing questions.

As Callum left the house, he felt like a hero and six feet tall, rather than the five foot two caused by a lack of meat and poor nutrition. He revved up the engine to impress everyone, as he let out the clutch. But the car went nowhere. It was winter and the road was frozen hard with packed ice. It had been cleared in town by the snowploughs, but in the four streets, as no one had a car, the area hadn't been touched. Callum's knowledge of driving was rudimentary and he pressed down harder on the accelerator, thinking that it would make the car move.

Fear crept into the pit of his belly and settled in, as he began to panic. He had to get the car back, before he was caught. His brother had already been sent down for thieving and Callum knew it would kill his mammy if the same happened to him. She would die with the shame. He now regretted, more than anything in his life, having taken the car. He heard a police siren in the distance, racing along the road, and imagined it was coming for him. It wasn't, but it made his heart beat faster in terror, nonetheless. The wheels began to spin on the ice and the car quickly gathered speed. Callum lost control and slammed his foot down hard on the brake, which made the spin worse.

He froze in fear as he saw people running down the street shrieking. He could hear a screeching noise coming from the engine, but didn't realize it was because his foot was now pressed down hard on the accelerator. It was all over in seconds, but, for years to come, Callum would play the scene out in his nightmares over and over, as though it had lasted for many minutes.

His mammy, as well as every child on the green and in the street, saw the car heading towards the girls, the pram and the children, and screamed hysterically for them to get out of the way. Suddenly aware of what was happening, Kitty pressed down hard on the handle of the pram, lifting the front wheels off the ground, and turned it round quickly to get round the corner, out of harm's way. Both Nellie and Kitty were in control and yelling at the kids to hold onto the pram, but the bigger ones had all scattered, terrified, as the car spun out of control. They had only just turned the pram round and moved it a few feet when they heard the screech of brakes.

As Nellie looked back over her shoulder, she and Kitty wailed with fright and ran, dragging the little children, still holding onto them.

That was when Nellie saw her again. Her red hair flew out behind her as she put both her arms out towards them and urgently whispered, 'Run, my darling, run.' At that moment, Nellie felt as though their feet left the ground and they were propelled twenty feet forwards, just before the car hit them – straight in the back – and then came to an abrupt halt.

Callum saw the look of horror on both of their faces as they went down like rag dolls, and the Silver Cross pram, with both the babies inside, lurched violently forward, before slowly meandering up and down over the cobbles, stopping only when it reached the kerb, taking itself home, like a trusty old nag. And, just for a tiny moment, all was silent.

Harry, even though he was in a state of shock, raced in through the back entry door to the kitchen, for his mam and for Kathleen, and then ran with Peggy to bang on the pub door, in order to use their phone to call for an ambulance. Maura ran screaming like a banshee to Nellie and Kitty.

Once Nellie hit the cobbled ground, the blood from the back of her head soaked into the snow to form a large, bright red halo around her, making her look like a figurine in the Russian icon that hung on the altar at St Mary's church. Kitty was out cold, lying with her arm flung out to the side.

The street erupted into chaos. The screaming and crying could be heard along all four streets and beyond, as people began running out of their homes and gathering round, huddling together from the cold and shock.

In a matter of moments, Nellie's face became paler and her lips turned blue, until the colour of her skin blended with that of the snow on which she lay. Flakes were settling on both girls' hair and remained frozen. A dusting of fallen crystals.

Kitty came round quickly and began to cry with the pain in her arm, shrieking for her mammy. But there was no sound from Nellie. Unconscious and hurt, with no lively spirit to offer a defence or protection, her vulnerability and frailty were exposed for all to see. She looked closer to death than life. A tiny and beautiful bird, broken in the snow.

One of the boys had been dispatched to the dock to fetch Jerry and Tommy. The women were whispering amongst themselves that even though the accident had happened only three doors down from Jerry's house, Alice had not appeared. Nana Kathleen was on her knees next to Nellie, stroking her arms and whispering soft words interspersed with prayers fearing the worst, while Maura tried to calm Kitty down.

'She has the energy to scream, Maura, that's a good sign, she will be all right,' said Kathleen, but the wise words did nothing to stem the flow of Maura's tears or silence her wailing.

Jerry and Tommy ran up the steps from the docks and collapsed onto their knees in the snow next to their girls. Jerry grabbed Nellie's hand and sobbed at the sight of his small scrap of life. The life he was supposed to protect and care for. This couldn't be happening. No God would be this cruel, he thought. His mind was frozen, not by the icy wind, but by fear, as he looked at his baby and felt his mother's arm slip across his back. Nellie opened her eyes, slowly, blinked and then closed them again. Blood was coming from the corner of her eye, which was badly cut.

Her cold blue lips suddenly moved as she said, 'Da, I can't open me eyes.'

Jerry sobbed with relief when, at that moment, they heard the ambulance bell as the van itself screeched and slid round the corner. Within minutes the drivers had the girls loaded onto stretchers and into the ambulance.

'Get back inside now, all of you, it's too cold to hang around out here. They will be well looked after in the hospital,' they told the anxious crowd.

Maura and Kathleen were allowed into the back along with the patients, before the drivers leapt into the cab and sped away.

Silence descended on the street while everyone stared at the retreating ambulance. It had all happened so quickly.

Callum was already in the Anchor, out of harm's way and close to passing out. Tommy and Jerry would likely want to kill him with their bare hands. Everyone now focused their attention on how to get Callum out of this hole and return the car to its rightful owner. The street looked after its own. Michael from the garage was sent for, then the police were telephoned and told about a mysterious car that had suddenly appeared on a garage forecourt.

As the ambulance pulled away, Jerry looked up to see Sheila with the pram, looking after the babies, and Peggy coming towards him and Tommy with mugs in her hand. As she walked up the road towards them, Brigie was shuffling along the ice with a bottle of Irish whiskey in her hand and a wake of little girls trotting after her.

'Hot sweet tea for ye both, for the shock,' Peggy said kindly.

'Here ye are,' Brigie said, as she poured the last drops from the bottle into both mugs. 'That'll help with the shock.'

Tommy, standing at Jerry's side as he knelt in the snow, said, 'Thanking ye, Peggy, and ye, Brigie.'

Jerry was speechless.

'C'mon, mate, we can't lose a day's pay,' said Tommy, trying to break into Jerry's thoughts. 'Let's get back now. They will be all right with Maura and Kathleen.' They both drained the mugs of sweet whisky and tea.

Tommy turned and walked towards his house in order to give instructions to the kids and to hand the mugs back to Peggy, who was talking with the other women. Jerry slowly got up from the ground and stood upright, wiping tears from his eyes that he could never have let Tommy see. The hot tea and whiskey burnt into his stomach and brought him to his senses.

Where was Alice? Why wasn't she here at his side? He looked at the road in front of the houses. The grit had been churned by fear and shock. The ice and snow stained with Nellie's blood.

As Jerry rose, he didn't see the extra, almost indiscernible, imprint of another pair of knees in the snow, alongside his own.

Upon admission to hospital, both girls were dispatched straight to the operating theatre. Several hours after the accident, they had been operated on and admitted to a cheerful children's ward, where they found themselves lying in beds, side by side.

The walls were painted white halfway up and then a pale blancmange pink to the top. Starting six feet above the ground so that no one could see in, huge Georgian windows reached up to the high ceiling. White iron-framed bedsteads were lined up against the walls in a regimental fashion, placed precisely six feet apart. Each top sheet was turned down over the pink counterpane by exactly eighteen inches. The rigorous attention to detail imposed exacting standards on the nursing staff and left no room for sloppiness.

Long, highly polished oak tables ran down the middle of the ward on which sat tall jars of flowers, books, cards, board games and the occasional toy. Around each bed stood a set of curtains on wheels, decorated with white bunnies playing in green fields, interspersed with the occasional bunch of yellow flowers. On a fine day, beams of sunshine tumbled in through the high windows and fell down onto the beds, radiating warmth, calm and innocence, in what was often the setting for high drama and despair.

The busy nurses' office, situated at the ward entrance, offered a clear view of the young patients almost to the very end of the ward, but not quite. The last bed, the 'night before home' bed, was tucked away around the corner. It was every child's aim to sleep in that very grown-up bed and to be on their way home the following morning.

Poorly and post-operative children slept in the beds nearest to the office and, as they recovered, were moved further down the ward. Recovery was measured in a daily physical progression, as beds were wheeled into new positions. Each morning, nurses would walk onto the ward in multiple pairs, like a small army, and cheerfully announce, 'Musical beds time, children.' It was the highlight of the day for those who were recovering and eager to go home.

Maura and Kathleen sat on long wooden benches in the corridor leading to the ward, waiting for the two girls to be returned from the operating theatre. Every time the ward door swung open, Maura would crane her neck to catch a glimpse inside.

Kitty's arm was broken and Nellie needed surgery, having caught one eye with force on the pram handle. Maura and Kathleen huddled together, talking in whispers and looking exactly how they felt when in the presence of authority:

invisible and inferior. The antiseptic smell of the Lysol disinfectant, used to clean the hospital floor, left a distinctive aura that hung heavily in the air and added to the sense of fear and the unknown.

A sweet young nurse approached them, carrying a wooden tray. Her hair was swept into an immaculate bun, which provided a throne for her tall starched cap. She had brought them a metal pot of tea and two sage-green national issue cups and saucers, a little milk jug and sugar bowl, and a plate with four biscuits. She rested the tray on the bench beside Maura and Kathleen and then squatted down to be at a reassuring eye level with them both.

'Don't worry, they won't be much longer,' she said. 'Sister says you will be allowed to see them for five minutes but then, I am afraid, visiting is from two to three in the afternoon and six until seven-thirty at night.'

She smiled gently, almost apologetically, as though she could recognize mothers who would be torn by leaving their children in such a scary place as a hospital.

Maura was so overcome with relief at the nurse's kindness, she began to weep.

'Shush now,' said the nurse, 'there really is no need to cry. We are moving the beds around so that when they arrive back from theatre, we can put them next to each other for company and they really will be very well cared for and looked after.'

She put her hand in Maura's and squeezed it, as Kathleen put her arm round her shoulders. The resolve that had kept Maura calm and upright for the last three hours was disintegrating.

Kathleen was well aware that, even though she loved Nellie, she wasn't her mother. She was her nana and it was different. Maura had the right to be the more upset, the one who needed to be cared for, and the thought crossed her mind: poor Nellie. Kathleen loved her granddaughter and would do her best for her, and she would always be there for Nellie for as long as God spared her, but no one could replace a mother's love. Kathleen comforted Maura, knowing that, of the two of them, only Maura had an irrational fear sleeping in the pit of her stomach.

They thanked the nurse for the tea and then both stared at her straight back and precise walk as she glided back through the ward doors, her crepe-soled white shoes squeaking on the highly polished wooden floor.

'She was nice, considering she probably knows we are Irish,' said Maura matter-of-factly, wiping her eyes. 'Peggy's cousin is working on the roads in London and he says the boarding houses have signs in the window that say, no dogs, no blacks and no Irish, can ye imagine that?'

'Well, we could have been a pair of monkeys for all that nurse cares,' said Kathleen. 'She had a good heart and it helps to know she works here, where the girls will be.'

Kathleen poured the tea and handed a cup to Maura. They drank it gratefully, waiting to be summoned, and discussed how difficult visiting was going to be. No one on the four streets owned a car, and the route involved taking three buses. To be at the hospital for two o'clock would take up the whole day in travelling and the fare would seriously eat into the housekeeping. It was hard enough to make the money stretch until the Friday-night pay packet as it was. Everyone lived hand to mouth, week to week.

'If he's not dead already, I will kill Callum with me bare hands,' said Maura coolly. They both considered the possibility, and drank the remainder of their tea in silence.

Nellie could hear voices around her in the dark. The strong smell of Lysol from the operating theatre had got up her nose, causing her to cough and panic. As she lifted her hand to touch her eyes and felt the crepe bandage wrapped around her face, fear took over. Kathleen had never known her granddaughter scream before, but she recognized it was Nellie just as soon as she heard it.

Kathleen didn't wait any longer to be invited in; she ran through the ward doors and followed the scream. Nellie was in the first bed; in the second, lying quietly and half asleep with her arm in plaster, was Kitty. Three nurses stood round Nellie's bed, two holding her down to stop her from thrashing around, whilst one tried to refasten her bandages. Nellie was furiously trying to kick her legs free from the nurses who were holding her down, either in pain or in terror, fighting to break free from their grip.

As Kathleen approached the bed with Maura in her wake, she saw something that made her stop dead in her tracks. The nurse holding Nellie's leg lifted her hand and slapped her hard across the thigh.

'Stop your thrashing about, you little bog jumper,' she hissed.

For a moment, the child's screaming stopped dead, both

from the shock of the new pain in her leg and the insult. Confused by the throbbing in her eye, she was stunned by the fact that she was unable to see who had slapped her.

In that moment, Maura grabbed hold of Kathleen's hand. 'Steady, Kathleen, we want to stay and see them both, say nothing.'

The smack turned Nellie's crying into a desperate whimper, as Kathleen shouted, 'I'm here, Nellie, I'm here.'

Kathleen ran to the end of the bed, her face red with suppressed anger. When Nellie should have been cared for, at her most vulnerable, she had been slapped and hurt. But Kathleen, who, as a 'bog jumper' herself, felt the insult keenly, had not the confidence or the ability to challenge someone in uniform.

Swallowing both her pride and her boiling rage, she noticed the name badge: Nurse Antrobus. At the sound of Kathleen's voice, Nellie's cry became more urgent and needy. Kathleen unceremoniously pushed past the nurse. Nellie threw her arms round her nana's neck and cried her little heart out.

Maura and Kathleen were allowed only ten minutes but managed to leave with both girls settled. The ward sister, who had looked at them over the top of her spectacles and straight down her large, upturned nose, spoke to them both as though English were not their first language. She explained that the bandages would be taken off one of Nellie's eyes that night and the other a week later. Kitty would also stay in hospital for a week and would be sent home wearing the plaster cast.

Both women were left in no doubt that they were expected to leave immediately and not return until the following morning. As they travelled home on the bus, they thought they were at least leaving their girls in a place of care and safety. If they had known the truth, they would rather have taken their own lives than knowingly leave Nellie and Kitty exposed to the danger that faced them.

# Chapter Twelve

THANKFULLY, THE MAJORITY of nurses on the ward resembled kind Nurse Lizzie, who had brought the tea to Maura and Kathleen.

From the very first morning after their operation, free from pain and reassured by each other's closeness, Nellie and Kitty began to absorb their new environment.

They relished food they had never eaten before, such as mashed bananas and ice cream. The kitchen lady, Pat, who was also Irish, had a soft spot for the girls and heaped up their plates at mealtimes.

Nellie adored the nurse's tall stiff hats and the white starched aprons they wore over pink-striped uniforms with white frilly cuffs. She loved the shiny fob watches pinned onto the front of their aprons and the big, shiny, gleaming buckles on their deep-pink petersham belts. She would let her hand slowly drift across the pale-pink counterpane and crisp white sheets, after the nurses had made her bed in the morning. This spotless, happy, hospital ward was luxury.

Her immediate thought on seeing Nurse Lizzie was how beautiful she looked.

'God, they are like angels,' she exclaimed to Kathleen.

'The one who smacked ye wasn't such an angel,' replied Kathleen under her breath, not so convinced. But Nellie had no recollection of being smacked by Nurse Antrobus.

It was only a nurse's uniform, but she had never before seen anyone wearing anything so clean and pretty. She became swept up in the romanticism of the profession. Nellie quietly observed Lizzie soothing poorly children and helping the doctors, and she secretly knew: one day she wanted to be like Nurse Lizzie.

Nurse Lizzie was also Nana Kathleen's favourite and she always popped over for a chat when she saw Kathleen visiting.

'I haven't seen Nurse Antrobus since the day the girls were admitted,' said Kathleen to Nurse Lizzie on one of these occasions – only just managing not to betray herself and preventing outrage from flooding into her voice.

'Oh, gosh no,' said Lizzie, 'and you won't either. The poor woman went off duty that night, slipped on the wet floor in the kitchen and broke her own arm. She won't be back at work for a while.'

Lizzie walked on to take the pulse of the child in the next bed, as Nana Kathleen turned to Nellie and said, 'Well now, who says there isn't a God, eh?'

'God doesn't have red hair,' laughed Nellie.

'Doesn't he now?' Kathleen laughed with Nellie, but didn't ask her what she meant. She didn't need to. She had seen the flash of red hair hovering over Nellie as she struggled on the bed that night.

Nana Kathleen visited every day and brought tales to Nellie of how Alice was coping with Joseph.

'I know it's often an ill wind that brings bad luck,' she said to Nellie, 'but Alice is doing really well with Joseph. In fact, Nellie, fingers crossed but if you ask me it seems that she is finding it hard to resist the little fella's cheeky face.'

Nellie was open-mouthed, hungry for every detail. 'How, tell me how, what is happening?' she demanded to know.

'Well, I kid ye not, but when I got back from the hospital yesterday, they were both asleep on the chair in front of the fire. Him lying full across her chest and she looking as contented as ye like with her arm across his back. It's her mother's love, sneaking out whilst she is asleep, so it is.'

Nellie gave Kathleen a hug. Her nana was a miracle worker.

Both children, but especially Nellie, loved the daily life of the ward – the hustle and bustle, the comings and goings of the cleaners, porters, doctors, kitchen staff and nurses – and it wasn't very long before they knew everyone by name.

But not everyone and everything was as it seemed …

Stanley had worked as a hospital porter at the hospital since he had been demobbed from the army at the end of the war in 1945. He had seen the job advertised in the *Liverpool Echo* four days after he returned home and applied immediately. His old mum, who was alive at the time, wasn't happy.

'Try and get on the buses,' she said. 'It's not bad money and free travel, you won't ever have to pay a fare again, and neither will I, when they get to know I'm yer mam. Or what about the English Electric on nights, that's good money?'

Stanley needed to look after his mam. His father had been killed in what was supposed to have been the war to end all wars and she had spent every day of World War Two in fear of a telegram arriving. Stanley was her only son and had been wrapped in cotton wool since the day he was born, eight months after his father had volunteered for Kitchener's army and been dispatched to the Somme, where he survived for just two days. When Stanley's father left, he had boarded the train at Lime Street with his head held high.

When Stanley's own dreaded call-up papers had arrived, he had burst into tears.

His mam had a point about the money at English Electric, but Stanley wasn't interested in money. The buses weren't a bad option. Lots of children used the bus to get to and from school, so there would be plenty of opportunity for the illicit contact he sought. He would be able to look at and talk to them and, if he was lucky, make friends with some. However, the hospital job was calling him: vulnerable children in a hospital bed who might need his help in some small way. Stanley closed his eyes when he read the job advert. Could there possibly be a more alluring option?

He also knew he couldn't be the only one. There must be others who thought like him. And if there were, then surely they would look for exactly the same kind of job and maybe he would recognize a kindred spirit, someone he could share his dark and secret thoughts with. Maybe Stanley could find a friend.

It took him only months to realize that in Austin, another single porter who still lived with his mam, he had a mate. Austin looked at the younger girls in exactly the same way Stanley looked at young boys. Stanley had looked for the signs when the porters were gathered in the X-ray department to be allocated children to take back to the wards.

A number of conversations were taking place between X-ray staff, parents and porters, but, like Stanley, Austin found it hard to concentrate on the adults talking, because his gaze would rest on a particular child, sitting in a wheelchair, waiting to be returned to the ward. Stanley knew that gaze. The gaze that lingered on the bare legs or the soft blond hair.

Stanley saw that Austin always carried sweets around in his pocket. Stanley went one better. He asked his mam to knit him a little glove puppet teddy to put in his top pocket. The kids loved that. They couldn't wait to jump into his arms to see if the teddy was asleep. His mam came round to the idea of her son as a porter and thought he was a hero. When he got home after a shift at the hospital, he was treated like a prince.

'I hope they know how lucky they are at the hospital to have a man as kind as you working with them children?' she would say, at least once a week. Stanley thought it was he who was the lucky one. His decision to apply for the hospital porter's job had been a stroke of genius.

Once he had plucked up the courage to make the connection with Austin, letting him know that he and Stanley had a shared interest, his life transformed overnight. It wasn't an easy thing to do, and Stanley had to wait for the right moment to come along, but, sure enough, eventually it did.

One busy theatre day, they were taking a little girl from the operating theatre directly to the nurses' station. Only five years old, she lay on the theatre trolley semi-conscious, naked, and with tubes and drips everywhere. Stanley saw how long Austin's gaze lingered on her exposed limbs.

Even when Stanley spoke to Austin, his eyes kept darting back, until the theatre nurse placed a gown and a sheet across the child's body, for the journey back to the ward.

'OK, lads, quick as you like. They are waiting for her right now on ward two,' snapped the theatre nurse, in a businesslike tone, as she moved on to receive the next child coming through the operating theatre doors.

As they walked down the centre of ward two, with the empty trolley, having delivered the poorly patient to her bed and the care of the nurses, Austin came out of his trance and said, 'What did you say, mate?'

'Nowt,' replied Stanley, smiling to himself.

On the way they passed a child, aged no more than three, crying, sitting alone on the edge of her bed. Stanley watched Austin look around the ward to check if there were any nurses nearby, but they were all busy with the child they had just brought back from surgery. Having made sure that he was not observed, Austin moved over to the little girl.

'Eh, eh, Queen, what's up?' he said, picking her up and swinging her into his arms. 'What do you think is in my top pocket, eh? Go on, look.'

Her tears began to subside and immediately turned to

giggles when she put her hand into Austin's top pocket, and he pretended to growl and bite at her hand as she brought out a sweetie. Having stopped the tears, Austin moved on to the next stage.

'Come on now; give Uncle Austin a big cuddle.'

She put her grateful arms around his neck and her legs around his waist. She was wearing only a loose hospital nightdress. Facing him, with each leg around his middle and her arms around his neck, Austin put his hand on her tiny bottom and pressed her body into his stomach.

'There, there, Queen, Uncle Austin is always here for a cuddle.'

Stanley was talking to the child in the next bed, but he hadn't taken his eyes off Austin. He saw the tear in Austin's eye and the look of ecstasy cross his face, before they heard a nurse's footsteps approaching. Austin put the little girl hurriedly back onto the bed.

As they walked away, they put on an exaggerated clowning act for the children, Austin pretending to beat Stanley for being slow, making the children roar with laughter.

'Oh no,' the men squealed, 'Nurse Helen will tell us off, now what are we going to do?' They winked at the nurse walking past, who laughed and shook her head.

As they made their way back to the porters' hut for a cup of tea, Stanley plucked up the courage and said to Austin, 'I like the little lads, myself.'

Austin looked at him sharply, Stanley winked, and that was it: a whole new world of opportunity and delight opened up to him from that day on.

Years later, very little had changed. Austin had introduced Stanley to others who had the same predilection.

'There is nothing wrong with us,' said Austin to Stanley, 'we just like something different from others, that doesn't mean it's wrong.' They all felt the same.

Austin had introduced Stanley to the Sunday meeting that took place in secret at Arthur's house on County Road.

'Homos will be in the law soon,' said Arthur, often. 'We will be one day too.'

Stanley supposed that, as he liked boys, he was a 'homo' too. The difference was, he liked them from the age of two to twelve. Once they reached puberty, they were of no interest to him.

Every week they paid to have pictures sent to a postbox delivery address. Each person in the group took it in turns to collect them before meeting the others at Arthur's house. They circulated the envelopes of photographs amongst themselves, most of which came from abroad and were of varying quality, but they paid the money happily. This was the darkest of secrets and those that shared it were well practised in keeping any knowledge hidden. The code was that if anyone was caught collecting the pictures, the rest were protected. They all knew that one day maybe one of them would have to take the rap, but they also knew the others would be safe.

Over the years, Austin and Stanley had learnt a new technique: to make friends with the families of children they liked. Today, Austin had gone to a child's birthday party and he had been invited to sleep over. The last time he had done that, the father had caught him taking a photograph of the daughter in the bath and had asked him to leave. Austin sailed too close to the wind sometimes. He had been out of his league with that family. After that incident, they spent two nervous weeks being extra careful, wondering if the father truly suspected anything and had written to the hospital.

Stanley was always telling him, 'Stick to the poor kids. They are the ones whose parents are too busy or neglectful to notice. They are the kids who don't get any affection and always need a cuddle. No one buys them presents or sweets. They are always more grateful and if they squeal, no one will believe them or be bothered anyway. Do as I do, stick to the poor kids.' That was Stanley's fail-safe.

Austin loved his new Kodak Brownie and couldn't stop taking pictures to sell on. It was so easy in the hospital. The children thought they were smiling for the camera alone. Sometimes, they were sitting on their parent's knee. Stanley was amazed that never once did a parent ask why a hospital porter was taking a photograph of their child.

Poor people were unused to, and lapped up, attention.

A camera was a novelty. It paid attention.

Stanley was on nights, he had his usual job to do for one of Austin's mates. He thought it was probably the priest, but he was never told whom he was helping. They all preferred it that way and he knew that if someone was helping him, they never knew who he was either. Secrecy was king. What you didn't know, you would never be able to tell.

Stanley's job tonight was to ring one of the children's wards at midnight and tell the nurse someone would have to go to the pathology department to pick up some test results for the doctor who was coming on night duty, and that they needed to hurry because the pathologist had to leave. He would say that he was sorry, the porter would have done it but he was run off his feet.

It took a good ten minutes for a nurse to walk to the pathology department from the ward. Five to work out what was going on and think they had missed the pathologist, ten to walk back and then another five for the cigarette she would smoke outside the ward door before going back in. That was thirty minutes when it was guaranteed there would be no ward round. If there was only one nurse on the ward, she usually stayed in the office until her colleague got back, in case the phone rang. It always did. That was the second stage. To ring the ward again, seven minutes exactly after the first call.

If it was the priest, he hardly needed help because he was known on all the wards as a regular visitor. According to Austin's instructions, Stanley had already checked that the fire-escape door to the car park was unlocked and left slightly ajar, a spanner in his hand in case a curious nurse popped over to ask what he was doing.

Before he pulled the curtain across, he took a peep at the bed closest to the door. Lying there was a young thin girl, barely into her teens. Stanley found that a bit odd. Austin liked them younger even than Stanley, as did most of the men in their group. Age two to eight was Austin's preference. Ah, thought Stanley, then it must be the priest; he seems to like them from quite young to right into their teens. Dirty bastard, he thought, as he put the door back with the bar not quite catching the lock. The irony was totally lost on him.

As soon as they were recovering and up and about, Kitty and Nellie begged to be put in charge of the night-time drinks trolley, while they helped the night nurse settle the younger patients down to sleep. The trolley had jugs of hot chocolate and Horlicks with plates of biscuits. They had never had anything other than tea at home. Hot chocolate was a luxury to be marvelled at.

Nellie and Kitty asked the nurses to keep their beds together and they moved progressively up the ward each morning. They pulled the curtains round to make their two beds into one when the doctors did the ward round. They had been like sisters before and, even with the age difference, they were more so now. Everyone loved them; they brought joy into a ward that could often be a heartbreaking place for staff.

They became so close they even got into each other's beds where they would chat for hours. When the nurses came round they made them squeal with laughter, as Nellie would lie flat on her tummy and hide in Kitty's bed under the covers. They were such a happy and pleasant pair, the ward staff would be sorry to see them both go, even Sister, who never laughed.

Kitty was very happy until, on the third day, Father James paid them a visit. Without warning, he suddenly appeared at the foot of Kitty's bed, where Nellie was also lying, and offered them a jelly baby out of a crumpled white paper bag, which he took out of his cassock pocket.

'Say no,' Kitty whispered urgently, as he approached.

Nellie looked at Kitty in amazement. She was expecting Nellie to say no to sweets?

'Do as I say,' said Kitty, with such urgency in her voice that Nellie didn't dare defy her, even though she loved jelly babies and didn't get sweets very often.

Father James sat on the end of the bed in which they were both lying.

'Your mammy asked me to pop by, Kitty, and say prayers with ye both for a speedy recovery, even for ye, Nellie,' he said, looking at Nellie sneeringly. Father James had not forgiven Nellie for having the cheek to kick the door shut in his face just after Joseph was born.

Kitty said nothing. Nellie turned sideways and looked at her in amazement. Kitty was being rude in not speaking to Father James and Nellie knew that wasn't allowed in the Doherty house.

Father James turned to Nellie. 'I would like to have a quiet word with Kitty on me own. Nellie, would ye like to go and see if the nurses need ye for anything? Do ye not have your own bed to go to now, whilst Kitty has a visitor?'

Nellie immediately threw back the corner of the counterpane, ready to dive out of the bed and dash to the nurses' office. Anything to get away from a strange and uncomfortable situation.

'No,' said Kitty so loudly that Nellie pulled the counterpane back in shock and didn't move. Nellie always did everything Kitty told her.

Father James made small talk on his own for five minutes and then, after offering them the jelly babies again, took his leave to talk to another child at the top of the ward who went to the same school as the girls.

For the rest of the day, Kitty hardly spoke. Nellie had noticed that whilst Father James had been sitting on the bed talking, his hand had been pressed against Kitty's thigh. While he spoke, Nellie stared at his hand and, when he became aware of it, he pulled it away sharply. Nellie watched Kitty's face and thought she looked scared.

As he walked away back down the ward, Nellie took hold of Kitty's hand and said, 'I hate Father James so much.'

Kitty put her good arm round Nellie's shoulders and hugged her.

'God, I love you, so I do, Nellie Deane,' she said and they both laughed.

Nellie asked Nurse Lizzie why Father James was in the ward so much.

'He comes to pray over all the poorly children,' said Lizzie. 'Do you know him? Isn't he just fantastic, he's always popping in.'

Nellie didn't know what this information meant, but she knew it wasn't good. She knew the people she trusted the most in the world didn't like Father James and that included Kitty and her Nana Kathleen. If they didn't, neither did Nellie.

Each evening there was excitement on the ward, as the name of the child going home the next day was written on a board. Kitty and Nellie both cried when they discovered that Kitty was going home the day before Nellie.

Nellie wanted to go home. She desperately missed Joseph and Nana Kathleen and her da. Her da brought Joseph into the ward some nights, but she could see he was missing her too. Suddenly, now that Kitty was going home, everything had changed; she was very keen to leave herself.

Nellie and Kitty parted to sleep in their own beds on Kitty's last night, after discussing how they would live in the same street when they grew up, become wedding-dress designers, or famous actresses, and marry two brothers so that they could become properly related.

They had lots of hugs from the nurses, but Kitty was nervous. She didn't want to sleep alone in the going-home bed at the end of the ward. She begged the nurses to let her sleep with Nellie, but they wouldn't agree. The two children finally parted when the nurses came to give Nellie a sedative, in preparation for her visit to theatre in the morning, to have the final bandages removed from her eye. As she left Nellie's bed, Kitty wept. She told Nellie she was frightened, but Nellie couldn't reply; the sedation had worked on her like a sledgehammer and she went out like a light.

Even though the ward was mainly in darkness, above each bed a nightlight dimly illuminated the faces of the sleeping children.

In the early hours of the morning, Nellie woke to see the curtain pulled round Kitty's bed. She thought she had heard the fire-escape door click open. The drugs had made her very groggy and she tried to say Kitty's name, but her tongue felt huge in her mouth and no sound came out. Kitty was in the going-home bed, tucked into the L-shaped bay at the end of the ward, the only bed away from the nurses' line of vision. But it could be seen from Nellie's bed, the last in the row running down the ward.

From the bed were sounds Nellie had never heard before. Desperately trying to fight the fog in her brain, she looked down the ward to the nurses' office and then, unable to sit up or speak, she managed to roll herself onto her side to face Kitty's bed, prop herself up on her elbow and rub her eyes.

Below the curtain, she saw what looked like a long black skirt and a pair of men's boots.

Almost at the end of the ward, she could hear the low hum of female voices, as the night nurses, who had worked together for years, exchanged news and chatted in muted tones. Tonight was Sunday, which brought with it a nocturnal atmosphere of calm. No operations, no distressed relatives and no one's child about to go to an early grave. The nurses were making the most of a quiet shift.

The telephone in the office suddenly rang and the sound glided down the ward, bouncing off the dreams of thirty sleeping little ones. It was quickly answered, before anyone woke, and Nellie heard the whispered tones of the night nurse swiftly followed by the ting of the bell, as she replaced the black Bakelite receiver.

Nellie heard the sound of the ward door swishing open and shut, followed by crepe-soled footsteps retreating down the corridor. She realized they would now be down to one nurse.

Nellie heard a new noise coming from behind Kitty's curtain. The bed began to slowly creak as though a great weight were pressing onto it. The shoes and the black skirt had vanished.

Nellie couldn't lift her head and her gaze seemed to be fixed down to the floor. She considered calling the nurse, but her tongue wouldn't work properly. She knew she was desperately fighting a battle with the drug to stay awake. She also knew instinctively that Kitty needed help.

Suddenly she froze, seeing the wheels on Kitty's bed moving slowly, backwards and forwards, straining against the brake on the wheel at the foot of the bed. Was someone taking Kitty's bed away?

The noise of something falling caught her attention. She saw a red jelly baby plop onto the floor, and then straight after it, a green one. The bed began creaking rhythmically, faster and faster. Nellie stared in groggy amazement as brightly coloured confectionery rained down from Kitty's bed and then, with an abrupt thud, a white paper packet of jelly babies fell and spewed its contents across the polished wooden floor. Just as the bed suddenly stopped moving and she heard a muffled gasp, she could fight the sedation no longer; her eyes closed as the drug did its work. She slept deeply and didn't even hear the second click of the door.

The following morning, Kitty appeared quiet. Her sparkle had gone and Nellie, still groggy and having been given more sedation to prepare her for theatre, couldn't remember what had been odd about the previous evening.

She and Kitty hugged tightly as the trolley came to take Nellie to theatre. When she returned to the ward, with all her bandages gone, Kitty's bed was clean and made up. Maura had been to collect Kitty and left a note on Nellie's bed.

Nellie's eyes were still blurred and she couldn't read the note.

'God please, ye will be back with us tomorrow. Daddy coming to see you tonight, Maura XX.'

The nurse who read the note to Nellie said, 'Well, there is no need for you to stay now, Nellie, your eye is healed beautifully and if your daddy is coming tonight, he can take you back home with him. You will be able to read in the morning and back to school on Monday.'

Nellie didn't know why, but she cried with happiness. She no longer felt safe with Kitty gone. She wanted to go home to see Joseph and get back to her own world on the streets where she felt as if she was related to everyone.

That afternoon, Father James came to say hello. He told her she was a naughty little girl going home early. That he would have liked to come and give her a special goodbye that night, one that was reserved for little girls in the end bed. He had been looking forward to giving her the treat he said he saved for all the pretty little girls on the ward.

'Why don't you ask the nurse if you can stay until tomorrow and then I will come and see you tonight, with a goodbye surprise?'

He put his hand on the top of her leg and she stared at it, not knowing what to say. There was a note of desperate conspiracy to his voice, as though he was discussing something that Nellie already had knowledge of, something they had already talked about together, a plan she was already a part of. She looked on in silence. She knew something was very wrong, but didn't know what.

'Go on,' he said, 'it will be our special secret.'

Nellie looked to the ward door for her da, who was coming to collect her after work. She prayed sincerely, for the first time in her life, asking God to please not let anything stop her da from coming to get her. She saw Nurse Lizzie, taking the temperature of a child further up the ward, holding onto her fob watch to count out her minute.

Nellie suddenly shouted, 'Nurse Lizzie!' very loudly, and, like a black serpent, Father James gradually uncoiled himself. Whilst Nellie's heart beat in terror at something, she did not know what, he rose and moved slowly away from her bed.

# Chapter Thirteen

ONCE THE GIRLS were both home from hospital and Callum had done his penance, which was to clean the windows of both houses inside and out, life settled back to a normal pattern.

For everyone except Kitty.

For the last few years Kitty had been in an ever darker and more threatening place. She knew what Father James had done at the hospital. Stella McGinty had told Kitty the more specific facts of life in the playground only weeks earlier. It wasn't a discussion that had taken place in Maura's home, but Kitty knew Stella had been telling the truth.

Everyone made such a fuss of her when she came home from the hospital. Even Alice, who as a result of the accident had learnt the basic art of caring for others. Alice had imbued the raw concern emanated by Kathleen and Maura, and, on occasion, had found herself being needed and useful.

It didn't happen automatically. She made a conscious effort on some days to look for something positive to do for someone else, but when she did she was well rewarded. After years of living within her own lonely capsule of solitude, she sometimes found herself smiling with pleasure.

Alice wrote Kitty a handmade card. It was the first she had ever written and it took her an agonizing hour to write her message. Kathleen watched Alice, sat at the table bent over her card, but offered no help. Ironically, Alice had to do this alone. Kathleen knew that the second time would be easier. When Alice put her pen down and folded the card, she felt exhausted.

'A cuppa tea, Alice, for a job well done,' said Kathleen, as she put a cup and saucer down in front of Alice and gave her a gentle hug as she walked away.

Peggy brought Kitty an opinion.

'Jeez, Kitty, ye look so pale. Are ye sure she should be home yet, Maura?' Peggy had demanded, when she came to the house to see Kitty for herself.

Her friends from school called round to visit and brought her handmade cards, letters from the teachers and home-made gifts. Her best friend Julia had made her a pincushion in the sewing class and had embroidered her name across the top in a pretty chain stitch.

'It took me forever and a day!' said Julia, as Kitty opened the little parcel.

'Oh, Julia, 'tis so beautiful indeed,' said Kitty, without a hint of enthusiasm in her voice.

Julia looked at Kitty oddly. As the girls walked home after their visit, they commented that Kitty was still not well.

'Knocked the stuffing right out of her, that accident, if you ask me,' said Julia thoughtfully.

She had noticed a huge change in Kitty of late and, although she couldn't put her finger on it, she knew that there was something more than a stay in hospital and a broken arm upsetting Kitty.

Kitty felt as though she lived in a parallel world to everyone else. Between her and those she knew and loved there was an invisible screen. Her family and friends spent their days rooted in reality, whereas hers were rooted in fear. They lived … she existed.

Up until now she had found clever ways to thwart Father James and stop him finding opportunities to be alone with her. She had been permanently on the run from his zealous pursuit and had outfoxed him. But now she was done for. That was it. He had won. He had turned her into a repulsive sinner and there was surely no one who lived on the four streets as disgustingly dirty and unworthy as she was.

Kitty didn't feel glad to be home. Kitty felt nothing but shame and self-loathing. It was all she could do to put her feet onto the floor each morning, once she had woken and realized, with acute disappointment, that she was still alive. She knew she had no choices and, as if she were an actress, it was a role she had to play each and every day.

Life on the four streets was getting tougher for the families who lived there. There was less work on the docks for the dockers, and little or no money. Boys who would have followed their da onto the docks were now heading into the big factories, such as Plessey's and Ford. The winter had taken its toll on industry everywhere. It was now March and the ice had only just begun to thaw.

For those houses on the four streets that had kept the ranges ticking over, water hadn't been too much of a problem. In other parts of Liverpool, in homes that had replaced ranges with cookers, and lost their back boiler, they had the misery of burst pipes to contend with. Kathleen wasn't able to keep the range lit all through the night. She filled the bath with water before she went to bed so that if her pipes did freeze, as they sometimes did, they were never short. The bath quickly formed a layer of ice that she cracked each morning to fill the kettle. The danger of frozen and burst pipes was a constant source of worry and anxiety. They tried their hardest to avoid catastrophe by putting extra coal on the fire before they went to bed.

Each night, Kathleen took a secondary precaution and left the kitchen tap dripping to keep the water moving to help prevent the pipes from freezing. There was nothing more miserable and difficult to cope with than a burst pipe in freezing weather. As if life wasn't hard enough. The weather was just another hurdle to overcome for those who were used to dealing with adversity on a daily basis.

Today was only Thursday, the day before pay day, and everyone had already run out of money. For many families on the streets, this meant going hungry. But Kathleen had a plan. She knew Peggy had a big ship's catering pan on her landing under the eaves and she sent Jerry round to collect it. Then she popped in to see Maura.

At the Doherty house, Tommy was fed up. The dockers had been laid off for yet another day and it was not a situation he liked, although it was no fun working in below-freezing temperatures. They had been dipping into the bread-bin 'back-up' money over the last few weeks and it was now running low. This always made Maura nervous and irritable.

Tommy was never miserable for long, though; it took only a neighbour or a fresh face to pop in through the door and he was a happy man again.

'Ah, Kathleen,' he said as she walked in. 'Ye are a sight for sore eyes, come over here and cheer me up.'

Kathleen sat down at the table with Tommy, smiling at the sight of his paper spread out in front of him.

Was there ever an Irishman more proud that he could read, she thought to herself.

If Tommy had read the paper by the afternoon, he would go back to the beginning and start it again. Reading the trivia of Liverpool life in the hatched, matched and dispatched columns gave Tommy somewhere to put his mind, whilst the hullabaloo of a house with well-loved and noisy children carried on around him.

The back door opened again and everyone looked up at Alice, nervously standing in the doorway. For a fraction of a second, the room was silent. This was the first time Alice had stepped inside another house on the four streets.

Alice had no idea why she had followed Kathleen. She was driven by new feelings and emotions over which she had little control. She wanted to belong. When Kathleen left the kitchen after sending Jerry to collect the pan and had thrown over her shoulder, 'I'm away to Maura's,' Alice had wanted to shout out, 'Take me with you.' But she hadn't. She had stood there and thought to herself, I want to go too. And so, that was what she had done.

Walking up Maura's back path was one of the most terrifying things she had ever done in her life. Her fear was overcome by the desire to be with Kathleen. To be like Kathleen. She wondered, should she knock?

Before she lifted the latch she took a deep breath. Perspiration had formed on her top lip and her brow, yet her mouth was dry. She looked at the pale blue, cracked, painted door and stepped inside. Just like everyone else.

Maura looked straight at Alice. She had been touched by the card she had written for Kitty when she came out of hospital and, since that day, her heart had thawed towards Alice.

Tommy, himself shocked for a moment, broke the silence.

'Jeez, how lucky a man am I, with the three best-looking women in the street all in me own kitchen. Alice, come and sit down with me at the table and save me from Kathleen and Maura naggin' at me, will ye?'

Everyone laughed, as much with relief as at Tommy's joke.

'Maura, it's going to have to be a pan night,' said Kathleen, in a resigned voice, as she picked up the tea Maura had placed on the table for both her and Alice. With her other hand, she reached under the table and gave Alice's hand a gentle squeeze. 'If I don't do it, some of the kids in this street will go to bed hungry tonight and we can't have that, so. I will do it in our kitchen, Maura, but if I'm doing the cooking and serving, ye need to do the organizing.'

Kathleen had spoken. It was more of an instruction to Maura than a query.

'Aye, Kathleen, I will that,' said Maura, drying her hands on her apron and sitting down at the table to take instructions. 'How much do we need from each house?' she asked.

'Threepence will do it, but if they don't have it, Maura, don't push it. We will have enough for everyone, so don't make anyone feel bad. Some of these women have been away from the bogs for too long and aren't as good at managing as they would be if they were back home with help.'

'And that's the God's truth,' Tommy chimed in.

'It's not just the women, Kathleen, some of the fellas are straight into the Anchor from the dock after work, spending the food money. The shorter work is, the more they want to drink the money away.'

'Aye, thank God for the family allowance,' said Maura. 'I don't know how we would manage without it, ye drinking as much as ye do, Tommy Doherty.'

She shoved Tommy on his arm, laughing as she spoke. Tommy always put his kids first and the only time he called into the Anchor was on the odd occasion when times were flush and Maura had given him a few bob extra. Every Friday night he walked into the house and put his pay packet on the kitchen table in a small brown envelope. Maura opened and checked it, then gave him his paper, betting and ciggies money. It was all Tommy needed; he didn't ask for any more; he worked for his wife and his kids, not himself.

The family allowance, which was paid out from her book at the post office on a Tuesday, gave Maura over two pounds a week extra, which usually got them over to Friday if things were harder than usual, but this week she had been helping everyone else out, with the odd bit here and there, and now she was shorter than usual herself.

Tommy got his pencil out and they counted up the number of children on their street. Kathleen knocked on the kitchen wall with the mop end for Jerry to come in from Peggy's, and promptly dispatched him down to Mrs Keating, Mrs McGowan and Mrs McNally, the keepers of the ship's catering pans on the other three streets, to let them know what was happening. Jerry came back and confirmed the other women would follow suit. They had done this before and they would no doubt do it again.

Maura went out to collect the money from each house on the four streets. Kitty and Nellie went with her, together with Harry and Angela, wheeling Joseph's empty pram to the shops. There were eighty-three children on the four streets, of varying ages. Maura needed forty pounds of potatoes, twenty pounds of carrots, fifteen of the large Spanish onions, which, to everyone's excitement, had just started appearing in the greengrocer's, and thirty pounds of neck end of lamb from Murphy's.

'Don't ye be giving me no spuds with black eyes in now,' said Maura sternly to Bill, the greengrocer. 'I don't want none of ye rubbish dumping on me, because I'm buying for everyone today.'

The greengrocer was English; if he could, he would palm the rubbish off on Maura and they both knew it. The greengrocer felt bad, knowing what Maura was doing and as she

NADINE DORRIES

had done many times in the past. Once he had taken her money, carefully counted out in threepenny bits, he said, 'Hang on a minute there, Maura, I've got something for you.'

He disappeared into the back of the shop and came out with a wooden box full of uncooked beetroots.

'I will have to throw these out at the end of today, so if you can get them cooked quickly, you are welcome to them.'

'Aye, so we can and thank ye, Bill, ye aren't all bad.' He and Maura exchanged a grin.

The cheeky mare, he thought. He had a soft spot for Maura, though. She had been Bernadette's best friend and, like every other man who had been blinded after laying eyes upon her, he had been in love with Bernadette.

Maura placed the box of beetroots across the top of the pram and walked on to the homes in the other three streets that would become communal kitchens for the day. When she reached the door, she called out through the back gate from the entry, 'I've an extra treat,' and handed over to each one their share of the vegetables and meat, plus eight big beets. 'Chop them into slices after you've boiled them, that way everyone can have a share.'

'Ye got beets for free from that thieving git?' said Mrs Keating. 'Well, ye never know, maybe pigs do fly.'

Now, everyone was happier. They might have had nothing. They might all have been poor, and this morning they had been facing misery and hungry bellies. Some were smoking what was left of old fag ends in dirty ashtrays and, as a result, they were bad-tempered. Now, everyone was pulling together and an atmosphere of something close to joy had settled on the four streets, as the kids played together, wrapped up against the March wind, aware something close to a party was about to take place.

Kathleen's kitchen became a hive of activity, as did the three others. As a result of Kathleen's thinking, each child would go to bed on a full belly of Irish stew. The women tripped in and out of each other's houses, sharing out the vegetables to be prepared and chopped. Once the beetroots were cooked, they were peeled and put into a large bowl, another gift from a ship's kitchen, and then the ingredients for the stew were put into the pan to cook. The neck end of lamb needed to simmer all day to soften and then break down into stringy lumps. The carrots were put in at midday and then the potatoes in the last hour before the stew was thickened up with flour and gravy browning. The women had also made soft floury bread, which was still warm and ready to be dipped into the gravy.

At suppertime each child brought a bowl and a spoon into Kathleen's kitchen, where she and Alice were dishing up. On the top of each bowl of Irish stew they laid slices of beetroot and on top of that a warm floury cob. You could hardly hear yourself speak for the excited chatter of children sitting on the stairs, as well as all over the kitchen and living-room floors.

'Thank ye, Auntie Kathleen, thank ye, Auntie Alice,' they all shouted, after they had taken the first mouthful, before getting down to the serious business of eating. As each child slurped and ate, silence descended on the house.

This was thrilling for the children. They had none of the worry of making ends meet. To them, this was an adventure, a break from the usual routine, underpinning the fact that they were all one big family and would always look after each other. Mothers wove their way among the children, helping the little ones to eat, making sure they were safe and could manage to spoon the food without spilling any. The women exchanged happy smiles with one another. This was a job well done. This was what their community was about. Together, they could beat anything.

Kitty did her bit to help, but she was feeling ill and the smell of the stew turned her stomach. She had helped to look after Joseph and, earlier in the day, once the pram was empty of vegetables, she and Nellie had taken him for a walk. They both kept looking over their shoulders for runaway cars as they ambled along the cold streets, wheeling Joseph to sleep after his lunchtime feed.

Nellie had noticed Alice was helping out in the kitchen, peeling carrots, which she thought was nice. Alice didn't see that Nellie and Kitty had taken Joseph and they didn't bother to tell her. Nana Kathleen knew where they were, that was all that mattered.

Nellie knew Kitty wasn't very happy. She didn't talk much and she didn't laugh at Nellie's jokes. This was unusual and confusing, but then Nellie had a grand idea.

'Kitty, did you know that Nana Kathleen makes everything better?' she piped.

Kitty laughed for the first time. 'Aye, she does that,' she replied.

'So, why don't you talk to her and tell her what's wrong?'

'Who says there's anything wrong with me?' said Kitty sharply. Nellie noted that her eyes had filled with tears.

'No one, Kitty, just me. But I knows ye better than anyone and I know summat's up.' Adversity had gifted Nellie with wisdom way beyond her years.

Silence descended upon the girls.

Kitty wondered, would she dare tell Nana Kathleen? Her mind toyed with the idea. It was a ray of hope. She looked troubled again. How could she tell her, though, if she really would badly hurt her mammy and daddy by telling them what had occurred? Even if they did disown her, maybe a life alone in a convent would be better than feeling like this?

Last week Tommy had read out a story from the paper to Maura, whilst she was at the kitchen sink. Tommy often did that, now that he was better at reading. There was a time when he could only read the horses. He progressed onto the names and dates on the hatched, matched and dispatched and now he was full of himself and read at least one story out of the paper to them all at least once a day. Kitty had been teaching him and he read her school books with her, when she had brought them home. When she was younger, and Tommy used to put Kitty to bed, she would read him a goodnight story and test him on his letters. No one knew from outside the house and no one ever would. He liked to read items from the paper out loud to show off, especially if Jerry came into the kitchen. Jerry was visibly impressed by Tommy's reading skills and assumed he must be much cleverer than he was.

'Would ye listen to this,' Tommy would always begin and waited for silence to descend on the kitchen, for effect. 'A young woman aged seventeen was found in a house in Boswell Street, Toxteth, hanging from a rope attached to the ceiling, where she had remained undiscovered for approximately eight hours. The police have said that it was an unlawful act of suicide and no one else was involved. Now, why the hell would a young girl, with her whole life in front of her, do that, eh?'

Kitty had listened intently. She wanted to tell him that she knew a reason, but she couldn't. She wasn't sure what was right and what was wrong any more. If it was so wrong to tell her parents about Father James and what he did to her, what on God's earth was right?

Her own life was becoming blurred and she knew she wasn't doing as well with her schoolwork. She no longer had any self-confidence and was snapping everyone's head off. She knew that, but she couldn't help it. She carried around with her the darkest, dirtiest secret, which made her feel horrible and sick every day, but if she told someone, she would be a bad person. Nothing that happened any more could make her happy whilst this was the life she had to lead.

What Father James had done at the hospital had shocked her. She hadn't seen him since, but she knew if he tried to do that once more, she would rather kill herself – she couldn't let that happen to her again. She would rather be dead, like the girl from Boswell Street. That would be preferable to carrying round a guilty secret. Over the last three years, he had become bolder and bolder, and now he had done *that*. Every time she thought about it, she wanted to cry. She was so desperately alone.

After feeding the entire street Maura and Kitty were helping to clean up Jerry's house. Jerry had put Nellie and Joseph to bed. Alice had gone up hours ago and Jerry himself was turning in. He and Tommy would be down at the docks early tomorrow, in the hope of a ship coming in and them both being taken on. They wanted a fatter pay packet next week.

Kathleen put the kettle on for the final cup of tea, while Maura finished scrubbing the big pan with a Brillo pad. Kitty startled Kathleen as she flew past her and down the path to the outhouse, yet again.

'That kid's not well,' said Maura to Kathleen, nodding her head towards Kitty as she ran.

'Really?' said Kathleen. 'What's up with her?'

'She has a stubborn tummy bug, which I think she picked up in the hospital weeks ago, and it won't leave her.'

'I'd take her to Dr O'Cole if I were you,' said Kathleen, opening the back door and looking down the path to see that Kitty, who hadn't managed to close the outhouse door, was throwing up in the toilet.

Kathleen was amazed that Maura hadn't cottoned on. She herself had, days ago, but then there wasn't much that got past Kathleen. She thought she had better make a joke of it, since Maura was obviously blissfully unaware.

'If I didn't know better, I'd say she would be pushing that bug around in a pram in six months,' said Kathleen, studying Maura's face for a reaction.

Maura looked up from the pan and laughed. 'I know, me too, just shows we aren't always right, eh?'

I know I am, thought Kathleen, and you will be too before long, Maura.

On Saturday night, everyone on all four streets had a wedding to attend at the Irish centre. It was an excuse for a big get-together. Half of Dublin had come to Liverpool for the celebration and nearly every house on the four streets had a guest sleeping over. Mrs Keating's daughter, Siobhan, was marrying the son of a Dublin republican who owned a pub overlooking the Liffey River and he would inherit the pub from his da.

The men saw it as one of the most fortuitous matches any child from the four streets had ever made. The blissful thought of it ... a free pint of Guinness always ready and waiting on a bar in Dublin, should they ever turn up. It didn't get much better than that. The four streets buzzed with excitement and those who couldn't fit into the church lined the path to St Mary's and the road outside, armed with rice and confetti to throw at the happy couple.

Early that morning, a crate of Guinness and a bottle of Irish whiskey had been delivered to every house on the four streets so the guests could begin celebrating with the happy couple at breakfast, along with a box of boxty bread and a whole peat-smoked salmon. Tommy thought he had died and gone to heaven.

Everyone was giddy with a happiness that can be found only in an Irish home where, for every stranger, there are a hundred thousand welcomes.

The wedding breakfast began at three o'clock in the afternoon, straight after the church ceremony, and carried on into the early hours of the morning. Nellie loved a party. She loved Irish dancing and she and Kitty were part of a group of girls who had put together a number of dances for the wedding party. They had been practising on the green for weeks without any music and had no idea how fabulous the dancing would be on the day, with the band playing behind them and the huge audience stood in front, cheering and clapping them on. As the girls left the dance floor, everyone pushed money into their hands.

'Oh my God, we're rich!' shouted Nellie, as they passed through the crowd, and they were indeed. Nellie had never seen so much money before. She put it straight into her pocket to give to her da the next morning; he would put it in the tin in the bread bin where all the savings were kept.

This was Nellie's first ever contribution to the tin.

By ten o'clock, Kitty was feeling dreadful and decided to take some of the little kids back to the street. Nellie offered to help. When she heard they were leaving, Alice said she would walk back with them and put Joseph to bed.

Jerry was thrilled that Alice had not only agreed to come but had even seemed to enjoy herself, in her own way. He hadn't even needed to persuade her. One word from Nana Kathleen was all it had taken and when he saw Alice laughing and clapping along to the girls dancing, his heart felt warm. His mother had worked her magic.

When they reached their own street, Alice took Joseph

indoors. Kitty and Nellie put Paddy and Peggy's kids to bed and then said goodnight with a hug.

'Get a good night's sleep, Kitty, and ye will feel better in the morning,' said Nellie.

Kitty could barely smile as she went in through her back door. Sleep was not her problem; she could hardly stay awake as it was.

They were all tucked up in their own beds and fast asleep within fifteen minutes, while the adults carried on partying.

Kathleen might have been a grandmother, but she had staying power. She loved to watch the young ones enjoying themselves and having a dance. The Guinness was flowing, the craic was wild, and she had caught up with some of her friends from home who had come over for the wedding. But having had five glasses of Guinness, she was now beginning to feel exhausted herself. The big feeding operation on Thursday had taken its toll and she thought about heading back home.

Kathleen couldn't stop worrying about Kitty, but for the first time in her life she was stumped. The two families were close. She knew Kitty's movements as well as she knew Nellie's. What the hell had gone on? Because there was one thing she knew, for sure: Kitty might have only been fourteen, but she was pregnant all right. It's not a bloody immaculate conception, she thought. Someone put that baby there and I cannot for the life of me think who.

She had no idea how to approach Maura and Tommy about it.

They could tell me to get lost, she thought. An accusation like that, especially if she were wrong, could spoil many years of a good close relationship. To be pregnant out of wedlock carried the biggest stigma. It was a shameful thing. Maura's children were like brothers and sisters to Nellie. Kathleen would have to tread carefully or, even better, say nothing at all, just be there to catch the pieces and clear up the mess the day it did all become clear to Maura and World War Three broke out across the street.

Kathleen put on her coat and took so long to say good-night to everyone that it took her half an hour to get out of the door. As soon as she stepped out of the club onto the street, the heavens opened. Kathleen crossed herself and thanked God Nellie had got home with Joseph and Alice before the rain had begun, while cursing herself for having stopped so long and had the extra glass of Guinness.

She pulled down her hat, tucking her hair tightly in, and then pulled up her collar to stop the water from running down her neck. With hands thrust deep into her pockets, she began to walk the half-mile home. There was no wind and the rain was heavy; the cobbles were black and drenched within minutes. Kathleen's path home was lit by the yellow sulphur glow from the street lights reflected off the glistening black of the wet path.

She could smell the river on the air as she lifted her head and breathed in. That mist has washed over Ireland on its way here, she thought, I can smell the peat bogs on the edge of it.

She could hear the band playing a folk song from back home. It got her in the back of her throat when she recalled that it was a song Jerry and Bernadette had danced to at their wedding. They had all stood in a circle and clapped and cheered while the besotted couple, who couldn't leave each other alone, danced and held hands. Tears began to escape from Kathleen's eyes and mingled with the rain as she walked along.

'God, I'm getting soft in the head as I get older, so I am,' she said to herself, as she took a hankie out of her pocket and wiped her face.

She missed Bernadette and thought to herself that, if things had been different, she and Bernadette would have been walking home together now, laughing and joking as they used to all the time. She knew her Jerry still went into the yard and talked to Bernadette. She smiled to herself as she thought, maybe she would give it a go and try it herself.

'Bernadette, I need a bit of help,' she said, into the wet night air. 'I'm worried about Kitty and I've no idea what to do, perhaps ye can show me the way, my lovely?'

Kathleen smiled. Holy Mother, she thought to herself, I've only had five glasses of Guinness and I'm as bad as me son. I'm losing me head already.

Suddenly, Kathleen knew she wasn't alone. She hadn't imagined Bernadette gently slipping her arm through hers. Bernadette was walking beside her, but she wasn't happy. Bernadette was urging Kathleen to hurry. Kathleen felt as though she were being implored and pushed to move faster and faster, as though she were being propelled along.

'Oh my God, Bernadette,' gasped Kathleen, 'I'm an old woman, my lovely, I can't catch me breath, slow down.'

Kathleen felt as though she had been flung round the top corner of the entry when suddenly, blinking in the dark and through the pouring rain, she saw a man in a black hat and cape lift the latch to Maura and Tommy's back gate. She stopped dead in shock.

'Holy Mary, Mother of God, what's going on?' Kathleen whispered to Bernadette, but almost before the words left her mouth, she realized she was once again alone.

The feeling of a presence, of someone she knew and loved being right with her and by her side, had gone, as had the intense feeling of urgency. She was now truly alone as she slowly walked down the entry and in through Maura's gate.

Kathleen didn't rush, she was too afraid. Her limbs felt like lead and she wanted to move in the opposite direction. Her throat and mouth had become dry with fear and her heart was racing, as adrenaline surged through her veins. The penny had suddenly dropped.

'Poor Kitty, the answer was under me very nose.'

She lifted the latch and crept into the kitchen. The main light was off, but the lamp had been left on for Maura and Tommy returning. Kathleen noticed that the door at the bottom of the stairs was slightly open and off the latch.

'Oh my Holy God, little Kitty,' she whispered, feeling like screaming.

She put her hand over her mouth, frozen to the spot. What should she do? Should she run back to the Irish centre? Should she wake Alice across the road to come? She heard a floorboard upstairs creak heavily and she knew she had no time. She looked frantically around the room for something to help her and picked up the poker, leaning up against the range. Far slower and quieter than the faintest heartbeat, she opened the door wide and crept very carefully up the stairs.

He never saw her coming, so engrossed in his own lust that he didn't hear a thing. Kathleen stood still for a moment to let her eyes adjust. The bedroom was pitch black and the only light reflected off the whitewashed wall. She could see his black shape in relief against it and hear Kitty whimpering in terror.

'Please don't, ye will wake Angela, please don't do that again.'

Kathleen felt as if she had no strength in her arm. The poker suddenly felt so heavy she thought she would drop it, but she knew what she had to do. As she raised the poker, she screamed to give herself strength. Just before it came down on the back of his head, he suddenly turned round and, for one second, looked at Kathleen with utter shock on his face before slumping across the bed.

Kathleen couldn't tell who was screaming now, there was so much of it. She dragged Kitty out of the bed by her arms. Kitty was crying and wailing as she tried to lift Angela, who was yelling about being woken up as she was pulled from under Father James, out cold on the bed. Kathleen picked up Niamh and woke the boys in the next room and got them downstairs. Then they ran, carrying the half-asleep twins and Niamh between them, out of the front door and leaving all the doors open behind them, fleeing across the road into Jerry's house.

'Lock the door, lock the door,' screamed Kathleen, when they got inside. 'I'm going back to the club for the others, hold on till I get back, Kitty.'

Kathleen was scared to death at what she had done to Father James. Had she killed him? If she hadn't, surely to God, Tommy would.

Just as she turned the corner at the top of the entry out onto the street, she saw the three of them dancing along. It was raining stair rods and yet they were laughing and singing without a care in the world, Maura linking arms with Tommy on one side and Jerry on the other. Kathleen almost fell to her knees with relief as she put her hand out and held onto the wall to support herself. She had run so hard, she could hardly breathe. Jerry saw her first, then all three of them stopped dancing and broke into a run.

As soon as they got into Jerry's house, Kathleen made Maura and Tommy sit down whilst she held onto Kitty and told them how she had just caught Father James in Kitty's bedroom and what he was attempting to do.

The impact of Kathleen's news was so devastating that it was received in a shocked silence while it sank in. Maura clung to Tommy's hand, both with the same thoughts racing between them. They needed to hold onto each other for strength.

Kitty never spoke. The tears ran down her cheeks while she clung onto Maura, dreading that she might be rejected and shaken off. She felt a huge relief that Father James had been caught, but was sure that now she would be punished.

Then Kathleen added very calmly, 'And, God help me, I think I've killed him.'

Jerry tapped Tommy on the shoulder, picked up the poker from his own fire and rushed ahead of Tommy through the door and across the road, into Kitty's room. Jerry knew that he needed to keep control of the situation, while Tommy's anger burst forth as they ran, not one word intelligible.

'The fuckin' kiddie-fiddling bastard fucking cunt face fucking ...'

His insults were in vain. When they reached Kitty's room and switched on the light, there was no sign of Father James. Tommy ran into the boys' room, but again there was nothing. Father James didn't even have the decency to be lying on the bed, injured. He had slunk off into the cold, wet night.

Jerry picked up from the bedroom floor the poker Kathleen had dropped, took it downstairs and put on the kettle.

'What the feck are ye doing?' said Tommy, already on his way out of the door.

'The police can tell who has touched things, Tommy, so they can. Let me do the thinking, man, you go and see to Kitty,' Jerry said.

When the kettle boiled, he poured the hot water over the poker and scrubbed it with the scourer from the kitchen sink. Then he plunged it into the hottest part of the fire where it would remain red hot until the embers burnt down in the morning. Jerry was worried. How injured was the priest? How hard had Kathleen hit him? Father James was powerful. When it came to his word in law against Kathleen's, an uneducated Irish immigrant, Father James would win every time.

Tears, tea and recriminations were flowing in Jerry's kitchen when he returned. Slowly and nervously Kitty told them everything. Jerry courteously stood in the background, facing the fire. Kitty's story was almost too painful to listen to and his stomach was knotted. He could only think how he would feel if this was Nellie sitting here, recounting to them all a story of living hell.

He turned round, about to suggest that he and Tommy go down to the police station, when he noticed that Tommy was no longer there. He felt a chill run down his spine. Tommy was no different from Jerry and Jerry knew exactly what he would want to do right now. He ran to the sink where the meat knife had been resting on the drainer ever since it had been used to cut up the lamb on Thursday. He didn't need to ask where it was now.

'Where the hell is Tommy, Maura?'

She looked up at Jerry as though she had seen a ghost.

'Tommy!' she screamed, when she realized he was no longer at her side. She leapt up from the arm of Kitty's chair and ran back into her own house. Jerry was right behind her.

'He isn't here, he's gone!' she said, as she came back down the stairs and went to grab a coat from the hooks on the back of the kitchen door.

'Oh no you don't,' said Jerry, taking hold of her arm firmly and steering her down the path. 'Go back in to Kitty; this is man's work, leave this to us.'

Maura shook in fear. 'Jerry, what's happening, I'm scared!'

'Well, don't be. This may be a test, Maura, but we will all pass it if we are strong. Go away now back indoors and look after Kitty, that's ye job. The rest is ours.'

Paddy's son, little Paddy, stood at his bedroom window, half asleep and rubbing his eyes, and watched Jerry disappear down the entry. The rain hadn't let up and there were no street lamps in the back alleyways. It was pitch black outside, but it was definitely Jerry.

Little Paddy had been woken earlier by the screaming from next door. He was a light sleeper. When he first woke he had thought it was his da choking. He wondered where Jerry was going at this time of night before he took himself back into bed. He was asleep again within seconds.

# Chapter Fourteen

I T WAS FOUR in the morning before the two men returned. Maura had put Kitty to bed with Nellie, holding her in her arms as she rocked her to sleep. She was her mother and she needed to know what her daughter had been through, but there would be time for all that. Now, the poor child needed sleep. It still hadn't dawned on Maura that Kitty was pregnant.

Later, Maura and Kathleen sat by the fire in the kitchen, waiting. Kathleen did her best, but Maura was distraught and in shock. They both were. Kathleen had never before almost killed anyone and the realization was beginning to dawn on her of what she might have done.

As they walked in through the back door, the men didn't say a word to the anxious women.

Jerry pulled out the copper boiler from the shed as he came through the yard and then shouted at Tommy to go into the outhouse, strip off naked and to throw his clothes out into the yard floor. Maura noticed blood on Tommy's jacket, which he was unnaturally holding tightly closed across his chest. She put her hand to her mouth and stifled a scream. She was shaking uncontrollably and her legs could barely hold her up.

Kathleen, no stranger to a crisis, flew into action. She dragged the mop bucket in from the outhouse, filled it with hot water and Aunt Sally liquid soap and then ran outside and doused the water over a naked Tommy who was shaking as much as Maura. He began rubbing blood off his body with the floorcloth that Kathleen gave him. Now was not a time for modesty.

She fetched a clean sheet to wrap Tommy in and sent him indoors, then she washed down the outhouse and the yard, forcing the red rivulets down the drain with the yard brush. Jerry submerged part of Tommy's jacket in the boiler as he scrubbed it down. If he fully washed it, someone would notice. He then put Tommy's trousers and underclothes in the boiler, and his blood-soaked shirt on the fire. No one would notice a missing shirt even if it was his best.

No one said a word, but the looks that passed between Maura and Tommy were agonizing. Both were incapable of speech. Maura stood and rubbed his arms vigorously through the sheet, in an attempt to warm him and halt his violent shivering. They had been ripped from their ordinary lives and plunged into hell within minutes and they were struggling to cope.

Jerry unwrapped the blood-stained meat knife, which he had bundled in his own shirt, dropped it into the sink and poured boiling water over it. Then he threw his own shirt straight onto the open fire in the range with Tommy's.

Filling the sink, he plunged his arms in and began scrubbing. Kathleen, having put everything back in order in the outhouse, helped him.

'Thank the Holy Lord it's raining hard,' she whispered to Jerry. 'The rain will have finished off washing the yard by daylight.'

Kathleen was now calm. This was about strength in adversity. The four streets looking after their own. The crime was irrelevant. The poor would always look after each other; they had to; they had the strength of a judgmental society to beat. And now they had this – an evil that stalked their homes and threatened their children.

'Give me ye boots,' said Jerry to Tommy. He dunked both pairs into the boiler, by now bubbling furiously, and then laid them by the fire. It was a wet night. Of course the boots were wet.

Kathleen opened the whiskey that had arrived yesterday morning, although it already felt like weeks ago, as so much had happened in a short space of time. They had been going to keep it for a Christmas treat.

'Feck Christmas,' muttered Kathleen, filling four mugs and pressing one into Maura's hand.

Jerry took his mug and looked up. 'None of us will ever mention this night again,' he said firmly. 'We will not speak of it to anyone. Do we all understand?'

Tommy, Maura and Kathleen nodded.

'Tommy and Maura, away home now to bed. We will be safe as long as no one knows. Don't be seen as you go. We will decide what is to be done with Kitty tomorrow, when we are calm and have all had some sleep.'

Maura and Kathleen had no idea what had been done with Father James, but they knew better than to ask. They were all now shaking violently with shock, even Kathleen. Now that her jobs had been done and there was nothing to focus on, the trembling took its hold.

Between chattering teeth, she said, 'If you had just put the evil bastard in a room full of young mothers, he would have got his punishment.'

'Sh, Mammy,' said Jerry, who, despite his shaking, was thinking with absolute clarity.

They each picked up their mugs and knocked the whiskey back, to stop the tremors before they parted from one another. Kathleen had filled the mugs to the brim and the amber liquid scalded as it slipped down, flooding them with warmth.

Tommy and Maura staggered back into their own house, having first checked that the street was quiet, Tommy still wrapped in the sheet, carrying his soaking clothes, with Maura clinging onto his arm.

The following morning, Alice woke early. As she came through the door into the kitchen, she saw the meat knife still on the draining rack. Thinking it best to put it away, she ran the knife under the tap and noticed a spot of blood on the end. She boiled the kettle and poured boiling water over it, then dried it and popped it in the knife drawer, before making herself a cup of tea.

She had heard every word that had been spoken last night, but had lain in bed, still and quiet. To Alice, it was normal to observe events from a distance.

The rooms upstairs were full of children sleeping, four girls top to tail in Nellie's bed and two sets of twins on the floor. The air was heavy with night breath. Alice tiptoed over sleeping children and opened the window on her way down to let in some of the fresh damp morning air.

Jerry was still sleeping off the Guinness and the whiskey when there was a knock on the front door. Alice took a breath, smoothed down her skirt and opened the door.

'Morning, miss, can we ask you a few questions?' enquired a young, fresh-faced policeman, one of two standing on the scrubbed doorstep.

Alice looked him straight in the eye and answered as cool as a cucumber. She told the policeman how everyone had been at the wedding party, then come home and gone to bed at about two in the morning.

'Was that just you, miss?' asked the policeman.

'Oh no,' said Alice calmly, 'it was all of us.' She reeled off the names of those living in Maura and Tommy's house, as well as their own.

She asked the constables why they were asking, but they wouldn't tell her.

She smiled sweetly, offered them a cup of tea she hoped they wouldn't accept, which they didn't, and then went back inside.

The policemen – Howard, originally from Wales, and Simon, a little older and second generation from Belfast – marked both house numbers in their little black book with the words 'alibi for all occupants' and went on their way. The lady in the house was English. She had a very nice accent. One of those proper types, upright and honest. 'Definitely not a bog jumper and obviously telling the truth,' said

Howard, as they walked away. He didn't notice Simon flinch at his words as he snapped his notebook shut.

When they went down the other side of the road and came to Maura and Tommy's door, they didn't even bother to knock.

'Leave that one,' said Simon. 'They came home with number forty-two.' If they were friends of the well-spoken lady, they were probably proper English types too.

'You sure?' asked the new and very keen Howard.

It was almost time for a brew and Simon wanted to get inside the car and head back to the station.

'Yes, I'm sure,' Simon replied. 'When you have been around as long as me, you get a nose for these things.'

Inside the house, Alice was feeling an unfamiliar rush of excitement and pride. For the first time in her life, she felt as though she had fulfilled a purpose. She was now relevant, important even. Her moment had come and, without conscious pre-thought or planning, she had risen to the occasion and shone. Even she knew that.

Jerry and Kathleen had looked after Alice. They had been good to her. Over time she had learnt the significance of her differences from most other people and had begun to realize that, as someone who lived on the four streets in the home that she did, she was very lucky indeed. For the first time in her life this had been her big chance to do something for someone else. Kathleen's ways had rubbed off on her. She wasn't going to let them down.

Every member in every household on the four streets gathered round their small black and white television sets that evening, from the youngest to the oldest, and watched the report of the gruesome murder of a priest in Liverpool. They listened in silence as the solemn newsreader described how he had been found on the path to the Priory with a stab wound in his chest and a significant body part dismembered, which had been found later in the day, mauled by a cat, ten yards away in the graveyard. No murder weapon had been found and the police had no clues.

'The local community has been paralysed by the news, because the priest was a well-known figure around Liverpool. He had a particular calling to aid children who were suffering in poor communities, as demonstrated by his work at local schools and the children's hospital.'

On Monday morning, while Kathleen had her cup of tea with the Granada TV rentals man and sliced him a piece of fruit loaf with the meat knife, he told her all the fanciful theories that were flying around the four streets about who had done for Father James. Naturally, not one of them included Maura and Tommy's house, where the Father had been treated like a saint. Or their own house, where the Father never came. They were all safe in their secret. And a secret it would remain, she hoped.

Meanwhile, over at the school, the police were talking to the children in the morning assembly, asking questions about Father James.

'Did any of you see anything unusual on the night Father

James was murdered?' asked Howard of the rows of children sitting cross-legged on the wooden parquet floor in front of him.

A complete dead end to their inquiries had driven him, under pressure from their Chief Superintendent, to try a more novel approach to gathering information.

Simon had moaned and groaned and resisted as much as possible. He was not keen on change. He also felt embarrassed. Sister Evangelista was openly crying. Simon had been taught by the nuns when he himself was a boy. He didn't like to see women weep. Nuns were a special breed of women, so he hated that even more.

Howard had considered this a smart idea when he first thought of it; at the very least it would look good when he reported back to the Super and help him on his race to become a sergeant. But now that he was here, standing in front of so many sombre faces, he wished he was anywhere else.

One little boy was wriggling and enthusiastically thrust up his hand.

Nondescript, slightly dirty, wearing a sleeveless pullover with no shirt underneath, despite the cold, and with a huge hole in the front, with what looked like half a ball of wool unravelled and hanging down in long loose threads exposing his skin underneath, he had been squirming on the floor since the police officers walked in. The tide mark across his neck was as black as the leather on his shoes, which were three sizes too big and only just still attached to the soles.

'Here we go,' said Simon disdainfully, 'he saw Donald Duck going into mass.'

'I did, I did!' shouted little Paddy, punching the air with his hand excitedly – innocently trying to curry favour with Sister Evangelista, who scared him so much he would do anything to be in her good books. 'I saw Uncle Jerry running up the back entry in the middle of the night.'

Simon and Howard both stared at the scruffy boy, wriggling about on the floor with the unwashed hair and grubby face.

'Paddy,' said Sister Evangelista in a stern voice, 'the officers have no time for your nonsense. Shut up, boy, and sit straight in your line.'

By the time she had reached the word 'line', Sister Evangelista was almost screaming. Sister Evangelista had no time for dirty children and must have told Peggy a hundred times, cleanliness was next to godliness. The boy smelt and had head lice, and she had no patience with him whatsoever.

The shock and horror of Father James's death had affected them all. The unanswered questions, along with revulsion at the manner of it, had set their nerves on edge.

When the police officers had told Sister they wanted to speak to the children at assembly, she had almost refused. She had barely slept, as confusing thoughts and questions to which she had no answer kept her awake well into the small hours.

Simon and Howard looked at each other. 'May we borrow your office, Sister?' asked Howard, who was already motioning to Paddy to join him at the front.

The children sat still and unspeaking as they watched the policemen hold open the large wooden and glass doors for Paddy to pass through from the hall on the way to Sister

Evangelista's office. There was no need for the teachers or nuns to remonstrate with those who wriggled as though they had ants in their pants. Everyone was silent and still as they stared at the departing backs of the tall policemen.

Alice was taking her knitting out from behind the cushion on the comfy chair, which was where it lived, when she heard three loud, ominous knocks on the front door.

The Granada man was packing away into his case his little black book and large grey bag of sixpences, and Kathleen was on her way to the sink with the cups and plates, when they all stopped dead in their tracks and stared towards the front door.

'Blimey, that's an important knock,' said the Granada man. 'It'll be a vacuum cleaner salesman. I saw the Electrolux men on Vauxhall Road yesterday.'

Kathleen and Alice looked at each other without a word. Alice slipped her knitting back behind the cushion and walked purposefully to the front door to open it. She was growing in confidence every day.

Down on the docks, the men were unloading the merchant ship, the *Cotopaxi*, which had sailed in from Ecuador early that morning. As he was one of the shorter and tubbier men on the docks, Tommy's feet had left the quay as he jumped up to catch a guide rope for a bag of jute, just above his head and out of his reach. Tommy travelled through the air for the twenty feet it took him to reach Jerry. It was time for their ciggie break and Tommy thought it was about time

Jerry knew. As his feet touched the ground again, he looked up towards the jute sack and his eye was caught by two policemen talking to the guard at the top of the steps.

He saw the guard point in their direction, as both policemen tipped their helmet peaks in a gesture of thanks and began to descend the steps.

As Tommy landed, he pushed the rope into Jerry's hand and squeezed it tight, pushing his nails into Jerry's skin, forcing Jerry to look at him in surprise.

'Let go of me hand, you homo,' Jerry said in annoyance as he tried to take the rope from Tommy.

'The fecking bizzies are coming down the steps, Jer,' Tommy almost spat at him. 'If it's us they is after, neither of us say a fecking word. If we don't say nothing, they don't have nothing.'

There was an urgency to Tommy's voice. They both knew which was the guilty of the two, but Tommy also knew they would never let one another down.

Jerry didn't glance at the steps, but looked Tommy straight in the eye as he said, 'Aye, right, to be sure I will say nothin' now, neither of us, nothin'.'

They took a long hard look at each other, as they heard Howard's voice ring out behind them, 'Oi, Jerry Deane, we want a word with you.'

Jerry and Tommy clasped thumbs briefly, then Jerry let go of the rope and turned round.

Alice walked up Brigie's path with ease. Her heart no longer beat faster when she stepped out from her lonely world. She was still not one for small talk and she knew that no one would ever seek her out for a shopping trip to St John's market, or indulge in baby chatter, but she did at least feel as though she was somewhere she belonged.

Brigie had been pacing up and down the kitchen floor all morning with a teething baby daughter who screamed louder than the rest put together. She didn't hear the back door open and could have dropped the baby when she saw Alice walk through it. Alice smiled conspiratorially in greeting, closed the door and then, from under her skirt, produced an almost empty whiskey bottle.

Brigie walked over to the kettle. This was going to be interesting.

Simon and Howard had pounded Jerry with repetitive questions for almost two hours, and yet he had remained silent.

The police station, old, large and forbidding, with its distinctive blue light over the door, was in Whitechapel. The cells were small and noisy and, on a Saturday night, full to overflowing with the same prostitutes who had spent so many nights in the cells that they called Whitechapel station home.

Jerry had been held in one such cell for four hours and, so far, hadn't said a word. He was trying the patience of Howard and Simon, who decided to take a break.

They took themselves off to the station canteen for a drink and a game of billiards, to help them decide what to do next. They were coming up against a brick wall. With the best will in the world, no judge was ever going to accept the word of a filthy, witless little boy who obviously wasn't the sharpest knife in the box. And what did they have anyway? Under questioning in Sister Evangelista's office, the kid had moved from having definitely seen his Uncle Jerry to possibly having seen his Uncle Jerry.

They were holding Jerry in the cell on spurious grounds, but once they had him in the cell, he suddenly reeked of culpability for no other reason than he wouldn't speak.

'If he was innocent, he would talk and tell us why he was running down the entry,' said Howard.

Simon, who rarely got anything right, pulled on his cigarette and, as the smoke swirled around his face, replied, 'Aye, I smell a stinking great rat all right. That man is as guilty as hell. The problem is, how? Why? What's the motive? The Sister said he didn't even go to the church.'

'We need to at least pin a motive on him soon or we will have to let him walk,' said Howard, who was not looking forward to the prospect.

The Super had been delighted that at least they had someone in the cell to question for the mystery murder of the priest. Simon and Howard had been feeling pressure as if it was coming from someone much higher up in the force.

'Let's go back in,' said Simon. 'Let's start the good cop, bad cop routine and see if that makes him start talking.'

'We will,' said Howard, 'but I will tell you this: we may have no motive and we may have nothing other than that feckless kid but all the same, that man reeks of guilt.'

# Chapter Fifteen

B Y THE TIME Tommy arrived home from work, the four streets were buzzing with the news that Jerry was being held by the police. It had been the longest day's work while he had counted down the minutes until he could run back up the steps and confer with Maura and Kathleen. When Maura told him what Alice had done, he felt a shiver run down his spine – and then, 'Jeez, Maura,' he shouted, 'why didn't ye wait for me to get fecking home?'

Tommy was having trouble weighing up the consequences of Alice's actions. Maura had never known Tommy to swear as much as he had since the worst night of their lives; in fact she had heard him shout on only a handful of occasions during their married life. Maura needed reinforcements and sent Kitty across the road to fetch Kathleen and Alice.

'Calm down, Tommy,' said Kathleen with authority, as soon as she came in. 'It's a grand idea if Brigie and Sean will play along with Peggy and Paddy, but you need to get your head together and go and see Paddy. It will work only if ye all agree.'

'Let me get this right,' said Tommy. 'Ye are all asking Sean, Paddy and meself to go down to the police station and say Jerry was sneaking down to Sean's house for a card school and to drink up the wedding whiskey, whilst ye lot was asleep in ye beds?'

Maura, Kathleen and Alice nodded. When it was put into Tommy's words, coldly and with an edge of scorn, it didn't sound so good.

Tommy exploded. He and Jerry had a pact, to talk to no one.

'Ye just couldn't keep ye's gobs shut, could ye,' he shouted. 'Me and Jer, tell no one, we decided. If we can keep it that way they have nothing and nowt, and youse have told the whole fecking four streets. I'm done for, Maura, I'm a fecking goner now.'

Tommy was losing control. Maura felt scared. Normally, Tommy was putty in her hands; she had never seen him like this before. His anger seemed to have erupted from nowhere. She felt the blood drain from her face as she began to think Alice had done something very, very stupid.

Both sets of twins and Angela began to cry, setting Niamh off too. Kitty had no idea what was going on, but she gathered up the children and took them across the road to Nellie, who was sitting in front of the TV on her own. Joseph was already in bed.

Kitty felt a pang of jealousy shoot through her. She had never in her life had a room to herself. As one of seven, she could only dream of such a luxury.

Nellie had no idea what was going on either, but the

whispering between Kathleen and Alice had set her on edge. She knew something was badly wrong.

They had told her Jerry was helping the police, but Nellie couldn't understand that. Helping them to do what?

Nellie got up from her chair and took the biscuit tin out of the cupboard. She and Kitty gave a biscuit to each of the little ones to encourage them to stop crying. Kitty felt jealous again. The biscuit tin was rarely full in her house.

When the children had calmed down, both girls sat in a comfy chair together, with their arms round each other. The rest of the Doherty brood sat on the mat and they all stared at the TV, which offered an escape from the frightening atmosphere around them. Nellie felt more settled than she had all evening, now that she was no longer alone, but in the company of her lifelong friends.

Sean, who was over six feet tall, had had to remove his cap as he bent to enter Tommy's kitchen. He was a mystery to every man on the street. Sean was as broad as he was tall, a fine specimen who spent his weekends at the boxing club. He worked on the docks by day and was in the boxing ring by night.

'Ye can't blame him,' Tommy had once said to Maura. 'If I had that many daughters, I'd be on a ship to Mexico, never mind the bloody boxing club.'

Sean had a formidable reputation and it went back as far as his street-fighting days in Tipperary. The word on the four streets was that Sean had arrived in Liverpool whilst on the run from the Gardai for having nearly beaten a man to death in a Tipperary pub brawl. No one dare ask Sean if the rumour were true.

'He beats the shite out of anyone who dares go near him in that ring,' laughed Tommy, after he and Jerry had gone along to a match to support their friend, 'the big man'.

And yet he and Brigie had produced only daughters, and lots of them. Eight little red-headed females in one house. Sean was living proof of the street folklore that it was the women who decided the sex of the baby. Unless, of course, she produced boys – and then it was all down to the virility of the man.

Sean hadn't liked what Brigie had told him about Alice's visit earlier in the day. It had perturbed him greatly.

Sean liked to take his wash-down upstairs at the press. The first thing he did every night, when he came home, was to carry his jug upstairs and strip off.

Every one of his daughters had been conceived during the end-of-day wash-down. Brigie looked at the other men on the streets and, with the exception of Jerry who was known for his good looks, she knew how lucky she was in Sean.

She didn't like the number of young girls who hung around the boxing club, and she was no fool. As exhausted as she frequently was, she kept her man happy and paid for it with a lifetime of pregnancy and breastfeeding.

Tonight, whilst Sean was washing down, Brigie had stopped downstairs. He thought over what she had told him and remembered times that Father James had visited his own house. Images flashed into his mind of the Father holding his daughters in his arms. He had often fleetingly questioned why Father James called round to the house so often.

Sean had no idea what had happened on that night or why Jerry was being questioned. He only knew what Alice was asking him to do. There were plenty on the four streets who revered Father James.

Sean told Brigie it was very important to keep her mouth shut. Some would find what they were doing difficult to understand.

'If I do what Alice has asked, Brigie, we need to keep safe.'

Brigie didn't need to be told. The people she lived amongst were as good as her family, but she knew that many were devastated by Father James's death. The Dohertys and the Deanes were good people. She would tell no one.

When Sean stepped into the kitchen, Paddy was already there. The women had left and the men sat down.

The women had talked Tommy round and, the more they had talked, the more he realized their plot made good sense. They were in greater danger without an alibi for Jerry. They needed to source one quickly, get him out of the police station and safely home as soon as possible. They needed help from their friends.

The kettle began to whistle on the range and, as Tommy stood to take it off and mash some tea, Paddy roared, 'Feckin' hell, imagine that, lads, no women and just us men living in one house now, how grand would that be, eh?'

Despite the seriousness of the situation, all three burst out laughing.

'Yeah, but I'm not going to bed with you, Paddy,' said Tommy, carrying a pot of tea over to the table. 'Ye snore.'

They laughed again and the atmosphere lightened momentarily.

'Now, lads, you don't need details, trust me, but Jer needs our help and we all need to be singing out of the same bloody hymn book to do that. Are ye with me?'

Sean and Paddy picked up their tea and looked at each other. They had both moved onto the four streets at around the same time and between the two families they had attended too many baptisms to count. They had both clasped their arms together and held Jerry upright underneath Bernadette's dead body as she lay in her coffin on the day they buried her. One of Sean's daughters was running around the street right now in Angela's old shoes, and the two girls were best friends.

Sean took both sets of Tommy's twins down to the boxing club with him on a regular basis and they had all pooled their resources together on many an occasion to make sure the kids were fed. When Paddy had run out of money before the end of the week, Jerry had often slipped him half a crown.

It didn't matter what Jerry had done. They were his mates and they would do whatever was needed, regardless of the danger to themselves.

'I'm in,' said Sean.

Paddy felt guilty as he looked at his two friends and drank his tea. Peggy had told him what little Paddy had done and big Paddy had taken his slipper to him. He wouldn't open his mouth again, the stupid little fecker. Too much like his mother at times. Spoke rubbish before putting his brain in gear.

He had been home for a full half-hour before Peggy told him what had happened, and the stupid woman had told the lad to hide in the outhouse, out of his da's way.

It took Paddy a full minute for what Peggy was telling him to sink in.

'He did what?' Paddy roared. 'He did what? Are ye telling me Jer is sat in a police cell, being questioned about the priest's murder, because that gobshite of a kid wanted to look clever?'

Shame and anger convulsed Paddy in equal measure. The men had talked about nothing else on the docks other than how ridiculous the police were. They had laughed at the ridiculous notion that Jerry could have anything to do with it.

'Stupid feckers, the bizzies are. Jer didn't even go to fuckin' mass since the day he buried Bernadette,' Brian, his gang mate, had said. 'He's even married a Protestant. God knows when the last time was that Jer even spoke to the priest. What a fuckin' laugh it is.'

Paddy ran up the stairs as quickly as a man could run who smoked forty a day and had worked nine hours straight. There was no sign of his son.

He ran back through the kitchen, picked up his slipper from in front of the fire and went out into the yard. Now he could hear little Paddy whimpering in the outhouse.

Maura could hear the shouts in her own yard as she took down the washing. She stopped unpegging and held onto the line with her eyes closed. Neither Maura nor Tommy ever hit their kids and it made her feel sick to hear poor little Paddy's pathetic pleas for Paddy to leave him alone.

'No, Da, don't hit me with the slipper,' he screeched, as the outhouse door flung open.

It was too late; his pleas were followed up by loud thwacks, screams and even louder crying. Paddy must have slapped his son at least a dozen times. Maura heard him swear as the slipper flew out of his hand, but that didn't stop him; he then resorted to his fists. The guilt she felt at hearing little Paddy take a beating made her stomach turn sour. Maura loved little Paddy. She often fed him at her own table and had deloused his hair as often as she had the twins. He was one of life's innocents and he never failed to make them all laugh with his antics. 'What has little Paddy done today then,' she would ask her boys at some stage of the evening. She often pulled him to her for a quick hug each time he said 'I wish I lived with ye, Maura.' She wished he did too. Never more than today.

Maura wanted to lean over the wall and plead with Paddy to stop, but she didn't dare. The four streets survived in harmony on the basis of unwritten rules and one of them was: you never interfered or stuck your nose in when it hadn't been asked for.

'I'm in,' said Paddy, relieved to have the opportunity to compensate for the perceived stupidity of little Paddy.

Jerry had been in the police station for eight hours and the police were getting nowhere.

Howard and Simon should have gone home three hours since, but they didn't want to leave this to anyone else. Neither could say why, they had no evidence other than a witness statement from a ten-year-old, but both knew they were on to something.

Their trained noses could smell it. They could taste it. The aroma of guilt filled the station. It was at its strongest in the cell in which they held Jerry and yet they didn't have a single fact to go on.

'Maybe we should let him go, put a watch on him and call it a night,' said Howard, who was imagining his tea, which was always on the table at six-thirty sharp, sitting there congealing.

'Are you joking?' said Simon. 'Look, mate, we both know we are on to something here. That man is playing us like a fiddle. He hasn't said one flaming word since we handcuffed him. We have to keep going until he cracks first.'

'We are running out of time,' said Howard. 'We will have to let him ...'

His words trailed off as, from the window, they saw Tommy, Sean and Paddy march in through the station doors.

Brigie had just got the youngest off to sleep when Howard knocked on her front door. She looked surprised to see him and with a warm and welcoming smile, invited him straight in. He made no small talk and looked as though he was in a foul temper.

He opened his notebook and took out his pencil. 'Would ye like some tea?' said Brigie sweetly. Howard appeared not to hear and got straight to the point. 'Did you, on the sixteenth of this month, receive a bottle of whiskey as a gift from the wedding family?'

'Aye, we did,' replied Brigie. 'And so did everyone else.'

'Can I see your whiskey, madam?' said Howard, feeling more officious than usual.

Neither he nor Simon believed the card-school story. Now they needed to check whether or not the whiskey bottle had been opened. If it hadn't, it would be their only lead. And a big one too. They would be able to prove that Jerry's neighbours had been lying and that was a serious offence indeed.

Brigie looked at Howard questioningly and slowly moved to the sideboard in the front room. Howard followed her.

Brigie bent down to open the cupboard door, looking sideways at Howard and, as she lifted the bottle of whiskey out, she let out a high-pitched squeal and gasped, 'Oh Jaysus, someone has drunk the bleedin' whiskey, there's nothing here.' She turned and faced Howard with the empty bottle in her hand. A look of pure amazement sat on her face and took a bow.

Howard snapped his book shut and stormed out of the kitchen.

At exactly the same time in Kathleen's kitchen, Simon was asking the same question.

'Sure,' said Kathleen as she went to the kitchen cupboard, 'we are saving it for Christmas mind, here ye are,' and she took out a full and unopened bottle of whiskey.

Within an hour, Jerry walked in through his own back door. Everyone had gathered in his kitchen, even Brigie, as once again Kathleen poured out whiskey for all. 'Bugger Christmas,' she laughed as she cracked open the seal. 'Easy come, easy go,' said Sean.

He and Paddy had both told the police that there was a card school, playing for money, in Sean's house that night, well after the women had gone to bed.

They had embellished the story with the admission that they had drunk almost the whole bottle of whiskey between them. They were both prepared to sign a witness statement to that effect. When Paddy said firmly, 'Aye, and my lad wants to withdraw his, so he does. Now he thinks it was me he saw leaving the entry, not Jerry,' Howard's heart sank.

Gone was his promotion.

Simon and Howard knew they were back to square one. With no evidence they had to let Jerry go. He had an alibi with two witnesses. He was safe.

Nellie and Kitty were back together on the comfy chair. Nellie had refused to move from Jerry's arms until Kitty came back in through the door.

Everyone lifted their glass to drink in relief, when Kathleen tapped her glass with a spoon and spoke.

'Before we drink,' she said, 'we need to say thank you to someone. To Alice.' Everyone turned and smiled at Alice.

Alice beamed, feeling swamped by a sense of pride. Her face flushed red and tears pricked at her eyes when everyone lifted their glass and said loudly, 'To Alice.'

It was the happiest moment of her life.

Nellie and Kitty hugged each other, grinning. They had no idea what they were grinning at, or what had just occurred, but everyone was happy and so were they.

Suddenly, without warning, Kitty leapt from the chair and raced through the back door to the outhouse.

As Kitty leant over the pan to throw up the first time, she felt someone holding back her hair from the vomit and stroking the back of her neck. She could hear the voices wafting down the yard from the kitchen, laughing and chattering away. Celebrating. Everyone joyous and happy.

Another shot of whiskey, she thought, and they will be singing next and pushing the chairs back to dance around the kitchen. They wouldn't miss her. She was shaking with cold and felt clammy as she knelt on the floor and clung onto the wooden seat, a long, polished plank that stretched across the top of the toilet. Next to the seat stood a large pile of cut-up pages of the *Echo*, to use as toilet paper. The smell from the printer's ink made her heave again.

The soothing, ethereal whispers calmed her panic. She knew everyone was in the kitchen, and there could be no one with her in the outhouse, but the nausea made her feel so deathly that she was beyond thinking or caring.

Just as she leant over to vomit for the second time and felt her own hair being lifted clear, she saw a long strand of red hair sweep past the side of her face.

Kathleen looked at Maura to see if she had noticed Kitty dashing out of the back door to the outhouse. She had.

Maura went white. She put her hand to her mouth and held onto the back of the chair to steady herself as the realization hit her with the force of a truck.

Kathleen moved over to her side and put an arm round her waist.

'Oh my God, Kathleen, 'twas before me very eyes and I never knew. Jesus, Mary and Joseph, what next? What will we do?'

'Sh,' Kathleen replied. 'Let's enjoy tonight, Maura. That problem is ours to share, tomorrow.'

# NADINE
## DORRIES

*Hide*
*Her Name*

*Chapter One*

'STOP LYING ON his pyjamas now, Peggy, and let yer man out to earn an honest crust!'

Paddy's next-door neighbour, Tommy, yelled impatiently over the backyard gate as he and the Nelson Street dockers knocked on for Paddy. They stood huddled together, in an attempt to hold back the worst of the rain as they waited for Paddy to join them.

Much to her annoyance, Peggy, Paddy's wife, could hear their sniggering laughter.

'Merciful God!' she said crossly. 'Paddy, would ye tell that horny fecker, Tommy, it's not us at it every five minutes.' She snatched the enamel mug of tea out of Paddy's hand and away from his lips before he had supped his last drop. There was not a second of silence available for him in which to protest.

'The only reason he and Maura have two sets of twins is because he's a dirty bugger and does it twice a night. I'll not have him shouting such filth down the entry, now tell him, will ye, Paddy?'

Peggy and Paddy had spawned enough of their own

children, but Peggy had never in her life done it twice on the same night. Every woman who lived on the four streets knew: that sinful behaviour got you caught with twins.

'I wonder sometimes how Maura holds her head up without the shame, so I do. Once caught doing it twice, ye would know what the feck had happened and not do it again. He must be mighty powerful with his persuasion, that Tommy. Answer me, Paddy, tell him, will ye?'

'Aye, I will that, Peggy,' said Paddy as he picked up his army-issue canvas bag containing his dinner: a bottle of cold tea and Shipman's beef paste sandwiches. Rushing to the door, he placed a kiss on Peggy's cheek, his shouted goodbye cut midway as the back gate snapped closed behind him.

Each man who lived on the four streets worked on the docks. Their day began as it ended, together.

It took exactly four minutes from the last back yard on Nelson Street, down the dock steps, to the perimeter gate. The same amount of time it took to smoke the second roll-up as ribald jokes and football banter rose high on the air. When the sun shone, their spirits lifted and they would often sing whilst walking.

The same melancholy songs were heard in the Grafton rooms or the Irish centre on a Saturday night, sunk into a pint of Guinness. Melodies of a love they left behind. Of green fields the colour of emeralds, or a raven-haired girl, with eyes that shone like diamonds.

The Nelson Street gang were often delayed by Paddy at number seventeen and would pause at his back gate and stand a while.

Each morning, wearing a string vest, which carried the menu of every meal eaten at home that week, Paddy sat up in bed, picked up his cigarettes and matches, lying next to an ever-overflowing ashtray on the bedside table, and lit up his first ciggie of the day.

Paddy smoked a great deal in bed.

He would often wake Peggy in the middle of the night with the sound of his match striking through the dark, providing a split second of bright illumination.

'Give us a puff,' Peggy would croak, without any need of the teeth soaking in a glass on the table next to her. Not waiting for nor expecting a reply, she would warily uncoil her arm from under the old grey army blanket and, cheating the cold air of any opportunity to penetrate the dark, smelly warmth beneath, grasp the wet-ended cigarette between her finger and thumb, put it to her lips and draw deeply.

'Ah, that's better,' she would say. 'Me nerves are shot, Paddy,' and within seconds she would drift back to sleep.

This morning, the squall blew across the Mersey and up the four streets, soaking the men waiting for Paddy. They stood huddled against the entry wall, trying in vain to protect their ciggies from the downpour.

Paddy appeared through the gate, Peggy's words at his back pushing him out onto the cobbles.

'Yer fecking bastards, ye'll get me hung one day, so yer will,' said Paddy only half seriously to Tommy and the rest of the gang.

'I was only joking, Paddy, I've seen a better face on a clock than on yer missus,' said Tommy. 'I knew ye was just stuffing yer gob with another slice of toast.'

'Leave Peggy alone or I'll set her on yer,' joked Paddy. 'She was kept in a cage till she was five. Ye'll be sorry if I do.'

They all laughed, even Paddy.

Tall Sean, a docker by day and a boxer by night, joined in as he struggled to light up.

'Never fear, Paddy, he laughed. 'yer a lucky man with your Peggy, her titties are so feckin' big, ye could hang me wet donkey jacket off them with a bottle of Guinness in each pocket and it still wouldn't fall off.'

They roared with laughter and, with lots of matey reassuring pats on the back for Paddy, continued on their way down the steps to face another day of hard graft on the river's edge.

Boots on cobbles. Minds on the match.

From an upstairs window in the Priory, Daisy Quinn, Father James's housekeeper, studied the dockers marching down the steps towards the gate, just as she had done every single morning since she herself had arrived from Dublin during the war.

In an hour, once she had cleared away the breakfast dishes, she would take her damp duster and move to another room, across the landing on the other side of the Priory, and look down on the mothers and children from Nelson Street as they walked in the opposite direction to that of the dockers, towards the school gates.

The Victorian Priory, large, square and detached, stood

next to the graveyard, and from each of the upstairs windows Daisy could alter her view: of the docks, of the graveyard, of the school and the convent, or of the four streets. Daisy had her own panoramic view of life as it happened. There wasn't very much about anyone or anything Daisy didn't know. They all turned up on the Priory steps at some time, for one reason or another.

'Daisy, have ye any coal to spare? We have none and the babby is freezing.'

'Do ye have any potatoes or bread? A coat for the child to go to school?'

They were always wanting something and, sure enough, Father James could often solve the problem. They had cupboards in the Priory stuffed full of the clothes people donated for him to hand out to the poor.

But the father never gave. Mother's had to ask.

'I am here to do God's work, not the corporations',' he would often boom in a bad-tempered way when Daisy asked should he take a coat or a pair of shoes to a family, after she had noticed the welfare officer knocking on their door.

But pride never stood in the way of a mother needing to warm a child, so beg they often did.

Occasionally people came for happy reasons – to ask for the father to perform a christening or a wedding – and when that happened, the father would take them into his study and Daisy would carry in a tray of tea and a plate of her home-made biscuits, just as Mrs Malone had taught her.

She almost always took back an empty plate. Hardly ever had Daisy returned a biscuit to the kitchen.

If ever a mother was too polite or too scared to allow her children to take one, Daisy would press a few into her hand at the front door, wrapped in greaseproof paper and tied up with string.

'Go on now, take it,' she would say. 'Have them for later.'

Daisy would have loved to have had children of her own.

She had arrived in Liverpool from Dublin to take her position at the Priory whilst still a child. She became an assistant to the fathers' cook, Mrs Malone, and like most young girls she had a head full of dreams and plans.

Father James had disposed of those faster than a speeding bullet.

'You will have one day and one night off per month,' he told her, within moments of her being summoned to his study.

Daisy was a little disappointed by that news. She had been told by the sisters at the orphanage in Dublin that she would have one day a week to herself and a week's holiday each year, during which she could travel back to Ireland and visit the only place she knew to be home, the orphanage where she had been raised since she was a baby.

Now, all these years later, Daisy could count the days off she had taken on one hand.

'You must work hard and help Mrs Malone in the kitchen,' the sisters at the orphanage had told her. And, sure enough, working hard was what she had done every day since.

Without a moment's pain or illness and certainly without any warning at all, Mrs Malone had dropped dead, almost ten years to the day following Daisy's arrival.

Mrs Malone had often told Daisy what a good worker she was.

'I don't know how I would manage without you, Daisy,' she had said, at least once a day. 'The sisters may have said you were simple in the head, but I didn't want you for brains, brawn was what I was looking for and you have plenty of that.'

Daisy smiled with pleasure. Being told that she was simple was not news to her, sure, she had heard it so often before. But the sisters had also said, 'You can hold your head up with no shame, you were born to a very good family, Daisy Quinn.'

Daisy never thought to question why she was in an orphanage and not with her family. She had no real under-standing of what a family was.

Being a good girl and coming from a good family must have been why she was sent to take up such an important job in England and for one of the fathers too.

'You have simple ways, but they can be put to good use if you can be protected from the sin that preys upon girls like yourself,' the sisters had told her. Daisy had no idea which sin would prey upon her or what it would do, but she was grateful for the protection.

Neither the sisters nor Mrs Malone had ever mentioned to Daisy the other reason that she had been sent to the Priory.

Daisy presumed that they could not have known, because Father James forbade Daisy to speak to anyone about it.

'To speak of anything that occurs in this Priory would be the greatest sin for which no forgiveness would be ever be forthcoming. Ye will be left to burn alone in the eternal flames of hell and damnation. Do ye understand, girl?'

She was asked this question on a regular basis and her answer was always the dutiful same: 'Yes, Father.'

Daisy took over the housekeeper's role in full. She coped well and never took, nor was offered, a day off.

However, there had also been a number of welcome changes following Mrs Malone's death. Neither Father James nor any of his friends had bothered her again, and the nuns began to invite her over to the convent for tea.

She had only the bishop to tolerate now.

She sometimes wondered if Father James would have preferred someone other than herself as housekeeper, but on the night of Mrs Malone's funeral, on her way to her modest room, she had overheard raised voices coming from the study.

'The money for the Priory would stop if she left. It must follow her wherever she is and, anyway, the sisters in Dublin would have too many questions to ask should she be moved.'

That was the bishop speaking. A fat man, distinguishable by his thin, weedy whine, which, as it whistled into the air, struggled past the blubbery folds of lard gathered under his chin.

'I suppose we are safer if she is here,' said Father James in a tone loaded with disappointment.

'Aye, we are that, but anyway, she is simple. No one would ever believe a word she said. I will write now that she is happy and improved. That she is running the show and, sure, isn't that the truth? Wasn't that just the grandest bit of rabbit pie we ever ate for supper?'

Daisy grinned from ear to ear with pleasure. They had loved her rabbit pie.

On this wet morning, Daisy padded across to the opposite side of the empty house. Sister Evangelista had popped a note through the door late last night to let her know she would be visiting the Priory this morning to help Daisy pack up the father's room, ready to send his belongings to his sister in America.

The murder of Father James in the graveyard had taken place only feet away from the Priory and everyone was still in a state of profound shock.

Everyone except Daisy, that was.

Daisy wasn't sad and didn't miss the father at all. Not in the way she had missed Mrs Malone when she died.

In fact, Daisy missed Mrs Malone a great deal. She had always told Daisy what she could and could not do, and with no one to guide her, Daisy was lost.

Father James had told her what she could and could not say.

What should she say now and who to?

Her mind was in torment.

Daisy pressed her forehead against the cold window and, looking down, watched the children walking to school. She saw Sister Evangelista close the convent door, make her way down the path and turn right along the pavement towards the Priory. The Reverend mother waved to Kitty Doherty from number nineteen, who was making her way towards the school steps on the opposite side of the road to the convent. Kitty was herding along the two sets of twin boys and that lovely girl, Nellie Deane, from number forty-two was helping her. The girls waved back to Sister Evangelista, all smiles.

The Kitty girl. Daisy had often seen Father James visit her house, very often at night, but he never visited Nellie's.

Nellie, whose mother, Bernadette, had died so tragically young and whom Daisy still saw sometimes in the dead of the night, running up and down the four streets.

It was Nellie's nana Kathleen who had woken Daisy up late on the night the father was murdered. She had been talking to Bernadette as she left the Keating girl's wedding and followed the river, down towards Nelson street.

Daisy wasn't scared to see the ghostly Bernadette with Kathleen. She often saw her in the graveyard and up and down Nelson Street, as she flew straight through the wall into what had once been her home, at number forty-two.

Daisy, uneasy, had been unable to return to sleep on that particular night. She had wandered out of her bedroom, the static from her peach, brushed-nylon night-dress crackling and snapping at her feet as she walked. She had leant over the dark, swan-necked banister that swept away steeply, and gazed down the long stairwell. The hall light was still on. The father had yet to return home from the wedding. He would switch the light off when he returned to the Priory.

From the window, Daisy had watched Nana Kathleen and Bernadette, and waited. And then she had seen the father in his large hat and cloak, turning the corner into the back entry just ahead of them both. He hadn't come back to the Priory as ususal that night.

Daisy knew she should tell someone what she had seen. But Daisy wasn't allowed to tell anyone anything.

'I might be simple,' she had said to herself as she got back into bed on that fateful evening, 'but I'm not an eejit. There's no way I am spending eternity stood in the fires of hell.'

When the bell pull rang, Daisy almost fell down the stairs as she ran to open the Priory door for Sister Evangelista. She had been unhappy sleeping in the huge house on her own since the murder. Today she would beg Sister Evangelista to take her to cart it all away. She would be safe there, just as she had been at the orphanage.

'Morning, Daisy.' Sister Evangelista sounded brighter than she felt.

She was dreading this job but the bishop had been very strong indeed on the telephone.

'Make sure you clear up every single thing that belonged to Father James, Sister, and I shall be with you later in the morning in my car to take everything away to send on to his sister in America. Everything, do ye understand?'

Of course Sister Evangelista understood. Did the man think she was witless?

'Yes, Father, there will be no problem. The housekeeper Daisy will help me and it shouldn't take long.'

'Ah, yes, Daisy, the girl is a bit simple, is she not, Sister?'

'She is, Bishop, but she is a good housekeeper. Mrs Malone trained her well.'

'I am sure she did, but she is bound to be very upset indeed and may be prone to rambling. We must be careful to protect her, as she has no family of her own, except for us. I wonder if a spell in the peace and quiet of the convent might be a good idea?'

This had never crossed Sister Evangelista's mind and she was far from happy. Disruption in the convent always upset the nuns' routine and, sure, didn't she have enough to do with a school to run as well?

However, even she dared not argue with the bishop.

'Aye, well, I'll see how she is, Father, when I get there, shall I? She will need to prepare the Priory for the father's replacement.'

No sooner had the words left her mouth than her throat began to thicken with emotion and tears swam across her eyes.

'I mean, what are the arrangements, Bishop? Where is Father James to be buried? We need someone in authority here. Everyone is dreadfully upset. Will you definitely be coming soon?'

The bishop had promised to visit days ago. But something both mysterious and urgent had occurred daily to prevent him. Sister Evangelista had carried the entire burden alone and now she felt exhausted.

She had almost broken down earlier in the morning when speaking to her friend, Miss Devlin, a teacher at the school.

'Our own Father James, found murdered in the grave-yard, and the bishop still hasn't arrived to help deal with the police or bring some authority to the church, and now, here I am, about to pack up all his personal possessions in the Priory with only simple Daisy to help.'

Into one of her hands Miss Devlin had quietly placed a hankie, and into the other a cup of tea with a couple of Anadin on the saucer.

Tea and Anadin, hailed as a miracle cure by all of Liverpool's women. A headache? Take a cuppa tea and two Anadin. A toothache? A cuppa tea and two Anadin. A priest found murdered in the graveyard? A cuppa tea and two Anadin. Anadin sat on the wooden shelf next to the Woodbines in the local tobacconist's and they sold almost as many of one as the other. Acknowledged as an effective alternative to gin to help with the pains of afterbirth, mastitis, monthlies and the constant headaches brought on by looking after a dozen unruly children.

Miss Devlin had spoken in her customary gentle tone. 'It has been very hard indeed on yourself. Drink the tea and take the Anadin now, Sister, and it will all be easier to face. The bishop will be here soon.'

Sister Evangelista's distress on the telephone had been apparent. Sensing that she was losing patience, he tried to pacify her as an adult would a three-year-old child.

'I will be there this afternoon, so keep calm now. Everyone must keep very calm. We cannot bury the father until the police release his body, but we know how the police can behave. You know how pushy they were about coming into the school and upsetting the children. You must say nothing to them about anything. They will be looking for someone to blame and we mustn't let that be us, Sister. Of course when I say us, I mean the Church. This is all a dreadful mess but be sure, Sister, we have a responsibility to protect our work.'

Sister Evangelista was speechless. She had no idea what the bishop was talking about. The police didn't have anyone in their sights'? He was right. In fact, they had taken themselves down a few embarrassing blind alleys, but none of them had led towards the school or the convent.

She replaced the receiver with a prayer that the bishop would arrive soon. As God was her judge, if she had to deal with much more on her own, likely she would go mad.

## A letter from the publisher

We hope you enjoyed this book. We are an independent publisher dedicated to discovering brilliant books, new authors and great storytelling. Please join us at www.headofzeus.com and become part of our community of book-lovers.

We will keep you up to date with our latest books, author blogs, special previews, tempting offers, chances to win signed editions and much more.

If you have any questions, feedback or just want to say hi, please drop us a line on hello@headofzeus.com

 @HoZ_Books

**HeadofZeusBooks**

**www.headofzeus.com**

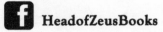 HEAD *of* ZEUS

**The story starts here**